Resonance Surge

Resonance Surge

A PSY-CHANGELING TRINITY NOVEL

NALINI SINGH

BERKLEY
New York

BERKLEY
An imprint of Penguin Random House LLC
penguinrandomhouse.com

Library of Congress Cataloging-in-Publication Data

Names: Singh, Nalini, 1977– author.
Title: Resonance surge / Nalini Singh.
Description: New York : Berkley, [2023] | Series: A Psy-Changeling Trinity novel
Identifiers: LCCN 2023003572 (print) | LCCN 2023003573 (ebook) |
ISBN 9780593440704 (hardcover) | ISBN 9780593440728 (ebook)
Subjects: LCSH: Shapeshifting—Fiction. | LCGFT: Paranormal fiction. |
Romance fiction. | Fantasy fiction. | Novels.
Classification: LCC PR9639.4.S566 R47 2023 (print) |
LCC PR9639.4.S566 (ebook) | DDC 823/.92—dc23/eng/20230130
LC record available at https://lccn.loc.gov/2023003572
LC ebook record available at https://lccn.loc.gov/2023003573

Printed in the United States of America
1st Printing

This one's for Geri.

Resonance Surge

Ruins

SILENCE HAS FALLEN.

For the Psy race, emotion is no longer a crime.

They are free for the first time in over a hundred years.

So free that perhaps they have forgotten those who cannot walk into freedom, who cannot even see or understand that freedom. The ones who were irreparably destroyed by Silence.

Where are the "rehabilitated," those Psy who were sentenced to a psychic brainwipe, those Psy who were left nothing more than shuffling blanks?

Where are the people who are a living indictment of the cruelty of the Silence Protocol?

Who watches over the most broken of them all?

Chapter 1

Theodora, I'm being told by your handler that you're refusing to follow orders. Do you or do you not realize that the act you're being asked to perform is the *only* way in which you can ever be useful to the family? If you continue to refuse, you become nothing but a drain on our resources, a failure of genetic potential that will need to be addressed— and do not make the mistake of believing that the fact you're the twin of a Gradient 9 gives you a protective halo.

You are now seventeen years old, far beyond the point where the loss of one twin will in any way impact the other. Pax has long forgotten you and is thriving free from the burden that was his bond to you. You are on your own.

—Private message from Marshall Hyde to Theodora Marshall
(12 December 2072)

BLOOD, THERE WAS so much blood on her. It spurted through the hands she'd clasped desperately to her throat, dripped down the bone white of her fingers to stain them a rich scarlet. Her eyes were stark when they met his. And he knew.

She was dying.

Yakov Stepyrev jolted awake, his heart thunder and perspiration hot and damp on the mid-brown of his skin. He whipped his head around, searching for *her* . . . but of course his room was empty.

Heart yet a bass drum, he dropped his face into his pillow and mumbled, "*Govno*, Yakov, you're losing it."

It was an effort to flip over onto his back, but once there, he couldn't stay put. He was a bear—usually he liked to linger in the warmth of the bed while hitting the snooze button on his old-school alarm clock. Usually however, he didn't wake with his adrenaline pumping from a violent dream about a woman who didn't exist and had never existed.

He flexed his fingers on the sheets . . . and only then realized his bear's claws, thick and glossy and deadly, had pushed through his skin. Fur brushed against the inside of his body, the animal that was his other half as unsettled and agitated as the human half of Yakov.

Shoving off the sheet, he gritted his teeth and managed to retract his claws, then decided to work off his frenetic fight-ready energy by doing push-ups on the thickly carpeted floor. He did pull on a pair of boxer briefs first, though. He was no blushing violet—he just didn't want his cock kissing the carpet with every rep.

But even the strenuous physical activity did little to redirect his mind from the track on which it was fixated. *Her.* The woman he'd been dreaming about since he was sixteen.

Never like this, however.

Never with blood, with fear that was chill sweat on his skin.

It had been fun in the beginning, when he was a teen. He'd bragged to his fellow juveniles that he knew exactly what his mate looked like, that he was a step ahead of them when it came to the mating dance. His great-grandfather had been a foreseer, hadn't he?

After the odd experiences both he and his twin had had over the years—when they'd just *known* things even when those things hadn't yet come to pass—Yakov had been certain his dreams were a glimmer of foresight. It had made sense to him that the dreams were so powerful because they related to the woman who was to be *the* one for him.

His mate. His heart.

But he wasn't a teen any longer, and he was beginning to question his sanity. The dreams had stopped for years . . . only to return with a bloody and brutal vengeance this past week. Every freaking night. Always the same dream, too—of Yakov in his bear form, walking through the mist of early morning until he realized that he wasn't alone, was walking beside a woman with hair of softest gold and eyes of haunted blue.

She knelt beside him at some point, her hand fisted in his fur as she cried into his neck. Her tears were so hot they burned, and all he wanted to do was change form, take her into his arms. But he couldn't disturb her in her pain, so he just folded his legs to come down to the ground, and he let her cry until all her tears were done, and she could look him in the eyes again.

"I'm sorry," she always said, her voice husky. "It's too late, don't you see?"

Then, without warning came the blood, the terror . . . the dying.

Yakov's muscles quivered as he held a plank, but he couldn't hold back the memory of his rage in the dream, the echo of his bear's growl of repudiation ringing in his ears.

One thing he knew—the dreams hadn't been like this back when he'd been a kid. His mystery woman had been younger then and he'd been in his human form, and though they'd met in the same misty clearing, she'd smiled at him in delighted surprise before they'd run through the flowers like small cubs playing a game.

It had been a thing of sunshine and joy.

Not a horror of scarlet blood and a man made helpless to save his mate.

Giving up on the push-ups when they did nothing to halt his thoughts of her, he sat back on the carpet he'd installed himself despite the ribbing from his clanmates about getting soft. Hah! Hadn't the big, furry *mudaks* all been jealous afterward and sidled up to him one after the other asking about where to get the same plush carpet?

"Why are you haunting me?" he demanded of the girl become

woman he'd never met, never seen. He was starting to wonder if she was someone his great-grandfather had known. Déwei Nguyen had been a powerful F-Psy, the *real* deal. Yakov and Pavel, in contrast, had only inherited a drop of his talent. With them, it was more a sense of intense intuition, rather than a manageable ability.

To Yakov, it felt like an itch under the skin when he knew he *had* to do something. He'd learned young not to fight the drive, because it never led him astray. That whisper of foresight had saved his and his twin's skin many a time—whether by warning them that their parents were approaching and they'd better hide all evidence of their illicit activities, or by making them halt in their tracks right before they walked onto a cliff destabilized by a storm.

But Pavel didn't dream about a woman with haunted eyes. Not like Yakov.

"That's because I like boys," Pavel had joked as an older teen, then waggled dark eyebrows identical to Yakov's; his eyes were a distinctive aqua green behind his spectacles, Pavel's vision the only physical difference between the two of them. "Maybe your future mate is Psy and is seducing you with telepathy."

Back then, with the Psy keeping a firm distance from changelings as well as humans, the idea had made Yakov roll his eyes. "It's probably just some kind of weird psychic memory inherited from Denu." The word he and Pavel used to refer to their great-grandfather didn't officially come from any of the languages spoken inside their family unit.

Not Pavel and Yakov's native Russian. Not their great-grandfather's first languages of Vietnamese and Mandarin Chinese that their beloved babushka Quyen had taught them pieces of, not the English spoken by their wickedly funny babushka Graciele, nor the Portuguese spoken by their paternal grandfather, Wacian.

According to their mother, as toddlers, they'd heard family members talking about their great-grandfather and tried to replicate his name, but in their baby mouths, Déwei Nguyen had come out sounding like "denu" and that was that. Their grandmother Quyen, one of Déwei's two children with his bear mate, had refused to allow anyone to correct them, and so he was forever Denu to Yakov and Pavel.

The two of them had been born after their denu passed, but their grandmother had told them stories about him that made him come alive. "He was so handsome and he had such a laugh, boys," their babushka would say. "His eyes would crinkle up at the corners, and it would just spill out of him." Her own lips curving, her eyes awash with happy memories.

Later, when they were older, she'd told them the other side of her father's life. "He was a man of heart and honor, my papa, but he had such sorrow inside him." Déwei, she'd told them, had already been mated when the Psy race embraced Silence, his home the Stone-Water den.

"He never once considered leaving my mama—he adored her to his dying breath." A smile potent with memory. "But he did miss his own parents and siblings terribly. I was born after the Psy embraced Silence, so I never met them. As an adult, I asked him about them, and he said they were afraid they wouldn't be able to maintain an emotional distance if they continued to stay in touch."

She'd shown them a picture of her parents in the twilight of their life, Déwei Nguyen's hair a shock of silky white and his face creased with laugh lines as he stood with his arm around his laughing mate, her hair a tumble of silver that yet retained a hint of the vivid red from images of her youth.

"You two love as fiercely as he did." Their grandmother's eyes had shone wet, her throat moving as she swallowed. "Always hold on tight to you and yours—and don't allow politics to come in between. That's what my papa taught me. Love is a far greater gift."

"I could use your help today, Denu," Yakov said now. "Who is she? A girl you had a crush on as a youth? Good thing your Mimi never knew." According to their grandmother, that had been his affectionate pet name for his mate, Marian Marchenko.

"Hot-tempered, my mama was," Babulya Quyen had said with a

laugh when they'd asked about their great-grandmother. "She apparently chased him down with a skillet once during their courtship, after she mistakenly thought he was making eyes at another bear. Shows you my father's charm that he not only got her to put down that skillet—but convinced her to make him pancakes on it!"

It was one of Yakov's favorite stories of his great-grandparents' enduring love affair. Smiling at the memory of the story, he rose off the floor, and seeing that the hand-knitted blanket on his bed was trailing over the side, he threw it back up. The blanket was terrible. Full of dropped stitches and wild lines. But their mother knit to "relax, damn it" and it always made Yakov grin when he woke and saw her efforts.

Mila Hien Kuznets was the least relaxed person Yakov knew, and he'd have her no other way.

But today, even the sight of his mother's knitting had no impact on the tension knotting his veins. He flexed his hands, unable to forget the blood. No matter what he might want to believe, this wasn't about a childhood crush of his great-grandfather's. It was too grim, held too much portentous weight to it.

Jaw clenched, he walked into the bathroom, stripped off his briefs, then stepped into the shower. A wet room carved out of the stone of the den, it featured a lush fern that thrived in the natural light system that ran throughout the den except where it had been overridden on purpose.

Yakov was happy to shower in the soft glow of cool dawn light that echoed the world outside. *Who was she?* The question would no doubt—

A *scream* pierced his eardrums, so harsh and pained that it took him a split second to realize it was coming from inside his own fucking mind. Hand slamming against the stone of the wall, he tried to gasp in a breath, but it was too late. The waking dream accelerated, and suddenly, he was standing in front of a weathered gate of wrought iron through which coiled thick green vines, a sense of urgency pumping inside him.

He twisted toward her, but she was already turning away to double over, her arm pressed against her stomach as if wounded. Yakov's bear threatened to take over, make him run to her, help her.

But he couldn't.

Yakov struggled against the invisible ropes that held him in place, but no matter how much strength he put into it, he couldn't move . . . *because he had no right to touch her.*

"Fuck!" He snapped out of the nightmare or whatever the hell it had been to find himself still standing under the water.

Claw marks scored the stone.

30 August 2083

BREAKING NEWS

Second Victim Fits Profile

Authorities in Enforcement continue to refuse to confirm speculation of a serial killer after yesterday's discovery in the Izmaylovo District of a second victim who fits the same victim profile as the first: Varisha Morozov, age 29.

The name of the second victim has not yet been released; however, Enforcement did verify that this victim, too, was a Psy woman in her twenties with blue eyes and blond hair.

When asked if young Psy women, especially those with blond hair and blue eyes, should be concerned, Enforcement Commissioner Yaroslav Skryabin stated that there is no reason to panic. "We are in the very early stages of the investigation. To throw around wild theories at this juncture would be both precipitous and inappropriate."

The commissioner also stated that at this point, there is no evidence of the killer being a fellow member of the Psy race. "Given the method of murder, they could as easily be human or changeling" was his only further comment on the subject.

That method of murder has not been released by the authorities. While the *Gazeta* does have sources close to the investigation, the *Gazeta*'s internal ethics board has agreed to Enforcement's request not to publish that information so as not to prejudice any future judicial case.

To be updated as further information becomes available.

Chapter 2

The restricted rider to Coda 27 of the Silence Protocol applies here. Pax and Theo can be—and *must* be—separated the instant they hit seven years of age. I'd recommend doing it sooner but the risk of psychic collapse is high. To chance that with a Gradient 9 would be reckless in the extreme.

—Report by PsyMed specialist Dr. Kye Li to Councilor Marshall Hyde (1 January 2061)

THEODORA MARSHALL BUTTONED up the crisp white of her shirt, erasing the view of the strip of smooth and pale skin in between the two panels. That skin was so inoffensive, so normal. Look at that and you'd never know what crawled over her back—and twisted inside her mind.

She could live with the physical marks of what had been done to her, but the only way to live with the mental marks was to enforce a rigid aloneness.

Except that was impossible.

Pax needed her. Her twin, the golden child, the one who was supposed to survive, to make it, had ended up kicked by their genes. Scarab Syndrome they called it. A disease that was the greatest irony of their race. Psy who were born so powerful that their minds effectively ate them up; prior to the advent of Silence, such Psy had imploded and died as children.

Then had come a protocol that put chains around all that chaotic power. Silence might have crushed and murdered millions, but it had *worked* for those like Pax who would've otherwise burned up in the conflagration of their abilities. Then Silence had fallen . . . and there was no putting the genie back in the bottle, no way to reinitiate Silence once Scarab Syndrome took hold.

Doctor Maia Ndiaye, one of the lead medics on the Scarab team, had framed it thus: "Once a susceptible Psy enters the Scarab state, it is a permanent shift. Literal alterations to pathways in the brain that mean the subject is no longer capable of initiating Silence on any level."

In short, her brother's vast power had become a voracious monster lurking in the back of his brain.

Theo's stomach lurched at the idea of Pax vanishing from her mind. Because that was what no one in their family had ever understood: their grandfather might have separated Pax and Theo on the physical level, but even Councilor Marshall Hyde had never quite managed a clean break on the psychic.

Pax had saved her life time after time.

Theo would do anything to save his. With that in mind, she picked up the bracelet she'd manufactured using knowledge gained in her prior job as a medical-device technician who moved tiny components using her very limited telekinetic abilities.

Made of two pieces of dull metal polished to an unexceptional smoothness except for the intricate pattern she'd hand-carved in the center, the bracelet was designed to clip over her wrist. She'd been careful to ensure that it mimicked a popular low-price comm device, complete with a tiny screen.

Snapping it shut on her wrist, she checked that it was fully charged. One hundred percent.

Good. The shock it was designed to send into her system would *hurt*.

Satisfied, she finished dressing in preparation for meeting Pax. Her brother needed her to handle something for him. No matter how much she'd prefer to vanish into the murkiest of shadows, she couldn't.

She had debts to pay.

Blood debts.

It still took all her willpower to drive through the imposing metal gates of the Marshall estate just outside Toronto. The blades of grass on the lawns on either side of the driveway were clipped to a precise length, the asphalt itself clean of anything as mundane as moss or dirt.

The two-hundred-year-old marble fountain in front of the house lay silent, but it, too, was pristine. As were the box hedges by the wide front steps. As if the gardener in charge walked around with a ruler in his back pocket.

There were no flowers.

Parking her small vehicle in the circular area at the top of the drive, she ignored the imposing bulk of the estate house of traditional red brick and walked around one of the wings to the green area beyond. If she'd ever experienced true freedom in this place, it had been in the small wilderness beyond the back lawns.

For a moment, as she stood in the silence behind the house, staring out at the green, she could almost hear the sound of her and Pax's mingled laughter as they chased each other into the trees.

"Theo."

Unsurprised that her brother had found her so fast, she touched the deep and glossy green leaf of the decorative plant that bordered the path that now cut the lawn in two. "It's changed a lot." She hadn't been back to the family residence for . . . a long time.

"Yes, I suppose so." A glance over the manicured green with eyes as blue and as cold as her own—neither one of them understood warmth. "I try not to spend much time here."

She didn't need to ask why; she knew. The grand old place full of antiques and an endless warren of rooms at their backs wasn't a home. It held too much poison and dripped too much treachery. "Why did you bring me here?"

"Because you own half of it."

Theo snorted; she didn't pretend to be Silent around Pax. He had an excellent idea of exactly how "good" she was at the protocol that had conditioned emotion out of Psy for over a century. "Pax, I know full well that Grandfather left everything to you." After Theo's place on the Gradient of Psy power was confirmed, Marshall Hyde had never even publicly acknowledged that he had a granddaughter.

Privately . . . in the darkest shadows, it had been another matter.

He'd had quite the use for Theo there.

"And," she added before Pax could speak, "I hope to hell you're not about to saddle me with any of it. You know the entire vicious lot of our 'beloved' family would be out for me with knives sharpened." They had no idea what Theo could do, no reason to believe that *she* was the more deadly twin—but that didn't mean she wanted to spend her life looking over her shoulder.

She already had too many ghosts chasing her.

"I wouldn't do that to you." Pax slipped his hands into the pockets of his black cargo pants. His black boots were scuffed and his simple sweater of dark green wool hugged a well-muscled body devoid of any ounce of fat.

Some would call the latter a result of discipline. Theo knew Pax had plenty of that. She also knew that Pax had never been permitted to fail, not even by the minutest fraction. He'd never been given any room to grow out of the brutally defined box into which their grandfather had put him.

Her twin didn't know how to be anything but unflinchingly perfect.

As it was, the world rarely even saw her brother dressed as casually as he was today; Pax was known for his bespoke suits and razor-sharp elegance, his "utter precision of form"—words she'd actually seen in a magazine article.

Why had she been reading an article about her brother?

Because he was the only person in the entire world who mattered to Theo, and—even though he'd never expect it—it was her turn to protect

him. Even from outwardly harmless journalists who seemed to be paying a little too much attention to a Psy who kept his focus on the business world. It could be a hapless individual caught by his magnetic
charisma—or it could be a stalker.

"What I've done," he said now, "is set aside a hidden trust. The details on how to access it are in our PsyNet vault."

"Our" meant the vault that Theo and Pax alone could access. Created of building blocks of pure psychic energy and embedded in the vast
psychic network that connected all Psy on the planet but for the rare
rebels, the vault was locked to their mental signatures. To the psychic
echo that ran through both their brains. Because those brains had de-
veloped together in the womb and never fully lost their entwined nature.

Their invisible bond was the only thing that had saved her all those
years when her grandfather would've rather disposed of this "defective"
member of the extolled Marshall family. Too bad for him that to erase
Theo would've been to fatally damage Pax.

Some Psy twins were like that.

"You've already given me enough money to last me multiple life-
times. And I earn an income from my work." Theo didn't need
much, didn't *deserve* much after what she'd done. "I have no use for
more. Especially after you gave me a position at your side, with the
commensurate pay."

Theo would've preferred to remain occluded, hidden by the shield of
their grandfather's machinations and her and Pax's apparent personal
estrangement. It had been far easier to help Pax as a lowly tech no one
was watching, but her twin needed someone he could trust without
question at his right hand—so here she was, a monster walking out in
the open.

Poor Pax. Tied to a twin with no power, and death her only gift.

"We need to prepare you to go under if I die." Flat, hard words, a
reminder that her outwardly healthy brother's life hung in precarious
balance.

Theo looked away, her stomach clenching so hard it hurt.

"*Theo.*"

She shook her head. "I don't want to talk about it." Not yet. Not when they'd had but a heartbeat of time together after the cold and lonely desert of their childhoods. "I don't like this place. Let's get out."

"Wait, I did have another reason to bring you here. I wanted to talk where we had no chance of being overheard—and no one ever comes out into the grounds." Halting on the far end of the path, where the land merged into a small stand of trees and other foliage that blunted the impact of the high walls beyond, he pulled a slimline organizer about the size of a phone out of his pocket.

"I've been researching Grandfather's interest in the Centers." His eyes were ice chips now. "We own significantly more of them than I realized."

A chill deep inside Theo's chest, a shiver of awareness over her spine. "I'm not surprised. That's exactly the type of business Grandfather would've considered a good investment." The truly sickening thing was that until recently, Marshall Hyde would've been correct.

Psy families had paid good money to have their "malfunctioning" members "rehabilitated." Such a clean word for the destruction of all a person was and all that they might've become, nothing but shuffling blanks left in the aftermath.

"The records are complex and I'm still digging my way through them," Pax said, "but I found a fragmented file with your name on it."

"What?" Theo blinked, frowned. "Why would my name be on anything to do with the Centers?"

"I don't know." Pax brought up a document on the organizer. "This is all I could pull up—looks like the file was deleted but the system glitched and so it was only partially erased."

Taking the thin datapad, Theo stared at the jumble of black letters on white. Most of it was so fragmented as to be gibberish, but she could clearly see what Pax already had: *Theodora M—*

There were no other Theodoras in the current line, but—"Wasn't I named after a great-great-grand someone?" Theo had zero interest in her family's history; aside from Pax, they were nothing to her. "Maybe she was the one who made the original investment in the Centers." A second later, she corrected herself. "No, it can't be that. Her death would've predated the Centers."

"Yes, but look here." He pointed out a fragment she'd missed in her initial scan.

A date: *November 2, 2055.*

Her and Pax's shared birthdate. Theo was exactly two minutes his elder.

She checked the entire document again, this time with intense care, but found nothing else legible. "You've already run a program to see if you can work out the rest of the scrambled words." Not a question because that was exactly what she would've done, and in things like this, they thought the same way.

A short nod. "From what I can tell, multiple files were deleted at the same time and hit the same glitch, so what we're seeing is a scramble."

Just when she'd begun to breathe again, sure that her name had nothing to do with any Center, he said, "The only thing that I am certain of is that *all* the documents in that particular file dump had to do with the family's interest in a specific Center."

Theo's hand clenched on the organizer, her bones pushing up against her skin. Rage simmered just beneath the surface of the person she'd patched together from the ruins left by her grandfather.

It took conscious effort to force herself to breathe and relax her hand, return the organizer to Pax. "There's no reason I should be in those files. Grandfather never took me to any of his business enterprises."

She looked away from her brother's incisive gaze, not wanting him to see, not wanting him to know. Pax had always believed she was angry with him for being the favored son, the family's shining scion.

His guilt was enormous.

How much worse would it be if she told him what Marshall had forced her to become?

Better that he believe her to be holding a grudge than realize that the reason she refused to permit him any closer was that she couldn't bear for him to see the ugliness of her. Because Pax had a heart far less warped than her own; he'd protected her even when he was so small he shouldn't have been *able* to protect her.

She'd die for her brother. More importantly, she'd kill for him.

"What do we know about this particular Center?" she asked when she could speak again.

Pax hadn't interrupted. He knew about this part of her, this splintered chaos that boiled deep within and exploded as rage.

Uncontrollable. Deadly to anyone in the vicinity not as powerful as Theo.

Not a problem since she was a 2.7.

Unfortunately, she had an instinctive and inseverable connection to a Gradient 9. And in her rage, she could access some of Pax's power.

They'd both tried to shut off the valve. It didn't work.

When under the influence of a rage attack, she became a violent and murderous 9. And there were very, *very* few people stronger than a 9 on the Gradient.

"That's just it," Pax said, making no comment on her tense frame or rigid features. He had no idea of the root of her rage, but he knew the price she paid to keep it contained, keep up the meek and mild avatar she'd perfected so she could hide in plain sight. "We know nothing. The Center isn't even a ghost in the main system. It's nonexistent.

"What I did unearth," he added, "I found in one of his private archives that he must've been in the process of decommissioning when he was assassinated—the job was half-done, a door left partially open."

Nausea, inexplicable and bitter. "Grandfather hid it even from you?"

"Maybe he was planning to tell me. But then he got killed." Pax said the latter in the same way he might mention a business acquisition.

Where others would see a ruthless predator with no emotions and no heart, Theo saw only the twin who'd had to survive a different kind of abuse. Being Marshall Hyde's favorite grandchild and heir had been no gift. At least Theo had been able to spend the vast majority of her time out of her grandfather's sight.

Now, her twin, the boy who'd refused to let go of her no matter what, held her gaze. "What's your status? Are you able to take on the task of checking out this Center? I can't be away from HQ with our dear cousin attempting a leadership coup, so it has to be you. Grandfather hid this because it's important."

"I'm in control." The last rage storm had hit three months ago, and she usually had six between strikes. "I need to know why I'm in those files." There was no reason, no reason at all for Theo's name to be anywhere near that of a Center.

She had full mental capacity.

She hadn't ever had a brainwipe.

Hadn't ever been rehabilitated.

Cold in her veins. Ice that crackled as it spread.

Are you sure, Theo? asked the cruel phantom of her dead grandfather.

Chapter 3

Gradient 1: Baseline—no one below a full level 1 has ever been able to link to the PsyNet.

Gradient 2: Minor useful ability but 2s do not work in fields that require psychic ability, unless the power requirement is negligible.

Gradient 3: Beginning of beneficial levels of power, though 3 remains in the low range.

—From the introduction to *Overview of Gradient Levels* (24th Edition) by Professor J. Paul Emory and K. V. Dutta, assigned textbook for PsyMed Foundation Courses 1 & 2

Twenty Years Ago

THEO STOOD OUTSIDE the door to her grandfather's study in the large family home that they were all supposed to live in before they turned eighteen and moved to their own places in either a high-rise owned by the family or, if they'd "achieved positions elsewhere," in "suitable" local apartments.

Theo knew that word for word because all children in the Marshall family knew that. Just like they all knew that while Grandfather's last name was Hyde, he was *the* Marshall. It was complicated and she didn't quite understand, but her mother had once said that Grandfather's surname was Hyde because he'd been meant to be raised in the Hyde family.

"The agreement didn't work as intended," her mother had added absently while she finished up a piece of work, "and Father returned to our family. He was old enough at the time that he didn't want to change his name, and because he'd won various accolades as a teenager under that name and was already building an excellent profile, he was permitted to retain it."

Theo still didn't know what "accolades" meant. She kept forgetting to ask the computer. What she did know was that her grandfather had grown up to be the head of the Marshall family.

He was the boss of everyone in this house.

Theo had watched her older cousins leave at eighteen, known that those cousins would no longer have to follow the rules of the family home. She and Pax had whispered about it, deciding what they'd do if they could do anything. They'd thought they had years and years to make their plans.

Then Grandfather had made Theo leave only days after her and Pax's seventh birthday.

Theo hadn't understood why. She'd cried. She'd tried not to, knowing that Silence said she shouldn't cry, but she wasn't very good at Silence then, and so she'd cried and asked her mother why she was being made to go away from Pax.

They hadn't even let her say good-bye to her twin.

Her mother had given her a firm look out of eyes the same color as hers and Pax's. "It's for the best, Theodora. Now stop embarrassing yourself and go wash your face."

Theo knew to obey her mother when she spoke like that, so she'd gone and washed her face. She'd tried to telepath Pax, but just like all the other times she'd tried to 'path him since the time they'd last seen each other, the pathway was blocked.

It had panicked her.

Pax had *always* been there. They were *always* in each other's heads. He was stronger so he could reach her from farther away, but she'd never had trouble reaching him either because Pax did the work of bridging any gap between them. Only now he was gone, and she couldn't find him, and no one would tell her anything.

Theo didn't panic anymore. She didn't cry these days, either. And she knew why she'd been moved from this house and into the apartment of a foster "parent" who was paid to look after her. The place she lived in wasn't a Marshall high-rise. It was also nothing like this big house with its many rooms, antique carpets, and large green spaces.

Theo's apartment had two bedrooms, the smaller one of which was hers.

She stayed inside her room nearly all of the time.

Her hands wanted to fist. She kept them flexed straight. Someone might be watching. She remembered that about this house. People were always watching and reporting back.

That was the only good thing about where she lived now.

No one watched her.

Colette, Theo's foster parent, spent her time in her room or in the living area, doing administrative tasks for the family, because that was her real job, her fostering of Theo an "addition to her duties for which she was paid a substantial sum"—that was how Colette had put it once, when Theo had screamed and cried and accused Colette of kidnapping her.

That had been right at the start, when Theo had still thought it all a mistake.

She hadn't thought that for a long time, and she behaved herself with Colette. Because after so many months, she understood that if she made Colette's job easy, then Colette would leave her alone.

That was better than being watched, being punished.

Now that Theo had learned how to feed herself the right amounts of nutrients for her age, Colette didn't even interrupt her work to make sure Theo was fed.

The only time they interacted was the daily one-hour walk that they took outside the apartment. Colette had told her it was a mandated health walk, the second part of Theo's exercise regimen. Theo was very careful to behave on those walks, the air freedom in her lungs. She couldn't risk losing the walks. Otherwise the screaming inside her head might come out.

Except for those scheduled walks, as long as she behaved and did her schoolwork on the computronic system in her room, no one cared what Theodora Marshall was doing.

That was how she'd managed to hack into the family's systems.

She knew she was too young to do it. That was probably why no one had thought to firewall her school system from the main system. But Theo had a lot of time. She didn't have Pax to talk to or play with anymore, and she made sure to finish her schoolwork right on time or just after. Before, she'd used to finish early.

And learned that the school program would give her more work in return.

So now she dragged things out while using a walled-off part of the system to hack into the family's files. It had taken her a whole month to set up those walls. She'd learned how to do it by going on the human and changeling Internet.

Her gut got a gnawing feeling. Like a small animal inside was biting at her.

She'd stolen the tablet she used to go on the Internet. It had been on one of the walks; Colette had been distracted by a colleague who'd stopped to chat with her. That was when Theo had seen the tablet abandoned on a park bench.

She'd had it in her coat pocket before she could think about it.

Her heart had thump-thumped all the way home. She'd been so scared of being found out that she'd waited until Colette was asleep before she took the tablet out of the hiding place where she'd shoved it after getting home.

Even though it was an old and cheap model, she'd known she

shouldn't have taken it. She should've handed it in somewhere. She'd felt a little better when she'd powered it up and seen that it wasn't registered to anyone and had no password. It was too basic to even have a fingerprint lock, but it wasn't so old that she couldn't charge it using the charging table she used for her school tablet.

It looked like someone had used it to read the news sites and play games.

Theo had told herself they wouldn't miss it if they had a tablet just for that stuff, but she still felt bad. She wasn't a thief. She'd never been a thief. But Colette had blocked the Internet from her devices except for authorized educational sites. Theo had known that if she tried to break through that block, it would set off an alarm, get her in trouble.

At first, she'd planned to use the Internet to connect to her brother. She *missed* Pax so much. They'd never been apart from each other for this long and it hurt her. She'd thought she could set up an email and get him the address and then he could set up an email, and they could talk that way.

Only . . . she didn't know how to get her email address to him.

Colette never took her to the family house. And all of Theo's psychic pathways were muffled, as if someone had thrown a big blanket over her. She wouldn't even have any idea if Pax was alive if she didn't have the knowing inside her. That, nobody could block. She knew her brother was alive the same way she knew she had two arms and two legs. It was just a knowing.

That was when she'd decided to hack the family's systems.

It had taken her a long time.

And what she'd found was so confusing. She wasn't listed as Pax's twin anymore. They had her down as a younger sister. She'd also seen a note about someone of whom she had no memory: Keja, a sixteen-year-old sister of their mother's who'd died when Theo and Pax were about two years old.

Like Theo, Keja had been a Gradient 2, though she'd been 2.3 to Theo's 2.7.

It had taken another month for Theo to realize what she'd found.

She'd been cut from the family because she was weak. Maybe that had happened to Keja, too. Only Keja hadn't survived. She'd died. And no one had cared. No one *ever* talked about her.

Her heart had been thudding so hard then. She'd wondered if she'd die, too.

Now, only two weeks after she'd broken into the system, she stood outside her grandfather's door and she tried not to run through these rooms screaming for Pax. He wasn't here. She'd always been able to tell when her brother was close by, and so she knew he wasn't here.

A lump grew in her throat, threatening to make her eyes burn. She'd been so good about not showing emotions; she'd been hoping that her family would forgive her for being so weak, that they'd take her back.

But Pax wasn't here. And Colette hadn't told her to pack her things.

She blinked really fast in an effort to fight her tears.

That was when her grandfather's aide, a short woman with gray hair who'd been his aide as long as Theo could remember, came out from his room. "You can go inside now," she said to Theo, and for a moment, Theo thought she saw a softness in her expression, and she wondered if she could tell the aide her email address and she'd give it to Pax.

Then the woman's face turned all hard again, and Theo knew that whatever had made her face go soft had nothing to do with Theo. The woman belonged to her grandfather, would tell him anything she said. And Theo would lose even the small possibility of meeting up with her brother.

"Thank you." Her voice came out quiet, but calm.

She checked that her knee-length black coat was neatly buttoned, her socks pulled up and her black shoes shiny, then turned and walked into her grandfather's study.

The door clicked shut behind her.

Chapter 4

Dear D,

It's so good to hear from you. I'm sorry I missed you when you visited Mom and Dad. My trip to Paris got extended because I've been promoted to supervising engineer! I'm now in charge of the entire Paris project. I'm so excited I might self-combust!

I'm going to call Mom and Dad tonight. But I had to tell you first! I would've never passed my exams without your advice and support. I'll never forget your patience as you helped me find my feet. I wouldn't be the confident woman I am today without having such an amazing big brother.

I hope you and Marian are having the best week. I can't believe my big brother is mated!! And at only 24! That ceremony was amazing. Now that you two have had six months of mated bliss, I want you to seriously consider visiting me in Paris. I'll be here for at least two more months, and they've given me a spacious two-bedroom apartment. There's plenty of room. Do come, D!

Your favorite little sister (who I hope you'll notice is writing you an actual paper letter in her terrible penmanship, *and* who will be paying the exorbitant rates for a telekinetic courier, rather than sending you a message via the Internet).

P.S. The discussion about shifting the aims of Silence is really heating up. I don't know what I think about it—what are your thoughts on it?

—Letter from Hien Nguyen to Déwei Nguyen (19 February 1972)

. . .

DAY FOUR OF the same nightmare and Yakov couldn't stand it anymore, couldn't stand watching *her* die over and over again! All while he lay in screaming helplessness, unable to go to her aid.

Yakov wanted to strangle someone and punch them at the same time.

Freshly showered but still pissed—and awake far too early—he went to grab coffee and pastries from the den's main kitchen. He met no one in the hallways, and even the Cavern, the huge central hub of the den, was empty. Weird time between shifts, he realized.

Fifteen more minutes and there'd be a steady flow of people in and out.

The brawny clanmate on duty in the kitchen grunted at him before going back to his breadmaking, his biceps flexing as he kneaded the dough like he was imagining it to be his worst enemy. Yakov had no idea why someone who absolutely *was not* a morning person had chosen to be a baker—but he was a damn good one.

As showcased by the array of fresh pastries ready for the taking.

"Thanks, Dan." Yakov's whisper had Bogdan waving a flour-dusted hand that said, *Get the hell out of my face, you infuriating morning person.*

Leaving his clanmate in peace, Yakov went to wake his twin. He didn't bother to knock since he knew Pavel was sleeping alone today. Pavel's lover—and the man for whom he was head over paws crazy in love—was on the final day of a work contract for a tiny Psy family unit out of Ecuador that could surely not pay him what he was worth.

Mercants had a way of making unusual choices.

Pavel proved to be lying facedown in bed, one foot out of the blanket and his arms above his head. "If that's not a croissant I smell, I will murder you," he muttered before raising his head. His bedhead might've been extreme if not for the silky weight of his hair—it fell back into place around his face at once.

They'd inherited the texture of their hair from their denu.

After turning on the lights using the touchpad by his bed, Pavel blinked owlishly at Yakov, his eyes identical to those Yakov saw in the mirror every day, but for one crucial difference: Pavel had bad vision. He also refused to get surgery to fix it. He didn't trust anyone with a laser near his eyes.

He slapped his hand at the shelf Yakov had built for him beside his bed, managed to snag his glasses. Vision now corrected, he sat up with his back to the headboard and his lower body covered by the blanket—but for that one foot. They might be changelings at home in their skin, and twins to boot, but it was rude to just let your junk hang out, and the two of them weren't *that* rude to each other.

Yawning, Pavel held out a hand.

Into which Yakov thrust a coffee before placing the croissant in his brother's other hand. Then he got the rest of the tray full of pastries as well as his own coffee and placed it on the bed. When he sat, it wasn't in the single chair in the room, but at the end of the bed, in a position from which he could talk to his brother about the nightmare that haunted him.

Only his stomach lurched at the memory and he found himself searching for a distraction. "I thought Stasya offered you a bigger room in the section for couples?" Pavel and Arwen might not have mated yet, but the two were a committed pair—any bear with eyes in their head could see that.

Pavel shrugged one shoulder. "We're not technically living together yet. Felt sneaky to switch rooms when Arwen's still figuring things out." His voice softened on his lover's name.

Yakov felt for his brother. But he also understood Arwen's need to know himself before he dove headlong into the mating bond that hovered in the air between him and Pavel. Unlike Pavel and Yakov, Arwen hadn't grown up free to live his life out in the open; this, *now*, was the first time in over a hundred years that E-Psy like Arwen weren't only accepted but treasured.

A cataclysmic shift even for a man who'd been brought up in the heart of a fiercely protective family. "I was raised in love," Arwen had said to Yakov once, "but I had to hide my truth from everyone outside my family."

"Arwen still enjoying his work in Ecuador?" he asked his brother now.

But Pavel scowled. "You didn't wake me up at the ass-crack of dawn to chitchat about my love life like a nosy babushka." His brother gulped coffee. "Spill."

Yakov exhaled, made himself say it. "I'm having flashes again."

His brother's sleep-hazy eyes sharpened, and suddenly he wasn't a lazy bear anymore but one of their alpha's top people. "Like when we were sixteen?"

"Yeah—but more intense."

"Back then, we were on our own," Pavel said, half the croissant already gone. "Now I'm sleeping with a Psy, and so is our alpha."

Yakov rolled his eyes at his brother's shit-eating grin. "TMI, bro," he said, even as his bear smiled at seeing his twin so happy. "But yeah, we have avenues for info. You think any of them know a foreseer?"

"Ena knows everyone and their ancestors," Pavel said dryly, referring to Arwen's powerhouse of a grandmother, then shoved the rest of the croissant into his mouth.

Sounds of bliss followed.

Yakov fiddled with his mug. "It's her." Quiet words.

"The woman of your dreams?" Pavel whistled. "Damn, she must finally be on the way to you."

"It's an echo of Denu's memories. We decided that, remember?"

"We were hormonal kids who knew shit," his twin pointed out. "Does this dream girl still look like a girl?"

Heart thumping, Yakov shook his head. "She's grown-up . . . and I see her bleeding, dying."

All humor erased from his face, Pavel said, "Tell me."

Because this was his brother, his *best* friend, he did, down to the most agonizing detail. "It's fucked up."

"Yes," Pavel agreed. "But if it *is* foresight, then it's also a warning. Remember what Babulya Quyen told us about what Denu always said."

"That the greatest gift of foresight was the chance to alter the trajectory of events terrible and dark." He sat forward, his arms braced on his thighs. "But, Pasha—she was so fucking scared and I could do nothing to help her."

Pavel took a long drink of his coffee, picked up a second croissant, and nodded. "Right, we start from the top. Work out why you might be immobile—then work out how to circumvent that."

HIS twin's idea had been a good one—until they'd run headlong into Yakov's lack of any detailed information about the blood-drenched situation. As a result, he was still in a foul mood when he drove into the city to meet with Silver. His alpha's mate had gone to her office in the middle of the night to coordinate an emergency response to another catastrophic PsyNet collapse.

Yakov knew the Psy needed the PsyNet to survive. All their minds were connected to it, and it provided critical biofeedback to their brains. People like Silver who were linked to others outside the Net would survive a collapse, but the vast majority of the psychic race was unconnected to anyone on the outside.

And now, their PsyNet was failing.

Each time the Net fractured, it forcibly ejected Psy minds from it. People died, crumpling on the streets, in their workplaces, at home. Yakov had witnessed it once—seen Psy go down like marionettes with their strings cut. No warning. No way to assist unless you were a Psy with a mind powerful enough to throw people back into an undamaged part of the network before they went terminal.

It had been horrific.

So when Silver shot him a message asking him to come in, he'd figured the fallout must've hit a nearby area and she needed more brawn on the ground. Worst case, it would be to help with body retrieval. Best case would be to provide security because the collapse had been caught in time, but people were injured and agitated.

Turned out he was wrong about that.

"It wasn't a major fracture," Silver told him from where she sat at her desk, while he sprawled in a chair on the other side, Moscow waking to a misty morning in the floor-to-ceiling window behind her. "Nothing compared to the chaos of the incident that led to the creation of the PsyNet Island."

The Island, as everyone was terming it, because it was the only one in the entire PsyNet, had been created in a maelstrom of violence. From what Yakov understood, that piece of the Net now floated in the network but was separated from it by "dead" air.

"The best metaphor we have for non-Psy is that of a moat," a talking head on the local newscast had explained. "The dead air around the Island creates that moat. The only difference is that we can't build a bridge over it, nor can we swim to it. There is no way to the Island, or off the Island."

Yakov's brain hurt at times when it came to PsyNet information, but the moat reference was an excellent one and had allowed him to visualize the situation. "I saw on the latest newscast that it's considered stable now."

"Yes, Ivan's done an excellent job in only two weeks," Silver said, pride a hum beneath the words, "but there's so much he doesn't know, and we can't help him, since none of us can even get to the Island."

"Well, the man is a Mercant," Yakov said in an effort to ease her concern—because he got it. The Mercants were as much a clan as Stone-Water. Not being able to help a clanmate? It hurt. "I'm sure a member of Spies R Us will find a way to get the data he needs."

Silver's lips twitched. "Do not repeat that around my grandmother or I can't vouch for your safety."

Despite the amused warning, there was no hiding the worry that hovered near-constantly in the silvery blue of her eyes.

"You should go home," he muttered. "You need the embrace of clan. I'm surprised Valya didn't just haul you back when you tried to leave." A reference to her first stay with StoneWater when they'd all assumed that Valentin had given in to his basest bear instincts and kidnapped her.

"He tried to make me stay." Silver's smile was subtle. "I, however, am made of sterner stock—and he has duties in the den today. Several of the tiny gangsters are starting school and you know how much strength they gain from him."

"Yes. They need him." Changeling bear cubs might be ninety percent feral and utterly fearless most of the time, but they were babies, too, and going to school—even the small school in the heart of bear territory—for the first time was scary. Valentin literally held their tiny hands and walked them in, cuddled them if they needed it, and hung around until they'd settled in with their friends.

Of course their parents or guardians were also present, taking pictures and gushing, but Valentin's presence was far from an intrusion. Every adult in the den knew that for a predatory changeling, an alpha's touch and guidance was, at times, a stark necessity. And their Valya was a good alpha not only for his strength and intelligence but because of his enormous heart.

"I can't remember my first day of school," he told Silver, "but my father says that Pasha and I exchanged glances on the doorstep, hitched our daypacks up our backs, and strode in like we were trouble and we knew it." Akili Stepyrev's hazel-brown eyes had been bright with laughter and pride against the warm brown of his skin as he told that story.

Today, Silver's expression grew even warmer. Look at her like this and you'd never know her for the ice-cold telepath Valentin had first courted. "Funnily enough, my grandmother says something similar about me. That she'd never seen such a small and determined child—I appeared ready to take over the class."

Yakov grinned. "Ena's heir in more ways than one." Silver Mercant wasn't the director of EmNet because she was anything less than ruthlessly organized and meticulous in her goals. "So, what do you need me for?"

Silver told him.

Making a face, he folded his arms across his chest. "*Izvinite*, Siva," he said, though he wasn't really sorry—his parents had just raised him to be a polite bear. "That's a big *nyet* from me."

Silver Mercant was well used to dealing with growly and uncooperative bears, didn't bat an eyelash at his response. "Even if it gains you entry to a highly secure facility with the warrant to poke about at will?"

Yakov scowled. "You fight dirty."

That was when she pushed across the box of fresh donuts he'd been smelling since he walked into this meeting that was really a cat-sneaky ambush designed to make him spend a lot of time with a person he most assuredly was *not* going to like.

"I hate you," he muttered with zero weight behind his words as he picked up one of the glazed circles of fried goodness and finished it off in two bites. "So," he said now that his stomach was happier, "you want me to babysit a Psy who might be a psycho?"

Silver rubbed her temples as she had a way of doing when dealing with recalcitrant bears. He might actually buy it along with the pinched expression in her eyes except—

"You like us." He grinned and spread out his arms. "You are, in fact, enchanted by our beariness."

Lips twitching in one of those still-rare expressions of emotion, Silver dropped the act. "I need help," she said simply.

Chapter 5

Councilor Adelaja brings up an excellent point. While the pre-Silence generation of adults is beginning to thin out due to age and the cognitive dissonance created by our people's new way of life, we do have a problem with young individuals who continue to fail to achieve satisfactory levels of Silence. It's time to talk about a solution.

—Councilor Vey Gunasekara to fellow members of the Psy Council (circa 2012)

YAKOV GROANED ON the heels of Silver's confession that she needed his help. "Grr, now I can't say no." He ate another donut in revenge, *and* reached across to steal the mug of hot coffee she'd just poured for herself. "So—how do the Americans say it?—lay it on me."

Leaning back in her chair, every single blond hair contained in an elegant twist at the back of her head, and her upper body clad in a white shirt and a gray suit jacket, Silver said, "What do you know about the Centers?"

"Not much." Yakov put down the misshapen coffee mug that looked to have been made by one of the cubs. "Nova told me once that the Psy sent people they considered 'defective' there to be brainwashed." He made a face. "I mean, it sounded about right for what we knew of the Psy under Silence so I never questioned it."

Silver made no effort to don the mask she wore around outsiders. Her anger was as cold as a Siberian winter. "Nova was close but she didn't go far enough. Silence was all about conditioning emotion out of Psy—those who wouldn't or couldn't conform were sent to a Center for rehabilitation." Her jaw was a hard line against the cool white of her skin. "Such a detached word."

Yakov wished he hadn't eaten those donuts now. "It wasn't brain-washing, was it?"

Silver shook her head. "It was a brainwipe." Her hand flexed, pressing down against the top of her desk. "They literally erased people. If they'd gotten their hands on Arwen, my brother would—" Silver bit off the words but Yakov didn't need them to understand.

Arwen—sophisticated, snobby, and painfully *kind* Arwen—was an empath. A being whose entire world was made up of emotion. The very thing the Silence Protocol had made illegal for the Psy. "These victims," he said, because fuck if he'd use the word "patients" for the horror she was describing, "did they die?"

"Some," she said, "but that tended to be unintentional. The survivors were left as little more than vegetables who could move and do menial tasks at best. Their real job was to be a warning to the rest of us to toe the line—or else."

Gut churning, Yakov shoved back his chair and got up to prowl around the room, his bear wanting to explode out of his skin. He was by no means one of the more impulsive bears in StoneWater. He couldn't do his job as one of his alpha's seconds if he were prone to flying off the handle, but neither was he a Psy trained to hide his emotions.

"How could *anyone* have agreed to Silence knowing that was one of the consequences?" he demanded.

"It didn't begin that way." Silver's tone shivered with fury. "It was the first generation raised in Silence—the first Silent natives—who founded the Centers."

That made a terrible kind of sense to Yakov, that this abomination had been founded by people who'd been shown no love, who'd actually been taught that to feel was to make a mistake.

They had been raised in coldness without heart.

And ended up flawless in their frigid logic.

Given the very public fall of Silence and the ensuing documentaries and reports that had begun to come out about the previously reclusive race, the world now knew that the parents who'd made those decisions for their innocent children had thought they were doing the best for them, that their choice would save their beloved cubs from the madness and violence then annihilating the Psy.

What *wasn't* public knowledge was that their desperate choice had created a people where psychopaths sat at the top of the power structure. How could it be otherwise when the perfect Psy was meant to be an unfeeling machine?

Yakov remembered coming up to his grandmother Quyen one day in her prized vegetable garden, her features soft with sadness. "Babulya?" he'd asked, crouching down beside her in the dirt. "What's wrong?"

She'd smiled, patted his cheek, then said, "Plant with me, cublet."

He'd been sixteen, a juvenile on a quest to catch the eye of a girl in his class, but he'd given up all thoughts of romance to stay close to his grandmother. She wasn't a sad person, and it had worried him to see her that way.

"It's only a memory," she'd told him. "It struck me because I'm getting to the age my father was when he spoke it to me. I found him right here, in this very garden—he started it, you know?" A proud smile. "He was crying. My papa . . . he was a proud man. I never saw him cry that way before."

She'd planted a seedling, patted the soil gently into place. "I hugged him. I was full-grown then, with cubs of my own, but I felt unmoored. He squeezed me close and he told me that he'd suddenly remembered how much his sister loved his homemade kimchi and he'd missed her until it hurt."

Another seedling tucked into place. "He never talked much about the PsyNet or his family to us when we were growing up—he was *such* a good father, so present and interested in our lives, a man who was delighted by his cubs and who adored his mate. I never once saw the old and weathered sadness that lived in his heart. Not until that day."

She'd sat back on her heels, her dirt-dusted hands on her thighs. "After the Psy retreated from the world, his mama and papa, his younger brothers, and his sister, Hien, told him it was better he forget them, that their paths had diverged too far."

"That's Mama's middle name," Yakov had interrupted.

"Yes, cublet." A brush of her hand over Yakov's hair, both of them too much the bear to be bothered by a bit of dirt. "I named her after my papa's sister. He told me that day about their closeness as siblings. It broke his heart that her children would never know his cubs, the separation carrying on through the generations."

His grandmother's description of Denu's pain had left a poignant mark on Yakov's young heart. He hoped his great-grandfather never knew about the Centers, but from all he'd learned over the years, Déwei Nguyen had been an intelligent and connected man.

He'd have known. And mourned.

"Why don't we see more of these wounded people?" he asked when he could speak rationally again. "These rehabilitated?"

Silver was on her feet now, too, cool and collected—and with an icy fire in her eyes. "Prior to the fall of Silence, the rehabilitated were kept confined to the Centers, where humans and changelings never went. As for now"—she took a jagged breath—"when it became clear that Silence was about to fall, someone gave the order to do a 'deep clean.'"

Yakov barely stopped himself from punching a hole in the nearest flat surface. "Siva," he said, using the diminutive that the cubs used for her and that had caught on with the entire clan. "I can't be inside walls right now."

Nodding, she strode out from behind her desk, her knee-length skirt slim and her heels at least four inches. That put her a few inches above his five-eight as they walked side by side out of her office and, bypassing the elevator, headed down the stairs that eventually spit them out into the cold fall air.

He inhaled deep breaths of it, his skin hot even though he was wearing only a short-sleeved black tee with his jeans. Changeling bodies ran hotter than Psy. "You should get a coat," he said to his alpha's mate.

"I'm too angry to need one," Silver said, and began to stride down the sidewalk already coated in the colors of autumn, the fallen leaves brown and red and orange and even an unexpected pale yellow.

He knew her intended destination: a park maintained by StoneWater.

Worried about his own anger, he let her go ahead for a minute before he ran to catch up. He had no trouble doing so—bears might not be the fastest of the changelings, but they were faster than a woman in heels. Even when that woman was his alpha's beloved Silver "Fucking" Mercant.

His bear finding solace in the thought of his clan, he didn't shrug off Silver's touch when she took his hand for a heartbeat of a moment. Because she was of StoneWater, carried the scent that centered his bear.

"I'm okay," he said before releasing her; he knew she remained less comfortable with touch than most bears. Only the cubs and Valentin had free rein—but all of StoneWater knew she was there for them to the death. "So someone—I'm guessing a team—went out and murdered a lot of these 'rehabilitated'?"

She gave a nod. "Kaleb didn't know. Neither did Nikita or Anthony. Aden definitely didn't authorize his Arrows to do it, as they were already independent from the Council by then."

Yakov bared his teeth, accidentally scaring a man walking toward them into hurriedly crossing the street. "I'll trust you on Kaleb." The cardinal telekinetic, a power beyond power, had once been Silver's boss, and from all Yakov and StoneWater knew of him, the man didn't play games with the lives of ordinary people.

Kaleb only played with other predators. Which was, to a bear's mind, fair enough. "And Aden's Arrows have proven who they are." The black-clad special ops soldiers had thrown their full weight behind the empaths, vowing to protect them to the last breath.

Yakov had zero doubts that the Arrows had done awful and even unforgiveable things while under Council control, so he wasn't about to paint them as lily-white. But he also understood that a choice made under duress was no choice at all. Regardless of all else, as Silver had pointed out, the Arrows had said "fuck you" to the Council well before the fall of Silence; no way they'd have done the Council's dirty work.

"Don't know about the other two, though." His bear curled its lip inside him.

"Sascha Duncan confirmed that her mother had nothing to do with the Centers businesswise—that Nikita, in fact, kept as wide a berth of them as possible in terms of her Councilor duties," Silver said. "Too much of a risk with Sascha being an empath."

"Nikita knew her daughter was an E?"

"Mothers always know."

Yakov whistled, not sure what that did to his thoughts on the former Councilor. Nikita Duncan was a coldhearted bitch with blood on her hands, but bears respected parents who protected their cubs.

"As for Anthony," Silver added, "he came into the Council too close to the fall of Silence to have had those connections—and also, he had no need to dirty his fingers in that ugly pie. Per capita, his family makes more money than almost any other family group in the PsyNet. Foreseers are highly sought after, and NightStar foreseers are the best of the best."

A pause before she added, "I found a little tidbit about your great-grandfather while I was researching this subject. He was once head-hunted by NightStar."

Yakov's bear strutted in smug pride inside him. "We always knew he was good, but he was *that* good?" *Everyone* knew about the NightStar group and their foreseeing empire.

"According to my contacts, yes. He turned them down because he'd already met his mate, knew that he'd be leaving the PsyNet."

"Yeah, everyone says he was crazy in love with his Mimi." Yakov felt a little more of the pressure ease off his chest as they walked into the green space yet swathed in fog that was the simply named City Park. He could handle the metropolitan area fine, but he loved the forests that were his home, and this was a little piece of it in the heart of Moscow. "Who does that leave?"

"Three other Councilors. It could well have been any one of them. Though, if Marshall Hyde had been alive at the time, I'd have fingered him."

Yakov screwed up his eyes. "Old guy, right? Got blown up." He mimed an explosion using his hands. "Family group's now headed by a blond android who looks like he walked out of central casting for the perfect bipedal specimen."

Silver shot him a sharp look . . . before amusement lit up her eyes. "I happen to think Valentin is the perfect bipedal specimen."

Yakov clutched at his heart. "Oh, ouch! And I'm right here next to you. But you know what I mean. Pax Marshall is about as physically flawless as it's possible to get. He's also . . . flat. It's creepy."

"Yes, I know what you mean." Silver kept to the paved path through the rustling hues of the autumn-kissed forest, while Yakov walked on the grass lush and green.

"Getting back to the Centers," she said, "they got . . . not forgotten, but overlooked in the transition from Silence. The Ruling Coalition has had to deal with multiple crises, including the current fragmentation of the PsyNet, and well, there remain rotten areas in the power superstructure that Kaleb and the others haven't yet discovered."

"Did this murderous deep-clean squad succeed in their task?"

Silver shook her head. "Not after the initial purge." Ice in her tone again. "The ones carrying it out appear to have run scared once they realized the old Council was dead in the water."

"No one around anymore to protect the vicious bastards."

A curt nod from Silver. "At that point, the Centers were left in a holding pattern—those who ran them didn't dare raise their heads above the parapet, lest they get those heads ripped off."

Yakov might've been surprised at the bloodthirsty remark except that there was a damn good reason why Silver was mated to Valentin. Honor and protectiveness ran bone-deep in both. "Which brings us back to what you want from me."

"Yes. Pax Marshall has just informed the Coalition that he's finally untangled the part of his grandfather's operations to do with the Centers. It's a mess. Turns out the Marshall family owns over fifty percent of all Centers across the world."

Chapter 6

To earn the trust of not just the humans and changelings but of our own battered people, we can no longer act as a closed system. We *must* welcome others in, as observers, as advisors, and quite simply, as sets of fresh eyes who will see the mistakes to which we've become blind because those mistakes are our reality.

—Ivy Jane Zen (president of the Empathic Collective) to fellow members of the Ruling Coalition (7 June 2082)

"FUCKERS." YAKOV SPAT out the word. "Monsters, one and all."

Silver didn't disagree. "Marshall Hyde's family has never been one my grandmother liked—but we know very little about Pax's personal ethics. It does speak well for him that he came to the Coalition with the information about the widespread nature of his family's holdings in Centers as soon as he had the information in hand."

"Seems fishy it took him this long." Yakov narrowed his eyes at the black-and-white house cat that had the temerity to pad up alongside Silver and give him the gimlet eye. *Cats.* Thought they owned everyone.

Lifting its nose and tail into the air, the cat looked away like Yakov wasn't there and continued to walk with Silver.

"No, I understand that part." Silver's words had him glancing at her in surprise. "Psy family businesses of that magnitude are incredibly complex, and Marshall Hyde was assassinated when Pax was only twenty-four.

"While he was raised as his grandfather's eventual successor, everyone assumed Hyde would be around for another two or three decades at the very least. There are rumors Pax was taking over more and more from his grandfather up to a year before Hyde's death, but I don't believe it."

Silver shook her head. "No matter how old he was getting or if he might've offloaded certain duties onto Pax, he wouldn't have laid all his cards on the table. There is no way Pax would've been given access to or told of all of his family's holdings at once—first, he'd have had to prove himself with smaller and less sensitive operations."

Yakov pushed himself to look beyond his instinctive revulsion at the entire "business" of the Centers. "I can see that," he admitted grudgingly. "Like proving yourself as a junior soldier before taking on more senior duties. So do I have it right? He's asked the Coalition to give him unbiased observers as he starts to audit these Centers?"

"Basically," Silver said. "In most cases, the Coalition has sourced medical personnel, human and changeling, to go in as impartial observers and consultants. However, this one situation is different—which is why Pax reached out to StoneWater."

Yakov ignored the house cat, which had come over to twine around his ankles now that they'd stopped walking. Everyone knew felines were contrary. He'd probably get clawed if he dared pet the slinky creature. "I've got basic medic training like all of Valya's seconds, but my studies were in chemistry, with a minor in pharmacological compounds."

Every one of Valentin's senior people had multiple skill sets—Yakov's knowledge as a chemist was more esoteric than most, but it was part of why he handled anything to do with the clan's natural resources.

He also had a brain that thrived on patterns and order; that was why he'd volunteered to handle all logistics when it came to shifts, training, and general organizing. Yakov was the reason StoneWater always had backup security equipment, and why their juniors never missed out on external training courses. Valya called him the "quiet engine" at the clan's heart, and Yakov wasn't mad about it. He liked being the reason things ran like clockwork.

"I don't want you on this for the medical side of things," Silver said. "Your partner has the necessary medical expertise." Her frown was faint, but Yakov had been around his alpha's mate long enough now that he could pick up on her micro facial expressions.

"My motivation for pulling you in," she continued as he gave in to the damn cat and crouched down to risk life and limb in petting its sleek pelt, "is protection and your knowledge of how a major organization runs from the top down—you know every nook and cranny, see every option, and can be counted on to think of things another person wouldn't."

"Got it. You want brawn with brain," Yakov said as the cat purred and pretended it liked him.

Hah! He wasn't falling for that. Next thing you know the beast would be expecting fresh tuna from the local fishmonger.

Silver's lips curved a fraction. "And a little slyness."

Insulted, he said, "I'm a bear, not a cat."

"But you can be subtle for a bear," Silver pointed out. "And you'll need to be with the Marshalls—even my grandmother isn't sure of Pax's overall motives. But as she says herself, she never liked the family when it was under Hyde's rule, so she could be biased against his successor."

"I trust your grandmother's instincts." He'd keep his guard up, make sure he wasn't taken for a fool by a Psy who thought him a stupid lumbering bear. Though he might well put on the act to ensure that the Marshall involved underestimated him. "So what's the deal with this particular Center?"

"It was hidden," Silver told him as he rose from his crouch and they began to walk again.

The cat padded beside him.

"The only reason Pax unearthed it was that he noticed a subtle but constant drain on the family's finances. Given the size of their coffers, it would've been easy to dismiss it as an accounting error—but Pax is too smart for that. He dug. And he discovered a Center that wasn't on the list of Centers he'd already found, *and* one that was being funded by the family rather than turning a profit."

Yakov fought off his instinctive revulsion at the idea of making money from torturing and maiming people. "They still do that? Make a profit, I mean?"

"They are now care facilities." Silver's jaw worked. "The people already rehabilitated . . . the vast majority of their families continue to reject them, would rather pay a fee for their long-term maintenance.

"The only good thing is that now, with empaths in charge of oversight, the care is the best—with enrichment a compulsory part of the service. Many human and changeling specialists with expertise in dealing with those like the rehabilitated work in the Centers these days. They're . . . gentle in a way my race has forgotten how to be."

"Not all of you, Siva." He nudged her with his shoulder.

Silver didn't soften, but neither did she put distance between them.

"None of the rehabilitated will ever come back, not when part of their neural structure was purposefully destroyed, but they can have far more fulfilling lives with an enrichment program than when they were left to vegetate."

Yakov's stomach clenched against the urge to throw up. "Your Council was flat-out evil."

"Yes. Each and every one on the road to what we eventually became." A pause. "Yet I won't be a hypocrite. I wonder what path I would've walked had I not had Grandmother to guide me. What path *she* would've walked without the guidance she received. We all begin as children, pliable and defenseless."

Neither one of them spoke again for several minutes.

Because Silver was right. Who would Yakov be had he not been raised by his parents and grandparents, his childhood awash in love and mischief? What if he'd been raised by a psychopath like Marshall Hyde?

The thought made his skin crawl. "Right," he said, telling himself to shake it off, "so it's Pax Marshall's sister who's coming to investigate the hidden Center on the outskirts of Moscow?"

Silver nodded. "Theodora Marshall has close to no footprint on the PsyNet. So much so that I'm sure it was done on purpose—especially given that she's listed as a Gradient 2.7 Tk on the records I did manage to find; Marshall Hyde wouldn't have wanted news of such a weak member of the family to get out. Quite frankly, I'm astonished he let her live."

Yakov bared his teeth; he hated how the Psy *ranked* their family members. Especially when it didn't have to be that way—he saw that with the Mercants. While they were a generally psychically powerful family, he'd met two of Silver's relatives who were lower-Gradient—but who held high positions in the family due to their non-psychic skills.

And no one would ever say the Mercants were anything but a power-house.

Still, he couldn't feel too sorry for this Theodora. She'd been raised in the same snake pit that had spawned Pax, was apt to be as ruthless. "Interesting that Pax is sending her for such a big job if she's that low down in the pecking order."

"Yes, that intrigued me, too. I assumed at first it was because of her medical training—apparently, she's a fully qualified nurse with a specialization in the manufacturing side of medicine, and previously worked in a part of the family's operations that makes medical-grade equipment. She used her telekinesis to move tiny components."

"I hear a 'but' in there."

"I reached out through my various connections and got an interesting response from Ivan."

"You know," Yakov said, diverted, "if you'd asked me the name of a person least likely to mate with a changeling, I'd have picked him." Ivan Mercant was cool and sophisticated and clearly thought bears were lunatics who'd escaped the asylum—but then again, the latter was the default conclusion of many people.

"I think being in a pack of cats suits him just fine," Silver said with another one of those slight smiles.

"Hmm." Yakov rubbed his jaw. "I see it. Mercants are as slinky as cats. Is he up for visitors of the bearish variety?"

Silver's smile deepened the slightest fraction at his grin. "Leave Ivan in peace, Yasha. At least for the moment. Arwen is hovering over him as it is."

"Oh well, then, job done." No one hovered better than an empath. "So, what does Ivan have to say about this Theodora?"

"He mentioned Theodora to a DarkRiver sentinel after I told him she was coming here. You know Ivan—given his skills and power, the cats are treating him as a shadow sentinel even as he focuses on handling the situation with the Island."

"I figured." Ivan was too strong to be left outside a changeling pack's hierarchy; it'd have messed with everyone's heads. "So he's trusted, has access to senior-level data?"

Silver nodded. "His sentinel friend shared that the cats have some dealings with Pax—as part of that, they unearthed the fact that Theodora was actually born on the same day and year as him."

Yakov's eyes widened. "Twins?" He whistled as the house cat pounced off to go about the rest of her important business. "That puts a whole new slant on things. No wonder Pax is sending her." Yakov would die for Pavel and vice versa.

Their bond was a thing of granite over titanium.

But Silver made a negative sound. "From all I know of the Marshalls, Pax and Theodora weren't raised together. I didn't even know about her until recently. Neither did my grandmother. They might be twins, Yasha, but don't make the mistake of thinking they're like you and Pasha."

Yakov nodded, but though he tended to bow to Silver's advice and knowledge when it came to the Psy, he wasn't sure she was right this time around. Because Pax Marshall could've sent anyone to investigate this sensitive and hidden part of their operations.

He'd chosen to send his twin.

"I'll do it," he said.

"I've got her ID photo for you back at the office."

Only after they got back and he looked at the image did he realize that he'd been braced to come face-to-face with his dream woman. Despite everything he'd said to his brother, some small part of him had begun to believe that the reason he was dreaming about her all over again was because he was about to meet her.

But while his dream woman had blond hair and blue eyes, that was where the similarity with Theodora Marshall began and ended. Yakov's dream woman was vibrant, *sparkled* with life. This woman's expression was flat. Her hair was pulled severely off her face, and her eyes, while technically blue, were so dull as to be dishwater.

To be fair, his own ID shot was only passable because Pavel had made him laugh right beforehand, so his eyes were still bright with it, and there was color in his face. Otherwise, ID images washed everyone out. But Theodora Marshall was beyond washed-out—it was as if she had no life to her at all, no kind of personality.

Another android.

Fun. So much fun.

His bear groaned inwardly and slumped down to have a good grump.

Chapter 7

Break the bond
Break the heart
Break the soul
Hollow, hollow, hollow

—"Steps to Cruelty" by Adina Mercant, poet (b. 1832, d. 1901)

Twenty Years Ago

THEO FELT SMALL and weak as she stood in front of her grandfather's desk while he sat behind it and stared at her with his ice-colored eyes. He was *powerful*. A Councilor. She wasn't sure exactly what a Councilor did, but she knew they were the most powerful people in the whole world.

"Colette tells me you've been behaving," he said at last.

Theo's heart filled with light and warmth. "Yes, Grandfather."

"You've completed your required educational modules to date, I see." He glanced at a tablet on his desk.

"Yes, Grandfather."

Putting down the tablet, he steepled his hands on his desk. "Unfortunately, you continue to fail your Silence tests."

The lump in her throat returned, her eyes all hot. "I'm working very hard, I promise. I'll pass next semester."

He made a grunting sort of sound. "That's not good enough. Pax has already achieved near-perfect discipline over his emotions. That was why we had to separate you—you were a weight on him, pulling him down."

Theo gulped back the tears that wanted to escape. Pax would *never* think she was a weight. He was her best friend. He'd always been her best friend.

"As it is," her grandfather continued, "we'll need to find you something to do that keeps you out of the spotlight. Our line does not birth Gradient 2s." His eyes were like a cobra's.

Theo had only ever seen pictures of cobras during her biology lessons, but she thought that if she saw one in real life, it would have eyes like her grandfather right then.

"I am, however, pleased at your facility in hacking."

The words were hammers smashing into her brain. She just stared.

His smile wasn't a real smile. She knew that. Her grandfather's Silence was perfect. His smile was a pretend thing . . . and it made her back go cold, her chest so tight she could hardly breathe.

"Oh yes, I know," he said with that scary smile still on his face. "You should grasp by now that nothing happens in this family without my knowledge." Leaning back in his chair, he said, "Did you really believe we didn't have alerts on your entire system? You're such a pathetic power that the alerts were to ensure you didn't embarrass the family. But this . . ."

Another one of those pretend smiles that were worse than the cobra eyes. "I wasn't expecting this level of expertise from someone so young. I wonder if it's a side effect of your particular ability." He waved that off. "Regardless, at least you show promise in the area. I'm adding a computronic coding and hacking module to your educational requirements."

Stunned, her mind abuzz, she stood there dumbly.

"Theodora."

She snapped up her head at that cold tone. "Yes, sir?"

The cobra eyes held hers again. "Pax doesn't exist for you now. As you don't exist for him. He is going to soar, while you're so far below the surface as to barely exist. No one will even know you're part of the Marshall family. Forget Pax. I assure you that he's already forgotten you."

Chapter 8

But here's the thing, before a bear attempts to feed you, they'll probably try to make you laugh. They'll succeed. Because bears have the best sense of humor in the entire changeling kingdom (and yes, I will fight my fellow columnists if any of them challenge my claim).

And see, after you're weak from laughter and utterly in thrall to their gorgeous, *gorgeous* smile and wicked humor, *that's* when your bear will offer you your favorite sinful dessert of choice. While your guard is down. Radar up! Remember, those gorgeous bear smiles are dangerous to your status as single Wild Women!

—From the March 2080 issue of *Wild Woman* magazine:
"Skin Privileges, Style & Primal Sophistication"

THEO WAS ON board her flight to Moscow three days after Pax first spoke to her about the hidden Center when she got a telepathic message from her twin. *Theo, can you take a look at my mind on the PsyNet?*

Theo responded without hesitation, wondering if he was worried about visible instability. *Entering the Net now.* A heartbeat later and she was in the sprawling psychic blackness dotted with countless stars, each star a Psy mind. Mere years earlier, the highways of the PsyNet had been a pure and unadulterated black, the minds islands in the darkness.

Now, streamers and sparks of color proliferated, and a honeycomb of fine gold connected people to each other and to the empaths who'd brought emotion and color back into their world. Despite it all, Theo's bond to Pax remained invisible. Forced to be hidden so long that their pain had become a permanent scar.

She didn't need it to find him. He was right next to her. It had always been this way, the reason why their grandfather had effectively psychically muzzled her for much of her early life. So she couldn't reach out to Pax on the PsyNet. Now, she did a careful examination of his mind.

It was dazzling, the brightness searing.

Clearly the mind of a Psy on the top end of the Gradient.

No fractures, no instability. Nothing but crisp clarity.

All stable, she told Pax. *What's the matter?*

I've received thirteen telepathic pings in the last hour. All from unknowns. I was wondering if I was somehow drawing them.

Theo scanned the area around them. While Pax's mind was visible in the Net, it was also so heavily shielded that it was a silent deterrent against unwanted contact. "Pings," as he'd put it, could be sent by any mind to any other mind. It was a request for communication, no threat.

It could be innocuous. Teenagers playing games. She'd heard rumors of such annoying but harmless games as her people began to come out of Silence. *But keep me updated. If it gets really distracting, you can always just turn up on the Net and catch them in the act.* No kid wanted to come face-to-face with an aggravated 9.

It's a minor irritation at most—I can easily set my shield to ignore any pings by unknowns for a period, Pax said. *Hopefully that'll send whoever it is off elsewhere. I'll let you know if it goes any further. You have two more hours in flight?*

Yes. I'll report back once I've been to the facility.

Upon landing, she decided to make that first visit right away. According to the city's sunset clock, they still had at least three hours of daylight left, she wasn't tired, and she needed to know what she was facing.

She didn't, however, know if her assigned partner was available—and though technically, she was within her rights to go to the facility on her own, Pax had made it clear that this was a question of politics as well as accountability.

"Our grandfather did a lot of damage," he'd told her. "We have to be cleaner than clean if we're to dig the family out of the mud. I have no desire for Marshall to become a backwater family—and I refuse to let Grandfather's actions define us for generations to come."

Having had firsthand experience with certain members of their family, Theo thought Pax was on a fool's errand. "Our family is tainted from the inside out," she'd said. "Even you were ready to cross some dark lines before."

Before he became aware he suffered from Scarab Syndrome.

Before an empath connected to the SnowDancer wolves became his only link to sanity.

Before his protectiveness toward Theo reasserted itself as a driving force in his life.

Pax was still far better—far *cleaner*—than Theo, but that didn't mean he had no skeletons in his closet. And Theo wanted him to face those skeletons. Secrets that dark needed to be exposed to the light or they turned toxic and poisoned a person from the inside out.

Theo knew that better than Pax ever could.

Her twin hadn't flinched at her blunt words. "I know. But that doesn't mean we can't be better. It'll take time, but we'll be better."

Strange as it was, she thought her ruthless sibling might even believe that. She didn't. The rot in their family hadn't started with Marshall Hyde. Back in her late teenage years, she'd dug into their family history in an effort to find a hero on whom to focus, some member of her family who'd done good instead of evil, who'd chosen compassion instead of cruelty.

But theirs was a line of darkness.

She'd gone back, so far back, and all she'd found was a thirst for power and for cruelty. They'd been conquerors who'd crushed uprisings, doctors who'd done horrific experiments in the name of progress, CEOs who'd wiped out entire towns in their hunger to be the best and the only.

Marshalls were evil.

At the end of her research, she'd sat there shivering in the small room that was her own . . . and she'd felt a whisper of a touch that was of her twin. Not the instinctual bond nothing had ever broken, but a more conscious attempt at telepathic contact. She'd rejected it not because she didn't trust Pax—that had *never* been the issue between them—but because she'd come face-to-face with the fact that she was just one more cog in the machine of evil.

Just another ugly Marshall.

But Pax thought they could be better. And . . . her brother was dying. There was no cure for Scarab Syndrome. This attempt to bring the family into the light might be the last thing he ever asked of her.

Theo's chest hurt, the pain sharp and hard. She'd tried to make herself stone long ago, and she'd succeeded with everyone but her twin. The far better half of their pair. Any lines he'd crossed couldn't compare to her crimes.

Not willing to look head-on at a loss that would signal the end of her own life, too—for there was no reason for her darkness to exist if Pax was gone—she exited the plane, then slid her phone out of the pocket of her calf-length skirt. She paused on the way out of the passenger area to send a message to Yakov Stepyrev.

Her phone rang in her hand mere moments later, the same name on the screen. "Theodora Marshall speaking."

"I figured you'd want to check out the site," said a masculine voice in accented English that held an undertone of warmth. "I'm your ride. Look out for a big furry brown creature as you exit."

Theo blinked, took the phone away to stare at it, then said, "I have your ID photo. Unfortunately, it only features your human face."

A pause from the other end before he said, "In which case, look for my ugly mug when you leave the secure area," in a voice that held a thread of something she couldn't quite pinpoint.

Shaking her head at the odd interaction, she slipped her phone back into her pocket. She'd undertaken basic research on bear changelings during her flight—most of it via the digital archive of a magazine called *Wild Woman*. She'd learned that while bears were intensely territorial, they were also considered one of the most good-natured of the changelings—as long as you didn't attempt to harm them or theirs.

The various columnists had often referred to the bear sense of humor, but she hadn't expected to run headlong into it the instant she set foot in Moscow. Of course, an article by "Aunt Rita" had stated that while bears found great amusement in acting like "lumbering trunks of fur with a limited number of brain cells," they were ruthlessly intelligent.

"Only a fool underestimates a bear" had been Aunt Rita's final words on the subject.

Theo hadn't needed the columnist's advice on that point; she'd figured it out on her own. No pack or clan would've survived existing in—much less holding territory in—the same region as Kaleb Krychek if they were anything less than dangerous and smart.

Aunt Rita had also stated that "bears appreciate spine" and weren't easy to offend—unless a verbal opponent targeted the vulnerable under their care. Theo had found herself compelled by the latter, unable to imagine a people so good-natured and even-tempered.

Psy might have aimed for peaceful minds with the emotionless regime of Silence, but all they'd achieved was a frigid control that wore on the psyche until people began to snap.

Murder rates hadn't gone down under Silence. The crimes had just been concealed better. She knew that because her grandfather had never bothered to hide information around her; he'd thought it was fear of him that kept her mouth shut. Theo had allowed him to believe that. Far better that than he realize she did it for Pax.

Marshall Hyde had never understood her profound allegiance to Pax—and her brother's equally visceral loyalty to her—which was why he'd never realized that he could use one twin to manipulate the other. A small mercy.

Today, she'd be interacting with a man as different from her grandfather as night from day.

She'd survived a Councilor. How hard could it be to deal with a bear?

Armed with her research, she had her guard up and her senses on alert when she exited through the doors that spilled her out into the public area. She'd ended up on the tail end of a group from a commercial flight and expected to spot Yakov Stepyrev well before he spotted her; Theo was hardly a woman who stood out. Her grandfather had taught her to never stand out for reasons of his own, and she'd taken those lessons into adulthood because they suited her.

Except the instant she walked through the automatic doors, she got a prickle on the back of her neck that told her she was being watched. She looked up . . . and met eyes of a stunning aqua green across a good ten meters of space.

He lounged against the white of the far wall, one booted foot kicked up against it and his arms folded. Faded blue jeans. Black T-shirt. His biceps were defined but not in the overt fashion of a man who'd made it a point to get those muscles—these were the muscles of a changeling used to the physical. His hair was thick and silky and the color of polished mahogany, his skin a shade closer to dark honey, his face put together in a way that had multiple women sending him smiles as they passed by.

Right now, however, Yakov Stepyrev, StoneWater bear and Theo's partner for the duration of this task, was focused absolutely and totally on Theo.

YAKOV exhaled against the visceral punch to the gut that was Theodora Marshall.

The woman of his dreams was staring straight at him, her eyes an intense and electric storm blue and her features set in lines that told him nothing . . . yet there was a potent power to her, a sense of that storm contained. So much fucking emotion hidden beneath an outwardly calm surface.

Barely able to breathe, he tried to settle his racing heart.

Stupid ID photo. Lying ID photo. Probably taken by a cat.

How had anyone managed to snap such a flat image of a being who fucking *radiated* energy? Oh, it was kept under tight lock and key, much like with Silver . . . but no, Theodora Marshall wasn't the same as Silver.

His alpha's mate had never given off this impression of an explosion barely contained, the veneer on the surface the merest patina. Silver's calm was internal, the reason why she could be the unflappable director of EmNet—and a senior member of a clan of bears who liked to misbehave.

Theodora Marshall, however . . . She was a powder keg.

A single trigger . . . and boom.

His bear stretched, ready for the boom. For everything. Because it was *her.*

The woman who'd been haunting him since he was sixteen.

Pushing away from the wall with what he hoped was a commendable show of lazy relaxation, he strode over to her. "Theodora Marshall."

"Yakov Stepyrev." Her voice held a slight huskiness, and she didn't offer her hand.

The latter, he'd expected. Psy who'd grown up under Silence weren't easy with touch. As for the huskiness, it affected him the same as when he'd spoken to her on the phone: straight to his dick.

Real evolved of you, Yakov, muttered his internal prude. That prude, however, was soon swatted away by his bear. A bear that really, really, *really* liked Theodora Marshall and her tightly pent-up energy and her unexpected and sharp comeback to his comment about looking out for him in bear form.

Woman had claws.

The bear was intrigued. It wanted to stroke her until she went boom for him.

Forcing himself to breathe and to keep his bear in check, he took in the rest of her. She was shorter than him by at least a couple of inches, maybe more. At five-eight, he was somewhere in the midrange for changeling males, but even though she was technically shorter than him, with fine features, there was nothing small about her—Theodora Marshall had what his babushka Graciele—his father's mom—would call a *presence*.

This, despite the fact that she wore generic black flats, a wraparound calf-length skirt in the same color, and a plain white shirt with long sleeves. No studs in her ears, no sign of piercings at all. Her only jewelry appeared to be the metallic comm device on her wrist. Her nails were clean and unpolished, her hair pulled back into a severe knot at the back of her head. Even her purse was nothing but a large black square with no personality.

Everything about her said *Don't touch.*

His bear was all about touching, but skin privileges were a serious matter. To be given, not taken. So he wouldn't assume anything. But he also intended to charm the heck out of her.

Hold on, hold on.

A screeching sound in his mind, a reminder that she was part of a family that had made a business out of lobotomizing people.

She was a child for most of that, another part of him murmured, but the earlier reminder managed to cut through his knee-jerk reaction to his dream woman. He might think he knew her, but all he knew of her was a figment of his imagination, visions caught between sleep and wakefulness.

Yakov didn't know the real Theodora Marshall.

He still intended to stick to her like glue—because if she was real, then so was that vision of her jugular spurting blood. His bear paced inside him, hunting for a threat neither part of him could see.

This woman who was both a stranger and not, he vowed, would not die under Yakov's watch.

He fell in step with her as she walked toward where the system would spit out her luggage after she scanned her ID. It didn't matter that she'd flown on a private jet—all luggage went through the airport's security systems and could only be collected by the person to whom the luggage was linked. At which point, it would either be handed over, or Theo would be pulled into a private cube to be questioned about items inside.

Moscow had a number of the most secure ports of entry in the entire world. A result of the fact that Kaleb Krychek, the StoneWater bears, and the BlackEdge wolves all called it home and had worked in concert to put those precautions into place.

"I'll grab it," Yakov said when her suitcase appeared in the waiting area behind the collection points.

He didn't realize what he'd done until she said, "How do you know it's mine?" Her ID was still in her hand.

"Scent," he said, though he didn't need to be thinking about the enticing lushness of her scent, all heat and dynamite and vanilla. Definitely a hint of vanilla in there. He just needed a closer sniff to be certain.

Sending a stern signal to his dick to behave and to *not* get all energetic about taking a deep draw of the scent at the delicate curve of her nape, he said, "Yours is all over the suitcase."

A pause, her eyes staring into his, as if she expected him to sprout claws at any moment, go rampaging through the airport. "Of course," she said at last, and scanned her ID so the luggage could be released. "That makes sense. By the way, you can call me Theo. My full name is a mouthful."

"You pack bricks in this thing?" he muttered as he picked up the case with ease, his bear sniffing at the idea of turning on the hover function.

Also, in Theo's defense, certain bears *had* been known to run amok in Moscow. Perhaps even Yakov. When he was much younger, of course. But even his *kretin* juvenile self had known better than to do it at an airport or any other port of entry. The alliance that held the city took no shit where security was concerned, and he'd have had his skin flayed off his body by his alpha *and* the wolf alpha.

Theo Marshall—and yeah, "Theo" suited this contained explosion of a woman far better than the antique-sounding "Theodora." Though the old-fashioned name was pretty, he supposed. Yet this sleek creature with her composure and her chilly blue eyes behind which stirred a dark inferno was far more a Theo.

She also wasn't as invisible as she clearly wanted to be, given her choice of clothing and her austere grooming choices. People looked her way, frowned as if they didn't know quite why they were doing so.

He could have told them: Theo was magnetic.

Charisma, he thought with an inward suspicion. A lot of bad people had charisma. Then again, so did a number of talented, good, and smart people. Like his own alpha.

He'd have to watch and listen and learn if he was to figure out whether Theo Marshall was a friend or an enemy seeking to slide under his defenses.

Or a lover, his bear suggested. Just get her naked, figure it out from there.

Groaning silently, Yakov shoved the ursine heart of his nature away from the surface of his mind. If he'd had any doubts, he now knew the primal half of his nature clearly couldn't be trusted here.

Chapter 9

Dear Hien (my favorite little sister),

Congratulations! We're so proud of you—we hope you enjoyed the flowers we sent. We told the florist to make sure they included your favorite tulips. And of course we'll visit you in Paris. Marian is already talking to her alpha about scheduling time off, and I'm just planning to run away from my duties too fast for anyone to catch me.

We can't wait to congratulate you in person.

And you might think I helped you, but all I did was hold your hand a little bit now and then. You put in all of the hard work and you deserve every ounce of success.

As for the modifications to the Silence Protocol, I attempted to be rational about it, but the truth is that that's an impossibility for me. It made sense when it was just about eliminating rage from our minds, with the aim psychic peace, but to cut all emotion out of Psy lives?

Where would that leave families like ours, where not every member is part of the PsyNet? Would you, Ma, and Pa have to cut me and Marian off? Would I even be able to see any of you? I feel like none of these questions are being addressed . . . And yet, I see the pain of our people. I see how much death there is, how much mental instability. I accept that something must be done, but I can't agree to Silence as the solution.

I'm sure we'll have plenty of spirited debate about this when we're together in Paris. But what I most look forward to are at least a hundred of

your hugs. I can't believe my little sister is all grown-up and writing me
letters on fancy embossed stationery.

With love from your favorite brother,
D.

—Letter from Déwei Nguyen to Hien Nguyen (28 February 1972)

THE VEHICLE YAKOV Stepyrev had brought to pick her up was large,
the manner of all-terrain vehicle that was no doubt necessary in bear
territory, but Theo still felt compressed inside it, as if he'd stolen all the
air and replaced it with a primal energy that brushed against her like fur.

Theo was always aware of those around her—a survival strategy
honed long before her exile—but this was far beyond that. Far enough
beyond that it could become a weakness.

She had to learn to think past the impact of Yakov's presence.

The good thing was that, bear personality or not, she was fairly certain he wasn't doing it on purpose. His actions so far had been relaxed,
and a grin creased his cheek when he stopped the vehicle to talk to the
security guards who kept an eye on the airport's incoming and outgoing
traffic.

The grin revealed one of the dimples she'd first glimpsed inside the
airport. She had the same inexplicable reaction as back then: the insane
urge to touch. It was nothing, she told herself, just a physical response
to such close proximity with a strong changeling. He was . . . potent.

Wrenching her attention away from the dent in his cheek that somehow made him even more astonishingly handsome, she forced herself
to concentrate on his conversation. Thanks to her family's interests in
the region, she had ninety percent fluency in the local tongue. It had
been a nonnegotiable part of her study program, even after she was ejected
from the family. Another one of Grandfather's little exercises in control.

"You asshole," one of the guards said in response to a comment of Yakov's that Theo had missed in her preoccupation with a man's dimple of all things, but the guard's voice held laughter and her pale brown eyes . . . weren't quite human.

Bear? Wolf?

Those eyes landed on Theo right then, and the woman nodded a polite greeting before murmuring something to Yakov at such a low volume that Theo had no chance of picking it up. Yakov responded back as quietly, then waved to the guard before driving on.

"Sorry about that," he said. "Silkie wasn't being rude. Personal matter she wanted to update me on."

It took all of her hard-won calm not to jolt in reaction. No one ever bothered about insulting or offending Theo. The ones who knew Theo's place at Pax's side pretended they did, but it was blindingly obvious that it was *Pax* they didn't wish to offend. The powerful twin. The one who held their life or death in his hands.

At times, she fantasized about showing those individuals exactly what she was capable of . . . but the desire for petty revenge never lasted long. She could be far more useful to Pax as a vicious weapon unknown and unseen.

Hidden from even her twin himself.

"I didn't take any offense," she said, and it was the truth; she'd assumed the guard was asking about why Yakov had a Psy in the passenger seat. "Does your clan know you're working with me?" It was far easier to deal with Yakov Stepyrev if she kept matters surface level and related to the business at hand.

"My senior clanmates, yes," he said, turning out of the airport area to join the flow of traffic. "I'm sure word will get around—damn nosy bears."

Theo had no idea how to take his last words even though she was much better than most Psy at understanding subtleties of emotion; her Silence had never exactly been perfect. She was almost sure she'd heard affection in those apparently harsh words, but his face gave nothing away.

"My research on bears states that you're communal by nature."

"There's communal," Yakov said darkly, "and then there's *bears*. A man just going about his business, and suddenly ten babushkas are on him about a little public disorder that never harmed anybody."

She was certain now that he was amusing himself by playing up to Psy perceptions of changelings being violent by nature. The irony of her murderous people judging anyone else would be laughable if it wasn't so tragic.

It was a long second later that she realized she was staring at his profile.

Waiting for the dimple to reappear.

A flush creeping up her neck, she jerked her attention to the large purse in her lap. "I need to go over some details of the facility before we arrive," she said to him, her voice too thin to her own ears.

A playful bear either (a) likes you or (b) is messing with you.

Despite everything, Theo had forgotten Aunt Rita's astute warning and fallen into a stealthily placed bearish trap. If she kept on going with this conversation, she had the distinct feeling she'd reveal far more than she'd gain.

Pretending she was acting normal and that she hadn't already memorized all the information, she pulled out her organizer. And tried not to breathe in the rough heat of him with every breath. She'd never realized *heat* could have a scent until she was inside a vehicle with a changeling who pulsed with a wild energy that made the hairs on her arms prickle and her skin tighten.

"Sure." Deep, relaxed, his voice felt like fur over her already sensitized flesh. "You want me to turn off the radio?"

She clutched at the matter-of-fact topic. "No, you have it at a very low volume. I can hardly hear it."

He tapped his ear in a silent reminder of his far more acute hearing. "Just tell me if you ever want it louder. With the various tonal corrections built into most audio media, it isn't uncomfortable for changelings even at higher volumes."

Though Yakov didn't interrupt her with words after that, his mere presence continued to be a rough buzz against her skin, a pressure akin to a building cyclone. She turned the pages on the organizer without seeing the text and images, her heart a staccato beat and her senses full of *him*.

Her leg began to quiver from the built-up tension.

She didn't understand her chaotic response, especially now that he wasn't luring her into conversation. It wasn't as if she'd never been around changelings. She went to most of Pax's appointments with E-Psy Memory Aven-Rose, and Memory never came alone to those appointments. Most times, it was her wolf mate who accompanied her, but every so often it'd be another dominant wolf.

Once, it had been a sleekly feline woman with long black braids. Desiree. No one had mentioned her animal, but she was apt to be a leopard, since the wolves had an alliance with their feline neighbors. Desiree might've been cat rather than wolf—but her dominance had been as violent a pulse. A silent warning that Memory had deadly backup.

Because the wolves weren't friendly when it came to Pax. It was more that they tolerated her brother because Memory was willing to work with him. In contrast, they were receptive and even kind to Theo—to the point that she'd exchanged conversation with the dominants who accompanied Memory.

Even then, face-to-face with a predator who was primed to attack if Pax even breathed wrong around Memory, she hadn't come anywhere close to being overwhelmed. Yakov, in contrast, was the most laid-back changeling she'd ever met. There was no sense of tension to him. He drove with one hand on the wheel, his other placed against the window and the wind riffling hair that glinted with concealed threads of red under the afternoon sunlight.

No taut muscles, no hardness to his expression, that dimple that fascinated her a suggestion in his cheek even when he wasn't smiling.

She should've felt at ease. Instead, the knot in her belly grew, her muscles so tight they were about to cramp. She was overloading in a way she only usually experienced during one of her episodes—but there was no cold prickle of blinding fury, her mind clear but for the fog created by her fascination with the bear beside her.

Swallowing hard, she pinned her eyes to the organizer screen and fell back on her oldest and most well-utilized focus technique. At seven years of age, tormented at being separated from her twin, she'd taken to creating his name in her mind using dots of mental light.

Pax created of tiny imaginary stars.

It was a child's trick, a child's need. She should've long ago moved to using her name, or any other random word, but this was what had worked when she'd needed it most, and her brain had become conditioned to it.

Inhaling quietly—only to be hit by the wildness of Yakov's scent—she placed the first dot in the black backdrop created by her mind.

Two. Three. Dot after dot.

Too late, she realized she wasn't writing out Pax's name after all. She was *drawing a bear*!

Chapter 10

Human horticultural expert Danil Yaslav tells us that in his opinion, the topiaries are the work of a master landscaper and their apprentices. "Brilliant, absolutely brilliant," he stated. "And such a lovely homage to the ursine inhabitants of our city."

—Excerpt from "A Beary Big Surprise," article in the
Moskva Gazeta (18 June 2068)

YAKOV'S PASSENGER WAS dead silent, her head bent over her notes.

And while Yakov might be the quintessential bear, being social his default, that didn't mean he couldn't deal with quiet. He'd already gone over the documents on the Center that Silver had forwarded him, wondered if Theo had more.

He'd ask her later.

For now, however, he kept his attention on the road and his mind on the task ahead . . . only his bear *still* wasn't in the mood to cooperate. The stubborn animal half of his nature had decided that dream vision aside, Theo Marshall was captivating in her own right.

Yakov growled at his own bear self inside his mind.

Things that fascinated him always got him into the worst possible trouble. Case in point: his teenage fascination with the den's solar-power grid. Yes, he'd crashed the entire system. Even worse, he'd taken his twin into his disgrace. Pavel, of course, had stood stalwart next to him, but Yakov had not been impressed by himself.

His bear stretched inside him, acting like it was just a casual movement. Until it nudged him to take a discreet sniff of his passenger. Because quite contrary to popular belief, canines did not in fact have the best sense of smell in the world. That honor belonged to elephants, thank you very much, and the herds were quite proud of it. But bears? Bears had a keener sense of smell than even bloodhounds. *Seven times* keener, to be precise.

So he could tell that Theo Marshall wasn't wearing perfume, and that the soap she'd used on her skin was a basic blend with such a faint undertone of vanilla that she likely hadn't even scented it. Having warmed up against her skin since her shower, however, the scent was rich enough to have his bear taking appreciative breaths.

Her shampoo carried a similar scent; had to be the same brand.

Sniff!

Ignoring his bear's demand—a bear that had no sense of boundaries— he played a game he and Pavel had done as children, seeing what they could figure out about a person from the tapestry of scents that clung to each and every individual in the world. The game was a popular one among cubs, one fostered by their parents.

Only later in life had he come to understand that the "game" was actually an important part of their education. Through it, they'd built up a database of countless scents. Not only that, they'd learned to interpret the intense amount of information they picked up simply by existing.

He already knew that he made Theo Marshall nervous.

She wasn't sweating, but her body chemistry was nonetheless clear: she found him disturbing.

Yakov wanted to scowl. He didn't enjoy going around scaring

women. Then again, this could be Theo Marshall's stock response to any predatory changeling. Many Psy had a tendency to believe that bears, wolves, leopards, and the like lived life on the brink of going feral.

No reason for him to take it personally.

Theo also carried a scent that wasn't an element of her—it was of another person. Given how light it was, he might've assumed she'd picked it up during her journey except that it held a fine strand identical to her own.

Not similar. *Identical.*

Family, but a special kind of family.

Twins.

So now he had Pax Marshall's scent, too. Excellent.

Other scents swirled around Theo—the fabric soap she'd used to wash her clothes, the polish on her shoes, the plas of her organizer, the food-based aromas that had followed her from the airport and were already fading.

The vast majority of those scents were such a normal part of life that his brain had long since learned to filter them out from the important data points. Else every bear would spend its life in a state of overwhelm.

But with Theo Marshall, he found himself worrying at each element, taking it carefully apart, then putting it back together. Trying to figure her out through his nose since she refused to talk to him.

His bear couldn't understand it. *It* hadn't scared her. It blamed that on the human half of Yakov's nature. The bear's suggestion was that Yakov stop the car, shift, and show her how handsome he was in bear form.

The human side of Yakov considered it: it *was* true. He was a very handsome bear. And Theo would probably be disarmed by the plushness of his fur. Much less threatening than his human skin.

He was still gnawing on the idea when his attention was caught by the news bulletin on the radio.

Enforcement has released the name of the homicide victim found on August 29 in the Izmaylovo District. Jelena Sekko, age 27, was a patternmaker at a bespoke tailoring business that specializes in menswear. She'd been in her position for the past five years and was in line for promotion to manager.

A clip played, of a woman saying: *"She was the best of the best at her work. Punctual and detail oriented . . . and kind."* The last came out hesitant, a Psy who was still uncomfortable with emotion but who'd made the effort for her friend.

Then the bulletin carried on:

Enforcement continues to refuse to speak on the possibility of a serial killer, but the mood on the ground in the city is nervous. Hair salons are reporting an influx of young blond women coming in to get their hair colored to darker shades.

Yakov's mouth tightened as the news bulletin moved on. Enforcement might not want to say it out loud, but Moscow had a serious problem. As did Theo, a slender, blue-eyed blonde . . . who Yakov saw bleeding out in front of him night after tormenting night.

Jaw clenched so hard that his muscles ached, he made a note to alert Theo to the danger stalking the city just as his eye caught the street sign up ahead. "Fifteen minutes to our destination."

His instincts stirred, his bear snapping into full hunting mode. It was time to find out what Marshall Hyde had buried on the far outskirts of Moscow. Far enough from any real population centers to fly under the radar—but close enough to the airport to move cargo . . . and people, at will.

He'd intended to come to the facility prior to Theo's arrival, do a reconnaissance, but had then decided to spend his limited time going over the data Silver had forwarded him. No point driving all the way out here when there was no way the staff would allow him to enter without Theo's presence at his side.

His brother had also dug up local records for him, to supplement Silver's information, but neither one of them had found any clue as to the facility's true purpose. To all outward appearances, and according to the business permit granted when it was built, the place was a Center, same as any other.

Aware of Theo raising her head from her notes as he slowed down, he pulled up to the locked gates of the facility. His information said it sprawled over a large area, but he couldn't see anything beyond the gate—the place was thick with foliage heavy and green. Ivy crawled over much of the gate itself, and enough trees thrived beyond that he couldn't see even a glimpse of the main building.

Unexpected for a Psy facility. The psychic race tended to go for manicured lawns and hedges pruned to within an inch of their lives. As juveniles, Yakov, Pavel, Valentin, and their felonious friends had once snuck into the landscaped area of a fancy Psy hotel and pruned their pristine squared hedges into the shapes of bears.

Standing bears. Sitting bears. Sleeping bears.

Bear balancing on one leg.

Bear thinking deep thoughts.

Thanks to literal *months* of practice in the lead-up to the prank, their topiary artworks had looked exactly like the aforementioned bears, but the best thing was that they'd never been caught. And the hotel hadn't noticed it fast enough, either—a human with a bearish sense of humor had snapped photos and the next thing they knew, their masterpieces were on the front page of the *Moskva Gazeta*.

Moscow residents had been despondent when the hotel ordered immediate "remediation of the damage."

"Wasn't damage," Valya had said at the time. "It was *art*."

But there was nothing of Psy perfection up ahead . . . or when it came to the intercom. Placed on a plinth on its own beside the drive, it was smothered in moss and cracked on one side. That was not standard operating procedure for powerful Psy families; they were slick and shiny as a rule.

Wondering if it was all part of the facility's camouflage, he reached over and pushed the old-fashioned button that should connect him with someone on the inside.

Theo took a ragged, gasping breath at the same instant.

On immediate alert, he jerked his attention to her.

She was stark white, her eyes fixed on a point he couldn't see.

Chapter 11

I suggest we attempt the procedure on another young subject in their teens. While our first such attempt wasn't a success, neither was it a total failure. Pre-adulthood neural plasticity may be the critical element.

—Message from Dr. Upashna Leslie to Councilor Marshall Hyde
(6 January 2063)

Nineteen Years Ago

THEO HAD BEEN excited when her grandfather picked her up for a trip. She'd been doing so well in her coding and hacking lessons. The computronic instructor had given her top marks and progressed her to a level beyond her age group!

She'd believed the trip a reward for working so hard.

But she realized she'd been very, very wrong the instant she got into the back of the vehicle with Grandfather. Every tiny hair on her body had stood up, her mind telling her to *run!* But the driver had shut the door behind her, and she'd known that even if she did get out, it would only anger her grandfather. He'd have no trouble finding her.

People liked to tell Councilors things they wanted to know. Sometimes, she made up stories inside her head of running away to live in a changeling pack—but she knew the changelings wouldn't want her.

They didn't like Psy. Her teachers tried to teach her that it was because the changelings were "savage beings with no intellectual curiosity," but Theo wasn't stupid.

Sometimes, people in her family had tried to make her believe she was stupid, but she *wasn't*. Her test scores in mathematical and science subjects had always been better than Pax's. Her brother had never minded; he'd been proud of her. As she'd been proud of him for always being the best at languages and pattern-based studies.

Because she wasn't stupid, and because she had access to that data-pad that was the one thing about her life that her grandfather didn't know, she'd done her own research. She'd found her way onto forums with changelings and humans, and she'd learned two things:

First, that changelings were as smart as the Psy.

And second, that changelings hated the Psy because Psy had done bad things to changelings. She hadn't been able to get into the forums that discussed the details of those bad things, but she knew enough to understand that Psy were bullies. And her grandfather was one of the most powerful bullies of them all. No changeling pack would want to hide Theo. They'd hate her for being his granddaughter.

No one would believe that he wished she was dead.

Grandfather turned to stare at her. "You failed another semester of Silence, Theodora."

She twisted her hands together in her lap. "I'm sorry, Grandfather." It wasn't that she didn't try. She did! But it was as if she had a hole inside her that kept on allowing emotions to drip through.

That hole, she'd come to realize this semester, was shaped like Pax. Her brother had shielded her from her inability to be Silent without her ever realizing it. He couldn't have known, either. They'd always done things like that—just . . . balanced each other out so that they were better together than they were apart.

Only now did she understand that he must've done the bulk of the balancing. Grandfather was right. What could a Gradient 2.7 possibly do to help a Gradient 9? Nothing, that's what. It hurt Theo to think that, but she had to be honest with herself. Because she was all she had now. Even if she imagined she could feel Pax inside her mind at times.

"Sorry isn't enough," her grandfather said, his voice flat with nothingness—as if Theo wasn't worth any part of his attention. "I think it's time you understood the consequences of failure."

She sat in frozen silence until the car pulled up to the shiny silver building that was the family's business HQ. She'd been shown it before she was sent to live with Colette. Grandfather had told Pax it would all be his one day. She'd been happy for her twin, hadn't understood then what Grandfather's words really meant.

Today, she kept her head down as she followed him into the building, then into the elevator. He took her directly to his office, where another person was waiting. A woman with skin as white as snow and eyes brown and empty who wore a gray suit with pants and black high heels.

Grandfather put his hand on Theo's shoulder, digging in his fingers hard enough to hurt. "To the central location. We'll drive from there."

"Sir." The woman put her fingers very lightly on Grandfather's brown coat . . . and the world tumbled.

Theo cried out and fell to her knees . . . except she didn't fall on the carpet of her grandfather's office, but onto cold concrete that scratched up her hands and made her knees hurt a lot.

"Sir, I didn't realize it was the child's first teleport. I apologize."

"There's no need. Bring around the car."

Her grandfather looked down at Theo as she got herself upright. Her hands were a little bloody and dirty; she pressed them against the black of her coat. The rough fabric felt better than the way he looked at her. As if she was a worm he wanted to crush.

"Pathetic," he muttered. "Get in the car and fix your hair. You're part of the Marshall family. Act like it."

Knees hurting, she nonetheless climbed into the back seat and tucked herself right into the corner. Though her hands trembled and her palms stung, she used them to straighten up hair that had become messed up when she fell.

She hadn't put it in a braid today, had wanted to look her best for her special trip. So she'd brushed it until it shone really bright, and then she'd added a black satin hairband that Colette had bought for her.

Theo hadn't been able to believe Colette would get her something so pretty. She'd asked why.

"Physical perfection is to be valued not for its emotional value," her foster parent had explained, "but because even Psy respond on a visceral level to beauty. While you'll never be beautiful, neither are you ugly. And considering how few advantages you have in life, I feel compelled to at least teach you how to present yourself as best you can."

Theo wasn't interested in things like that, but she listened to Colette's lessons, and she tried to follow them because she knew it mattered to her grandfather. He was always dressed neat and perfect, his hair cut and his short and pointed beard groomed. Back when she'd lived in the family house, he'd always told her and Pax off if they ran inside with dirty knees or untucked shirts.

She wished she had enough telekinetic power to 'port over her hairbrush, but wherever she was now, it was really far from her room. She couldn't *reach* that place with her mind. Not wanting to look at her grandfather and see the nothingness for her on his face, she just looked out the window at the strange city through which they were passing.

The people looked like at home, but their clothes were a bit different and the buildings were a lot different. Some of them seemed really old and had the style of round domes she'd seen in a geosocial lesson about India. But she didn't think this was India. The people didn't dress the way she'd been taught many people in India dressed, and their skin was mostly pale like hers.

Then the people disappeared and so did the buildings and they left the strange city behind, driving and driving until the teleporter who was the driver pulled up in front of a set of thick metal gates.

"This is why we didn't teleport in, Theodora." Her grandfather's voice snapped her to attention. "I wanted you to see these gates, understand that if you ever give me cause to take you through them again, you won't come back out."

Theo stared at the cold metal . . . and sucked in a breath when she saw the electricity that arced a searing blue at the top, above what looked like spikes sharp enough to stab a person straight through from one side to the other.

She'd never seen electricity like that, out there in the open.

"It's a warning," her grandfather said at the same time. "No one should be out this way regardless, since we own a large chunk of the area, but the visual warning should halt anyone curious enough to make the attempt."

Theo tried not to panic. He hadn't read her mind. She'd been staring at the electricity, so he'd told her why it was like that. "I understand," she managed to say in a calm voice.

Then the gates opened slow and smooth to show a long drive that disappeared around the corner. Once inside, their driver stopped and waited for the gate to close behind them before she started to drive again.

High security.

Theo knew those words and what they meant because their parents had made sure to tell her and Pax about security from when they were small. It was because Grandfather was so important and their family had so much money that they had to know about security. People might try to kidnap her or Pax.

Theo knew now that no one in the family would pay to get her back. She wasn't the important twin. Pax wouldn't say that. Pax always said she was his best friend. Or he used to. Back when they were together. It had been a long time since then, and maybe Grandfather was telling the truth and he'd even forgotten her.

Her chest hurt deep inside as they turned the corner and at last she saw the big white building with shiny windows out front. There were people outside. A lot of them wore pale green pants and shirts, while others wore pale blue ones with white coats. The ones in green looked sleepy, a little confused.

One almost stumbled and fell even though there was nothing to trip him up.

A white-coat person helped him up, and then they watched him try to walk again.

"Is this a hospital, Grandfather?"

"Of a kind." Her grandfather got out. "Outside, Theodora."

She scrambled out behind him because the door on her side was locked. It was only once she was outside that she saw the faces of the people in green. They were somehow . . . loose. And their eyes were all wrong. It was like they couldn't see.

Stopping on the tiny stones that lined the area, she stared at the person closest to her. As she stood there, a single tear beaded on the corner of the man's eye and rolled down his cheek. But his face didn't move, and he didn't make a sound.

"Why are all these failures still alive?" Her grandfather's voice had her staring at him, her heart thudding.

She didn't hear what the person in the white coat said, but whatever it was, her grandfather grunted and carried on. Feeling bad for the man who'd cried the tear, she looked at him once more. But he was no longer looking at her, was staring down at the ground with his empty eyes.

Theo ran after her grandfather over the tiny stones that crunched under her shoes, knowing he wouldn't be pleased if he turned around and saw that she wasn't following. She didn't look at any of the other people who wore green.

Her heart was thumping too hard and she had a sick feeling in her stomach.

Inside, the building was shiny and clean like the care center her parents had visited that time she and Pax got in trouble, and there were lots of people with white coats who all looked at Grandfather the way people mostly did: with slightly lowered heads even when talking to him. Because her grandfather was important.

There was only one woman who looked her grandfather straight in the eye. She had hair as gray as the cat that Theo often saw on the balcony of the neighboring apartment building. The lady who lived there waved at her sometimes and since no one could see Theo doing it, she waved back. She hoped the cat would visit her one day.

This woman was much older than the neighbor lady and so thin that her bones stuck out hard against her wrinkled brown skin. But she was strong. Theo could tell that from the way she stood, and how she moved as she walked down the hall toward Grandfather. "Councilor Hyde," she said when she reached them. "I'd like to reiterate my objection to the procedure. The risk is significant."

"So noted," her grandfather said, and the fact that he'd actually listened to everything the woman said without interrupting told Theo that this woman was important, too. Her grandfather didn't listen to many people at all.

The woman looked down at Theo. "How old are you?"

"Eight years and nine months," Theo answered after a glance at her grandfather to check if she should talk.

The woman looked back at her grandfather. "The brain is too plastic at that age. The procedure, even if successful, is unlikely to hold."

"Regardless, we'll do this. We need a child on whom to test the regimen and who better than my granddaughter? She's been displaying some rebellious tendencies. There's no need to look for an external subject."

Theo got a very bad feeling in her stomach. She knew they were talking about her, but she didn't understand why.

The woman went silent as they walked, but something told Theo that she was still talking to Grandfather, just telepathically. Since Theo couldn't hope to listen in on that, she tried to figure out what was happening by forcing herself to look around. But all she saw were more people with the dead eyes and the faces that looked like they had melted.

One woman stood facing a wall. She fell against that wall the next second, banged her head and bounced back. Then she did it again and again.

"Truly, Upashna?" Grandfather muttered as they passed that woman. "Why are we wasting research funds keeping these subjects around?"

"Each one teaches us something different," the woman named Upashna replied. "The female we just passed, for example, has retained all physical abilities. No hesitation when we can get her to walk. No shakiness. Full control over the body."

"Interesting," her grandfather said.

"Yes, I thought you'd see it that way." A pause. "Marshall, you're sure you won't reconsider? I realize she's only a 2.7, but she's still part of your genetic line."

But her grandfather shook his head. "Let's get it done."

Theo hesitated in front of the door through which her grandfather had gone. She wanted to turn, run outside and away. But even as the thoughts passed through her head, she realized the driver had come into the building behind them and stood watching her from only feet away. Theo couldn't run without being caught.

Then her grandfather came, gripped her shoulder, and dragged her inside.

Chapter 12

Keja Marshall
Date of birth: 19 August 2041
Date of death: 8 December 2057

—Entry for Keja Marshall in the Marshall Family Tree (current)

THEO COULDN'T BREATHE. She literally couldn't breathe, her lungs collapsing inward as she stared at the gates in front of them. Her mouth dried up at the same time that bile burned the back of her throat.

Images flashed to the forefront of her mind. Faces. Scrubs. Medical masks.

Screams.

Oh, God, whose screams were those?

Her grandfather's face, telling her that this was her duty as a member of the family.

Cold in her veins. God, she was so cold. It burned, the cold.

"Hey, hey! Theo!" A deep male voice, a big body leaning toward her own.

She knew she wasn't alone, that she should be wary, but she couldn't take her eyes off the gates even as lights began to spark behind her eyes from the lack of oxygen in her lungs.

"Govno!"

Movement, the slam of a door, then the slap of chill outside air as someone opened the passenger-side door. She was vulnerable, so vulnerable, but she couldn't break the loop in her mind.

Screams.

Cold that burned.

Medical masks.

Grandfather.

Screams.

Burning ice.

Straps, straps, holding her down.

Pain.

So much pai—

"Theo!" Arms coming around her, dragging her out of the passenger seat and into the bright cold of the fall day . . . and then he was literally lifting her up and turning her so she faced the other direction, his body behind hers as he put her down, then held her with her back to his chest.

She stared at the asphalt spreading out in front of them and away from that place of nightmare . . . and took a desperate breath. It hurt, shards of broken glass in her lungs.

"That's it, *pchelka*. Breathe. Slow and easy, slow and easy."

She couldn't follow the advice, had to gulp. But he kept on talking, and though she couldn't really hear him anymore through the roar in her ears, the calm and warm timbre of his voice got through, gave her something to focus on that wasn't the road.

She became aware of the power of his body behind her with a creeping slowness, the heat of him a furnace. Changelings burned hotter. She'd read that during her research using *Wild Woman* magazine. It had been in an article about how to deal with an argument about the temperature of the air conditioning between a mixed-race couple—human and changeling.

The human was too cold. The changeling was too hot.

She couldn't remember the advice given to the couple who'd written in, but right now, she understood why the human was cold at the temperature comfortable for her husband. Psy burned the coolest of all three races, and Yakov Stepyrev felt like a fire at her back.

She didn't pull away.

She needed his fire to melt the lumps of ice that had formed in her bloodstream, threatened to choke up her throat, cut off her breathing.

"That's it," murmured that voice so deep and warm, "you've got it. Slow and easy. Long and deep."

She took an inhale, released it quietly . . . and finally made herself step away from him. It was the closest she'd been to another sentient being since childhood. It hadn't felt odd, not in the moment, but now, she flushed. Not out of embarrassment but because of bone-chilling fear.

Because she didn't want to turn and look at the gate again.

"What is *wrong* with me?" The words spilled out past her lips.

Yakov shifted so that he faced her, while her back remained to the gate. "Looked like a panic attack to me." He examined her face. "Your eyes have gone black. Psy I know tell me it's a response to intense physiological, psychic, or emotional stress. One second."

He reached in through the open passenger door to retrieve something while she was still trying to come to terms with his short and succinct summary of the situation. Theo didn't have panic attacks. She'd never have survived in her family if she allowed panic to steal her breath—they'd have killed her. Literally. Most of her family had been waiting for her to die since she was first graded as a 2.7.

"Here." Yakov twisted off the top from a fresh bottle of water. "Get a little of this into you. It'll help clear things up."

Numb, she accepted the offer because water was always good, and took a sip. Only then did she realize it was fortified in some way. She kept drinking. Her muscles ached as if she'd been running full tilt for an hour.

She didn't stop until she'd drunk a third of the bottle. "Thank you," she said afterward, and wondered dully what Aunt Rita would say about accepting this food-related gift from a bear.

Shock, she was in shock. This was no time to be thinking about bears offering food. And the situation was so far beyond Theo's normal as to be anarchy. None of the usual rules applied.

Yakov took the bottle once she was done, put the cap back on, and dropped it on her seat. "No problem." Narrowed eyes as he looked past her shoulder.

Her skin crawled.

"You've been here before." It was a statement, not a question.

She couldn't blame him for the assumption. "If so, I have no memory of it." She held a gaze that had gone a striking yellowish amber, waiting for him to snort a rejection of her words.

But he nodded. "Yeah, I figured. No reason for you to panic that way if you'd prepared yourself for it."

Theo swallowed. Her normal mode of operations was to keep her mouth shut on any possible vulnerability. Even with Pax, she was careful, not wanting him to see the truth of what Grandfather had done to her, what he'd *made* her. It would break her brother into a million bloody shards.

Fingers shaking, she rubbed the bracelet on her wrist. And knew she had no other option but to trust this bear with her current state. "I'm having trouble making myself turn around." A noxious realization had begun to bloom in her brain, a horror so bad she could hardly face it.

Her name in the mangled file Pax had found.

Memories of medical masks and scrubs.

Echoes of childhood terror.

Yakov didn't tell her to stiffen her spine and get on with it. "Do you want to?" he asked instead, those bear eyes penetrating her thin skin. "Or do you want to get out of here?"

Screams.

Masks.

Grandfather.

Straps tying her to the chair.

Cold that seared her blood, made her scream.

"I want to," she said, her voice a rasp. She'd never sleep again if she didn't find answers to the nightmare images.

"Then we might need to take a break," Yakov said. "Maybe get an E out here to—"

Theo shook her head in a hard no. "I need to know what lies beyond. I'll go mad if I delay." There was no point in attempting to hide the depth of her reaction from Yakov, not when he'd witnessed it firsthand. "The terror will circle my brain until it cripples me."

YAKOV wanted to vehemently disagree. He'd never seen anyone go that stiff, every muscle in their body locked, their breathing halting as if a switch had been thrown. And her color. *Govno*, she'd gone so white her skin was parchment, the blackness of her eyes stark pools against the white.

"I'm not sure you can physically do it," he said, being blunt because he had no intention of allowing her to push herself into another panic attack.

A long breath, Theo's chest rising and falling before she put her hand on the side of the car, then began to swivel on her foot very, very slowly. He knew when she caught first sight of the gates. Her entire body went rigid; her breathing began to accelerate.

"Theo." It came out a warning rumble.

She held up a hand, palm out. It trembled, but she was still breathing, albeit rapidly.

And somehow, she managed to turn and face the gate full-on.

The woman didn't only have claws, she had steel for a spine.

The two of them stood in silence for several minutes as she worked on getting her breathing under control, her body no longer as stiff as a plank of wood. "I can do this," she murmured, and he wasn't sure which one of them she was talking to.

Regardless, and despite the confusion of protectiveness and suspicion inside him, he couldn't help but admire her courage. He wasn't sure it wasn't stupid courage—it was obvious she was putting herself through hell—but bears could often be bloody minded, too, so it wasn't as if he had a leg to stand on there.

"No response to the intercom," he told her. "Not even sure it's working."

Forehead creasing, she looked over at the dilapidated device. "The facility has been drawing funds continuously. That should have been fixed long before it got to that state."

"Do you have an override for the gate? It has what looks like a complex computronic lock." He began to close the distance to the looming metal bars.

"*Wait.*"

When he paused, glanced back at her, he found her staring up at the spikes at the top. "I . . . I think there was an electrical current once. Blue." Her voice was distant, as if inside a memory.

A second later, she snapped her attention back to him. "It's dangerous. Stay away from it."

Yakov's bear halted, startled at the clipped order.

Aside from his mother and father and grandparents, who had the privilege by dint of having diapered his baby butt once upon a time, there were very few people on the entire planet who'd dare give a bear of his dominance an order. For the most part, that number was limited to his alpha and Valentin's second- and third-in-command.

No one else would dare.

Except Theo just had.

He considered being insulted by it, but nope, that didn't feel right. His Psy dream woman with secrets in her eyes was trying to protect him. His bear wanted to cuddle her for it—though he didn't think he'd get that chance anytime soon, he was gentle with her when he replied, well aware her nerves had to be scraped raw.

"Easy enough to check if the security field is still running." He angled his head. "I can't hear the hum of an older system."

"I didn't know that was possible."

"Lot of changelings have the hearing range for it." Walking to the side of the drive, he picked one of the long blades of grass and touched it to the nearest part of the gate with care.

Despite the cold terror in her scent, Theo actually jerked forward until she stood within arm's reach of him.

Ready to drag him back if he got himself in trouble.

Astonished at the fierceness of her courage all over again . . . and seduced by the protectiveness that apparently ran so deep in her nature that she was willing to face her worst nightmare to shield his bear ass, Yakov had to fight not to turn around and wrap her up in his arms, nuzzle at her until she wasn't so afraid anymore.

He hated that this strong, brave woman was so scared that it had stolen all the light right out of her.

What the fuck had they done to her?

His bear growled inside him.

Chapter 13

While bear changelings have many talents, grace is not one of them.

—"Jocie's Opinions: Inaugural Column" in the June 2083 issue of *Wild Woman* magazine: "Skin Privileges, Style & Primal Sophistication"

IT TOOK ALL Yakov had to keep his attention on his task, his nape burning with the intensity of Theo's focus on him as he moved the blade of grass slowly forward. No telltale vibration, none of the hairs on his arms standing up. To be extra careful, he took off the metal ring he wore on his right ring finger and flicked it gently at the gate.

It pinged harmlessly off the metal to fall to the ground.

"Must've been turned off." He bent to pick up the ring that had been a gift on his and Pavel's eighteenth birthday from his maternal grandparents. He figured they'd be pleased he'd used it to assist in his safety.

Satisfied he wouldn't get fried, he went to examine the lock more closely. "Interesting."

A stir in the air, Theo coming to stand by his side. Much closer than he would've expected. But *chert voz'mi*, if she'd just give him permission, he'd cuddle her right against his chest and wrap her up in his arms.

Fear remained a strong thread in her scent. Whatever else this place turned out to be, it was obvious that to her, it was a horror. And no matter the suspicions he had about her family, his bear was not okay with allowing another being to suffer when gentle skin privileges would help ease their pain.

"What?" The question was air over the back of his neck as he bent toward the lock.

His bear stirred under the shivering caress.

Wrenching the animal within under control, he said, "This." He pointed to a patch of clean metal. "Someone's gone to great effort to make this lock look as overgrown and as old as the intercom, but it's undergone recent maintenance."

"I do have a code," Theo said, and he could all but hear her pulling the tempered steel of her soul back together, "but it won't work. This lock is a different kind than the one in the files."

Yakov considered bending the bars of the gate, but a single shake of one cylindrical piece of metal told him they were built strong—strong enough to repel even a bear's considerable strength. He next looked at the top of the gate.

Tall but not insurmountable, even with the spikes. "I can jump the gate, see if I can find a way through for you." Bears weren't the most limber or graceful climbers, but they were strong, and in human form, that strength made up for their lack of fluidity.

"No, wait." Theo put her hand on the lock, tilted her head to the side for a full minute. "Yes," she said at last. "I can unlock it."

That was when he remembered what Silver had said—that Theo Marshall was a Tk who could move tiny parts around with her mind. "Telekinesis?"

A curt nod, her attention clearly on whatever it was she was doing to the lock.

He actually *heard* a tiny click before she stepped back, rubbing the palm of her hand against her skirt. "It should open now. I didn't break the mechanism, so we can lock it back up when we leave."

Yakov whistled. "I didn't know Psy could do that." Computronic locks like this were considered highly secure, since they had few if any moving parts that could be "picked."

"Most can't." Theo's voice had gone oddly flat, devoid of the hum of contained emotion that was her trademark. "It's a skill so rare that there's probably less than five people in the world capable of it. I just happen to be one of them."

Yakov wanted the real Theo back. "Could you walk into a bank and unlock their vault?" he joked.

But her response was serious. "Likely."

"Paired with a teleporter, you'd make one hell of a heist team."

She shot him what should've been a flat glance—but there was too much mobility to her face, too much energy. "I'm not a criminal." Hard words.

Yakov realized that while he'd broken through the flatness, he'd also hit a nerve. Then again, it could be deflection, because what Theo had just done wasn't exactly a minor skill. It was, in fact, a *very* useful one for a family that wanted to keep secrets and take advantage of the secrets of others.

What exactly had Theo Marshall done while flying under the radar? And *who* had she done it for?

Bear rumbling inside him because the damn animal liked the scent of Theo Marshall, but also saw her as a possible threat—*and* couldn't forget that she was part of a family that had made a profit out of maiming people—he reached out to push open the gate. It stuck and he realized it had a redundancy in the form of two bolts behind it. "Can you move these?"

Theo tried, shook her head. "No. I'm only a 2.7." And that trick with the lock had taken a large amount of her power reserves—it was harder than it looked from the outside. "They're too heavy."

Yakov stepped back. "Guess I'm jumping the gate after all."

Theo's entire body tensed, her gaze jerking to the spikes, then back to him. Her hand lifted on the instinctive urge to grab him, stop him.

. . .

"HEY." Eyes kissed by amber meeting Theo's. "Bears aren't as clumsy as we look. We only run into things fifty percent of the time."

"Be careful of the spikes." Theo didn't realize she'd risen onto her toes until she settled back down. "They aren't decoration and you *are* a bear. My source on changelings states that bears constantly overestimate their ability to be graceful." He didn't need to know that her source was *Wild Woman* magazine.

A sudden grin from Yakov that made her stomach clench. "Watch this," he said, then jogged back several meters before running full tilt at the gate.

Her mouth fell open as he hauled himself up with a power and speed she'd never have expected from a bear changeling. Close to the top, he all but *vaulted* over the spikes and came to a firm landing on both feet on the grassy and cracked drive on the other side.

Wild Woman didn't know what it was talking about! She had half a mind to write a letter to the editor demanding a retraction of the slander against bears. But the magazine had been right when it had called bears "an arsenal of brute power." Yakov clearly had muscles atop muscles.

Her heart was still thumping when he began to slide open the bars that acted as deadbolts, his biceps flexing and the veins in his forearms standing out against the burnished brown of his skin. That took enough time that she had some control over herself when he opened one side of the gate. It was big enough to drive through.

"I'll drive in," he said, jogging back out, "then we should lock things up. There's a reason security is stringent—we don't want to risk others coming in, or getting out. For all we know, this place was hidden because it's where your grandfather housed dangerous criminals he had a use for."

Nodding, she stood where she was with her gut churning as he drove the vehicle inside. It took every inch of courage she possessed to make her feet move to the gate, but she couldn't cross the boundary between the outside world and whatever lay beyond.

Getting out of the vehicle on the other side, Yakov jogged back to her . . . and then he held out his hand. "Take your time, *pchelka*. This place isn't going anywhere."

"Did you just call me a little bee?" It came out a startled question, her voice strangled with a fear that infuriated her. She'd *fought* this, had won. She'd refused to be scared anymore, and in so doing, she'd stolen her grandfather's power.

A slow smile by the bear in front of her, followed by a wink. "You must've misheard . . . *zaichik*."

It had been rabbit . . . no, little hare, that time.

Bears.

And somehow, her fingers were touching his, and then she was sliding her hand into his and gripping with bruising strength as she forced her feet to cross the invisible dividing line between the outside and . . . this terrible, dark place behind heavy metal gates.

She would not let a long-dead monster defeat her.

Yakov's body so close to her, his breath brushing her earlobe as he said, "Not *mishonok*, I think. Not for a woman with a spine so fucking strong."

Mouse, she translated inside her head. He refused to call her a mouse, even in jest. And . . . it meant something. As it meant something that he stood there with her hand locked around the rough warmth of his until she could make herself let go. Even then, he ran his knuckles over her back in an act of comfort before he turned to close the gate.

The sound of the deadbolts sliding home made her flinch.

"You're doing great, Thela." A murmur far too close to her, the heat of his body pressing against her chilled skin.

Thela. Not Theo. He'd altered her name in a way that her language lessons told her was familiar, friendly. Such a Russian thing to do. The implied acceptance left her shaken. "What do your friends call you?"

"Yasha," he said. "My mother calls me Yakov Mayakovskevich

Stepyrev when she's about to give me a scolding, but otherwise, it's Yashka. My babushka Quyen calls me Mischief Bear One. You can call me Gorgeous."

No one in her entire life had ever spoken to her this way. So open and warm and amused. And that was when she realized she was gripping his hand again, and he was letting her. "How about Trouble?" she shoved out past the cold fear that crushed her throat with a skeletal hand.

Because Theo wasn't about to surrender to evil.

Not then. Not now. Not fucking ever.

A grin that revealed those dimples that were weapons of bearish distraction—and the antithesis of evil. "You honor me." He did a half bow before rising to squeeze her hand. "You ready to move on, *pchelka*?"

She'd have to ask him why little bee, but for right now, she jerked her head in a yes, ready to face this head-on. The worst of it wasn't the physical sensations of fear that crawled over her skin and blocked her breathing, it was that she didn't know why this place was a cauldron of nightmare for her—if that flashback by the gate had been a memory, she didn't have the rest.

I won after all, whispered the ghost of her grandfather.

Theo bared her teeth and slapped away the phantom. No, he didn't get to come back from the dead, didn't get to taunt her. He got to stay in pieces so small that his remains hadn't even filled a box of such trivial size that a child could've carried it with ease.

"Yes," she said to Yakov in a voice as hard as stone, "let's go." But before she could take a step forward, her eyes fixed on a crack, over which grew green moss.

Shifting her gaze, she looked further down what should've been a pristine drive, but while there weren't an enormous number of cracks or potholes, there were more than there should've been. And a lot of foliage had begun to creep onto the asphalt.

"This place must've been heavily planted to begin with," she murmured with a frown, "which is unusual in a Psy facility, but now it looks totally out of control." At last, finding her footing in the practical, she made her fingers let go of his.

Her digits cramped, used to the shape of him.

"Planting would've been to ensure privacy." Yakov hunkered down beside her, touched the growth she'd seen. "This stuff is fairly quick growing, but some of the other plants . . ." He looked up, eyes narrowed. "Two, three years without being trimmed at least, to get to this stage."

"My grandfather died roughly three and a half years ago." She didn't use the word "assassination" because to use that word seemed to imply that it had been a bad thing that Marshall Hyde had been killed. It hadn't been a bad thing.

The world was a better place without her grandfather.

"Hmm, and you say funds are still going out?" Yakov rose to his feet, rigid thighs pushing up against his jeans. "Might be a case of embezzlement. If it is a Center, they've unloaded their 'patients' and are siphoning money."

Ice crackled over Theo's skin because in Psy terms, "unloading" would mean only one thing. "We'll find out today."

She already knew hers was a family of monsters.

Today, she'd find out if they were also a family of mass murderers.

Chapter 14

Scarab Syndrome cases remain on the rise. Current projections—based on available historical data as well as data from the present outbreak—are that it'll be at least six months before we see a decline.

—Report to the Psy Ruling Coalition from Dr. Maia Ndiaye, PsyMed SF Echo (15 August 2083)

PAX STOOD NOT far from the river of dead air in the PsyNet, staring at the Island.

He'd responded to the initial emergency when the PsyNet tore away in that section. Despite the syndrome that threatened his sanity and his life, he remained a 9 on the Gradient.

And, thanks to Memory, he'd regained his usual control over his abilities—not a permanent state of affairs, but the two of them had scheduled his sessions with her so he'd never get too close to the edge.

Pax knew he hovered the merest breath from oblivion.

But that day, he'd been Pax Marshall, CEO and Gradient 9 telepath, and his help had been accepted. Even those who knew about his battle with the syndrome hadn't rejected his help.

So he'd waded in and saved as many lives as he could.

The work had been hard and dirty. He'd literally grabbed people as they fell screaming into the dead air, their lifesaving link to the PsyNet broken. At which point, he'd thrown them back into a more stable part of the Net. Not exactly subtle, but it had done the job.

Now, the island formed that violent day glowed with life.

Some of that energy whispered to Pax even across the abyss of dead air.

It *knew* Pax.

Scarab energy. An energy of false promises and madness.

Rubbing his eyes on the physical plane, Pax shook away the thought. Nothing could cross dead psychic air. This was only his paranoia speaking. And crossing the region wasn't his goal today; it was to check on the steadiness—or not—of the PsyNet on its edges.

Pax felt responsible for the lives he'd saved.

He'd done good for once in his life, and he wanted to see it through.

He would've preferred to be closer, but there was a heavy security presence around the circle of dead air. He understood why the Ruling Coalition had made that call. The Island was too tempting to the curious—permitting rubberneckers wouldn't only clog up the flow of this section of the PsyNet, it might lead to more deaths.

Pax, however, was strong enough to see the Island from a significant distance away. What he couldn't see, however, was the chaotic signature of the Scarabs he knew existed within it. He'd caught a single brilliant glimpse of their minds during the incident, right before a ripple of silver light spread over the entire island from the center, an unimaginable psychic bomb.

The Scarabs had vanished.

Yet the media hadn't reported a surfeit of deaths on the Island.

Part of him hoped the silver "bomb" had been a magic bullet, that it had cured the Scarabs . . . that it could cure him.

A stir in the PsyNet next to him, a mind black that shimmered with an obsidian mirage of colors.

Pax didn't react, Memory Aven-Rose's mind as familiar to him as Theo's. Unlike the vast majority of the people in the Net, the empath could find him at will, the two of them bonded on a level he knew the empath detested—because she detested Pax.

He couldn't blame her for that; he'd tried to murder one of her friends, had done such terrible damage that he'd put the man into a coma. There would've been no coming back, not even a chance of forgiveness without Theo.

His far better half.

"Is there a problem?" he asked Memory.

"No, I was out here with another E interested in the Island, and I felt you nearby." Her mental presence was intense, lacking the soft edge of most Es. Because Memory was a unique class of empath, the kind dangerous enough to deal with a mind affected by the syndrome. "Why the interest in our new breakaway state?"

Pax didn't share his inner landscape with anyone other than Theo, but Memory had earned his answer. "I suppose because it gives me hope. The Scarabs are under control there."

Memory exhaled next to him. "I've been liaising with the Es dealing with the patients on the Island. I'm sorry, Pax"—kindness, because whether she liked him or not, Memory was an E—"the Syndrome is still running rampant through their minds. It's just been contained to those minds rather than being allowed to leak into the network."

Disappointment tasted like ashes, he thought, dull and dusty.

Once upon a time, he wouldn't have acknowledged his reaction. Because once upon a time he'd put on the act of being the perfect graduate of Silence. Such a good act that he'd almost convinced himself of his lie.

But the truth was that he'd been born loving his twin, and that love had never died. He'd cut out his heart, sacrifice himself without a thought if it would save Theo. That he hadn't been able to protect her from their grandfather was the greatest guilt of his life.

"Thank you for telling me," he said to Memory, the ashes drifting in his vision as they floated up, motes from a distant fire.

"I wish I had more positive news." True sadness in her tone. "You're better than I thought you were once, Pax," she said unexpectedly. "I feel it, you know, your love for Theo, your need to protect her. I wish I had a solution for you—and for every other victim of the Syndrome."

Pax fisted his hands on the physical plane, struggling against the vulnerability of being seen so clearly. And yet, there was a freedom in that, too. He didn't have to pretend. "I'm setting systems in place for after my death, so that the worst of our family can't harm her."

But there was only so much he could do in advance. "Will you do me one final favor after I'm gone and keep an eye on her situation?" Memory was a SnowDancer, the wolves' power a feral and dangerous thing.

Theo would be safe under their watch.

"Yes," the empath said without hesitation, her mental voice thick with emotion. "But we're not done yet. Don't give up."

"No, I intend to fight to the bitter end." Until the madness wrapped in a beautiful promise of power ate up every last piece of who he could've been in another life.

Each and every day, that lying promise whispered in his ear, telling him he could be more, he could be everything, he could be the center of the Net if he only let go and set the power free . . .

Chapter 15

Dear D,

And the letter writing tradition continues! Today's stationery is from a company called Visions. I thought that was apt, given that my big brother is a foreseer. ☺

   I meant to ask—did you foresee that our parents would decide to adopt two little boys after seeing their story on the news? They're such adorable little munchkins. I'm excited to be the elder sibling for once! Fingers crossed the adoption process goes smoothly.

   I've just received word from the company that they want me to head a project in Zürich for the next six months. That'll mean a delay in my wedding to Kanoa, but he's excited about getting a chance to play in Switzerland. He's already put out feelers with the orchestras there, and given his reputation and experience, chances are high he'll soon have an offer.

   I'll send you our new address in Zürich once I have it, and of course I expect you to visit me again. I loved having you and Marian stay with me in Paris. I know it'll be different this time, with Kanoa in the mix, but you two already get along like a house on fire—and Marian is my soul sister. I know we'll have a blast.

   I'm assuming you haven't seen the Silence questionnaire they're sending out through the PsyNet, so I am attaching a copy for you. There are a number of thoughtful questions in there, big brother.

Love from your little sister, Hien

   —Letter from Hien Nguyen to Déwei Nguyen (1 September 1973)

. . .

BEFORE THEO COULD get back inside Yakov's rugged vehicle, he grabbed something from the back passenger seat and said, "Here. You're cold."

It was a leather-synth jacket in a deep shade of brown. Lined with what looked like fleece, it'd be incredibly warm. She wanted to grab at it, but kept her hands to her sides. "I have a coat in my luggage."

"Which it'll take you a while to open up and find," he pointed out. "Take the jacket. I only use it when it's snowing. You might as well get use out of it."

Theo shivered again, then felt her eyes narrow when he raised an eyebrow. Suddenly, she wanted to reject the jacket just because he looked so smug. So much like . . . like a bear! Which was utterly irrational. Then again, part of the reason her grandfather had so disliked her was that she *was* irrational. The most irrational member of the family.

Grabbing the jacket, she shrugged into it. The length of the arms would've probably been perfect if it hadn't had such wide shoulders—hers were far narrower than his. But that was an easy fix and she quickly rolled up the sleeves before giving him a grudging "*Spasibo.*"

"You're welcome," he said with a glint in his eyes that told her he could guess at her uncharitable thoughts. "Make sure you close up the throat. That's where you lose the most heat. Looks good with your outfit."

Now she was sure he was making fun of her. Her "outfit" was blandness personified. She'd made sure of that. Deciding that sometimes one had to ignore bears who were clearly amusing themselves, she got into the passenger seat without responding.

But once there and staring out at the drive, she was grateful to him for distracting her from the situation, even if only for a few moments. Because her stomach began to churn the instant she was staring ahead once again. She might've conquered her grandfather's ghost, but her own invisible memories howled.

Yakov glanced at her from the driver's seat. "Go?"

She made herself nod, the action bringing even more of his scent to her nose. He might not use this jacket much, but he used it enough that his scent was embedded in its weave and heft. She should've found it too much, claustrophobic. Instead, she took his advice and zipped the standing collar all the way.

If she tucked her chin down, she'd be breathing him in.

Ahead of them, the drive continued to whisper into shadowy darkness . . . before it curved to the right.

"Good way to ensure no sightline from the gate." Yakov's words were crisp, his body alert.

"There were light sensors here at some stage." She pointed out the small black box that had fallen onto the ground from its intended position. Likely on a large tree trunk close by. "No way to sneak up to the facility even if you bypassed the gate."

"A changeling could've gone through the forest," Yakov pointed out. "But we'd have had to have a reason to come poking around so far off the beaten path. Especially if everyone thought it was a medical facility."

His chest rumbled. "As a juvenile, I never knew Centers were for hurting people. If I ever thought about them, I figured they were Psy-only clinics. Made sense since Psy and changelings and humans don't have the exact same physiological needs."

"No." The three races were *almost* but not quite identical. Just enough minor deviations to make a difference when it came to medical care.

"I'm pretty sure my great-grandfather must've known the truth of the Centers," Yakov added, "but I want to imagine he didn't. I mean, Psy in Silence were pretty tied to the idea of keeping their secrets, so it's not out of the realm of possibility. From all I know of him, the truth would've broken his heart."

Before she could ask him why his great-grandfather might have had reason to be interested in the Centers, the landscape opened up enough to reveal a large and weathered building surrounded by more foliage.

Vines crawled over the walls, their roots a fine mesh beneath the red-gold of the leaves, and fallen debris covered the twin ramps and one set of stairs that led up to the wide front door. The roof appeared undamaged but the weatherproof coating had begun to peel off in patches that exposed the coppery underside.

Theo could tell the building had been white once upon a time, though it was now smudged with dust and dirt. While most of the windows were whole, a couple bore large cracks from what looked like accidental hits by broken branches and other storm detritus. Remnants of those branches still lay below and around the property.

The place echoed with emptiness.

Maybe that was why she didn't panic, curiosity overriding her wariness. Or perhaps it was because it looked so different from—

A clear flash of memory, of seeing this building from her grandfather's car.

Her heart thumped but there was no panic this time. Only a grim determination. She got out, her gaze going immediately to the right where she'd seen—She frowned, thought, but the fragment of memory, if that was what it had been, slipped out of her grasp.

Yakov, who'd been prowling around, came to a halt near her. "Certainly looks abandoned," he said, "but according to the map your brother forwarded, there's a large area at the back along with a shed and another outbuilding. I say we check that section out before we attempt entry into the building."

Willing to take his guidance on this because security had never been her bailiwick, she fell into step with him . . . a little too close for a Psy, but he didn't seem to mind or even notice. Because he was changeling, his standards of physical proximity were different than her own.

The fallen autumn leaves crunched beneath her feet, the sound painfully loud to her ears. "Am I making too much noise?"

"No, that's background. I'm picking up nothing—no scent, no sound—that indicates any other presence that isn't avian, and maybe a few mice."

No functioning medical facility would ever allow rodents so close.

Gut taut for a different reason now, she said, "Even Pax couldn't unearth the final count of those held here, but it was at least fifty people. Thirty patients to twenty staff, but that's the best guess he was able to make after running the financials."

Yakov's arm brushed hers as they walked, and she realized she was all but pressing herself against him. It was incredibly bad form in Psy society . . . but she couldn't make herself pull away. And he still didn't seem to really notice.

So she stayed. Warm and safe against his solid bulk, the quiet horror of this place held at bay.

THEO'S tension was an acidic burn against Yakov's skin.

No fear now, but rather the embers of a simmering rage as she considered the evil that might've taken place here.

Theo was *pissed*.

Angry enough that his bear made a note to never make her that mad at him.

But her anger didn't mean she wasn't also in pain. What had happened back at the gate? The panic attack? That had been no minor reaction. Stuff like that didn't just disappear—no matter how determined the person involved.

Still, at least she'd tucked herself against him.

He'd been around Psy enough now to know that was a big fucking deal, a signal of trust she likely wasn't even aware of transmitting.

His bear moved against the inside of his skin . . . right as they finally came around the side of the building and saw what was supposed to be a large courtyard area at the back. Fallen leaves of yellow and red and brown covered the mildewed paving stones, the furniture was stacked neatly to one side where it hadn't been pushed over by the wind, and the pergola was collapsed in one corner due to damage done by a tree that must've fallen in a storm.

But it was the far left of the courtyard that caught his attention. "That look like a greenhouse to you?"

Theo frowned.

Yakov wasn't surprised by the open expression of her feelings; it was clear that she wasn't exactly the perfect Silent Psy. Might never have been, given how easily emotion came to her.

Her brother might do a good impression of an android, but there was nothing hesitant or false about Theo's reactions—or about the raw violence of what she kept contained. He could almost feel the vibration of her anger against his skin.

When Theo Marshall blew, she might take out half the world.

"Yes," she said now in response to his question about the possible greenhouse. "A cheap one—looks like it's not glass but plas sheeting creating the walls."

"Yeah." Part of one "wall" was flapping in the light breeze, and when they got closer, he saw that an entire section had torn away and flown off to lie crumpled against the door of a closed shed. He checked out that shed first, found it empty of anything but a few rusty tools. "Must've been the landscaper's shed," he said on returning to the makeshift greenhouse.

Theo pointed. "Vegetables."

Yakov crouched down to touch the seedlings that had rooted on their own after the pots on the rickety metal shelving had fallen off. "I didn't see anything in the files that said this place was supposed to be self-sustaining."

A shake of Theo's head, her eyes scanning the area. "No, it was a normal facility in that sense. Regular deliveries of food and other supplies." She looked back at him. "Someone lived here. At least for a while. Properly lived here."

Rising, he said, "Let's do a quick recon of the one other building that's meant to be out here, then we'll go look inside the main structure."

Theo's gaze jerked to the main building before she wrenched it back. Her pupils were huge, almost overwhelming the blue.

Pretending he hadn't seen her visceral response—because this bear had manners and he was smart enough not to poke at a *very* angry woman, thank you very much—Yakov took the lead toward the other building he'd seen on the original map of the facility.

"We'll have to do a full sweep," he said as they walked through the overgrown vegetation. "Might be other temporary structures on the grounds." He pushed aside an overhanging branch dotted with small yellow flowers so Theo could pass through; the vegetation wasn't yet at the point that it was impenetrable, but it was making a good effort.

He took the lead again once Theo was past . . . and got a sharp look from her. Oh yeah, Theo Marshall was no submissive. In point of fact, she'd eat a submissive alive.

Good thing Yakov had the dominance to balance out hers—and that he was about as charming a bear as could be.

Grinning his best bearish grin, he said, "I have boots," and pointed out the thick and tall grass up ahead. "I can stomp a path through for you."

Theo's lips tightened, and he had the thought that she knew far more about bears than he realized. She might even bust him for being protective. But she gave a curt nod, and they continued on—with his bear keeping a wary eye on a woman who had far more layers to her than he'd initially realized.

Problem was that Yakov *liked* complicated.

"There it is." Theo pointed to a patch of grayish white just visible through the trees.

"Here." He made his way through another patch of grass. "Looks like the path's pretty clear on this side." Just moss and mildew—and the carcass of a dead bird.

Yakov was a predatory changeling, the hunt in his blood. But he didn't like to see an animal injured when it wasn't about food. So he paused, broke off the plate-sized leaf of a nearby plant, and gently scooped the bird's featherweight body onto it before laying it carefully at the foot of a tree, where it would decompose without being stepped on, its tiny bones crushed.

Theo had paused beside him, watching in silence.

When he rose to his feet after completing his task, she was looking at him in a way that he didn't understand. Her next words held a haunted echo. "We saved a bird once. Pax and I." It was a murmur. "We made its heart start beating again." A quick shake of her head, a blink.

"Theo?"

"No, it's nothing." Her tone was back to normal. "We should hurry so we don't waste the available daylight."

Deciding that little mystery could wait for the moment, Yakov continued on toward the building. It looked to have been a small residence. Neat and tidy from what he could see through the windows, with no sign of disturbance.

Then Theo put her hand on the front door lock, snicked it to the unlocked position . . . and opened the door.

Chapter 16

Claire, we need to discuss Theodora now that the twins' seventh birthday is on the horizon. In my office. 8 pm. No need for Miles to be present. This is a family matter.

—Telepathic message from Marshall Hyde to Claire Marshall
(1 September 2062)

IT WAS IMMEDIATELY obvious that the place was *too* clean.

"Someone lived here relatively recently." Theo wiped her finger along a tabletop, came away with a fine coating of dust. "This should be thicker if it was shut up after my grandfather's death."

"I'm not picking up any scents other than the normal odors of a house that's been closed up for a while." He opened the cupboards in the small kitchen. "No sign of food."

"The cooler is turned off." Theo opened the door to look into its interior. "Yakov."

"Smells like milk that's gone off." Face screwed up against the unpleasant but familiar odor, he joined her by the open door of the cooler. And saw what his nose had already sniffed—a small single-serve carton of milk forgotten in the corner. *Fresh* milk, not the kind treated so that it was shelf stable for long periods.

Picking it up, he checked the best-before date. "Expired two months ago."

Theo shut the cooler door. "Whoever it was is long gone."

"If you're serious about discovering their identity," he said, "we can get a forensic team in here, find fingerprints. We have people in the clan who specialize in that."

"No, that would involve too many individuals." Theo shoved her hands into the pockets of his jacket, and his bearish heart beamed at seeing her making use of the warmth. "For now, this is a minor matter. It could've been one of the staff—but if it was, their records are unlikely to show up in any search."

"Because you can't run a shadow operation without shadow people," Yakov said, putting the spoiled milk back where it had been since he had no way to dispose of it and, once closed, the cooler kept the smell contained. "Time to check out the main building."

Theo said nothing as they stepped outside, but he could feel the tension that was taut lines of wire throughout her body.

Judging that her balance was steady, he asked what he hadn't earlier. "You get a flashback during your panic attack?"

A single lock of hair that had somehow come loose from the punishing tightness of her bun settled to curl softly by her ear. But her voice when she answered held the same unyielding focus he'd glimpsed in her expression. "Jumbled and broken, but yes."

Stopping when they came within sight of the main building, she stared, her pupils once more inkblots against the searing blue of her irises. "My visual proportions are off in the flashes."

"Viewpoint of a cub?" Yakov said.

"Cub?" A frown that cleared quickly. "Yes, a cub. A child. Half my current height or so. Young then. Under twelve. I had my main growth spurt around twelve; until then I was in the shortest percentile of my age group."

Yakov hated the idea of a vulnerable child being in this cold and lonely place with its patina of old evil. "You have any conscious memories of the place?"

"No. Until the incident at the gate, I never knew I'd been here."

Yakov wanted to believe her. In her favor were his own instincts, and her reaction by the gate. No one could've faked that panic, including the chemical changes in her body that had screamed her fear. Against her was her family and their history.

The Marshalls were very good at hiding things.

Bear and man straining against the duality, he nonetheless offered her his hand once more. She stared, and he thought she'd turn it down. But Theo Marshall surprised him all over again, sliding one slender and too-cold hand over his, her fingers curling around his palm.

"You definitely need warmer clothes," he muttered as he enclosed hers in his much bigger hand, willing his heat to sink into her.

"Yakov?"

"Call me Yasha." It just came out, his bear making the decision about trust well before the more logical part of him could work through his dueling feelings.

Her fingers tightened on him. "I don't touch people." A statement coated in a hard shell.

"I'm not people." He winked at her. "I'm a bear."

A frown . . . followed by the faintest tug of her lips. "I stand corrected." She took a deep breath. "I'm ready."

A bird squawked loudly overhead at that instant and Theo's head jerked up, following its progress across the sky. When she looked back at him, he could barely see the blue of her irises. "Maybe it's a good sign."

"It's important to you," he murmured, "that memory of saving the bird."

"Yes. I think, in the end, that's what counted most heavily in favor of our family's decision to separate Pax and me. So maybe it's a bad omen." Her expression grew hard. "It used to be a secret, but I'm not keeping the Council's or my family's secrets anymore. We're a Harmony pair, my brother and I."

Yakov didn't know that term, but he had a feeling Silver would. Not that he was about to ask her. This, what Theo had just shared, was a private thing. "Tell me about it at dinner." Because he was damn well filling her with comfort once this was over. "After this is done."

She squared her shoulders, the anger in her a shield of fire. "After this is done."

They climbed the steps together, found the door locked—but that was no impediment, Theo unlocking it with her telekinesis in a matter of seconds.

Yes, that was one very useful skill in a family that liked power.

Yakov kept his mouth shut because he wasn't about to terrorize her—she might be tough and determined, his Psy, but this was the home of her private horror.

His questions could wait, he thought as they stepped inside.

Chapter 17

Harmonies are a gift, to be treasured and protected. These rare pairs—
often, but not always twins—hold within them the gift of *life* itself. No
Harmony pair is to ever be harmed. In harming them, we would be harming
the shining heart of us.

—Aleya, Psy philosopher (circa 1571)

Twenty-Two Years Ago

THEO WALKED OUT of the family house even though she wanted to
run. Her grandfather and parents had made the rules very clear: there
was to be no running inside the house.

"Any infractions will result in the loss of privileges."

That was what her mother had said. Theo hadn't understood what
the second word meant, so she'd remembered it and asked her and Pax's
tutor. So now she knew it meant breaking the rules. She'd told Pax, too,
even though he didn't get punished like her. Her twin had told her to
follow the rules, so they wouldn't lose their time outside—the time
when they were supposed to exercise in the way that they'd been taught,
but that they used to play.

Mostly no one checked on them during that time, since they were
inside the grounds of their grandfather's big estate. They played hide-

and-seek, or climbed trees, or played games that they came up with together.

I don't know why they punish you, Pax had said to her, mind-to-mind. *We do the same things.*

Theo might've only been five, but she knew the answer. *It's because you have lots of psychic power. I heard Mother say that you might be an 8 or a 9 and she couldn't understand why I wasn't strong, too.* Her mother's disappointment made her sad. *I keep on trying to be stronger so that when we do the tests, we'll be the same, but I can't make my mind bigger.*

But I like you just how you are, Theo! You're the smartest at equations and you always teach me!

Theo wanted to smile at the thought of what Pax had said to her. She knew he liked her. She could feel it inside her in a way she could feel no one else; Pax would never punish her or treat her bad just because she wasn't an 8 or a 9. And she knew he didn't go out and play by himself when she got punished and had to stay inside; he just did the exercises on the lawn outside, then came back inside.

So that we're both punished when you're punished, he'd said to her. *It's fair.*

Finally, she was out on the big deck with cold stone tiles and could see Pax sitting and waiting for her at the bottom of the wide steps that ended at the bright sunshiny green of the lawn.

Pax! She called out with her mind because she knew better than to call out using her voice. If anyone heard her, she'd be in trouble for not adhering to the "principles of Silence."

He turned around, waved, but didn't smile. They already knew not to smile except for when they were alone. Getting up, he dusted off his shorts. They were the same light brown as hers, and they also wore identical white T-shirts. "You chose the same clothes!"

She heard his laughter in her mind. *Again!*

She laughed inside, too, because they were always choosing the same clothes. Or if they didn't have the same things, they chose things that were almost the same. *Shall we pretend to do the exercises now?*

That was what they did every single time—just spend enough time on the lawn that people thought they were behaving. She couldn't always tell if someone was watching from the windows, but Pax could. His mind was so strong and he already understood lots about how to use it.

Yes. Grandfather is watching.

Her heart got quiet and her skin became cold. She didn't speak as they walked down the stairs and out onto the lawn to begin their stretches. She knew Grandfather was disappointed in her. He'd told her so.

"What a waste of excellent genetic material and intelligence if your Gradient rating tests come back as low as we believe they will," he'd said while going over her most recent educational report. "A true disappointment to the family."

He's gone.

She gave a long huff of breath at Pax's telepathic words. "I thought he'd *never* go!" But now that he had, she knew they were free. Grandfather only ever watched for a short time and he never came back. He had too much important business to do.

"Me, too!" Pax also huffed out a breath, because even though Grandfather wasn't disappointed in him, Pax thought he was too strict, too. He could feel how Theo's heart got all small when Grandfather called them both into his office and told Theo everything that was wrong with her.

Pax always tried to tell Grandfather that she was trying her best, but Theo was going to ask him to stop. Grandfather didn't like it, and she didn't want Pax in trouble. "Come on," she said. "Let's run to the trees before anyone else comes." If they weren't on the lawn, no one usually looked for them and if they did, Pax gave her enough warning that they could pretend they were just taking a nature walk. That was allowed, since it was a school activity.

The two of them began to run, Pax reaching back as if he'd take her hand.

No, Pax, she reminded him. *Not yet.* They weren't allowed to touch. It wasn't permitted under Silence.

Oh, I forgot. He dropped his hand, but he ran a little slower, so she could keep up.

Because he was turning back to check on her, she saw the bird before he did. *Look!* She stopped running.

He did, too, and they both went over to where a blackbird lay on the ground, its wings fluttering. "It's hurt," he said, going down on his knees on one side.

She sat down beside him on her knees, too. Tears burned in her eyes, even though she tried to make them go away. Grandfather would punish her a lot if he thought she'd cried. "I don't want it to die."

Her brother touched the top of the bird's head with a soft finger. "I think it hurt its head, Theo." He couldn't say her name properly still, so it sounded like "Tio." Grandfather didn't like that he had a "speech impediment," and Pax had to go to special lessons with a special teacher to practice talking, but Theo didn't see why it mattered.

She reached out to carefully pet the bird. "I think it's scared," she said just before her finger touched the silky black feather.

Her mind . . . opened. It was so clear.

Pax didn't stop her when she walked along the silver path that she knew he'd built. It was so strong, so bright. Just like her brother. Pax was shiny and bright inside and so was everything he built in the psychic world.

When she looked down at her hands in the black space lit up by his silver road, they glittered all silvery sunshiny. Smiling, she walked to the end of the road until she was in a room where things were broken and in the wrong place. It was a mess.

She began to put everything back where it should be, like how she sometimes filed things in her father, Miles's, study. He wasn't as disappointed in her as the rest of the family. She didn't know why, when he was an 8, but she was happy about it. When she needed to hide from Grandfather, she sometimes knocked on his office door and asked if he wanted her to tidy his bookshelves.

He always said yes unless he was going to have a meeting.

And his bookshelves were always messy. Even though she couldn't read as well as a grown-up, she could read enough to work out the words on even his big books, and the ones she didn't understand—like "astrophysics" or "cosmology"—she looked up on her study tablet. So she could file her father's books and other papers pretty good. The ones she really, really didn't understand, she put in a pile to ask him about when he was free.

But here, in this room where everything was tumbled and broken, she didn't need his help. She *knew*. The ones that were only a little out of place were easy to put back, but the broken pieces wouldn't fit so she had to sit down and fix them before she could put them back. It wasn't hard, but it took time and lots of energy.

Pax gave her his energy. *You're so clever, Theo*, he said, and she realized he was in the room, too, but he was just sitting in the corner, watching her. *I don't know how you fixed that.*

You built the road, she told her brother. *I don't know how to do that. Thank you for giving me your power.*

He smiled and she felt it inside her mind.

They stayed in that room until she'd fixed and shelved every broken and confused piece. Then she turned and walked back down the road, and though Pax wasn't with her, she knew he'd be there when she opened her eyes. He had to close the door behind her and erase the road.

She opened her eyes before he did.

The bird hopped up as soon as Pax opened his eyes. It fluttered its wings, squawked . . . and then spread those wings and flew away so fast that Theo almost felt a wing hit her face. She laughed. "We did it, Pax! We did it!"

Her brother grinned at her . . . and then the world went blank, both their bodies and minds shutting down without warning.

Chapter 18

"I could relocate with her to my family home."

"No, Father wants to closely supervise her education and growth. She's a Marshall and will remain a Marshall. That was part of our procreation contract."

"She's a child, Claire. Well-behaved and intelligent. There's no need to isolate her to fulfill the requirements of the Protocol—it works just as well if I raise her in the Faber home."

"The decision is made, Miles. Unless you wish to challenge my father?"

—Conversation between Claire Marshall and Miles Faber (15 October 2062)

WITH DARKNESS NOT far off and the electricity to the facility non-operational, Yakov knew they only had time to do one quick sweep. All they discovered in that rapid sweep was abandoned equipment, cobwebs, and zero sign of any computers, tablets, or organizers.

"We aren't going to find anything more today, especially with the light about to go," he said to Theo once they were back on the ground floor. "I've caught no scents that indicate recent passage by humans, Psy, or changelings."

Theo looked around, her gaze a touch wild. "We haven't found *anything.*"

"Exactly," he said. "Which in itself is a finding."

He barely stopped himself from reacting when Theo turned back to face him—with eyes that had gone wholly black. It should've been eerie and it was in a sense, but it was also beautiful in a haunting kind of way. "We won't do any good bumbling about in the dark. We need a plan and the time to do a deep search. Whoever scrubbed this place can't have eliminated every single piece of data."

"They've had a lot of time."

"Yes, but it's a large area and maybe not everyone did what they were meant to do."

Theo, her eyes yet black, refused to move. Jaw tight and shoulders bunched, that humming anger yet alive in her, she said, "I can't leave with only emptiness where answers should be."

Yakov shoved a hand through his hair. "I didn't want to tell you this while we're in this damn creepy building while the shadows are getting deeper, but I spotted old blood in one of the rooms. It was cleaned up"—because the people behind this *had* had time, years of it—"but I have a bear's nose. I hunted down the scent and found a large pool of dried blood inside a closet."

Theo stared at him. "As if someone was hiding in there and died?"

"That's what I figured. Body got removed first, and the cleaners either didn't know about the blood or just forgot." He folded his arms. "Either way, it doesn't sound like a fully controlled transfer. Things get left behind in a rush, get forgotten."

Theo stayed stubbornly put, as immovable as a bear. "What if someone enters now that we've disturbed it? They could have a silent alarm."

Yakov hadn't located anything of the like, and he was very good at spotting such security measures, but he wanted her out of here. Damn woman had started to tremble. The tremors were fine enough to almost ignore as being a figment of his imagination—except he knew they weren't.

He also knew the tremors weren't born out of fear. What he saw in Theo's expressive face was fury at being thwarted . . . and the anguish of a trapped animal with no way out. Only in Theo's case, it wasn't a trap

that held her but a hole in her mind populated only with echoes of terror and helplessness.

She wouldn't sleep tonight if he didn't figure out a solution.

Most people would probably say she risked another panic attack in
her refusal to leave. Now that he'd been around Theo for longer, however, he'd bet on her pacing the room as she ran investigative search
after investigative search while waiting for the sun to rise.

Pulling out his phone, he said, "I'll give the clan a call and see if we
have a couple of soldiers nearby who don't mind keeping an eye on the
place overnight. We'll come back tomorrow to do a comprehensive
search."

As it was, he didn't have high hopes of getting a yes. This place was
so far out of the way. But he had to make the attempt—because otherwise, he had the feeling he and Theo would be sleeping in the car until
someone could relieve them. His *pchelka* was in no mood to compromise.

His fears were proven correct. "No clanmates anywhere in the vicinity," Zahaan said . . . then sighed. "You could ask the wolves."

Yakov bit back a groan. StoneWater and BlackEdge were friends
now. Mostly. They were friends who growled at each other over a distance, snarked at one another at every opportunity, and would turn up
to help if the other was attacked. Once the fight was over, the growling
and snarking would, of course, recommence, to everyone's satisfaction.

"Yeah," he said, shoulders dropping. "Let me check if that's okay
with Theo."

"Theo, huh?" A waggle of the eyebrows that Zahaan somehow managed to put in his voice. "Have we got another Valya-Silver or Pasha-
Arwen situation on our hands, hmm? Does she have a scary badass
grandmother? It's one of the requirements."

"You need to stop watching daytime soap operas, you koala in a re-
spectable bear's clothing." After hanging up on his chortling fellow
second, he told Theo the option of calling in the wolves. "I'm not sure
who you want aware of this location."

Her response was an immediate shake of the head. "If we have to involve more people," she said, "I'd rather we keep it to your clan. My brother spoke specifically to Silver Mercant to organize this, and we trust her."

Which meant that, by extension, they trusted the bears.

Yakov got that. He was just about to bite the bullet and suggest they wait in the car while his clan sent someone to this location, when his phone rang in his hand. "Z," he said, answering the call. "Update?"

"Yeah, turns out I was wrong," Zahaan said. "I asked around and Moon and Elbek are on leave today and decided to head out that way to bird-watch."

"Bird-watch?"

"I swear the assholes told everyone they're bird-watching. I have no idea what they're actually doing, but when I called them, they said they'd be fine with keeping an eye on your location—they'll be there in ten, fifteen at the latest. They're already equipped for an overnight stay. With hyper night-vision goggles and all."

"For bird-watching."

"Owls, they tell me." Zahaan's voice was deadpan. "Rare miniature owls."

Lips twitching as he ended the call, Yakov shared the news with Theo. "We should meet them at the gate or they'll try to climb it."

"Right, of course."

After closing up but not locking the facility behind themselves, they drove back into the gloom of the tree-shadowed drive.

This place would be pitch-black at night.

Good thing the two coming over had those goggles. Most change-lings didn't need anything like that even in low-light conditions, but the goggles would give them an extra clarity to their vision in this level of intense darkness.

He put the headlights on low as they moved down the long drive.

"Did you call your clanmate a koala or did I mistranslate?" Words so tense they hummed . . . and yet she'd been curious enough to ask the question.

Yakov relaxed into his seat. "No, you didn't mistranslate," he said. "I was insulting him."

"Why would calling him a koala be an insult? As far as I know, most beings like koala bears."

"That's exactly it." He pointed a finger at her. "Koalas are not bears. Koalas are *marsupials*. Yet those furry gray Aussies go around acting like bears. It's not on."

"Is there a rivalry?"

"Nah. Koalas are pacific vegetarians. One time a bear I know tried to pick a fight with a koala family—you know what those *marsupials* did?"

He saw Theo shake her head in his peripheral vision.

"They invited him to a tofu dinner and gave him a handwoven shawl as a gift! Then they plucked their cub out of the carry pouch they wear in human form and asked him if he wanted to hold her! She *smiled* and goo-goo-ga-ga'd at him! He had no idea what to do with himself!"

Yakov threw up his hands for a second, while maintaining full control of the vehicle. "That's no kind of bear behavior! A man should be able to pick an honest-to-goodness fight with another!"

A strangled sound from Theo that he wanted to imagine was a stifled laugh, but knew he had to be imagining it. Especially when she went silent and still as they reached the gates a minute later.

Once he stopped, Theo got out to unlock those gates.

Leaning back against the grille of the vehicle, Yakov frowned. "I don't want our people trapped inside if something goes wrong at night."

Theo looked over, her face all angled shadows in the falling dark, a sudden evocative echo of his dreams. "You're right," she said as his bear's fur bristled at the memory of Theo bleeding, dying while he lay helpless. "But we need to secure the area for their own safety—the current deadbolts can be pushed back as you did. Do you have anything suitable?"

"I might." Heading to the back of the all-terrain vehicle while fighting off his urge to bundle her up and keep her safe, he lifted up the back hatch and looked through the toolbox that came standard-issue in most clan vehicles.

"Yes, here it is." He grabbed the heavy weight of metal chain. "It's meant to lock the tires if we ever run into an issue with the vehicle's computronic security, but it can be used as a secure lock on the gate. Moon and Elbek will have the override code."

After placing the chain in front of the vehicle as Theo opened the gates enough for it to exit, he stood and just watched her. His instinct was to assist, but he had a feeling Theo needed something on which to expend her energy. And for now, all she had were the gates.

So he just watched her move, this woman who had haunted him for years—and who was even more compelling in reality than she was in his dreams. That woman had been a fantasy. This Theo was *real* in every sense of the word.

Potent. Angry. Beautiful.

She wasn't graceful, however, though she moved smoothly enough. It was the contained explosion in her. It added a taut edginess to her motions—and it made him wonder what exactly it was that had birthed that blinding rage in Theo Marshall. Because no one was that angry without cause.

One thing he knew for certain now: none of this was an act. Theo was too expressive to hide her thoughts well. Her only obvious Psy trait was the fury of her need to contain her anger. Any bear in her position would've torn up a room by now, probably broken a chair or three.

Not Theo.

A thread of scent on the night air. Rough brown. And there was the second. Warm umber. Clan. Both of them.

Maybe his twin alone would understand Yakov's shorthand descriptions of his clanmates. He and Pasha had always *seen* scents in color. Apparently, their parents had only discovered their little quirk when they'd one day described their papa as sparkling red and their mama as juicy orange.

It had taken the two of them much longer to understand that their playmates didn't see the world of scent in vivid color. But, because they were bears, their quirk had always been treated as a joyful gift. Friends often asked them to describe what their scent was in color.

Today, Yakov's senses were dazzled in a deep, dark green with hidden undertones of ebony and sparks of flickering ruby. And that was just the first layer of the scent of Theo Marshall. A meld as secretive as the woman in front of him.

"Here they come," he warned her.

Chapter 19

Dear Aunt Rita,

I've read your previous advice on being wary of bears who come with delicious edible gifts, and I have to disagree. My sweet bear friend Sally-mae has been baking me fruit pies for the past six months, and she has no designs on my body or heart whatsoever.

Why, the other week, she even offered to iron my shirt for my date with another woman. It wasn't her fault the iron malfunctioned and she burned a hole in my shirt.

~Just a Friend

Dear Just a Friend,

Oh, you sweet summer child. Do write to me once you two are mated so I can say "I told you so" while eating my favorite peach pie.

~Aunt Rita

—From the February 2073 issue of *Wild Woman* magazine:
"Skin Privileges, Style & Primal Sophistication"

HAVING BENT TO examine a plant beside the gate, Theo now moved back to stand nearer the car.

Nearer Yakov.

He tried not to take that personally. Of course she trusted him more than the others. After all, he'd spent hours with her without doing her harm. It was a choice made out of logic. And still his bear grinned inside him, urging him to wrap her closer.

His damn bear was drunk.

"Yasha!" Elbek raised his arm as he walked into view, a small pack on his back and his rangy body covered in mud-splattered outdoor gear.

Slender and long-legged Moon was in much the same condition, though she also had mud in the curly black of her hair.

"Bird-watching?" he said dryly.

They both grinned.

"Energetic, those marsh birds," Moon said without any shame, before nodding at Theo. "*Zdravstvuyte*. I'm Moonbeam, but you can call me Moon. And yes, my name really is Moonbeam." Sparkling dark eyes in a face as delicate as a mythical nymph's, her skin as pale a hue as her namesake satellite. "This mud bear here is Elbek."

Elbek, all dramatic bones in a face that was just a touch too long for conventional notions of handsome—but that worked on him to the extent that the man was one of the clan's resident Romeos—gave a jaunty salute. His skin glowed a burnished brown under the fading light.

"Theo," Theo responded. "Thank you for stepping in on such short notice."

Moon waved off the thanks. "Sounds like an interesting place. You want us to stay outside?" A question directed at both of them.

"I think you should be fine camping inside if you stay right by the front doorway," Yakov said. "Not much to disturb there. Water's been shut off and I didn't manage to locate where, so you'll be mud bears overnight unless you can find running water."

"Already did." Elbek held up his phone, on which was a topographic map. "Map's old, but says there's a stream out back. We'll go one at a time, make sure the place isn't left unattended."

"*Spasibo*." Yakov bumped fists with first one then the other. "I'll bring you croissants and coffee tomorrow morning from the bakery." Because there was only one bakery in the city that mattered.

"Good deal," Moon said. "That lock for us?"

"Yeah. Only Theo can open the current gate lock."

"Got it. See you tomorrow."

"We'll be early," Yakov promised, knowing Theo wouldn't want it otherwise. "Hope the ghosts in that place don't keep you up too late."

Elbek gave him the finger. "I love ghosts. I have a ghost detector I'm working on. So joke's on you, Pashmina's less handsome brother, also known as Yashmina."

Laughing at the ridiculous set of names his and Pavel's teenage friends had found hysterical—and still did even now they were all grown—Yakov waved his hand in another good-bye before he got in his vehicle, with Theo doing the same, and they drove out.

He waited outside the gates until the others had successfully installed the lock and given him the thumbs-up in the rearview mirror. Sticking one hand out the window to indicate he'd seen, he drove away.

Theo, however, twisted in her seat to look over her shoulder. "Are you sure they'll be all right? That place . . ."

"They'll be fine. If they don't like it inside, they'll camp outside—worse comes to worst, they'll shift into bear form. *Proper* bears. Not fluffy koalas."

A sudden silence before she turned back to look out the windshield. "Bears. Right."

He realized she'd forgotten he had another form, was probably now imagining what he and the others looked like when they shifted. Well, even if he didn't talk her into petting him in bear form, she'd get a look at plenty of bears strutting about if she hung out in Moscow long enough. Bears had a tendency to be bears and walk into shops while wearing their credit chips on necklaces custom made for their thick beary necks.

A bear had to shop, after all.

He almost laughed aloud at the memory associated with the thought—of the time he'd dared his twin to walk into a women's lingerie shop that had a small stand of novelty men's boxers for women to buy for their guys. Yakov had challenged Pavel to buy a pair of boxers in the correct size for his human form while in full bear form.

Pasha had returned with boxers printed with sparkling red hearts in his mouth. In the right size.

A faint sound from the passenger seat. A stomach rumble.

Adorable in how quiet it was.

"We'll stop for food," he said while reminding himself never to say his earlier thought aloud—for surely this secretly angry woman would strike him dead for even daring to think she was in any way adorable. "We need to talk and strategize regardless—might as well do it over food." Even his easily amused bear knew that place was drenched in evil. If he could blunt a little of that for Theo by offering the comfort of food?

Hell yes, he was going to do that.

And no, it had nothing to do with the fact that he was finding Theo Marshall intensely more fascinating with every second that passed. So much fury to her. So much intelligence. And so *many* secrets.

Bozhe, but he wanted to feed her delicious desserts and charm each and every secret out of those lips so soft and full.

A wave of heat pulsed under Theo's skin, snapping the loop of memory and gnawing anxiety that had held her prisoner. Yakov had heard her stomach make that demanding noise. That was *not* something for which her research on bear changelings had prepared her. It was, quite frankly, mortifying.

Despite her discomfort, she clung to the sharp burn of her embarrassment—because otherwise, the darkness might return, the echo of screams might return, and with them, her realization that her life was a lie. "That sounds sensible," she said.

"Do you eat ordinary food or only Psy nutrients?"

"I can eat ordinary food." One good thing about being an unimportant member of the family without agency or power was that after a while, nobody had cared to watch her. "Though . . . I have been warned about accepting food gifts from bears." By Aunt Rita, who was clearly an extremely wise woman.

Yakov rolled his eyes. "It's all lies. Food is just food." Keeping his eyes on the road, he added, "I know a good place. Far away from rowdy bears. Only minor culinary subterfuge involved."

Oddly enough, she already knew this stranger better than she knew anyone else in her life apart from Pax. He was amusing himself with his words but not in a way that shut her out. Rather the opposite. Yakov was inviting her to play with him. He was . . . warm. Not only in the body, but in everything about him.

"I do believe I'm traveling with a rowdy bear," she said in such a solemn tone that he shot her an assessing look, his eyes kissed by amber.

"Funny," he muttered with a scowl, but she heard the laughter he did a bad job of hiding beneath. "I'll have you know Mischief Bear One has grown into a most well-behaved adult."

So *much* warmth and heart. Theo wanted to crawl into his lap, into him.

Her mind flashed with the memory of his piercing gentleness with the poor broken bird on the path, his big blunt-tipped hands carrying the fragile body with utmost care. Even as her chest squeezed against the surge of emotion that threatened to overwhelm her senses, her fingers curled into her palm in instinctive memory of her contact with him.

Being enclosed in his grip had made her feel *safe* in a way that was disturbing.

Theo had spent a lifetime relying on no one else to find balance, but right then, she knew it would be terrifyingly easy to rely on Yakov Stepyrev. *Pitiful*, she told herself. *He's only being polite. You're nothing but an assigned task to him, just like you were to Colette.*

Even brutally conscious of that, she couldn't stop herself from indulging in this moment with him where she could pretend to be a normal woman with a man who drew her like a bee to a pollen-laden bloom. No one needed to know of her internal foolishness. "I read an article that stated bears take pride in being unruly, but that beer is off-limits. Never to be spilled or wasted, no matter how bad the fight. Is that true?"

His wicked grin, the single dimple she could see, it made things low in her body clutch in ways unfamiliar and disquieting. "You should ask Nina Rodchenko sometime. She owns a club in Moscow that's a favorite with the clan. Her bouncers have broken up many a fight."

Squeezing her thighs together against the strange ache that was turning into a low, deep pulse, she found herself leaning a touch further toward him. Another small foolishness for a stolen beat of time. "In which you were a participant?"

The grin grew wider, a deep crease forming in the cheek she could see. "I told you, I am the very picture of good behavior." Pious tone at odds with his expression. "It's my brother who's the troublemaker."

So, they both had brothers. "Do you have other siblings?"

"No, just the one. You?"

"Pax is my only full sibling. Once we turned eighteen, our parents dissolved their co-parenting agreement." Which hadn't applied to Theo since she was seven, regardless. "After that, my father had two more children. We weren't raised together and I don't know them as anything but genetic half sibs."

As a child, she'd sometimes dreamed that her father would rescue her and bring her back to Pax; it had taken until she was a teenager to realize that her father had never held any true power in the Marshall household.

Miles Faber had been chosen as Claire Marshall's partner in procreation because of his Gradient level, high IQ, and pleasing appearance, and had been granted co-parenting rights as part of a business deal. Any kindness he'd had in him had stood no chance against the vicious coldness of her grandfather's reign—a reign in which her mother had always been complicit.

Part of her had always believed that her half siblings were her father's attempt to do it all over. Replacement children for the ones to whom he had no rights and that he'd "co-parented" only in name. It was her grandfather who'd made all major decisions when it came to her and Pax. She might've judged Miles for his inability to fight for his two firstborn, but it'd be akin to judging a sparrow for not standing up to a falcon.

Even teenage Theo had been tougher than Miles Faber would ever be.

"Big age gap." Yakov's voice was a warm brush of fur over her senses, an unspoken invitation to continue the conversation.

Perhaps that was why she carried on speaking of matters she spoke about to no one else. "I *do* wonder how things will change now that Silence has fallen. If it *will* change on any major level." Theo couldn't see her mother ever being anything but a cold and pragmatic machine.

"Love has a way of changing a lot." Yakov turned onto the main thoroughfare that would lead them to central Moscow.

"A parent who loves their child," he continued, "will move mountains to keep them safe. You ever try to take a child from a bear mother? She'll rip off your face, make a mask of it, then wear that mask to your funeral."

Theo blinked.

"Too violent?" Yakov winced when she didn't reply.

"No." Theo understood violence on the most intimate level. Only her grandfather had known the entirety of what she was capable of. And he was dead, bombed into innumerable fleshy shards that had then mostly been incinerated in the ensuing fire. The authorities had run his DNA from a blown-off hand that had survived the fire, done the secondary scan on a small piece of his skull that still had brain matter attached.

Too bad he'd been at one of his other residences at the time and not the estate.

Theo knew that there was probably something wrong with her for not being horrified by the mental images of Marshall's obliterated body, but all she'd felt at the news of her grandfather's demise was a soul-crushing relief—and a fierce joy. The fucking bastard was dead. She'd shake the hand of his murderer if she knew their identity.

"I suppose the idea of such parental protectiveness is strange to me," she said in response to his question, and her words were an understatement of mammoth proportions. "What are your parents like?" Her curiosity about him was a tree with ever-emerging branches, even if to him, she was nothing but an assignment.

"I'll introduce you to my mama before you leave Moscow," Yakov offered. "She's tough but friendly and she once tore off the head of a man who tried to kidnap me and Pasha."

Chapter 20

Do not ever get between a mama bear and her cubs. You will most certainly be in pieces before you realize your mistake and start to apologize.

—*The Traveler's Guide to Changelings* (revised edition, 1897)

THEO'S SPINE WENT rigid. "You were almost kidnapped?"

"No. Our mother was too fast—I guess they figured one small woman and two cubs in an isolated section of the park against four big males was fair odds."

He bared his teeth. "Two dead in seconds, third guy—she ripped his arm off. That leaves the one whose insides she clawed out while we cheered her on from the spot where she'd told us to stay put and keep out of her way. Wasn't even a close fight."

Theo was beyond fascinated at this point, her anger at the old incident no longer the dominant emotion. "How old were you?"

"Five. Had our claws out and were straining at the bit to go for the attackers, but Pasha and I knew better than to disobey our mother when she used *that* voice. So we just threw up our arms and cheered every time she got in a hit. Afterward, one of the injured men called us 'fucking bloodthirsty animals.' And our mama punched him in the face for daring to insult her sweet little babies."

Having twisted fully in her seat, Theo stared at him for long moments before she found her voice. She didn't know which question to ask first, went for, "Who was it? Behind the kidnapping, I mean?"

"Pissed my parents off but no one could ever figure it out. The guys were all hired muscle, paid through cash drop-offs. No real trail to follow. In the end, Enforcement said it was probably part of a trafficking ring that they'd heard about but that hadn't previously shown up in Moscow. Whoever it was, they never tried that shit again, not with any bear cub."

Having lowered his window, Yakov leaned one arm on the window frame. "With some of what we've learned about the Council since the fall of Silence, we suspect it might've been a Council-backed operation. Word is, their psychopathic scientists experimented on changelings in an effort to discover a way to break us."

Theo had zero trouble accepting that suspicion. "My grandfather once told me that changelings were about as intelligent as stray dogs—he would've thought nothing of abducting a changeling child. Because once he'd justified it to himself that way, the facts no longer mattered."

Yakov shot her an assessing look before returning his attention to the road. "You didn't like him much, huh?"

"I would cheerfully dance on his grave if he had one." But she didn't want to speak about the dead and never-mourned Marshall Hyde.

Theo wanted to know about bears. Warm, beautifully lethal-in-their-protectiveness bears.

"Did you need psychological assistance after witnessing the violence?" Theo didn't know why she asked that. Perhaps because she knew that she was damaged in ways nothing could fix . . . or maybe it was because she wanted to test his tolerance for rage-induced violence.

Yakov took his time answering. "I'm not human," he said at last. "I'm not Psy. I'm changeling. Violence is part of our life—and it's not always in a bad way. My animal hunts for food, takes only what it needs to survive. It feels no shame in that, because it knows that is the natural way."

Every cell in Theo's body resonated with the power of his words.

"A predatory pack isn't a soft place," he added. "Wolf, bear, leopard, hawk, it doesn't matter which predator, we all have so much physical power that it sometimes needs to be slapped down when it gets out of control.

"There are dominance struggles. And changelings have certain laws that if broken, result in an automatic death sentence delivered most often by the alpha—but that can also be delivered by other senior members of the pack or clan."

He continued on when she didn't interrupt. "Don't take me wrong— we're fierce in defense of our own, too. That's the other side of the coin. We love as ferociously as we fight. I grew up knowing that my parents and clanmates would kill to protect me, and that it's okay to fight back if someone tries to hurt you. It's the natural way. One predator against another.

"If it had gone wrong? If they'd hurt our mama? Yes, then we'd have been screwed up. But she won. To the small bears we were then, that was just the natural consequence of bad behavior by the would-be kidnappers. The worst possible time-out."

Theo batted away the whisper of hope flittering around her head, but it wouldn't vanish out of existence. Not now that Yakov had made it crystal clear that his tolerance for physical violence was far beyond what she might've imagined from her own experiences with the Psy race.

She didn't dare put her hope into words, couldn't reveal the stabbing need inside her, so she spoke another truth: "I would very much like to meet your mother." The woman sounded astonishing and amazing and like the kind of mother Theo would worship.

Yakov smiled—and thought that his mother would be highly interested in Theo Marshall, too. Because his *pchelka* was a study in contradictions, and if there was one thing Yakov's mama loved, it was a mystery. That was why she ran StoneWater's monthly mystery book club, the Beary Good Sleuths, and why she was an *actual* detective.

"She's a private investigator," he told Theo. "The stories she sometimes tells us." He shook his head. "She served as an Enforcement cop for ten years before going the P.I. route. Can you imagine that? A bear changeling in Enforcement?"

He chuckled. "She took no shit and, as a new recruit, threw so many bears into overnight jail that it became a badge of honor to have been arrested by Mila Kuznets."

"Bears," Theo said slowly, "are interesting creatures."

His shoulders shook. "Her colleagues *loved* her, and while she enjoyed the work, she hated the administration side of things. She's much happier on her own and she occasionally still gets called in to consult for the cops."

"How about your father? Is he an investigator, too?"

"No, he's a landscaper. A lot of the planting you see around Moscow? He and his team probably had a hand in it. I can still point out the trees I helped plant when I worked on his crew for a summer job. Then I did another summer with my mother, acting as her assistant while her real assistant was out for maternity leave."

Grinning at the memories and conscious of Theo's attentive interest, he said, "Pasha and I switched off, since my parents refused to have us both on the same job at the same time. Said we were menaces together." Which, in fairness, was the absolute truth.

One twin: fairly well-behaved, invested, and useful.

Both twins: demons who pulled every prank possible while still being useful and invested.

"How about you?" he asked as the light-studded buildings of central Moscow began to appear in the distance against the black cloak of night. "You do any fun summer jobs?"

"I worked for my grandfather," she said in a flat tone that made his fur bristle and all his doubts about the truth of Theo roar to the surface.

It took effort not to allow his bear's rumble to color his voice, demand she reveal herself to him. "Yeah? Filing and that sort of office stuff?"

"Something like that."

The bristling intensified. She was lying to him. According to what Silver had told him, Theo had been sidelined and considered unimportant during her grandfather's reign, such an insignificant cog in the machine that she had no psychic or digital footprint beyond the most basic facts.

Yet he'd put good money on the fact that Theo had done exactly what she said she'd done: worked for her grandfather. That wasn't the lie. The lie was in her answer as to *what* she'd done for Marshall Hyde, the man who'd been a Councilor during some of the Council's ugliest periods. The same man Theo herself had just told him would think nothing of kidnapping an innocent cub.

What then, Yasha, asked his internal bear, *did that man do to his unimportant and unnoticed granddaughter?*

A bearish rumble building in his chest, his emotions colliding. Because the Theo with secrets dark and perhaps ugly was the same Theo who'd once been a child held in a monster's punishing grip.

Chapter 21

"Mischief Bear One!"

"Here, Babulya!"

"Mischief Bear Two!"

"Present, Babulya!"

"Fall in line. It's time to go jumping in your favorite mud pool."

—"Three Bears, a Mud Pool, and a Rabid Squirrel,"
a true family tale as told by Quyen Kuznets

NEITHER ONE OF them spoke again until he pulled into a parking spot outside the small bar and restaurant that was a favorite of his. Set up by a human couple who'd moved from Mexico City to Moscow for a work contract and fallen in love with the city, Jorge's Cantina—named after a man important to both the owners—had a mellow vibe and gentle warmth.

And regardless of all he didn't know about Theo, what he did know was that she'd had one hell of a horrific day. Fuck if he was just going to drop her off at her no-doubt sterile Psy apartment to handle the aftermath all alone.

He was a goddamn Stepyrev on one side and a Kuznets on the other, with Morais, Nguyen, Li, and more in the mix, too. His ancestors would roll over in their graves, while his living forebears would keel over—after slapping him upside the head—if he did anything but feed her. And pet her.

Only *then* could he grill her.

And he would—because he was also one of Valentin's seconds, and he couldn't work with Theo without being able to trust that she posed no threat to the clan. For that, he needed total honesty.

"Best Mexican food in the city," he said to her once they'd exited the vehicle. "Owners are also happy to alter the spice level to their diners' needs." Some might say that made the dishes less authentic, but Juana, who ran front of house while her husband Videl ran the kitchen, said food was about comfort, and comfort came from being welcomed.

No wonder Jorge's had a steady clientele of bears.

Inside, the cantina was all earth tones, from the dark cream of the walls to the polished wood of the floor and the rugs thrown here and there. The rugs as well as the place mats were handwoven in Juana's hometown by an artists' cooperative, while the plates, mugs, and glasses were supplied by another cooperative in the same city.

He glanced around, spotted a group of five thirtysomething humans discussing the menu, a single elderly human enjoying a leisurely dinner, and two bears. Good, that was as he'd expected for nine on a Friday night. Jorge's was small and, despite its name, was set up more for food than as a bar, so folks in party mode tended to come by earlier, eat, then bounce to do their hellraising.

When one of his clanmates raised a hand, he raised one back with a smile but didn't go over. "They're on a date," he whispered to Theo, leaning down to speak close to her ear. "She's been courting him for months and I don't want to throw a wrench into the works by interrupting."

To Theo's credit, she didn't turn and look, but she'd clearly already noted the couple because she said, "He doesn't look like the skittish type."

"Don't get taken in by appearances. He might look like a bear in human form, complete with the pelt"—Simeon's beard was legendary for its lushness—"but she's a senior dominant while he's at the other end of the dominance scale." Yakov got the sweats even thinking about the balance Vana would have to maintain to create a relationship with Simeon, but love was a crazy thing.

His bear saluted her courage.

"Yasha!" Juana waved from the other side of the restaurant. "Grab a table. We'll be with you shortly."

Theo kept her silence until they were seated on the far side of the cantina from the other couple, a small candle between them. "How does it work," she asked, "with such a big power imbalance?" The candle flame flickered in the intense blue of her eyes.

It took him a second to realize he was staring, compelled by her energy. Energy so wild it was near to feral. "Trust and communication." His words came out rough with the bear's compulsion toward her.

Hell, who was he kidding? It wasn't only the bear.

Yakov wanted to take Theo Marshall home and unravel her. He'd probably end up with bruises, but oh, it'd be one hell of a ride. "And love." He held her gaze as he added that, his bear at the fore. "A ton of no-holds-barred love."

Theo's lashes glittered gold in the candlelight. "I understand." Leaning back, she picked up the menu. "What do you recommend?"

Yakov narrowed his eyes but permitted the unexpected retreat from a woman who had refused to retreat from even her own worst nightmares. "Anything. It's all good. I've been through the entire menu twice."

In the end, she didn't stick to the safest possible choice, as he'd half expected.

The waitress who took his order gave him a wink after turning slightly away from Theo.

Though he'd kept a straight face, Theo said, "Is she a bear?"

"No. But she's dating one." Dating seriously enough that she was all but clan at this point. "You're about to become a hot topic in bear circles."

"I'm hardly that exciting."

"Oh, I wouldn't say that." Then, and aware that no one was close enough to listen in to their conversation, he decided it was time to stop playing games. One way or another, he needed to discover if he could trust Theo.

His bear *hated* the idea that he might just be another man who hurt Theo. But he was also a StoneWater dominant, one of his alpha's most trusted people. He was honor bound and heart bound to protect his clan from all perceived threats. And right now, the woman of his dreams was an unknown, classified as a threat until and unless he learned otherwise.

He locked his eyes with the shielded blue of hers once more, and this time, it was dead serious. "I can't help you find what you need to find if you're not honest with me—and Theo? I'm not real comfortable with the idea of assisting a family that made a ton of cash off maiming people."

THEO froze, caught unawares. Yakov had been so easygoing and friendly that she hadn't been prepared for the steel in his tone. She remembered too late that he was one of Valentin Nikolaev's seconds. That meant Yakov Stepyrev was one of the most powerful people in the city of Moscow.

Steel was a prerequisite.

His eyes glowed amber with an edge of yellow in the candlelight, the animal that lived beneath his skin in full focus.

She should thank her grandfather. He was the one who'd given her the ability to hold even the most brutal gaze and not flinch. Because flinching meant pain. Her back tightened, her skin holding the worst echoes of memory.

I wouldn't have to do this if you'd cooperate, Theodora.

She rubbed her bracelet. *Hard.* "Are you saying you won't assist me unless I share everything?"

"I'm saying you're wasting me as a resource if you tie one hand behind my back." Eye contact so confronting it was more intimate than she'd ever before been with a man. "I also can't work with a partner who's hiding things that might get in the way of what we're trying to do."

Theo found herself flinching inside, all her stupid hopes shattered at her feet.

Partner. Work.

That was all she was and would ever be to Yakov.

But that didn't change the fact that he was right, of course he was right. She'd been useless while she'd had her panic attack—and she'd be even more useless should the bracelet activate. But she had time there. Enough time. "I apologize—" she began.

A rumble from his chest cut her off. She realized at the same time that the bear couple on their date had gone motionless on the other side of the restaurant, while every single human had fallen silent. That was when she *truly* understood the level of dominance possessed by the otherwise laid-back man sitting across from her.

His displeasure had affected people nowhere near them.

As if realizing that, he turned and smiled at the others. "Sorry," he said with an abashed grin, using those dimples of his like weapons, "we're arguing over dessert."

Everyone exhaled, laughed, and went back to their own discussions.

When Yakov turned his attention back to her, his eyes remained uncompromising in their intensity. "So."

She drank half a glass of the water the waitress had dropped off before Yakov put her on the spot. Then she narrowed her eyes at him, because there was one thing she wanted to set straight here and now. "I am *not* a submissive. You can't intimidate me."

The slightest tug of his lips. "I know. If you were a submissive, I'd have handed you over to a gentler clanmate hours ago. You have a spine made of iron, Theo." That slow smile deepened. "I like iron."

Her breath hitched, her pulse erratic. She wasn't so certain anymore that this was only about work. Not that it mattered. Her answer wouldn't change—because this was no longer just about her own questions. It was about that man with the empty eyes who'd cried that single heartbreaking tear, about the woman who'd banged her head on the wall in the facility, and all the others she'd seen that day.

Where were the patients? What had her grandfather done?

"It stays between us," she said, then shook her head when he would've interrupted her. "It's personal. Nothing your clan needs to know—but I'll allow you to make that call after I tell you."

The amber grew brighter, a prowling wildness to it. "That's a whole lot of trust, *pchelka*."

Theo had the sudden, primal urge to crawl over the table and into his lap, grip his hair so that she could look endlessly into his eyes, the need born from the same core as her rage. She wanted to force him to know her, *see* her: Theo Marshall, Tk 2.7, no one important . . . and the masterwork of a cold-blooded psychopath.

Masochistic. But she couldn't stand not knowing how he'd look at her once he knew all of her. Better to rip off the Band-Aid fast and hard. A little blood, a sharp stab of pain, and it would be over.

This . . . taut hope? It hurt worse.

"I did my research," she got out past the storm inside her. "Stone-Water bears have a reputation." She paused. "In more ways than one—but everyone agrees your word is your bond."

Throwing back his head, Yakov laughed, the sound a warm wave that had the others in the restaurant looking over with big smiles on their faces. The waitress bore the same smile when she dropped off their food. And Theo realized that this man wasn't just liked by his friends and clanmates. He was *loved*.

"Agreed, then," he drawled, while she was still recovering from the impact of his laugh, so open and generous. "I won't say a word to anyone as long as it's truly personal."

"We'll talk in the car," she said. "I can't risk anyone else overhearing." True enough—but also true was that she needed to build up her willpower and courage to walk back into the suffocating evil that made her hate herself.

Yakov held her gaze, as if judging the sincerity of her words, before inclining his head in a small nod. "Be careful of the serving skillet—it's hot."

The next few minutes were taken up with him explaining how she could put together her fajita, then offering her a portion of his soft taco to try. She felt overwhelmed, as if she was living another woman's life. A *normal* woman's. One who had nothing to hide and could enjoy the company of a beautiful, bearish man who seemed determined to feed her even if he didn't trust her.

Yakov had already ordered a couple more dishes.

"Sides," he'd explained. "I eat like a bear and this way you can try more dishes."

Now he said, "Thela, try this sweet pepper." He began to lift it to her lips, a slight flush kissing his cheekbones before he changed course to put it on her plate. "You won't believe how good it tastes."

The entire experience threw her.

Food was never this generous sharing among the Psy.

We used to. Pax and I.

A cascade of memories from their childhood, of her passing him his favorite nutrient bar rather than eating it herself, even though it was part of her allotment for the day, and him making sure the bags of dried fruit they got as treats ended up in her pockets.

The memories hurt.

Right then came the bite of heat on her tongue as the newest flavors penetrated. Feeling her eyes widen at the punch of sensation, she focused on that, on the external. Across from her, Yakov laughed again, generous and warm and beautiful in a way no man had ever before been to her, and said, "Go with it."

So she did, and decided that the food was delicious.

As was Yakov Stepyrev.

Far, far beyond her reach, but she could pretend he wasn't for this moment out of time. And she wouldn't wonder what could've been had she had a different life, been a different Theo. Because soon enough, he'd know the terrible, awful truth of her, something even Pax didn't know.

A stir at the door to the restaurant.

Glancing over, Yakov threw up his hands, a scowl on his face. "No, I got here first!"

Twisting in her seat at the comment that sounded like a reply to a statement that hadn't yet been made, Theo looked over her shoulder to see . . . Yakov standing there. Only, no, it wasn't Yakov. This man wore spectacles, and a checked shirt over jeans . . . and he was still a near-perfect replica of Yakov.

Chapter 22

Dear Hien,

Thank you for hosting us for Christmas and New Year in Zürich. We're still buzzing from the trip—and so excited for you to visit us in turn. We've already booked the guest quarters in the city for all four of us, so we can do every one of the sights! Though you must also come back to the den with us often. Everyone wants to meet my famous engineer sister!

And of course, we'll take our newest siblings out and spoil them so badly that Mom and Dad will pull out their hair. Seeing Otto and Grady settle into the family, begin to smile and act like cubs their age should, it makes my heart grow a size each time I see them.

Amidst all this joy, I do worry about what I hear coming out of the Net. It appears that there was a major shift in the tone of the response to the questionnaire this time around from the last time it was sent out.

It's clear that the recent spate of serial murders across multiple continents and cities has pushed people to the edge. But that isn't the right reason to make a decision this big. It's a decision that could impact generations and it should be made with thought and care.

And yet I know I'm prejudiced in my thoughts, that I resist the idea so much because I know that should the new Silence come into being, it would alter everything, perhaps even destroy the bond between us.

I want our children to grow up together, to become lifelong friends as we are. I want Marian and me to adventure together with you and Kanoa to our silver-haired years. It would shatter my heart to have you distance

yourself from me, Hien—and this is what I see in the specter of Silence: a
future without my little sister.

Your big brother always,
D.

                    —Letter from Déwei Nguyen to Hien Nguyen (17 January 1974)

EVEN AS THEO tried to make sense of suddenly seeing double, the
other Yakov scowled an identical scowl. "Hey, we booked it first!" he
protested. "Seriously? Again?"

Groaning in concert, the two—almost simultaneously—said, "I'm
going to pretend you're not here."

Laughter from the silver-eyed Psy in a sharp suit of a blue so dark it
was almost black, who stood beside the other man. Dramatic cheekbones, olive skin, perfect jawline paired with eyes tilted sharply upward
and hair of silky black, he was as close to physical perfection as a man
could get.

Yet nothing in Theo reacted to him as she did to Yakov.

Neither did she react to the man who was a carbon copy of Yakov,
complete with the dimples.

"You're hangry, my darling Pasha," the Psy man said. "Let's go eat."
He waved at Yakov, then shot Theo a penetrating look before nudging
his date to the back of the small restaurant, as far as possible from both
Yakov and Theo as well as the courting couple.

"Your brother," she said to Yakov, her voice husky.

"Pasha." He made a face in his brother's direction and, from the glint
in his eye, received an equally sour look in return. "Officially Pavel Pain
in the Ass Stepyrev."

"Twins." Her heart thundered. "You didn't say."

"What?" A frown. "No, I guess not. It's not something to say unless
it comes up."

Of course, he was right. People didn't go around randomly announcing they were a twin. "I'm a twin," she blurted out. "It's not in the records, but I'm a twin. The older twin by two minutes." It was suddenly so important that he believe her.

"I'm the younger by one minute," he murmured. "And I knew that—about you and Pax."

"Oh." It shocked her, that the world was starting to pick up on a fact the family had gone to such great lengths to hide for near to the entirety of her existence. "You must've been surprised at the differential in our power levels." Inside, the small girl she'd once been braced herself for what was to come.

But Yakov just shrugged. "Twins aren't the same people." Nodding over at where his twin sat with the extremely handsome man in the suit, the bear sprawled out in his chair while the Psy in the suit sat with perfect posture, he said, "Pasha's my best friend, but he's a totally different person from me.

"Our mother said she never had trouble telling us apart even when we were babies. Apparently, we laughed different, kicked our baby feet in different ways, and fell asleep to different lullabies.

"As adults," he added, "I love peppers, while he can't stand them. His desk in his workroom is chaos tinged with the aftermath of a hurricane, while I color-code my physical files, then head into numerical codes when it comes to the documents themselves." A grin. "He thinks I'm an over-organized lunatic. I think he's a chaos monster."

That was when Theo realized that this was the first time in her adult life that she'd spoken to someone who'd also been born a twin. She'd been forced to hide that part of herself for so long that the opportunity had just never come up. "Yet you're best friends?" she asked with a desperate hunger.

"Always." Simple. Absolute.

"Did your parents ever compare you to each other?"

"Oh, they're not perfect," he said. "I'm sure they screwed up a few times over the years. They tell us they did—but what I remember are parents who loved us both. I never felt less than or more than Pasha, and he's told me the same. We were just their cubs and they loved us."

His words kicked her deep in the heart. "You were lucky," she found herself saying, revealing a tightly hidden corner of her ruined soul. "My parents were beyond disappointed when I began to show signs of being a low Gradient. They expected another child in Pax's power range."

Yakov scowled. "That's shit parenting. A cub is a cub. End of."

"Perhaps that'll change with the fall of Silence, though I can't see it." Still, it was nice to imagine that any future Theo would grow up beloved. "My race has worshipped power for too long."

"Can't argue with that. What about the harmony thing you mentioned?" He took a sip of the beer he'd ordered, the liquid an inviting golden hue. "You said it influenced your parents' decision to separate you."

"Grandfather had the final say." Marshall Hyde was the architect of Theo's life. "Harmony pairs aren't always twins, but it shows up more in twins. Two abilities that effectively merge to become something extraordinary—the first time around, we saved a dying bird. The second time around, we woke a man out of a yearslong coma." As for the third, that was Pax's secret to tell.

Yakov whistled. "What's the downside? Because I don't see it."

"It flatlines our powers," Theo said. "Every single time. No one much cared with me, but nobody wanted a 9 to flame out and be useless to the family for up to a day or more. I was considered the instigator, the one responsible for the decision to Harmonize."

"Must've messed up your relationship with your twin. The dissimilar treatment."

"It hurt us both." She'd always understood that, always felt the guilt that gnawed at Pax. By exiling her and making Pax helpless to protect her, Marshall had broken a part of Pax that nothing might ever heal. "Before they separated us, we were best friends, too. I think . . . I think we're on our way back to that."

Some people might say she was fooling herself, that Pax was just using her and their bond to mitigate the effects of Scarab Syndrome, but she could *feel* her twin inside her, in the same spot where he'd been since they were born. He'd never left her. Not once. More, she knew her brother blamed himself for everything, and that he was doing all in his power to protect her should the treatments fail, should he die.

Her hand clenched on the cloth napkin.

Poor Pax.

He had no idea of the creature she'd become, the creature her grandfather had made of her. She was the one who should be under a death sentence.

YAKOV didn't push Theo to talk when she went quiet after that revelation about her and her twin. He wondered if she even realized that she got a fiercely protective tone in her voice when she spoke about her brother.

Interesting, when—per Silver—Pax Marshall was considered a serious power player in the Net.

But to Theo, he was just her brother. Her twin.

Yakov got it.

As he got her edginess when they finished up and headed out to the car. Not wanting her to feel cornered, he didn't immediately bring up the subject on which they intended to talk. Instead, he backed the car out of the parking spot, then drove to park on an overlook with a glittering view of Moscow.

The lights of the city fell onto the black ribbon of the Moskva, making the river ripple with infinite shades of color.

"The wild is far more home to me than the city," he said, leaning forward with his arms around the steering wheel, "but I do love its beauty at night."

Theo said nothing. Not for a long time. When she did speak, what she said made his bear's heart break.

"When Pax first came to me as an adult, I reacted with anger." Her voice was . . . toneless and gray, as if she'd retreated behind a mile-high wall. "He thinks that it's because I blame him for keeping his distance during the time when our grandfather was in charge—the truth is, I responded with anger because I didn't want him tainted by my ugliness."

Yakov's chest rumbled. *"Theo."* It was a warning. "You don't get to talk about yourself that way."

No flashing eyes in response to the possessive edge he hadn't been able to hide, no prickly retort. She kept on going in that voice monotonous and without emotion. "I knew he had his own scars, had survived his own hell. Imagine, if something horrible happened to your twin while you believed him safe. Perhaps not in the best situation, but safe at least?"

The question hit hard. "It would destroy me."

"So you see why I could never let Pax know what happened to me. After we were separated at seven years of age, he tried *so hard* to protect me, even though he was a child himself."

Yakov's chest ached; whatever he'd expected to hear, it hadn't been that. Pax Marshall wasn't supposed to be a good brother; Pax Marshall certainly wasn't supposed to be a twin who loved his sister enough that to know of his failure to keep her from harm would destroy him.

Theo, her eyes on the lights of Moscow glittering in the distance, rubbed hard at her bracelet. "The family chose that age to split us up because all the psychological data says that separating twins any younger could cause catastrophic damage. When I say separated, I mean that they cut us off from each other on the telepathic plane as well."

Yakov muttered a harsh curse. "Nothing? No contact?"

"Not as far as they knew. The truth was their attempts were ninety-eight percent effective—but they couldn't cut off the connection with which we'd been born. A connection so deep that I don't think there is any way to cut it off. It will exist as long as both of us are alive."

He was glad for her, that she'd had that at least.

"I was never good at Silence," she added. "Later, once Pax was able to get around some of the psychic blocks, he shielded me so that people wouldn't guess at the depth of my lack of Silence. So for the later years of my childhood, I was considered stable. The same can't be said of my earlier years."

Yakov was starting to get a very bad feeling that he knew where this was going. "Did your fucking grandfather take you to that place to be rehabilitated?" He spit out the last word, so angry that he had to remove his hands from the steering wheel lest he rip it off its mounting.

"I think so," Theo said. "The first flashback was jumbled, but it jarred other things loose. As if my mind has opened a door and now there's no stopping the return of memory. I don't see it all . . . but I see enough."

Her fingers moved even harder on the bracelet. Rubbing. *Rubbing.* "I see eyes dead of any hint of personhood. I see fear. I see—" Breathing short and sharp, her next words a taut whisper. "There was a chair. With straps."

Chapter 23

Miles, I commend you for your continued consideration for a 2.7, but the decision has been made as per our majority vote in the contract: Theodora has been rehomed in a situation far more suitable for her. She will be educated as is appropriate to her Gradient level.

—Message from Marshall Hyde to Miles Faber (4 February 2063)

Nineteen Years Ago

THEO WAS SCARED, so scared that it made her bones hurt. She tried to resist being put into that white chair that looked like the reclining chair she had to sit in when the dentist checked her teeth. It was white and leather and it had belt things around it. She wasn't scared of the dentist—she'd always found it interesting, all the tools he used, and the way he didn't mind talking to her about what he was doing.

But there was no white-haired M-Psy specializing in dentistry in this room. Only the woman named Upashna who was probably a doctor because she wore a white coat like a doctor, her grandfather, and a man who also wore the same blue clothes as she'd seen on the people in the corridor. Only he didn't have a white coat. That man looked at her when she tried to resist walking to the chair and suddenly she couldn't move at all.

Even as she opened her mouth to scream, her grandfather said, "I expect you to behave like a Marshall, Theodora." His voice was ice. "It's only necessary to incapacitate you because you refuse to cooperate as you should. Now stop with the theatrics, take off that coat, and get into the scrubs provided for you."

Theo didn't know what scrubs were; however, she could see that the man she didn't know had turned and was picking up a set of green clothes like the kind she'd seen on the man who'd cried and the woman who'd smashed her head against the wall. They didn't make a very big pile and she understood that those must be scrubs and the pile wasn't big because they were her size.

"I don't want to be like the people outside, Grandfather," she said to her grandfather, even as she struggled against the invisible force that held her in place. Her heart thudded, thudded, thudded. So hard, so fast. The man in blue, she understood, was a telekinetic just like the driver outside the door, and he was much stronger than Theo's 2.7.

Panic was a siren inside her brain, making high-pitched sounds over and over again that blurred her vision.

"We're not here to do that," her grandfather said dismissively. "However, you do need a little help with your Silence, so get in the chair."

But when the telekinetic released Theo, she didn't move to the chair. Instead, she turned and tried to run away. She only got a few steps before the telekinetic stopped her again.

"This is ridiculous," her grandfather said. "Get her out of the coat and up in the chair. We don't need her in scrubs as long as her arms are exposed for the needles."

It was the woman who took off Theo's coat and put it aside. Theo stared into her eyes, hoping that she'd help her. Dr. Upashna had disagreed with whatever her grandfather wanted to do. But Theo should've known better. It didn't matter how much the woman might disagree with Grandfather; he was the boss and Dr. Upashna would do exactly what he said.

No one touched Theo to get her to the chair itself; the telekinetic just lifted her up and put her on the cold white leather-synth. The landing was soft. He was very good at telekinesis, she thought in the part of her mind that liked to examine things, liked to take mechanical objects apart to see how they worked so she could then reassemble them.

Colette had even given her a game where Theo had to use her small amount of Tk to put tiny plas and metal pieces into holes meant for them. If she made a mistake and a piece touched the sides of the hole before slotting into the bottom, the board went red and she got a "strike" against her—she only had three strikes before she had to restart.

Theo spent hours playing it.

She was already on level twenty-eight.

Dr. Upashna went to a table full of bright silver tools. Theo's heart kicked like the horse she'd seen on the comm screen inside a compu-tronic shop once. She wished the man in blue wasn't one of her grand-father's people so that she could ask him what it was like to be a powerful telekinetic. Theo would never be able to stop anyone from moving. She could hardly even pick up a mug of nutrients and float it across the room. She could only move small things a little bit.

Now, the Tk used his hands to pull the straps on the chair across and over her so that she was tied down to the white chair. The straps were wide and they buckled tight on either side of her body, keeping her pinned in place even after the Tk released her from his power.

The worst was the strap against her forehead that stopped her from moving her head, making her stare straight up at the ceiling. It was pure white except for a small dot that she thought might've been a fruit fly. She hoped it was a fruit fly. If she pointed out that this room wasn't clean like hospital rooms were supposed to be, maybe they would stop.

But something pricked her inside her elbow even as she was opening her mouth to speak, and she realized that the doctor was putting some-thing inside her. Not a pressure injector. This was a needle all long and sharp and it hurt.

Why did she use a needle? No one used needles anymore, that was what she'd learned in her science lesson.

"C-cold." Her teeth clattered as she tried to speak, to tell her grand-father that something had gone wrong and that a burning cold was spreading through her body from the point where Dr. Upashna had injected her.

But she couldn't form words anymore. Her heart had started to race so fast that she thought it would jump out of her chest. The edges of the world went fuzzy, her spine tried to curve and lift her off the table. And then . . . Nothing.

Chapter 24

You've surprised me, Theodora. You might be useful to the family after all.

—Marshall Hyde to Theodora Marshall (9 December 2063)

"IF ALL THESE flashbacks are indeed pieces of memory," Theo said, while Yakov sat next to her vibrating with rage, "then when I came out of the anesthesia I did it faster than they expected. Looking back, I think it must've been because of my brother. He either did something, or that two percent of our bond did something, and I was a little stronger than I should've been."

"What did they do to you?"

"My head hurt. So much." She lifted her fingers to one temple, pressed. "Through it I heard them in pieces. The only thing I remember now is that they had to stop midway because Pax collapsed on the other side of the world."

She looked up, her eyes dark pools. "*Midway.* That means they got halfway through the procedure before my bond with Pax forced them to stop." Her chest rose and fell in shallow breaths. "And I have no idea what that procedure was."

Yakov couldn't sit in the car any longer. Shoving his door open, he stalked out into the cold night air and all the way to the edge of the lookout. It had no barriers, nothing to protect against a drop, but he was a changeling, the physical natural to him. A bear might not be as graceful as a tiger or a wolf, but they could take a lot of knocks and keep on going.

When he heard the passenger-side door open behind him, he turned to watch Theo walk toward him, a slender woman with golden hair and eyes made of shock—within whom lived a volcanic anger.

It spoke to his own.

"I knew Psy hurt their children," he said as the wind rippled through that single escaped lock of her hair. "But like *this*?" Cubs were to be protected; it was one of the founding tenets of life.

"I grew up in that culture," she murmured, her cheekbones sharp against her skin, "and even I can't believe my grandfather would do that to me. I still trusted him then. He was such an important part of my life that trusting him was habit. Like the sky is blue and the grass is green, Marshall Hyde knew best."

She swallowed hard. "Only . . . I'd begun to say no to things he asked me to do. Small things. But I knew they were wrong." Her eyes on Moscow, as if she'd rather look anywhere than at him, she said, "There are Tks who can affect the cells of the body itself. The rarest of the rare."

Yakov tried to clear his mind so he could think. "You're one of them?"

A laugh that was mechanical, a rusty clock left unwound too long. "If only. No, I'm exactly what I appear to be: an ordinary everyday 2.7. I know because I was tested intensively for Tk-Cell status because of what I *can* do: I have fine control over that 2.7. I could move tiny components with dexterity at an age when most Tks are still accidentally breaking cups or chairs or desks, depending on their strength."

Theo shoved her hands into the pockets of his jacket again, and only then did he consciously realize she'd put it back on after the restaurant.

His bear rumbled, pleased.

"Do you know how many things a 2.7 can do if they have intensely fine psychic control?"

The day ran through Yakov's mind. "Walk through locked doors, for one."

"Yes. At first, he had me practice with locks at home until I could undo almost any. It was a game. I liked it." Echoes of childhood pain escaped her rigid control. "Then late one night, long after I was asleep, one of his men came, drove me to a small apartment block, and asked me to unlock a particular door. I did it and they took me home.

"It was years later, long after I'd stopped doing anything my grandfather wanted, that I discovered that a man was found murdered in that same apartment. Under ordinary circumstances, Tks have excellent memories—I knew the date, the time I went in. He died within minutes of me circumventing his lock. No forced entry. Nothing to set off his alarm system. Unsolved homicide."

If Yakov had had any illusions about Psy under Silence, they lay in splinters at his feet—and Theo wasn't done.

"As a child, I thought it was a game or that I was helping Grandfather's friends get into their houses after they forgot their codes. Then the game changed. He gave me part of a car engine—I didn't know what it was then—and told me to learn how to fragment a tiny piece hidden deep within. Such a small piece that even a 2.7 would have no trouble at all with the force required.

"In such a situation, it's more about accuracy than strength." Theo continued to refuse to look at him. "A lot of high-Gradient Tks can't do subtle telekinesis. Their power is too unwieldy at that scale. Quite the opposite of mine. I felt important when he first told me that I might be able to be useful to the family after all. I thought he'd let me come home if I studied hard and did as he asked."

Yakov's claws thrust at the insides of his skin, wanting out, his bear enraged at this cynical and cruel manipulation of a child who'd just wanted to *come home*.

Theo carried on, as if she couldn't stop now that she'd started. "I was given access to a private garage in my apartment building where I could go anytime to look at the right model of engine so I could memorize the position of the part. Spatial placement is critical to a Tk."

Yakov felt a sick twisting in the pit of his stomach, but he didn't interrupt. Theo needed to get this poison out of her system. She'd been carrying it around for far too long.

"Then one day, Grandfather picked me up and said we were going for a drive. He told me he was very pleased with my results when it came to the telekinetic test he'd set me. I was so happy. And after a while, I saw that we were behind the exact make and model of the car I'd been ordered to study, and he asked me to 'disrupt' that piece of the engine."

Gaze still pinned to the Moscow skyline, her breathing ragged. "I said 'No, Grandfather. That will break the car.' Because I knew that by then. I've always been good at technical things and I'd looked up what that part meant. It was critical. Disabling it in high-speed transit would've meant certain death for the driver."

"Bozhe, pchelka." It was ground out through his teeth. "You were a damn baby!"

"I said no that day and another day." Her shoulders hunched in. "But you see, Yakov, I stopped saying no at some point." No distance in her voice now, just jagged shards rough and brutal. "I have only foggy memories of multiple years of my childhood . . . but when I came out of the fog, I did so with blood coating my hands. So *much* blood."

"No, fuck no." Yakov moved into her line of sight so she could no longer avoid his gaze. Then he took her chin between thumb and forefinger, because the two of them, they'd come to a silent understanding on a limited level of skin privileges. "You were manipulated and had your brain fucking *rewired*. This is *not* on you."

Theo wanted to clutch at his words and never look back, but it wasn't that easy. "Or is that what I want to believe, Yasha?" That affectionate diminutive of his name, it felt so easy on her tongue, as if she had the right to say it. "What if I said yes because I wanted to please him? What if I became a monster in order to earn the approval of a monster? And what if I don't remember because I'm too ashamed to remember?"

Yakov's chest rumbled, a distant thunderstorm. "You were a cub." He said each word with delineated focus. "No matter what, you are not to blame."

"But I need to know." She found herself gripping the solid heft of his wrist, squeezing. "I need to know if what they did to me in that place made me more likely to say yes. I need to know what damage they burned into my neurons. Maybe then . . . maybe then, I can forgive myself."

Forgiveness hadn't even been a thought in her brain for years upon years, since the day she came out of the fog and understood the horror of what she'd become. "I've spent years tracking down murders tied to my powers. There are so many. It doesn't matter that I was a child. The body count is too high for me to ever forgive if I *chose* that path."

He made a deep rumbling sound this time, and then he was hauling her against him and wrapping her up in his arms, and she'd never in her life felt so warm and safe and protected. And though she'd spent a lifetime teaching herself to rely on no one, she clung on. "I need to know." It came out a shaken whisper.

His hand cradling the back of her head, his breath warm against her temple. "Then we find out."

A vow that rang through her bones. And she knew this man would keep his word. He'd do everything in his power to find her the answers she needed. For better or worse. Because at the end of it . . . she might yet discover herself a murderer who'd traded the lives of others for her own happiness.

YAKOV wanted to hold on to Theo forever, tormented by the image of her as a tiny helpless child strapped down and subjected to hurt by the very person who should've protected her to his last breath. She was so slender and small even now. Back then? Fuck. His claws threatened to erupt.

Fine strands of her hair whispered up in the wind to cling to his face. And he realized she must be cold out here so late at night. Cold and tired and heartsick. That did it. "I'm not leaving you alone tonight," he said, willing to fight her tooth and nail on this. "And since I haven't checked the security on your place, we're going to a clan apartment we keep in the city."

Theo didn't stiffen, but said, "My apartment should be secure. It's maintained by experienced staff."

So much courage and steel to her. She left him breathless.

"I helped with the security on the StoneWater apartment myself," Yakov countered. "I know it's a fort." He continued to hold her, shattered that she let him; that told him far more than her words.

His complicated, smart, tough Theo's heart was broken. Had broken a long time ago and never healed.

"We also have hot chocolate and supplies of cookies," he cajoled. "And if you like, I'll turn into a bear and let you pet me."

Her head jerked up. He'd said the last as a joke, but from the wonder in her gaze, he was about to be a very happy bear. The thought of her fingers stroking through his fur? Hell, yes. "Deal?" he murmured.

"Will there be anyone else at the apartment?"

"No." Yakov could answer that without checking because he was the one in charge of the bookings. "Most places we have, it's for any clanmate to crash in if they need it, but this particular one we keep for guests of the clan who're only in the city for a short time and can't make it out to the den. It's empty this week."

"Then, deal." Theo's hand flexed against his back, curled in again.

He wanted to purr—not like a cat, like a *bear*. That was a real purr. "Come on, in the car before you freeze."

Chapter 25

LvrBoo: I've got a good one: Best cuddlers in the changeling world?

H2lmhot: Snakes. Tangle all around you silky and smooth and strong. You haven't been cuddled until you've been cuddled by an anaconda.

4cubs: Um, H2lmhot, different strokes but yikes! Isn't that how they kill their prey? Anyway, my vote is for tigers. They're so prowly and that fur . . . mmm.

BB: Bears! Of course the answer is bears! Why is this even a conversation?!

—Forum of *Wild Woman* magazine

ONCE HE GOT the engine running, Yakov made the mistake of turning on the radio—right as the reporter made an announcement about the killer they were now calling "the Moscow Ripper."

Wow, real original.

"That's another reason I want you safe and secure," he said after the bulletin was complete. "Blond hair, blue eyes, Psy, you fit the victim profile of the murderer stalking the city."

"I'll be careful, though if the newscast is correct and the Ripper stalks their victims for days prior to attacking, I'm unlikely to be a target—I haven't been in the city long enough." Theo yawned on the last word. "I don't know why I'm so exhausted."

Yakov wondered how she didn't see it—she'd taken emotional blow after emotional blow today. He wouldn't be surprised if she fell asleep in the car.

As it was, she was barely keeping her eyes open by the time he got them to the apartment. Grabbing her suitcase from the back of his vehicle after parking in the secure underground lot, he ushered her into the elevator operated by either a keycard assigned by building management or by an override code that Yakov was in charge of updating every month.

Because while StoneWater only used one of these apartments, they owned the entire building—and it wasn't their only property in the city. One of Valya's early business ideas that had taken off in serious fashion. Buy neglected properties with good bones, use clan labor and smarts to fix and polish them up to the highest specs, then flip them or hold them as long-term investments.

StoneWater properties were now some of the hottest on the market. Because bears knew how to build—and how to create homes that glowed with a sense of welcome. A few beers with friends on a lazy night in the den and Valya would proclaim himself a property mogul— but he only ever kept a straight face for about ten seconds.

Then that big, generous laugh of his would fill the air, making everyone grin.

Valya might find the idea of himself as a mogul amusing, but their entire clan knew their alpha's foresight meant a more secure future for their cubs. He wondered what Theo would think of the bear Yakov loved as a friend and respected as an alpha. But that was a question for another day.

Today, he ushered her into their apartment as fast as possible.

"Bedroom," he said, putting her case beside the sprawling bear-sized bed. "Bathroom and toilet are the next doors down. I'll take the couch."

Theo stared at the creamy white of the embroidered duvet that sat fluffy and warm atop a neatly made bed. Below that were cream sheets, but the assemblage of pillows provided bright pops of autumnal color.

"There is a large number of pillows." Theo's tone was painfully polite, but at least the pillow mountain had shocked her out of her numb state.

"Honest truth," he said, starting to throw the pillows over his shoulder and off the bed, "I don't get it, either. But interior décor is Chimeg's bailiwick and I'm not a stupid bear. I don't ask any questions." Was he ever going to get to the end of this pile? "Submissive, my furry ass," he muttered. "She's about as submissive as a feral squirrel. Those things look small and cute but they can claw your face off."

He'd wanted to make Theo laugh with his description of his short-tempered clanmate, but the woman who ordinarily shimmered with contained energy just stood there without moving.

Until at last, she said, "Yasha . . . will you stay? I'm so cold." A shiver rippled through her.

Yakov didn't need to think of his answer. "Of course, *pchelka moya*." Tenderness burned a fierce and wild need inside him. "Can you stay awake long enough to change into more comfortable clothes? I'll go do the same."

When she nodded, he went to hunt out the stash of spare clothes; such emergency wardrobes were a necessity in a race that occasionally destroyed their clothing with an inopportune shift. He found a pair of washed and folded sweatpants that would fit, as well as an old but clean T-shirt. When he heard Theo moving to the bathroom, he busied himself with other tasks so she wouldn't feel rushed.

But she was back in the bedroom quickly, and then he heard the sound of the mattress being compressed. Leaving his jeans and other clothing on the sofa after quickly getting into the sweatpants and tee, he padded barefoot to the bedroom to find her in bed, curled up on her side. She'd put her hair in a braid and had the sheets pulled up to her chin.

A shiver racked her frame once again even though the apartment was at a more-than-comfortable temperature.

Muting the lights to almost but not quite full dark, Yakov strode to the bed and got in behind her. She didn't resist when he tucked her against him, her body fitting perfectly into the curve of his own and the vulnerable slope of her nape bare to him.

His bear nuzzled gently at her as, the vanilla scent of her shampoo in his nose, he held her tight until she fell into a deep sleep. Only then did he turn off the lights. But he stayed awake far longer, listening to the rise and fall of her breath, this woman who'd destroyed all his doubts about who she was by telling him the worst of her secrets.

He believed her.

Every fucking word.

What Theo had told him could damage not only her but the twin she loved. It had been an act of desperation rather than of trust . . . but this, tonight, her so vulnerable in his arms, this was trust. "Sleep, *milaya moya*. I'll keep you safe."

But when he came awake in the dead of night, his heart pounding and perspiration sticking his T-shirt to his back, it was with the haunting certainty that he *couldn't* keep her safe. That Theo was destined to die, her blood soaking her hands as he screamed, helpless and frozen.

He squeezed his eyes shut, buried his face against the warmth of Theo's nape, and said, "Fuck that," under his breath as a gentle rain pattered against the windows. It didn't matter how many times that nightmare vision tried to convince him of failure, he wasn't about to buy into it.

No one was going to take Theo from him.

A vow that came from the primal heart of the bear within.

Chapter 26

It's working. What we considered a failure at the first pass has proved to be a total success. This is the project that'll put my name in the history books, never to be forgotten.

—Councilor Marshall Hyde to Dr. Upashna Leslie (17 July 2068)

IT WAS DIFFICULT to avoid bear surveillance.

The only reason the Watcher had tracked down their prey was pure unpredictable luck. They'd seen their prey in the bear's vehicle while driving in the opposite direction and, even as their heart raced, had made a slow turn that wouldn't attract attention.

It had been almost too slow. They'd *just* caught the tail end of the StoneWater vehicle entering the underground garage of an apartment building the Watcher knew was owned by the bears.

At the time, the Watcher had driven on.

Now the Watcher was on foot. They could never be fully confident that the bears didn't have eyes on the street. So the Watcher became just another person walking along the rain-washed street below the third-floor window where Theodora Marshall currently slept.

It had to be that apartment; the Watcher had passed by this building multiple times over the preceding week, absently noted the single set of dark windows. They had considered checking to see if it was available as a rental before shrugging off the idea; the central location was a drawcard, but the Watcher couldn't risk eliciting bear attention. Now, one of those windows glowed gently, perhaps from a light left on in a hallway.

A Marshall in the city after all this time.

Slipping off their backpack with the ruse of searching within it for something, the Watcher took one more glance at the window.

A Marshall.

In Moscow.

Could it be? No, surely not. Marshall Hyde had been as jealous as a spoiled child when it came to his special project. He hadn't told anyone.

No, this had to be about some other business matter.

Still . . .

"Theodora," the Watcher murmured under their breath as they walked on, their skin hot and their pulse rapid. "2.7. Pax Marshall's twin." The Watcher knew that because the Watcher knew everything about the Marshall family.

Had to know.

The entire operation hung on a steady supply of Marshall money.

They'd have to think carefully about their next step. And they'd have to keep on watching.

Chapter 27

Skin privileges aren't just about touch. They're about trust.

—"Skin Privileges: An Exploration" by Xandra Jabi
(thesis concept in progress)

THEO WOKE FROM the best sleep of her life. Her entire body felt heavy, but the kind of heavy that indicated a dreamless rest. And she was so wonderfully warm. The fur blanket was—

Fur blanket?

Eyes snapping fully open, she jerked around to come face-to-face with a thick wall of dark brown fur that was rising and falling in a steady rhythm. She probably should've been scared, but instead, all she felt was a wondrous fascination. Moving with utmost care so as not to jostle the bed, she sat up.

And took in the bear fast asleep next to her.

StoneWater was made up mostly of Kamchatka brown bears. She'd read that in her research notes on the clan. She'd also read that Kamchatka bears were some of the biggest in the world. She hadn't actually comprehended what that meant until she took in the astonishing living mountain next to her.

The mass differential made no logical sense.

She didn't care. She just wanted to touch him.

. . . *I'll turn into a bear and let you pet me.*

Her heart thumped as she remembered that he'd given her permission for what *Wild Woman* termed "skin privileges." She probably should let him sleep, but she felt like a child with a forbidden toy. She wanted to touch as she hadn't wanted anything in an eternity.

A little scared he'd react to her touch as a threat, she nonetheless moved her hand oh-so-carefully to his side. Her heart all but pounded out of her at the sheer wonder of touching this magnificent creature that was Yakov's other form, the other half of him.

Another kind of twinning, she thought to herself as she sank her fingers deeper into the luxuriant silk of his fur. She'd thought she'd never again feel warm or safe or even a little happy after the numbness engendered by her conscious acceptance of her grandfather's cruelty—but bubbles of excited joy popped in her bloodstream. A thing she hadn't felt for so long that it took her a while to pinpoint the emotion.

Yakov slept on as she petted him in long strokes, indulging herself in the feel of him. He was pure power and heat and wild. Right here in bed next to her. She looked at the fancy sheets, then at the claws visible on the paw on which he'd propped his head. Yet there were no rips in the sheets that she could see—and the bed was holding.

Built for bears, she realized. *Of course everything in this apartment is built for bears.*

Emboldened by her success thus far, she dared move her hand to his head, stroke the softer fur there. He stirred . . . and then he was yawning, that big and dangerous mouth opening to reveal equally dangerous teeth.

She'd frozen at his first movement, but yawn done and eyes still closed, he butted his head against her hand in a silent demand. Theo wanted to laugh in utter delight. She didn't know how to laugh, but the urge, it was rampant. Twisting to sit cross-legged next to him now that she knew he was awake, she petted him in earnest.

When he turned his head so that her hand ended up near an ear, she went with instinct and scratched him there. He sighed, then gave her his other ear. Theo wasn't sure she wasn't dreaming. "If this is a dream, I don't want to wake up," she said, leaning down to rub her cheek against his fur.

THE bear that was Yakov smiled, smug that she loved him in this form. He settled into her petting and would've happily gone back to his napping except that the human half of him knew they had to get moving if they were going to relieve Moon and Elbek early as he'd promised.

Finally opening his eyes, he allowed himself a moment to take in the happiness on Theo's face. She didn't smile, but there was a softness there, a light in her eyes. He felt himself turn to mush.

Chert voz'mi! He was going to be putty in her hands if he wasn't careful.

Groaning at having to be an adult bear, he lifted his head.

She slid her hand down his neck to lie on his side. "Time to go?"

When he nodded, she looked as disappointed as he felt, and then and there he decided he'd be a bear again for her the next chance he got. When he'd woken earlier with the desperate urge to change into his bear form, he'd hesitated, then thought Theo was tough enough to handle it.

Of course he'd wakened when she had; he was a bear second, his instincts finely honed. He'd been ready to shift back if she showed any signs of fear—but his *pchelka* was made of sterner stuff.

Proud of her in a way that told him he was heading into ever deeper waters, he considered how to get off the bed. It was built to take his weight in bear form, but Chimeg would set his hair on fire if he tore up her sheets, and while that was easy to avoid when he was dozing, walking on the sheets was another matter.

Theo patted his side. "I'll go use the bathroom so you can shift."

He rubbed his head against hers in thanks, and she clenched her hand in his fur for a second. He almost thought he felt her smile before she got off the bed and headed out.

Shifting the second she was gone, he pulled on his borrowed clothes. He had no trouble being naked, but neither was he an undomesticated dolt. Theo was Psy, hadn't been raised among feral bears. Though, to be fair, were he courting a bear woman, he wouldn't shift into naked human form in front of her, either—at least not until they were into the intimate skin privileges stage.

This depth of attraction? It altered things.

When he heard the shower come on, he used his time to make up the bed. No point in stripping it, since he had every intention of talking Theo into staying here again tonight. With him. Where she could pet him all over once more. Perhaps even on his human skin this time.

His cock grew hard between one breath and the next.

He groaned again. "Not now," he said sternly, but it still took teeth-gritted will for him to get his rampant body under control by the time Theo was done with her shower.

He went out to raid the spare clothes stash again as she crossed back to the bedroom, deliberately keeping his back to her. No doubt she was wearing one of the silky guest robes Chimeg stocked in the bathroom, but it'd be oh-so-easy to undo the fabric belt around her waist and un-ravel that robe, slide his skin over the smooth nakedness of hers.

His cock reacted again.

Clenching his jaw, he grabbed a dark green T-shirt that looked like it'd fit. He could wear his jeans again, just go commando. But since he planned to stay in the city with Theo for the duration, he'd have Pavel or another clanmate drop off some clothes for him.

For now, he had a quick shower, dressed, then finger-combed his hair and was done. "Thanks, Denu," he said with a grin in the mirror. Because it was his great-grandfather's genes that meant his hair didn't tangle, that it fell back into perfect lines no matter what.

"You okay with grabbing food at the bakery?" he called out to Theo after he exited the bathroom. "They stock nutrient drinks, too." Silver had taught him that Psy needed those nutrients to refuel the psychic parts of their brains—they *could* get the same through food, but it took a lot longer. Easier to just add nutrients to other meals.

Theo had also spent considerable energy unlocking the gate at the facility yesterday, never mind the emotional energy she'd expended when she'd walked into the past.

"Yes, of course," she said, emerging from her room wearing dark blue jeans, a gray sweater . . . and his jacket. She'd braided her hair neatly and once again wore that metal bracelet on her wrist. "We don't want to let down your clanmates after they stepped in to assist."

They put on their shoes side by side. And when he held out a hand, she slid hers into his. It was only after they were outside that he realized she hadn't even asked about moving to her apartment.

Bear and man both smiled, and for this misty morning, they didn't talk about the dark cloud that hovered above, and just kept everything light. Yakov did get an odd prickling sensation when he pulled out onto the street, as if they were being watched, but he saw nothing when he scanned the area.

Might just be the whole Ripper situation making him edgy.

That reminded him not to turn on the radio in the car; he didn't want news of blood and death to fill the vehicle when Theo looked relaxed for the first time since he'd met her.

When he pulled up in front of the bakery, he groaned. "Bears, fucking bears everywhere." He looked around. "It's six in the morning! Not even full light!"

"You're a bear and you're here," Theo pointed out.

He scowled. "I'm different."

Getting out, they walked into the bakery. A dark-haired male was leaning on the top of the display case, chatting with the owner, Gustav, while a bear cub in cub form clung upside down to his back. Another cub—this one a polar bear—was clinging to his leg like a barnacle.

Chapter 28

"Fitz and Nurlan, you gotta keep watch. Juji, Arkasha, you carry the bags. I'll put the cupcakes in. Ready?"

—Early-morning cupcake raid by five tiny gangsters, led by current chief tiny gangster Svetlana Valeria Kuznetsov (today)

"YASHA!" VALENTIN'S BOOM of a voice as he spotted Yakov.

The cubs saw him at the same time and released Valentin to run over to him. It was instinct to crouch down, grab them both. Throwing them over one shoulder each, where they chortled and clung on, he rose to his feet. "Theo," he said, "meet Valentin Nikolaev, alpha of StoneWater."

His alpha was an imposing figure—one of the biggest men in Stone-Water, all wide shoulders and taut muscle. Only his clan knew that he was a complete teddy bear. Unless, of course, you came after those under his care. Then Valentin Nikolaev would be the last thing you ever saw.

Valentin's night-dark eyes gleamed as he took in Theo. Damn it to all hells. Yakov's friend and alpha was too fucking clever for anyone's good. He'd either scented Yakov on Theo, or Yakov had given it away with his body language, but Valentin knew this was no longer just a business relationship.

But his alpha only grinned, and said, "*Zdravstvuyte*, Theo. If Yasha gives you any trouble, just come to me—I'll report him to his mother, and his furry butt is toast."

"Funny, Valya." He threw the polar bear cub at his alpha.

Only when Theo let out an involuntary cry did he realize what he'd done. Wincing, he turned to take in her shocked face. "They love it," he told her. "Look." Then he threw the other cub.

Both cubs laughed so hard they almost fell out of Valentin's grasp. A second later, they positioned themselves to be thrown again.

Yakov caught first Dima, followed by Zhenya, then kissed each laughing cub in the face. "My friend Theo thinks throwing you is scary. You want her to give it a try?"

When both cubs nodded, he turned and raised an eyebrow at Theo with a grin. "Want to try bear cub throwing? Get good enough and you might make it to the annual den championship."

Theo blinked, looked at the small bears in his arms. Who put on their best innocent looks. Hah! The tiny gangsters had no doubt been awake far too early and snuck into Valentin's truck when they realized he was about to drive into the city. Valya would've known of his illicit passengers—he was alpha, and they were babies. But sometimes, you had to allow a cub to think they'd gotten away with something, build up their confidence.

"They do love it," Valentin assured Theo as Gustav—long used to bear antics and a frequent guest at the den—put Valentin's boxed-up order on the counter and charged it to the account on record. The box was the largest the bakery offered, so their alpha was probably grabbing treats for the senior soldier meeting this morning.

Breath still not steady, Theo carefully accepted young Dima into her arms. The usually rambunctious polar bear cub sat quietly looking up at her. "Oh, he's so beautiful." Theo's voice was awed. "They're both so beautiful."

Zhenya stretched out of his arms so Theo could pet her, too, while Dima took some of his body weight off Theo's arm by lightly gripping the top of her jeans with his claws. Nova and Chaos's cub—and Valya's nephew—was a clever child. A mischievous one by nature, but kind with it. He'd end up either a master jewel thief or an alpha.

All bets were off at this stage.

Valentin caught Yakov's eyes while Theo was distracted by the cubs. A slight tilt of his alpha's head that Yakov returned with a shake of his. Nothing to report yet. The fact that Theo had been at the facility prior to this visit wasn't something Valya needed to know to maintain the clan's security.

That particular thread of this investigation was a private matter.

Valentin nodded before grabbing the distinctive pink bakery box. "Time to hit the road."

The cubs immediately jumped out of their arms and to the ground.

"Here." Having come around the counter, Gustav squatted down to put a small bag in front of each cub. "Don't tell your friends." A dark scowl. "Our secret, got it?"

He got pounced on with cub licks in thanks.

"Yeah, yeah." Grumpy words, but he petted both children with big hands that were painfully gentle, the backs marred with the small burn scars that ended up on many a baker's hands.

Picking up their bags of cookies with their mouths afterward, the cubs padded along behind Valentin as the alpha headed to the door. "We'll speak again, Theo," Valentin said. "Yasha, I'll get a few clothes sent out to the apartment."

When Yakov made a rude gesture, timing it so the cubs wouldn't see, Valentin just grinned and walked out. There weren't many people out on the street at this early hour, but each and every one stopped to gush over the cubs—who played up their cuteness to maximum extent.

"How did your alpha know?" Theo murmured after Valya and the cubs were out of sight.

Yakov put his hands on his hips. "Because he's too fucking smart. And don't let the cubs fool you—they're tiny gangsters, one and all. Whole tiny mafia going on back at the den. No candy is safe from their clutches."

Theo's eyes . . . sparkled, the taut anger of her replaced by delight. "Your clan seems rather wonderful, Yasha."

Yakov could suddenly see her in the heart of the den, surrounded by cubs. He groaned. "Theo, the tiny gangsters are going to take you for all you've got. You're not going to be able to say no, are you?"

"No," she said, without any sign of that being a problem. "Shall we order?"

Bemused and falling even deeper for her, he placed the order. One box for Elbek and Moon, one for him and Theo. "We need lunch, too," he told Gustav. "And throw in a few extras in case we have to be on-site longer."

Gustav didn't ask anything about that site. Unlike certain bears, the baker preferred to mind his own business. He was, however, a shrewd businessman. "Free samples," he said, and thrust a small pre-prepared plate in front of Theo.

"Hey." Yakov threw up his hands. "What about me?"

A snort. "I already got you bears addicted. She could be a new customer."

Laughing because Gustav really was a bear in human form, Yakov kept an eye on Theo's plate as she tested things . . . and ended up adding a box of donut holes to their order after she ate the freebie down to the last little bite, then licked her fingers.

His cock wanted to *react*.

Impeccable timing as always, he thought darkly.

Food order placed, he also ordered three coffees in the vacuum flask mugs the bakery gave out to regular customers on the understanding they'd be brought back after use. "Twelve hours," Gustav told him. "That's how long the coffee will stay piping hot in these new cups. Straight from a local manufacturer. Special deal for locals. You report back if it works in the field."

"Roger."

Theo walked back from the cooler with a nutrient drink to add to the order.

Gustav scratched his bristly jaw. "You want that heated?"

"I never—" She cut herself off when Gustav began to scowl. "Um, yes?"

Gustav grunted and went off to heat up the drink and put it in a separate flask. Meanwhile, Theo leaned in close to Yakov and whispered, "Is he a bear, too?"

"No, human. With bear tendencies."

"You want water?" Gustav yelled out from the back. "Free if you have your own bottle. I got a new purifier."

"No, we're set," Yakov said, having stocked his vehicle up with water earlier in the week. He'd also checked the supplies in all the other clan vehicles. It wasn't technically part of his job, but he liked knowing his clanmates wouldn't be without emergency supplies should they break down.

Gustav grunted as he returned with Theo's drink. He also gave her a free mini pain au chocolat.

"Oh." Theo looked at the gift wide-eyed. "Thank you so much. Your baked goods are the most delicious things I've ever tasted."

Gustav actually . . . smiled.

Bozhe moi! Maybe the world was ending and he'd been hit on the head by a meteor and was suffering delusions.

"Wow," he said with a mock scowl even as his bear delighted in the irascible baker's liking for her. "You're obviously the favorite here."

"Go away now." Gustav flapped his hand. "I have civilized customers soon." He looked over at Theo. "You can come back anytime. Do a proper taste test."

"Pleasure doing business with you as always," Yakov said, and grabbed the boxes of food, Theo taking the recyclable tray that held the drinks. As they drove out, it was pretty much a perfect day, with Theo trying a sugar-dusted donut in the passenger seat while Yakov bit down on his hot bacon-and-egg roll as they drove out of the city.

The world felt hopeful.

Then it all went wrong.

Chapter 29

Major incident unfolding in eastern quadrant of airport zone. Traffic at a
standstill. No official reports. To be continued.

—*Moskva Gazeta* livestream (today)

IT HAPPENED WHILE they were about a half hour out from the site—
which put them inside the airport's automatic driving zone. Yakov was just
about to take another sip of his coffee when he saw brake lights up ahead.

Not just one set.

Looked like a severe traffic jam. Unusual, when a major reason for
the mandatory automatic driving zone was to ensure a steady and uninterrupted flow; his vehicle had switched to that mode the instant he crossed
into the airport area—though Yakov had never mentally switched off.

Auto-driving in general might be safe, but it was still based on ma-
chinery. He needed to be in a position to react rapidly if his car suffered
a sudden mechanical failure, or if an unpredictable hazard impacted the
road. Today, however, his trusty all-terrain vehicle came to a halt at the
precise safe distance behind a sedan stopped in the road. In front of that
was a transit van to a rural area, and the line continued on.

When he flashed the car's navigation system up onto the dash to
check what was holding things up, he saw the red exclamation mark

symbol that indicated an emergency a quarter mile up ahead. "Most likely an accident," he said to Theo. "Must be pretty bad if traffic is this backed up." The first responders usually opened up one lane around the site of an accident, but from the lack of traffic on the other side of the road, the entire thing had been shut down.

"I hope no one was seriously injured." Theo lowered her window and tried to look around the side of the car. "I can't see anything from here."

Having mirrored her move, angling his head out into the crisp wind, Yakov said, "I can see the barest glimpse of flashing lights. A whole lot of them." He sat back, his gut tight. "Has to be bad." Injuries—even deaths—were highly likely.

Yakov's phone beeped at that moment, with StoneWater's emergency code. He answered it at once, putting the phone to his ear rather than on speaker. It was one thing to trust Theo on a personal level, quite another to bring her into the heart of his clan. One decision was his and his alone to make, while the other required the input and trust of his clanmates.

Valentin's voice in his ear, no humor to it as there'd been at the bakery. "Yasha, our system is showing that your vehicle is very close to the site of a major incident."

Yakov could've turned off that tracking—it wasn't a clandestine thing. He'd left it on because he was on clan business and one of the benefits of the tracking system was that the clan could find people when it needed them in particular areas. "Stuck in a queue of traffic. I can see flashing lights up ahead but that's all. What's happened?"

"Another murder." Valentin's bitten-out statement made Yakov's skin go cold. "Fucker is getting bolder. He laid his victim out in the middle of the road. Two drivers actually saw him do it, but no one was fast enough to capture him even though he escaped on foot. Enforcement brought in bloodhounds, but they lost the trail. They asked if we had a tracker nearby and you're the closest."

"Got it." While most people didn't know the extent of a brown bear's acute sense of smell, Enforcement in Moscow would've had to be brain-dead not to utilize it. StoneWater's relationship with Enforcement hadn't always been as good as it was these days, but the bears had always responded when the cops asked for their assistance when it came to tracking down dangerous predators—or vulnerable victims.

That was one of the many reasons Moscow loved the bears even when they misbehaved. They knew that should their child or another at-risk member of the family wander off, they could send out an SOS for bear assistance and it would be provided.

"Transfer the vehicle's controls to Theo," Valentin added. "If she doesn't drive, I'll have Enforcement send someone back to mark it off with emergency signs."

Yakov glanced at the passenger seat. "Hold on a second." He turned to Theo. "I need to get up to the scene of the incident. Can you drive this vehicle?"

Theo, incisive and quick, didn't ask questions that would've delayed him, just reacted with a nod.

"Theo has it," he said into the phone. "I'm heading to Enforcement now."

"Good luck. I hope you locate the bastard."

After hanging up with his alpha, Yakov quickly programmed Theo's fingerprint and voice ID into the car's system so that she had temporary authority to drive it. "If the queue starts moving, drive to where you see Enforcement vehicles, then pull off to the shoulder and park. Tell them you're with me. I'll explain everything after I get back."

He waited only until Theo had given him a nod before he got out and began to run between the rows of cars, his nose already picking up the scent of old blood and ice-cold fear.

THEO didn't bother to get out of the car. She just slid over into the driver's seat. It was easy since Yakov was bigger than her—she had plenty of space to get her feet underneath the dash. At which point, the automated seat controls reset for her height and asked her to either confirm the setting or make further changes. She confirmed the setting while her heart yet thundered from witnessing Yakov's sudden burst of speed. She hadn't realized that bears could run that fast.

It wasn't the kind of graceful and relentless speed she might expect from a feline or a canine. Rather, it had been a burst of raw power that propelled him down the road. No human or Psy would ever outrun him. And other changelings would be very stupid to pick a fight with an animal that big and strong and *fast*.

Once again, Aunt Rita's wise words reverberated in her head: *Never underestimate a bear.*

After her pulse finally slowed, she began to scan the highways of the PsyNet for any piece of information on what might've happened. She found it minutes later. A live feed into the network built of neural energy from a Psy near the front of the line.

Body on road. Murdered there? Enforcement officers everywhere. I think I recognize a detective from a news show. Maybe the body was dumped from a moving car? People in neighboring cars milling about. One woman says she's sure it's just a stunt. Fashion dummy on the road. Annoying. I heard dogs, though. And there's a forensics van. Oh, I see a dog! Such a floppy face.

Whoever it was uploading the information wasn't a person with a neat mind. Neither were they anchoring their data; it would disappear within a matter of minutes. Unless, of course, the feed was quickly picked up by one of the bots that scanned the PsyNet for news. Then it might end up in a more stable form in the *Beacon* or another reputable news organization.

Why, she considered, had Yakov run to the scene?

She'd heard that changelings tended to keep their distance from Enforcement because Enforcement was thought to be controlled by Psy. The latter wasn't just speculation; Theo had been in her grandfather's car more than once when he'd called up an Enforcement contact. Theo wasn't the only reason he'd gotten away with his murderous crimes.

—bear.

She snapped her attention back to the PsyNet stream. The person up ahead was now broadcasting that one of the StoneWater bears had just run onto the scene. Had to be a local to have pinpointed Yakov as a bear without hesitation.

Bears have an incredible sense of smell. Better than bloodhounds. Oh! That's the breed of dog the cops brought in!

That fragment of information about bear abilities was blurted out by the same person. It explained everything. As for the rest, Theo would wait until Yakov returned to find those answers. For now, she allowed herself to mourn for the nameless victim who'd lost their life for no reason except that someone felt the need to kill. She had never understood that.

Theo was responsible for more murders than she knew, her hands a permanent blood red—but she had never *wanted* to kill. *That makes you no less culpable*, said the part of her that would hold her to account till the end of her days.

For the first time, however, she fought back. "What if I didn't make the choice?" she said aloud. "What if the only person who made a choice was Grandfather? What if he broke my brain so he'd have a puppet?"

The questions hung in the air, the possibility of redemption a painful hope.

Theo? Her brother's crystal clear telepathic voice. *Is all well? I'm hearing disturbing things about events in Moscow.*

You set a bot to monitor the PsyNet for news from Moscow, didn't you? Of course he had; he'd been taking care of her for so long that he didn't know how to stop. *I'm fine*, she replied before he could answer, knowing that his powerful mind would pick up on her much weaker voice. *There's a possible serial killer roaming the streets, but I'm with a bear anytime I'm out.*

What's the word on the facility? Did you have a chance to visit yesterday?

She wasn't surprised at the lack of any emotional response from her brother. She and Pax, they'd both been damaged in different and equally terrible ways by their upbringing. *It's abandoned*, she said, not ready to talk about the rest of it; it would only hurt him. *We're going back there today for a more in-depth look. I'll send back anything I discover.*

Abandoned? I should stop the financial drain on our accounts. It has to be fraudulent.

Theo frowned. *No*, she found herself saying. *I don't want to risk alerting the person behind the financial draw—they might be our only hope of discovering what was going on there. I need to know.*

Yes, I understand, said the twin who hadn't been allowed to be her twin for most of her life.

Pax? Are you stable? Theo's headaches had stopped since Memory Aven-Rose began to work with Pax, but that meant she couldn't always tell when Scarab Syndrome was starting to go rampant inside Pax's brain.

Yes. No change.

She didn't tell him that he was to draw from her psychic energy whenever he needed it; he knew that, and he'd also go to the wire in an attempt not to do it—because it weakened her, and Pax didn't want her weak in a sea of predators.

There is one thing, he added. *Those telepathic pings I mentioned? I checked my filter today and they've increased in volume so I'm now getting multiple such contacts per hour.*

Theo looked into the Net, toward his mind, but saw no obvious disturbances or incursions. *Sounds like it might be more than a childish prank. Have you responded to any?*

Not yet. I've been busy handling the current bloodbath in the family. I'll let you know when I get around to dealing with it.

He then gave her an update about the power struggle going on in the family, but there was no concern in his tone. It was more, she knew, an annoyance than an actual threat. For better or worse, Pax had been trained for the CEO position by *the* Marshall. He was also a 9, multitudes more powerful than any other member of their line.

He could crush them like ants.

Why are you letting this continue? Theo usually left all the maneuvering up to him, but today she could hear the tiredness in his tone.

I'm hopeful that the situation will reveal someone who might prove suitable to take over from me should the need arise.

Theo swallowed hard. *There's no one as good as you.* Marshall might've molded Pax, but their grandfather'd had brilliant material with which to work.

There are children in the line. Maybe, before I go, I can put a CEO in place who'll ensure their lives aren't blighted as ours were—our entire family can't be poison. There has to be *at least one person with both empathy and the cutthroat ruthlessness required to survive at the top.*

Theo dropped her head against the seat, her hands clenching on the steering wheel. Because the only person in the line who matched that description was Pax. And yet . . . there *were* children. Innocents. *Is there anything I can do?* Emotion clogged up her throat, burned her eyes.

At times, she wanted to scream at fate until she had no more voice, and then she wanted to burn down the world, the rage in her an inferno. Forcing herself to breathe, she rubbed compulsively at the metal of her bracelet.

You do everything by just being there, Pax replied. *You're the one person in this world I know will never stab me in the back.* A pause. *Theo? Will you ever tell me the secret I sense in the shadows of your mind?*

She squeezed her eyes shut, her fingers tight on the bracelet, and then told the truth. *I don't know. I've kept my own counsel for a long time.*

Grandfather taught us well, didn't he? That tiredness again, so heavy and dark. *I have to go. Meeting.* His telepathic presence vanished from her mind.

That was one thing they'd done forever. Never said good-bye. Because it was never good-bye, that two percent bond functional even when everything else was gone. Theo would shatter if it ever disappeared . . . and her brother was dying. Being devoured by Scarab Syndrome, piece by brilliant piece.

Her internal scream grew ever louder, the rage within a feral beast.

She'd barely gotten her emotions under control when the traffic began to move. Slowly, but steadily. It looked like the authorities had opened up one of the three lanes on this side.

Her car started up, joining in the mandated flow.

Chapter 30

Black clothes. Maybe sweatpants and a hoodie with the hood pulled up? It happened so fast. But not a big person. Hard to tell if they were thin or just rangy with the baggy clothes, but definitely not bear-sized. Average, I guess.

No idea on height. I'm no good at that and they were on the road, with nothing to compare against.

—Eyewitness report as recorded by Detective Vo Zaitsev (today)

"EXIT ONTO EMERGENCY shoulder," Theo instructed the car once she was close to the scene.

As she'd expected, the system didn't question that order; it tended to be one of the built-in overrides when it came to mandated automatic navigation zones. Communicating seamlessly with the other vehicles around them, it shifted lanes with ease until it came to a stop on the emergency shoulder, mere feet from the Enforcement cordon.

The red beams of lasers sparked angrily against the morning light.

An officer in plain clothes immediately walked over to the window she'd already lowered. "You can't stop here," he said in rapid Russian. "Is your vehicle in trouble? If so, we can give you a ride out and you can organize to retrieve it once the area is clear."

"This is Yakov Stepyrev's vehicle."

The officer raised his eyebrows, then stood up and spoke into the microphone dotted at his collar. Leaning back down shortly, he said, "You're cleared to remain here. But don't leave your vehicle. This is a live scene. Understood?"

"Understood," Theo said, because she knew how to play the game when it came to people in power. No one ever expected trouble from the meek and mild persona she adopted in such situations—so no one watched her.

So easy it was to fool others into seeing her as not worth their attention.

In this case, however, she had no intention of breaking the rules. "Officer," she said before he could walk away. "Is Yakov all right?"

"Of course. He's a bear." As if that was all that needed to be said.

She found that strangely reassuring.

A little of the tension leaching out of her muscles, she relaxed into the seat and observed the scene in front of her. A white tent blocked any view of the body, for which Theo was grateful. She'd had enough death in her life, didn't want to see any more.

But not all of what was happening was obscured from view.

The forensic techs in their head-to-toe white coveralls, their faces covered with clear masks and their hair tucked neatly under the hoods of the coveralls, moved around the site in a quiet swarm.

Taking samples, shooting photographs, setting up evidence markers.

Enforcement officers outside the cordon wore the city's dark blue uniform. A number spoke into phones, while their colleagues directed traffic. But she was most interested in three people in ill-fitting suits— two women, one man—who stood on the far left of the road, their attention on the forested area on that side.

Detectives. Waiting for Yakov.

Who was too fast for them to follow.

Climbing into the rear section of the vehicle through the seats, she grabbed a bottle of water from the storage area for when he came back, then returned to her seat. She expected to sit there for some time, but Yakov appeared out of the trees less than ten minutes later. His face was grim, the shake of his head a hard negative. After a short conversation with the dejected-appearing trio, he looked around, spotted her, and jogged over.

Theo had already shifted to the passenger seat and now passed him the bottle of water. "You lost the trail?" she asked after he'd emptied it, his body so hot with energy it was tongues of flame on her skin. "At another road, I assume?"

But Yakov shook his head again, a pulse ticking in his jaw. "In the middle of the forest." Grit in every word. "I even went up a tree, thinking that perhaps he'd climbed up. Bears aren't the best climbers, but I checked the canopy on every side, and even did a wider circle just in case. Nothing."

Light dawned, the reason for his frustration crystal clear. "A teleport-capable telekinetic." A nightmare of a person to hunt. Someone who could vanish and appear at will, constrained only by the level of their power.

"That's not the worst of it." Exhaling, Yakov threw the empty bottle into the back seat. "This stays between us, Theo." Not a question. Not an order. Just . . . a statement of trust.

Warmth uncurled inside her stomach, flowed into her veins. "I won't say anything."

"I tracked one scent from the body to the place in the forest where I lost it—but I'm certain I scented two *different* individuals at that spot."

Theo sucked in a breath. "A teleport assist?" She could barely wrap her mind around it. "Serial-killing pairs are rare." A fact she knew because of her obsessive research about murderers and what drove them.

"Rare but they do exist." Yakov stared at the scene beyond the windshield, the tendons in his neck standing out starkly against his skin. "My nose doesn't lie. There are two people involved in this." His hand fisted against the steering wheel. "I can scent the victim's death from here."

Theo didn't know much about how to offer comfort, but she did what he'd done for her and reached out to take his hand. His fingers closed over hers, his body a furnace.

It did something to her that he accepted her faltering attempt at help without a pause.

"Unless Enforcement needs you to stay, we should go," she said, hating that evil had found this man so warm and *good.* "Get you some clean air." Now that she had a better idea of his sense of smell, she knew why he'd used the word "death" rather than blood. Because it wasn't blood alone that he was picking up.

"My nostrils feel lined with malice." With that, Yakov lifted Theo's hand to his nose and took several long breaths.

She'd been trained all her life to pull back from physical contact—but she'd never been truly Silent. And she liked touching Yakov and being touched by him. More than that, she understood that this wasn't about crossing boundaries. "My scent?" she asked softly when he raised his head at last.

Perhaps it was her imagination, but he looked calmer and more centered.

"Delicate and steely and lush and complex and far better than the mess outside." Rubbing his cheek against the back of her hand before he let it go, he started up the car and told it to merge back into the flow.

He only lowered the windows once they were some distance from the site.

"I'd better call Moon and Elbek," he said a couple of minutes later. "Give them a heads-up about our detour."

Theo nodded, scanning his face as she did so. The lines of strain had eased, his skin no longer pulsing with heat and anger. With his hair falling across his forehead, he could have looked young and boyish—except that there was too much determination and maturity in his expression. This was a man who could be relied on, a bear who was a foundational piece of his clan.

"Got you on speaker," he said when Elbek answered. "So act like you have some manners."

"You're just sore I won that award for Best Manners in fourth grade" was the growled comeback.

"It was a pity award," Yakov said with a sniff. "We're running late."

"Yeah, Valya called already. Bad situation. You okay?"

"Other than wishing I could rip off the fucker's head, yes. We're twenty minutes out, with coffee and baked goods."

"See you both then. Bye, Theo. No good-byes for you, you sore loser." The last words were followed by an apparently unfriendly grunt.

Yakov was grinning when he hung up, his bad mood vanquished—at least on the surface.

Theo did not understand bears. "Your clan has an unusual way of interacting."

"Can't argue with that." He drank some of the coffee he'd abandoned earlier; she'd closed up his cup so that it'd remain hot. "You'll get used to it."

Theo felt her skin tighten, wondered if he realized what he'd just implied.

From the way he went still for a second, she thought he did. Then he said, "I trust you, Theo," and completely cut her legs out from under her.

People didn't go around just declaring such things.

But he wasn't people. He was a *bear*.

And she was starting to realize what that meant.

"You're under my skin, *pchelka*." Taking her hand again, he lifted it to his mouth and pressed a kiss to her knuckles.

She sucked in a breath, panic beating at her because of how much she wanted this. "Aren't you afraid of how fast it's happening?" Theo had no ability to judge, had never before been—or wanted to be—in such a situation. "I'm a fractured creature of pain and shadows."

Another kiss to her knuckles, this one softer. "Oh, I think you're a lot more than that." He put her hand on his thigh.

Her heart thudded, her face hot, but she didn't break the intimate connection.

"As for the speed of things . . . I have a confession."

"Oh?" Theo froze.

And got a scowl. "Stop expecting a knife in the back." An order. "Bears don't do that shit. We'd rather punch someone full in the face than go about trying to be stealthy and sneaky. That's for cats. Never trust a cat who offers to sell you a life insurance policy, that's what my dedushka Viktor always says."

Theo found herself digging her fingers into his thigh in an effort to hold on to her footing. "Do cats often sell life insurance policies?" she asked, befuddled.

"No, but they could. Don't buy one." Yakov squeezed her hand. "So you know how my great-grandfather was an F-Psy?"

"*What?!*" It came out a shout.

Chapter 31

Dear Déwei,

I understand your reservations, brother, I truly do, but I don't think you can comprehend the chaos in the PsyNet right now. We're all going slowly mad, losing pieces of ourselves and pieces of those we love.

Even my beloved Kanoa is starting to show neurological issues. He's undergoing testing but is certain—and so are the medics—that the disorder in the Net is leaking through into his brain, causing irreparable harm.

How can you expect me to fight against the Protocol when it might save his life? And yet, at the same time, I would not lose you. Ever.

Your little sister,
Hien

—Letter from Hien Nguyen to Déwei Nguyen (5 March 1974)

"GUESS IT WASN'T in the files." He rubbed his jaw. "Makes sense. Most people outside the clan wouldn't know about Denu. Known to the world as Déwei Nguyen. A strong, empathic man who had his heart broken by Silence."

She heard the respect in his voice, and though she had no experience with such deep family ties, she also understood that her family was an aberration. "His memory means a great deal to you."

A nod. "The thing is, Theo, he left a little of himself behind in me and Pasha."

Theo felt her eyes widen. She'd never considered that changelings might have psychic abilities, but *of course* they must. Prior to Silence and the retreat of the Psy race from the world, Psy, changeling, and humans had all lived in the same society. They'd married, mated, and had intimate connections with each other. Children had been born of those bonds.

Which meant that not only did some changelings have echoes of psychic abilities, so must any number of humans. Today, however, she was only interested in one of those descendants of the past: the bear in the driver's seat.

"What did you see?" she asked, her voice a rasp.

"You. I saw you. When I was sixteen." His thigh flexed under her. "We played in a field under the sunshine." A glance at her. "So you see, *pchelka*, I've known you a lot longer than a couple of days."

Theo's mind spun, her center of gravity lost. But even with that, she felt the tension in his muscles. "What are you hiding?"

"I'm not hiding anything. I'm just choosing not to tell you everything."

Theo narrowed her eyes. "That sounds like sneaky logic. Like a cat."

His chest rumbled. "No need to insult me." Scowl heavy on his face, he said, "I'll tell you once I figure out the solution. Until then, it's just a mess it'll do no good to share."

Stubborn, she realized. He was very, very stubborn.

And once again, Aunt Rita was proven correct.

Deciding to drop the subject for the time being because what he'd shared was startling enough, she said, "Tell me more about your dream."

He did so without hesitation, and she felt her heart burst open with wonder at the joyous beauty of his vision. Then she almost knew how to laugh when he complained about her ID photograph and asked if it had been taken by a feline.

"What does it mean?" she asked afterward. "That we were always meant to meet?"

"It means what we make it mean." His voice was oddly solemn. "My grandmother Quyen passed on a lesson that her father taught her: that nothing is set in stone. The future is ours to shape."

The words rang in her head as they closed the final distance to the gates into what she was beginning to think of as her personal hellscape. Her mouth went dry. Her heart struggled to pump blood. "The future is what I make of it," she said to herself after Yakov jumped out to unlock the gates, and it was the most hopeful thing she'd thought for an eternity.

Yet her lungs still protested her need to inhale and exhale, the echo of terrified screams a painful screech in her ears. Not her own screams. No, not *just* her own screams.

Breath short and shallow, she frowned, tried to *remember* where she'd been, what she'd seen. Today, however, her brain refused to cooperate.

Perhaps it couldn't cooperate.

What damage had her grandfather done to her neurons? Had she been going through life believing herself whole when he'd cut out and thrown away pieces of her?

The idea made her stomach churn, but she forced herself to volunteer to close up the gates after Yakov drove through. If this was her hell, then she'd *live* in it, instead of allowing it to crush her.

"Done." She jumped back into the passenger seat.

Yakov shot her an amber-eyed look. "Tough as fucking nails." Lifting her hand to his mouth again, he kissed her knuckles in a way that had already become familiar—and wanted.

So painfully wanted.

The shadows pressed in on them as they drove on. When she lowered the window in an effort to dispel the sensation of being suffocated by the darkness, the rustle of the trees seemed a sinister whisper. "I think I remembered a fragment," she said, because she had to get it out. "Garbled. Less words than emotion."

"You want to talk about it?"

Only when Theo's back threatened a spasm did she realize how stiffly she'd been holding her muscles. The old injury rarely caused her trouble if she maintained her stretching routine and didn't tense up for long periods.

Flexing back her shoulders to ward off the attack, she said, "I'm not afraid like the first time." It was a revelation. "Now I'm just angry—not only for myself but for every other 'patient' at this facility."

She took a deep breath and admitted the rest. "All my life, I've known my family was evil. But this much? To the extent of sacrificing a child?" Her stomach threatened to rebel. "I *hate* that I'm one of them."

"Blood doesn't make a person, Theo," Yakov said, his voice a growl. "It's but one component. Would you condemn your brother for being a Marshall?"

Theo's response was immediate. "Grandfather tried so hard to break him, mold Pax in his own image, but Pax is *Pax*." Her pride in her brother's will was enormous. "And he's a thousand times better than my grandfather."

Stopping the car, Yakov reached over to squeeze the back of her nape with his hand. "Then so are you, *pchelka*."

"You don't know that. *I* don't know that. I could've been my grandfather's willing accomplice."

Removing his hand to put it back on the steering wheel but not restarting the car, Yakov emitted a very bearish growl. "Then so could your twin. You can't condemn yourself without condemning him, too."

"It's not the same!" Theo emitted a frustrated sound that came out sounding like a growl.

Shocked at her own behavior, she clamped a hand over her mouth.

Those deadly dimples appeared a second before Yakov's laughter filled the car, a boom of sound that might as well have been a hug, it was so warm and all-encompassing. "That's it, *milaya moya*, let out your inner bear." A glance at her, laughter yet creasing his cheeks, but his voice solemn as he said, "You deserve to have the same faith in yourself, Theo, that you do in your brother."

Theo's rib cage felt like it was crushing her heart. "I *can't*." A confession tight and painful. "Not until I have proof. I know too much of what I did for my grandfather."

Eyes of bearish amber touched with yellow held hers for long moments before Yakov gave a hard nod. "We'll get you your answers." Another squeeze of her nape. "Then I'll say I told you so—because I have faith in you, Theo, my Theo."

Theo couldn't speak, her lower lip threatening to quiver.

"If this was the drive to the den," Yakov said as he got the car moving again, "we would've been attacked by a few tiny gangsters by now."

She realized at once that he was dragging her into the light and out of the dark, with memories of joy, of a family that would *never* abandon or hurt its children.

"The cubs know we look out for them," he added, "so they like to hide up in the trees and then suddenly drop down while hanging from their feet. The aim is to make one of us scream or yell in surprise."

The whispers of cruelty and evil that haunted her were no proof against such wild visuals. "Do they ever succeed?"

"Oh yeah. Because they know not to do it all the time. Lull us into a false sense of security . . . then boo!" His shoulders shook. "Kids also know never to dart into the road, or to otherwise get in the way of the vehicles—which just leads to them coming up with increasingly inventive ways to achieve their nefarious aims.

"Last month, Stasya—she's our second-in-command—made the mistake of actually parking along the drive to take a call. Next thing you know, she's got a cub going splat on her windshield. She refuses to admit it, but she screamed."

He chuckled, the sound a kiss of warmth. "Tiny gangsters are still bragging about that—and every so often they jump out at Stasya from around random corners in the den. Last time around, she threatened to make bear fur rugs out of the lot of them and was immediately swarmed by a tiny attack force."

Laughter in the eyes that met her own. "I'd worry they'd grow up to create a criminal empire, but both Pasha and I were previously tiny gangsters and we turned out okay. Mostly."

Theo tried to imagine the adorable bear cubs she'd seen pulling such pranks. It seemed an impossibility. They were so small and so sweet. Surely, Yakov had to be exaggerating for effect?

She never got a chance to ask, because they'd arrived.

The facility loomed empty and sinister against the searing blue of the clear autumn sky.

Chapter 32

Intercepted: Encrypted message from Claire Marshall to parties listed at end of report.

Sent: September 4, 2083

Transcript: Pax is the only one with the ability to right the ship. My father was brilliant and he trained Pax. The problem is Theodora. I don't know how she wormed her way back into his life, but Father made it clear that *she* is the threat. I don't believe that status to have altered. We need to separate them without causing harm to Pax—though surely, the twin bond must have frayed to nothing by now?

Status: Urgent. Imminent threat to Theodora Marshall.

—Confidential report to Pax Marshall from ZDex Private Security Consultants (4 September 2083)

MOON AND ELBEK were already waiting out in front of the facility. They looked freshly scrubbed, their packs sitting neatly against the steps. Both gave Theo warm smiles, then took a seat on the steps and dug into the box of bakery items Yakov had brought for them, with enthusiastic sips of coffee in between.

Since the pair seemed in no hurry to head off, Theo felt comfortable asking, "Did you stay in the facility?"

Elbek, his black hair pulled back in a short tail, nodded. "Just inside the front door. Place is definitely haunted, though."

"But the ghosts didn't mind us," his partner added after swallowing a bite of a cheese and bacon roll, her own hair in pigtails that made her look incredibly young—and belied her air of extreme competence. "We played cards, invited them to join us, but they just wanted to watch."

Theo stared at the twosome, wondering if they were amusing themselves at her expense, but the two seemed very matter-of-fact in their expressions. Her shoulders prickled without warning, her nape cold. And she thought, yes, this place had plenty of ghosts. But unlike with the amiable bears, she didn't think the ghosts felt any sympathy with her. They knew what she was. Blood of the man who'd turned them into ghosts. Who'd stolen their lives.

"No signs of any attempted incursions," Moon was saying to Yakov now. "We took turns doing runs around the property throughout the night, didn't catch sight of anything that shouldn't have been present."

"But," her partner picked up, "there's something out back beyond that small house that you should investigate further. An oddly open patch with sunken areas. Didn't catch any suspicious scents, but . . ." He shrugged.

Theo didn't understand his meaning, but Yakov clearly did because he said, "Thanks." A new grimness to his tone. "I'll check it out."

"Moon might not have minded the ghosts," Elbek added, "but they creeped me out. I only stayed inside because it rained last night and I didn't feel like being a wet bear. I say the spirits seemed more malevolent than friendly."

Theo thought again of the woman who'd banged her head against the wall, of the man who'd cried. "Those walls witnessed a lot of pain. It's bled into the building, is barely hidden under its floors."

Moon held Theo's gaze. "Are you sure you should be here?" An oddly gentle question. "It makes your aura go dark."

There was so much Theo didn't know about changelings, and about what they could do, but she could recognize kindness and concern. "I have questions that need to be answered."

Bodies that needed to be unearthed.

. . . HIDDEN under its floors.

Yakov wondered if Theo had said that in response to Elbek's report about the land out back of the property, but he waited until after the other man and Moon had left to speak his thoughts aloud. He and Theo yet stood in front of the facility, the clouds dark overhead, and the leaves beneath their feet old and browned.

"Do you think there's a possibility that the victims of whatever it was that took place here were buried on the grounds?"

A sudden frozen stillness from Theo, her body an unmoving silhouette against the backdrop of tangled greenery all around them.

No, she hadn't understood the meaning of Elbek's report.

When she spoke at last, she said, "My grandfather was very good at covering his tracks. It wouldn't make rational sense for him to leave evidence lying around—especially in a region with such a heavy predatory changeling presence. A curious changeling might jump the wall and go exploring in the grounds."

Yakov nodded. Marshall Hyde hadn't reached the status of Councilor without being expert at presenting a certain face to the world; he'd never risk airing his dirty laundry. "Bodies moved out to be disposed of elsewhere?"

"He had telekinetics on his payroll," she said. "All Councilors did. He could've had them taken anywhere—straight into the heart of a crematorium, dropped into a volcano, or thrown into the deepest part of the ocean."

That she'd simply accepted that there must've been victims of whatever it was that had gone on in this place gave him another indication of just what kind of horror she'd witnessed as a child. But her experiences had blinded her to a stark truth. "Your grandfather wasn't in charge after his death."

Theo's pupils expanded. "No," she said at last, then turned to stare out at the grounds. "You think the staff—or at least some of them—murdered the patients and got rid of them."

"Would they have had access to the telekinetics?"

Theo shook her head. "Teleport-capable Tks are too thin on the ground. Even our privately contracted Tks are only available to senior members of the family." Tucking her hands into the pockets of his jacket, she said, "You're right. There are bodies out there."

"You sound certain."

"I read up on Centers during my flight to Moscow. About a quarter of the victims of a brainwipe, the ones who were the most functional, ended up being put into menial positions. Jobs that no one else in Psy society wanted."

That thrumming rage in Theo, it was back, and it was a hum against his skin.

"The others died." Flat words. "Slowly, and in a way that their deaths could be listed as natural, but the truth is that they died of medical neglect. While a few were kept around to show us what would happen to us if we stepped out of line, the majority were left to rot."

Yakov's claws thrust out of his fingertips, his bear in a rampaging kind of mood. It took everything to keep the ursine part of his nature under control. "You think that happened here?"

"I don't know, but I know there were a number of very damaged people in this place. Why would the staff spend time and money caring for them if they thought they could erase them from the equation and pocket the entire funding for the Center? After all, the families of the victims were never going to check up on them." Cold words, but her eyes were pure black now.

Yakov forced his claws back in with sheer effort of will—because one of them had to be rational, and he had a feeling his *pchelka* was in no

mood for that. The impending explosion he sensed in her? It was heading ever closer to the surface.

"We check the interior first, then the grounds," he said. "Lack of the
scent of decomposition isn't a surprise given that it could've been over
three years since any bodies were buried." Hands on his hips, he looked
out at the green. "And the dead have waited a long time. I don't think
they'll begrudge us another day."

Theo nodded . . . and then she walked into the past, into the world
of ghosts who hated the blood in her veins. She almost expected to feel
a shove against her when she crossed the threshold of the building, but
all she sensed was the musty scent of a closed-up building . . . and those
veins of agony and fear.

The walls pulsed with it.

The enormity of it threatened to crush her, but more than answers
for herself now, she wanted justice. For all those who hadn't made it out.
All those who might lie buried on the grounds.

Her anger felt old now, old and strong, and hot enough to burn
down this entire monument to her grandfather's evil.

This time, she and Yakov did a methodical search, deciding to start
on the top floor and work their way down. "Being at the top means it
would've been the hardest to clear," Yakov said after they reached
the third floor. "Everything would've had to be brought down via the
stairs or the elevator. People get tired of repetitive work; they make
mistakes."

Theo took in the scuff marks on the walls, the dents in the doorways,
the areas where things had literally been ripped off the walls. "Agreed."
She touched her fingers to a spot where the paintwork was badly scraped
and found herself releasing a withheld breath when no screams reverberated inside her skull. "Especially since this appears to have been a
rush job."

"Look everywhere," Yakov said. "Lift mattresses if they're still on
the frames. Tear open those mattresses. Screw open any air vents, and
look behind all electrical outlets." Putting down the daypack he'd

grabbed from the car before coming inside, he removed a slim packet of tools and passed them to her. "That should get you into most things."

Included in the set was a scalpel.

Cheeks going ice-cold, she closed the kit and went to move away, but Yakov stopped her. "Hey." A big and warm hand cupping her icy cheek, bear eyes looking into hers. "You're not alone, *pchelka*. Don't you forget that."

Theo found herself clenching her hand in his T-shirt, the warmth of him a welcome furnace. "I want to raze this place to the ground," she admitted. "The violence in me, it wants vengeance."

Those primal eyes flashed. "Later. Today, we take apart the monster's lair."

Her blood heated, and this time, it wasn't with rage. "Let's tear this hellhole apart."

"That's my *pchelka*."

Theo stayed true to her word as she tackled one end of the first room, Yakov the other. She didn't intend to leave a single corner unexamined. If there was anything to find here, she would find it.

It was only when she flipped open the toolkit to remove a screwdriver that the nightmares tried to crawl back in, carried on the gleam of the scalpel. She could feel the icy purity of the blade as it sliced across her palm, the scarlet so wet, the pain a dazzling shock of brightness.

This is what happens when you don't follow orders, Theodora.

"You're dead," she muttered vengefully under her breath. "Blown to so many pieces they had to scrape you up."

"Who's that?" asked the bear with preternatural hearing.

"My dear departed grandfather."

Yakov snorted from where he was on his haunches unscrewing a plate off the wall. "Sarcasm suits you, Thela."

Grinning—though it was likely a terrifying twist of the lips, complete with bared teeth—she continued on with her search, while Yakov worked with predator silence in another section of the room.

Every so often, she'd find herself in a position from where she could watch him—the flex of his thighs, the muscle of his shoulders, those fascinating veins on his forearms, the frown lines that formed between his eyebrows when he was concentrating, it all compelled her . . . aroused her.

Her breasts suddenly felt swollen, the skin too sensitive, the fabric of her bra an abrasion.

But it wasn't only how Yakov moved, the warm hue of his skin, the rich silk of his hair. It was the lines in his cheeks that said he laughed often and the sparkle in his eyes when he was amused. How he didn't condemn her for the rage within. How he'd lain quiescent and allowed her to caress his bear.

She could never imagine this man becoming cold and angry and distant.

Bears don't do that shit. We'd rather punch someone full in the face than go about trying to be stealthy and sneaky.

"Yasha?" She loved how that affectionate diminutive sounded on her tongue.

Concentrating hard on whatever he was doing, he just made a "Hmm?" sound in return.

"When you were small, did you ever go to bed mad at your twin?"

"No. We just stayed up fighting until our papa or mama came in to tell us to go to sleep. And then we fought in whispers until we figured out which one of us was wrong and needed to apologize."

A grin thrown over his shoulder, her favorite dimples on full display. "It wasn't until we were much older that we realized our parents could probably hear the whispering. They were either too exhausted to be bothered by it—or they decided to leave us at it. Conflict resolution. Bear style."

Theo swallowed.

No, Yakov wouldn't fight with silence or distance. He'd stand toe-to-toe with her and demand they have it out. After his answer about his twin, she was certain he'd refuse to move until they worked out the problem, a literal wall of stubborn, immobile bear.

Another woman might've found that overwhelming or aggravating in the extreme, an affront to her need for space to process her emotions, but Theo wasn't that woman. Her chest constricted at the idea of having a man like Yakov in her life, a person who'd never make her guess at his emotions, or who'd threaten to shut her away from his warmth as a punishment. If he committed, he'd *commit*.

One hundred and twenty percent.

Until it drove her crazy . . . but made her feel safe down to the bone.

Wanting that so much it hurt, she made herself remember why she was here, the answers she didn't know. Because she might yet discover that she'd sold out the lives of others in order to earn her grandfather's approval.

If she had, it wouldn't matter how much the idea sickened her now. She'd still have to pay the price of her evil, and part of that price would be to sentence herself to a life without joy. Especially when it came to a bear with a laugh that dug into her shattered and scarred heart and made itself at home.

Throat tight, she began to check the set of narrow drawers beside a patient bed.

Nothing.

And more nothing.

Until, at last, they moved on to the next room.

1976

Handwritten message from Bien Nguyen to Déwei Nguyen (3 May 1976)

Son,

I drove to the den to tell you this news in person, but your alpha says that you're out deep in the territory with Marian, with no plans to return for a week. She's promised me she'll hand-deliver this letter to you as fast as she can, and assured me that no one else will read it.

I must trust her, because you have to know the terrible news.

Kanoa died by suicide two days ago. We're only just hearing about it because your sister suffered a severe psychic break on finding him and was taken to the hospital, where she was put under sedation. It took the authorities in Hanoi this long to find our information and contact us. With Hien having just moved employers, no one seemed to have her emergency contact information on hand.

We don't know too much yet. We hadn't spoken to Hien for a few days, as she and Kanoa were having a little vacation break at home to recover from the move, and who wants their parents to intrude on that? We were happy for them. Things were going well, with none of the concerns of early last year.

Kanoa seemed to have come to terms with the neuro-logical damage that led to him being unable to play his instrument, and he'd just picked up a prestigious position as a senior lecturer of music theory at the Hanoi Conservatory (Hien asked us not to tell you, as the two of them were planning to surprise you and Marian with the news by sending you a clip of his first lecture).

That's the real reason why Hien transferred to Hanoi; you see. Kanoa was always so wonderful about moving for her work, and this time, she said it was her turn to support him. She was smiling so hard when she told us the news that I could hear it over the phone. And Kanoa, he sounded ecstatic.

But it's clear now that we were all wrong. His cello was part of Kanoa's very being. And you know he was a proud man, one who based his sense of self on both his art and his ability to be an equal partner to Hien.

I wish he'd understood that to Hien, he was the gift. She loved him more than life itself.

We're on our way to the airport. The boys are with your aunt Geri—this is not a situation their young minds can handle, and they love and trust Geri. I know you and Marian will be behind us the second you get this message, so I'll see you in Hanoi, my son.

*love,
Dad*

Voice message from Déwei Nguyen to Hien Nguyen (18 June 1976)

Anything you need, Hien, I'm always here for you. All of us are here for you. Please don't shut us out. I miss you, little sister.

Letter from Hien Nguyen to Déwei Nguyen (27 June 1976)

Dear D,

I'm sorry I didn't want to see you when you came to Mom and Dad's. I feel awful admitting this, but you remind me of all I've lost. We were meant to be four. You and Mimi, me and Kanoa. Now our square is missing a side and it's all wrong. My heart is shattered into so many pieces that the only reason I get up in the morning and do anything at all is because of the life in my womb.

My love's last and most precious gift to me.

Without the spark of our child, I would be a ghost, insubstantial and without meaning. I just float through life and all I see when I close my eyes is the torment on my husband's face when the doctors told him what the neural damage had done to his ability to play his instrument.

He kept on trying anyway. Over and over again. Until he was shattered into as many pieces as the cello he smashed to bits with an iron mallet one hot summer's day last year.

I should've known. I should've forced him to get more help. But he told me it was his way of saying good-bye to the past so he could move into the future. I stood with him as he burned the broken pieces of his cherished instrument, and I held his hand as he said a silent good-bye to dreams he'd nurtured since childhood.

My sweet, talented, beautiful husband. He tried so hard for me. But he couldn't bear the pain.

So much pain, D. How can it possibly be worth it?

So much suffering. You've been outside the Net these last terrible years. You'll never understand the agony of watching the person you love vanish piece by small piece as the madness of the PsyNet eats away at him.

I won't have that for my child. I won't.

I'm sorry, D, but I plan to vote yes should the authorities go ahead with the referendum they're considering about the change to the Silence Protocol. Please don't hate me for that.

Your little sister,
Hien

Letter from Déwei Nguyen to Hien Nguyen (30 June 1976)

Dear Hien,

I could never hate you. You will always be my little sister no matter what. If you need me, just call and I'll respond—whether that's today or ten years from today. Nothing you can ever do will stop my love for you. Or my love for the child you carry.

I plan to be the best uncle a kid could ever have. And I know that any choice you make for your child will be one with their best interests in mind, for your love is a bright flame, Hien. I will never attempt to gainsay you.

I'm leaving this letter with Mom, for whenever you're ready to read it. I understand why you can't see me right now, but I hope the day will come when to see me will be to remember all the joy Kanoa brought wherever he went. The cubs in the den still talk about the time he played bear games with them. He was a man of incredible talent and heart, and he shouldn't be gone from this world. I wish I could change the past, fix things for you as I did when we were children.

Your big brother,
Déwei

Chapter 33

Subject V-1 is showing significant neural "burns." We need to stop the alternating drug regimen before the subject begins to lose cognitive function.

—Message from Dr. Upashna Leslie to Councilor Marshall Hyde (5 May 2069)

AS HE AND Theo continued to search the facility, Yakov's bear nudged at him to move closer to her, dazzle her with his prowess. The human part of him told the bear to rein it in. Theo might've allowed him to cuddle her in bed and petted him with wild pleasure, but she wasn't yet ready to be dazzled as the bear wanted her dazzled.

Naked. The bear wanted naked. Lots of naked.

After all, it had spent years waiting for her to turn up. It figured now that Yakov knew Theo could be trusted, the courtship was done. Time to get naked. Naked skin privileges would also make her feel better, the bear argued. She was so sad and angry inside and what better cure for that than hard-core cuddling?

We have to be subtle, he reminded the bear. Valya had won Silver by being subtle, hadn't he? *Psy like subtle.*

Valya climbed up Silver's building and appeared outside her door, his bear pointed out helpfully.

Shaking his head to stop the argument going on inside his head, he lifted up the bed he'd already searched and stood it against the wall. And yes, he flexed a few muscles in the hope that Theo would notice, but he was *subtle* about it.

No ripping his clothes off, then strutting over to her and putting his hands on his hips to best display his assets as his bear suggested.

He didn't glance over to see if she had in fact noticed, which was as well, because his eye caught on something. One of the legs of the bed didn't look right. All the other beds he'd examined so far had featured a single continuous metal frame, but this one appeared to have legs that could be screwed on or off.

"Means a cavity inside," he said to himself, thinking aloud. "Question is whether it's deep enough to be a useful space, or just enough for the leg to be screwed in."

Unscrewing it was child's play—it hadn't been built to withstand bear strength. He pulled and it was off.

A cascade of color bouncing off the polished but dusty floor.

"What's that sound?" Theo ran over, her scent a welcome caress over his senses. "It sounded like pebbles." That was when her eyes fell on the colorful array at his feet.

They crouched down in concert, each picking up a different pill. Hers was long and red, a capsule in which tiny particles tumbled when she turned the capsule this way and that. His was a small and hard tablet, half green and half pink.

"A patient hoarding or avoiding medication," he murmured, picking up another jewel-like pill; this one was hexagonal in shape but a bland beige in color. "For a long time, too."

Theo stared at the array of color. "No," she said. "Look at the different varieties. If we say that the patient was given one of each every day, there are still only enough pills for four or five days. Ten days if we split the pills into alternate days."

Yakov realized he'd made a critical mistake; he'd assumed that no one would give a patient so many pills in a single day. "You were more on the tech side of nursing, right? Developing medical items?"

"I was a drone," she muttered. "I chose the nursing degree, thought I could use it to get out. But my grandfather punished me for rebelling against him by sticking me in a dead-end position that I couldn't leave without abandoning Pax—because if I left, I knew I'd have to go under, beyond deep.

"Otherwise my grandfather would've hunted me down out of spite; and by then, he'd learned how much pain he could inflict on me without my subconscious reaching out to Pax. He would've taken great pleasure in keeping me as his whipping girl after I conveniently made myself disappear."

Yakov went motionless, the bear's playfulness replaced by predatory rage. "He physically abused you."

A shrug. "I never cried." Fierce pride. "And I was bored out of my skull in my job, so I made it my business to learn as much as I could about what it was my grandfather manufactured in that particular facility. Including all of these pills."

It took teeth-gritted concentration for Yakov to focus on her words and not on the information she'd so casually shared.

"I'd built up quite the chemical arsenal simply by picking up detritus from the factory floor," she told him, a gleam in her eye. "I was planning to poison Grandfather at our next meeting, but an assassin blew him up before I could. It was the one murder I would've never regretted."

Yakov's bear rumbled in his chest, proud of her ferociousness even as he wanted to go out there and bring Marshall Hyde back to life so he could rip him to shreds with his claws. The bear's rumble yet in his tone, he said, "Any therapeutic reason a person would be given this many pills?"

Theo began to put the pills into groups. Seeing what she was doing, he helped her and they ended up with ten discrete piles. At which point, Theo leaned forward and put those piles into three groupings.

"None of these medications have been anonymized," she told him, then picked up a pill and showed him the stamp in the middle that bore a letter of the Cyrillic alphabet. "There was no reason for them to be anonymized or used in a generic form. No one was ever going to come here and do a prescription audit."

"You recognize them?"

Theo pointed to the first set of pills. "If I'm correct, those are basic sedatives. Relatively mild except for the dark pink capsules—one of those will hit a Psy hard. They'd be able to follow only the most basic commands at best."

She pointed to the second pile. "Those relate to digestion, more specifically to nausea control. Not an unusual combination. Some patients don't react well to sedation, and nausea can be a side effect.

"However"—she picked up one of the anti-nausea pills—"this specific drug is extremely heavy-duty. Furthermore, most of this class of medications have been phased out across the world." She pointed at the third pile. "Even so, those are the most unusual. The black one is the most hated medication possible among Psy."

Yakov thought of what side effect might elicit such a strong reaction. "Does it impact your mind? Your abilities?"

"That wasn't its initial purpose," she said. "In the time before Silence, it was a drug born of empathy—it was used to assist those who couldn't control their strong psychic abilities and their attendant side effects. I'm not talking about people who simply needed to learn control. I'm talking about individuals who didn't have the neurological capability to do so.

"The telepaths used to just scream and scream, their hands over their ears, because they couldn't block out the telepathic roar of the world, while the Tks often teleported themselves into horrific or deadly situations because they'd caught a random glimpse of an accident site on the comm, or seen a photograph a relative had taken of their climb in an ice crevasse. Do you see?"

Yakov whistled. "Yeah. Like a bear who has all the strength of an adult but thinks he's a cub so he doesn't know to protect others from his actions. But in this case, the Psy were hurting themselves."

"Not all of them," Theo clarified. "A powerful Tp could liquefy their parents' brains with a tantrum should those parents be less powerful. A Tk could kill a caregiver if they began to lift and throw things. A foreseer could grab hold of a child and spit out nightmarish prophecies."

"*Bozhe moi.*" Yakov had never once considered this issue when it came to the Psy. "The medication was a way to offer the patients peace, while protecting those who cared for them."

"Exactly so." Theo picked up the black pill, stared at it. "The problem with it is the significant side effect: it blunts awareness. The world becomes a blur, seen through a haze. More so than any other drug I've ever researched. One patient described it as being a zombie incapable of moving from the spot in which he was 'parked.'"

"Pretty significant side effect."

Theo nodded. "Which was why, once stabilized after an initial course of the drug, the patients with the capacity to understand their options, even if that understanding was limited, were weaned off it little by little until their cognition became more acute. At which point they were asked if they wanted to be on the drug. Led by empaths, our medics were far more ethical then. Those empaths also facilitated conversation with the nonverbal patients."

"How many said yes to continuing the medication?"

"Ninety-seven percent."

Sensing Yakov's surprise at her precise answer, she said, "I did a research project on this medication for extra credit—it was a course about Psy medicinal history. The drug has been out of use for over five decades." Because instead of helping their people, come what may, the Psy had begun to "dispose of" those they considered "imperfect."

Such clean words her people had learned to use to hide the weight of their evil.

From the way Yakov's body went still beside her own, she knew he'd come to the same conclusion. But what he said aloud was "So, it was helpful when used as designed to be used."

"Yes. For most of the patients on it, it was the first time in their life they'd been able to consciously experience the world in some capacity instead of being overwhelmed by their abilities, and that wasn't something they were willing to give up. Most asked for a dosage calibrated to give maximum benefits with minimum side effects—a little psychic risk in return for agency and conscious awareness."

Yakov nodded slowly.

"However," Theo murmured, her mind making the connections spark by dark spark, "it strikes me that using this pill would be an effective way to achieve a reversible chemical rehabilitation." She turned the innocuous-looking pill from one side to the other. "Unlike with traditional rehabilitation, this wouldn't erase the structures in the brain that make us psychic. It would instead put those abilities in a holding pattern."

Yakov whistled. "Pretty handy if you had a person whose abilities you wanted to use, but who it was too much of a risk to keep lucid and able the vast majority of the time."

Theo placed the pill back on the ground, her fingers feeling soiled. "Pre-Silence research suggests that if a person were to go on this medication, the dosage would have to be gently shifted up or down—no abrupt increases, no sudden stops. The latter was said to cause irreversible brain damage." So if a patient *had* been put on this and then taken off, over and over again, there was no knowing the current state of their brain.

She forced herself to pick up another pill, this one a capsule that was white on one side and yellow on the other. "I'm pretty sure this is a form of Jax." Glancing at Yakov, she explained the drug that had been formulated to control the Arrows, the most lethal soldiers among the Psy.

These days, it was also a street drug.

"How do you know about Jax and the Arrows?" Yakov said. "I'd figure the Council kept that information close to the vest."

She lifted one shoulder in a motion she would've never made had her grandfather been alive. It would've shown him too much of who she was behind the mask she wore in front of him. "Once you have a dog on the leash, there's no reason to watch your mouth around said dog." Because that was all Theo had ever been to her grandfather: a vicious dog trained to the leash.

Yakov's hand on the back of her neck, the hold gentle but firm—and his voice rumbling thunder. "Thela, you talk about yourself that way *ever* again, and I won't buy you any more of the donut holes you inhaled on the way here—and I'll talk Gustav into banning you from the bakery, too, so you can't buy them yourself."

Theo, braced for an altogether different kind of a response, felt her mouth fall open. She hadn't even realized he'd noticed how quickly she'd demolished the entire small box of the sugared treats; he'd seemed intent on his savory tarts the entire time.

Bears. Sneaky in a wholly bearish way.

She wanted to hug him for *noticing* her, even caring for her . . . and she was utterly bewildered by him. "Why does it matter to you?" she asked when she could speak. "What I say about myself?"

He leaned in so close that his nose brushed hers, the scent of him wrapping around her like a bear's fur. "Because I think you're mine, Theo Marshall. And I don't let people hurt those who are mine. You can't hurt yourself, either." A slight squeeze of her nape, his hand so warm, his skin a little rough. "You might as well get used to it."

Chapter 34

While a wolf lover will flat-out leave a bite on the curve of your neck like a cave dweller, so that everyone knows you're theirs, and a cat lover will scratch up your back for the same reason, bears are sneakier.
I know, I know, bears aren't sneaky. Accepted fact. Or *is* it?
Want to know my theory? Well, I think bears are the sneakiest of all the changelings when it comes to possessiveness. They've just tricked us all not to expect the sneaky—so when it happens, we just don't see it. But I have my eyes wide open now. No sexy bear is getting their secretly sneaky paws on me.

—"Jocie's Opinions" in the September 2083 issue of *Wild Woman* magazine: "Skin Privileges, Style & Primal Sophistication"

SHAKEN WITHIN BY Yakov's blunt claim, Theo nonetheless narrowed her eyes. "I think you should get used to a woman who knows her own mind and will do as she pleases."

An equally narrow-eyed look in return. "Oh, I *like* you just how you are, *milaya moya*. Except for the putting-yourself-down part. That's your grandfather speaking. And that bastard needs to be erased from existence—especially when it comes to you. He has no rights to your mind or your thoughts and I'm never budging on that stance."

She parted her lips, shut them. Because . . . he was right. She wasn't a dog on a leash. She was *Theo*, who had a twin who loved her even if he didn't understand love anymore, who was a nurse with all types of esoteric medical knowledge in her brain, and who had somehow become entangled with a bear who'd decided she was his.

Cheeks hot, she decided to ignore the confusion of her emotions to focus on the task at hand. "The thing is that Jax isn't usually administered orally. It's too weak in pill form. Even the street junkies inject it—or if they're really hard up, they buy the cheap pills the dealers make up and try to liquefy the stuff before snorting it."

"Used in concert with another drug for reasons unknown?" Yakov asked as he rose to get a resealable plas bag from his daypack.

"Unlikely." Taking the bag when he held it out, Theo began to put the pills inside—after she snapped a photo of each one. "I'll send the photos to Pax and have him ask a specialist to confirm my findings, but the thing is, we're looking at drugs that shouldn't go together—not even in mad scientist experimental terms."

"It's possible this stash didn't belong to one person," Yakov pointed out, then went to examine all the other legs on the bed. "This is the only bed with hollow legs in the entire ward. Could've been a hiding spot for multiple people."

Theo could see his point. "If so, they'd then have to have a way of getting rid of the excess. Flush it down the toilet?"

"I can see it." Yakov screwed back a leg that had proven empty of anything. "Here's another way if there was a risk the pills might not flush cleanly—like most big facilities, this place likely ran on schedules. Wouldn't take much to know when to secrete a few temporarily in your mouth just before being herded outside. Spit them out when no one's looking, grind them into the grass under your shoe."

Theo thought about the high ratio of staff to patients—and then she thought about the patient who'd been standing in the hallway knocking her head against the wall while no one paid much attention at all.

Yes, there'd been gaps, chances for a patient or patients to evade medication.

"If we have patients smart enough to hide pills," she said on a burst of hope, "there's a possibility they survived the deep clean, got out. They could give us the answers to all our questions."

Yakov nodded, but his expression was grim when he met her gaze. She knew he was right to be skeptical. It was one thing to get out of taking meds, quite another to escape a death squad. Especially if that death squad came in the form of medics with injections the patients couldn't dodge.

Shrugging off the cold chill that accompanied that thought, she put the bag of pills in the daypack, and the two of them continued on with their search. They found a few other pills but those looked to have been dropped and forgotten. Nothing like the first hoard.

"I don't think we'll have to wait long for the results from Pax," Theo said. "I'm guessing most if not all the drugs were produced by our pharmaceutical arm, so one of their senior staff should be able to ID them at a glance. It'll give us something to work with while we organize the analysis of the actual pills—in the unlikely scenario that the pills were bespoke, contain drugs we don't know about."

At this point, she wasn't taking anything for granted. "My brother can organize a telekinetic to pick up the samples, or we can courier them to him. The Marshall Group has the labs to make quick work of the task, but I'll ask him to also send identical samples to an unaffiliated lab." It was highly doubtful that her grandfather had taken a lowly lab tech into his confidence, but better to be safe.

"You mind me looping Pasha into the conversation regarding the drugs?" Yakov asked. "Be good to have a clear set of eyes on this—he's got no chemical or pharmaceutical background, has no biases there." A shrug. "Might see a link we wouldn't."

Accepting that she and Yakov were now too invested to be totally clear-eyed, she made sure that both Yakov and Pavel were copied into her message to Pax. Photos of the drugs sent, she carried on in her search, but that was it as far as drugs went.

They did, however, find several printed pages that had fallen behind a heavy metal filing cabinet. Given that most facilities such as this one were digitized, those either had to be archival documents or had been printed out by a member of staff who didn't want to carry a device.

The only reason they discovered the pages was that Yakov took one look at the incredibly heavy piece of furniture, put his arms around it, and just moved it. Like it weighed nothing.

When she stared at him, he grinned. "I'm not all brains, *pchelka*. There's plenty of brawn in this beautiful body." A grinning tap of his finger against her nose.

Skin heating from within, she busied herself with checking behind the filing cabinet to make sure they hadn't missed anything . . . and touched her own nose when he wasn't looking. Why had that odd little touch felt so good?

Answers first, Theo, reminded the more pragmatic part of her. *You don't deserve anything good until you know the truth.*

Breath catching at the stabbing pain of it, she nonetheless knew her internal voice was right. "Nothing else here," she said a few seconds later—right as a sneeze erupted out of her. "Just dust and cobwebs."

"You sneeze cute. Such a tiny sound." Yakov's cheeks creased once more. "Papers are in some kind of code."

Theo, flustered all over again, considered the page he was holding out. "Might be old-fashioned shorthand. I feel like I saw similar writing on the desk of my grandfather's aide."

"I can run the pages through our computer systems, see what it spits out," Yakov offered, his arm brushing hers. "Unless you're worried about secrets here."

Theo met the gaze of this bear who knew all but one enraged piece of her darkness. "No secrets," she said. "Not about this." She closed her hand over the cold metal of her bracelet, that unspoken truth choking her from the inside.

This, whatever was happening between them, it couldn't be based on a lie. She needed to tell him. But her guts froze up every single time she tried to open her mouth, force the words out.

It had been far easier to admit to being a murderer.

Chapter 35

Hello big brother,

I want to thank you and Marian for your grace and kindness,
your sheer depth of love, during the worst period of my life. I was so
ashamed after I came out of the fog at last, at how jealous and bitter I'd
acted.

Especially after I began to remember the good times, remember how
much Kanoa enjoyed being with you both. He said you felt like a brother to
him, too. I don't think I ever told you that.

The way you hugged me when I turned up at the den . . . I love you,
Déwei. And I miss you, but it's good for me to get back to work, even if I
couldn't bear to return to Hanoi. Paris is as lovely as ever, and my old
workplace welcomed me back with open arms, even if I do plan to return
to Moscow to go on maternity leave in three months.

We're taking this time to set things up so I can work remotely long
term, with short visits to Paris—my mind and heart feel more healthy with
the extra focus provided by work, and Mom and Dad have told me they'll
disown me if I dare hire a nanny when they're right there.

Otto and Grady are beyond excited to be uncles, just like their "wow-
to-the-max" big brother, Déwei—they're already going around boasting of
it to their school friends. I adore them—such hearts they have, D. And what
fun for my baby to grow up with uncles who will be only eight and ten
years older.

Plus, I want my baby to spend lots of time with her Uncle D and
Aunt Mimi. I know you'll be terrible in spoiling her, and I can't wait for that
for her.

As for what I said about my vote when it comes to the new brand of Silence . . . that was said in anger and grief. Any decision I make, I'll make with thought and care, for this will be my daughter's life.

See you in three months (when I'll be huge and nearly ready to pop)!!

Lots of love from your baby sister

—Letter from Hien Nguyen to Déwei Nguyen (18 October 1976)

SEARCH COMPLETE, YAKOV and Theo exited the building at eight that night to emerge into the pitch-black of a fall evening. Yakov had flashlights in the vehicle, but Pax—in his capacity as the Marshall CEO—had managed to get the power company to turn the electricity back on, so they'd been working under clinically bright lights for the last couple of hours.

"No point searching the grounds in this," he said, just as the land vibrated under his feet. Ignoring it, he continued on. "Especially without a scent trail. We'll come back tomorrow with the proper tools, do it right. And it's already eight. By the time we get back to the city, it'll be past nine."

Theo—who he was starting to realize wasn't the most patient of women—stared out at the dark but did eventually nod. "You're right. I'd probably trip on a root, fall on my face, and break my nose. Impromptu cosmetic surgery."

His bear grinned, delighted at her deadpan humor.

"Was that a quake?" she asked as he pulled the facility's door shut.

Yakov nodded. "We've had an increase in them over the past couple of years. Scientists were worried they were warnings of a much bigger event on the horizon, but all tests confirm no unusual activity underground, and the mini quakes never do any real damage."

The odd cracked road or bit of landscape was about it.

"So now we just shrug and move on. Pasha likes to joke it's Kaleb

Krychek having a laugh at our expense." Silver's ex-boss was one hell of a powerful telekinetic.

He thought Theo would ask him more on the peculiar phenomenon, but after she'd engaged the lock, she said, "It's strange, Yasha."

Loving the sound of his name on her lips, in that soft accent she had, he said, "What?"

"Knowing that if I didn't have a twin, I might've been one of the bodies carted out of here for disposal." Words unadorned with emotion on the surface, but her pain was a song in the air.

His claws sliced out, his bear in no mood to be calm any longer.

Yakov gritted his teeth, but his anger continued to rise and rise. He'd done a good job of controlling it at her dog-on-a-leash comment, but after witnessing how this place had stolen the shine from her through the day, he was *done*. His bear was so angry for her that it wasn't rational at all. He needed to burn it off, but no fucking way was he abandoning Theo to go rampaging in the forest.

"Your claws are out." Theo's voice, her body close to his. "Can I touch them?"

Of course she wasn't scared. Not his Theo. He held out one hand so she could examine his claws. "I want to punch something," he muttered in a low grumble because it was nice having her close and he didn't want to scare her off by being loud and angry. "Since I can't—would you like to go dance?"

She blinked, looking at him as if he'd taken up speaking in hieroglyphics. "Excuse me?"

"Dance. Move to music."

Theo parted her lips. Her instinctive reaction was to say no. Of course it was to say no. Theodora Marshall did not go about dancing with bears. She didn't go dancing at all.

But when she went to speak, she found she didn't want to say no.

Perhaps it was the anger on Yakov's face on her behalf. No one but Pax had ever been angry for her—but her twin was bound to her by bonds of birth, of genetics. Nothing bound Yakov to her . . . yet she mattered to him.

He'd made that crystal clear.

And now, he was inviting her to dance because he was a physical being and he needed to work off the anger inside him.

Theo thought of the rage that stretched her own skin until it felt as if it would explode. For so long, she'd tried to convince herself that she had it under full control, that she was an iceberg cold and contained, nothing inside any longer. But that was exactly the problem she'd always had—there was too much inside her.

Even before being separated from Pax, she'd been by far the more emotional of the two of them. She'd cried when she'd seen the bird wounded on the lawn, and she'd sobbed to Pax when they were punished for things no human or changeling child would ever be punished for—simply for being children.

And now, here she stood in a world where emotion was no longer illegal—and yet she felt locked in chains. Because her grandfather had painted her with his evil, made her an accomplice to his crimes.

Then the bear who'd invited her to go dancing said, "I promise we don't bite." Light words, but he simmered with contained fury.

For her.

And Theo found herself grabbing at this chance to be wild, to be *normal* for this moment in time where her whole future hung in the balance. In that space in between, she could allow herself to believe that she wasn't evil, that she hadn't made the choice for her grandfather's approval . . . and that she deserved a glimmer of happiness.

"I have no idea how to dance."

A sudden grin that lit up his face and made her stomach flip in an unsettling way that somehow wasn't unpleasant. "No bear has ever let a lack of knowledge or skill stop them from dancing."

Chapter 36

I appreciate StoneWater settling the bill for damages so quickly.
Thank you also for the crew of hungover bears you sent to clean up the
mess. I *almost* felt sorry for the lot of them, especially after they were on
their best behavior and didn't leave until they'd swept up the last bit of
debris.
At least they enjoyed one hell of a New Year's Eve party.

—Email to Anastasia Nikolaev from Nina Rodchenko, manager and
owner of Club Moscow (1 January 2083)

YAKOV KNEW HE should take Theo to one of the more refined clubs
in Moscow, the ones where people sat and conversed over cocktails and
only occasionally danced rather than all crowding onto the dance floor
in a mass of bodies and heat. But he didn't want to go to one of those
fancy clubs with their muted music and delicate furniture—tonight, he
wanted a bear kind of club.

Which was why they ended up at Club Moscow. It wasn't the least
bit disreputable—it had, in fact, recently been voted "the" club in Moscow by *Wild Woman* magazine—but it was built for hard use. Including
by bears who forgot their strength and got carried away.

Rather than a small and cramped space, Nina Rodchenko's prize
project was housed in a sprawling warehouse in the middle of an even

bigger piece of land. All sides of the warehouse featured accordion-style doors that could be folded back in good weather to leave the space wide open to the outside.

Bad weather? No problem. Nina's staff would pull the doors ninety percent shut. Never was the club totally enclosed while in operation—because while her more rambunctious bear and wolf guests might occasionally earn Nina's ire, she understood the needs of changelings.

It was all the more extraordinary because Nina wasn't changeling. She was, as she'd once told Yakov, "a full-blooded and proud-of-it human." Some might take that as an insult against the other races, but Yakov had understood the context of her comment—changelings weren't like how the Psy had been for so long, looking down their noses at the rest of the world, but his race, too, had a way of underestimating humans simply because humans tended to be less physically strong.

Petite Nina'd had to fight for respect when she first took over as the manager of the then-ailing Club Moscow. The place had been all but on life support. Which was probably why the owner had sold it to her for a song when she'd made him an offer. At which point, Nina had shut the entire place down for a month before opening it with a "free beer and vodka night" that had turned into the party to end all parties and firmly established the club as the hottest destination in town.

Club Moscow reflected her in every facet—including the efficiency with which she sent out invoices to StoneWater for bear-related damage to the glossy black décor. The walls of the club were painted that shade inside and out, as were the noise-canceling fences that surrounded it.

Any impression of a warehouse, however, was obliterated the instant you walked inside—and into a space accented by lights that changed with the mood of the club. Early on in the evening, most of it emanated from fairy lights, a sweetly romantic setting for folks who came to slow dance and grab dinner at the excellent restaurant that took up one-quarter of the floor area inside the warehouse.

With him and Theo having stopped at a food cart to grab a bite, it was past ten by the time he parked and they began to walk the couple of blocks to the club. This time of night, the lights would be a dazzling array of blades, blue and purple and pink and red, and every other color you could imagine. The restaurant would've also closed its tables, the kitchen switching over to quick and tasty bar snacks.

He felt the vibration of the music under his feet the instant he pushed through the gate in the fence. It swung shut automatically behind them, containing the noise within once more. Nina had to have spent an enormous amount on the soundproofing—but now she didn't have to pay fines to the city for breaching noise ordinances. *Especially* important in a city full of changelings with acute hearing.

Leaning in close to Theo as the two of them walked up to the door manned by two bouncers, both in slick black-on-black suits, he said, "Stasya figures Nina has to be in debt up to her neck with all the work she's done to modernize the club. But damn she got results. Place is never empty. Even doubles as an event venue in the daytime."

"Then any debt was a considered and smart risk."

"Yeah, but none of us can figure out who would've given her the financing. Won't have been the bank, not when all she had as collateral was a run-down club. I know she didn't come to StoneWater, and I've never heard any hint of the wolves being involved. And she wasn't born into money; nor does she have any shady connections."

StoneWater had done a background check as a matter of course once Nina began to rise in the city's entertainment district—a security measure to ensure she didn't have any unsavory ties that could lead to criminal activity. "Pasha and Stasya even dug through her public business filings. No hint of her backer in any of those records."

Theo gave him a look so affectionate that his bear was immediately her adoring slave. "It's driving all you nosy bears nuts, isn't it? The not knowing?"

Not even thinking about it, he nipped lightly at her ear, making her squeak. "It's not nice to laugh at people."

Eyes alight in the way they'd been in his dreams, she didn't tell him off for assuming he could just nip at her. His bear took note.

And adored her even more when she said, "Won't this be too loud for you?"

Lifting his hand to his ear, he removed one low-profile earplug to show her. "Created for changelings out of SnowDancer Labs. I put them in right after we got out of the car. Brings the sound below the pain threshold." Still much louder than normal life, but that was the point of a club.

"If we forget our own," he said after slipping it back in, "Nina's people are delighted to sell us a disposable set at an exorbitant markup."

Theo leaned in closer to his ear, the warmth of her breath a caress that made him want to be bad and lean in further and accidentally-on-purpose steal a kiss.

"All but invisible once in," she murmured. "Brilliant design."

Placing his hand on her lower back as they began walking again, he was struck by the slenderness of her body, the lightness of her being, this woman of steel and fury. "You still okay with hitting the club?" It came out rough with tenderness. "No foul if you want to back out of it. Drive calmed me down a bit." And he wasn't about to push her into a situation she found uncomfortable.

"From what I know of such venues, I'm not dressed correctly" was her response right as they reached the entrance.

About to tell her that it didn't matter, that she fucking blazed with magnetic energy regardless of her attempt to hide her fire, he was interrupted by a familiar female voice. Nina Rodchenko herself had appeared at the door. Tiny, dark-eyed, and dark-haired, her skin a self-described shade of "vampire white," she'd caused many a bear to quake in fear.

Tonight, she wore a dress with a high neckline that came to midthigh, had long sleeves, and hugged her body as if it had been painted on. The hue? A dark scarlet. The same shade as her lipstick.

Her shoes were skyscraper ankle boots in glossy black with laces that wrapped all the way up her calf.

"I can help you with clothes, honey," she said in the sultry tones that had beguiled admirers from one end of Moscow to the other. Nina, however, didn't date. She was too busy taking over Moscow's entertainment industry.

Yakov was grateful he wasn't susceptible to the Nina effect. It was just sad to watch her admirers make puppy eyes at her that she never noticed. He did, however, respect her economic and political nous. "Theo"—he made a gentle circle on her back—"this is Nina."

"I own the club and a number of other enterprises," Nina said. "Including a boutique down the road. Strange as it might seem, more than one individual has found their way to my club right after work. Which is why I keep an array of the boutique's offerings here for purchase."

"A shrewd business decision."

Theo's cool words seemed to please Nina; she smiled with more warmth than Yakov had ever before seen her display. "Exactly. Come, darling, I've got a dress or two in your size." A cool glance at Yakov. "Hmm, are you the one I banned for two weeks?"

Yakov gave her his best choirboy smile. "Ban finished three days ago, remember? Also, in my defense, I was breaking up a fight when I accidentally fell on the jukebox." In bear form.

He was a big bear.

The jukebox had been toast. Really flat toast.

"I know," Nina said with a gimlet stare. "That's why I only banned you for two weeks. The fighting idiots who shifted into their fur to fight are not welcome for the next six months. Amuse yourself. We'll be back when Theo is good and ready."

As Nina turned to walk away, Theo glanced back at Yakov with a question in her eyes. A sudden and bright tenderness bloomed inside him at the realization that she was checking with him that it was safe to follow Nina. He gave her a quick nod.

Not saying anything further, Theo left with the club owner.

Instead of going inside with her, Yakov shot the shit with the two bouncers. One the stereotypical hulking man, the other an average-sized woman with a *real* mean look to her. Both were, of course, bears.

Who else was Nina going to hire to keep the riffraff out of her club when the majority of said riffraff was stronger than any human, Psy, or even wolf?

Within StoneWater, the rules were clear: while on the job, Vadim and Calina were bouncers, not clanmates. They might be your best friend in the clan, but they'd boot you on your furry ass if your ass needed to be so booted.

Now, Vadim waggled his eyebrows. "The blonde is hot."

"I think you mean icy," his partner murmured, relaxing what she called her "resting assassin face." "That one's not for you to play with, little boy."

Vadim growled. "Are you insulting me?"

Calina rolled her eyes. Friendlier expression or not, she remained the more deadly of the two bouncers, her body ripped under the uniform black. "I'm protecting you, you big idiot. She's Yasha's. And even I can't put our pretty Yashmina here on the ground."

Her partner shaped his mouth into an O and looked carefully at Yakov. "Sorry, Yasha. Didn't mean to step into your territory."

"Maybe don't say that in front of Theo," he suggested, though secretly he liked the idea of thinking of her as his territory. And secretly was exactly how he'd keep it. There were some things you just did not say to strong women. "She might kill you dead, then flay me alive."

"Now you're just bragging." Vadim's shoulders drooped, his expression morose. "I want a dangerous girlfriend."

"You're only twenty-four, gorgeous." Calina patted him on one meaty shoulder. "Plenty of time to get yourself lassoed by a badass."

Vadim perked up. "Talking of which . . ." He beamed like the sun at the woman now walking up to the club.

Yakov had scented her before he saw her: Anastasia "Stasya" Niko-laev, Valya's sister and second-in-command of StoneWater. Tall, with eyes of greenish gray, and dramatic cheekbones under strikingly short hair she'd colored a vivid purple two weeks back, she was about as bad-ass as they got.

Now, she patted Vadim on the cheek and had him blushing. "Nina tells me that you're doing an amazing job." She nodded at Calina, too, including her in the compliment. "Making the clan proud."

Both younger members of the clan shuffled their feet a little, but they also squared their shoulders. Then Anastasia turned to Yakov, her expression altering in the most subtle way—because where the other two were subordinates, Yakov stood in the senior ranks right beside Stasya.

It wasn't about dominance. There was so much more to it. The acknowledgment that Stasya didn't need to protect him, as both of them would do with Vadim and Calina, the acceptance that she could lean on him as he could on her, and beneath it all, the deep bond of friendship forged by years working side by side with Valya.

"I thought you were babysitting a Psy today."

"I asked her if she wanted to go dancing."

Stasya rolled her eyes. "Funny, Yasha." Then she walked into the club.

Vadim waited until after their clanmate was out of earshot to grin. "I don't think Stasya believed you," he whispered.

"She will soon enough." His bear stretched, more than ready to party with Theodora Marshall, the woman of his dreams.

His smile faded on the thought, his mind flashing wet scarlet. Because Theo had died in his dreams last night, the reason why he'd shifted into bear form in the twilight hours. He'd needed to escape his human skin, his frenetic mind. But that didn't alter the truth of what he'd seen.

Theo's fatal future remained unchanged.

Chapter 37

Arwen, when are you planning to introduce me to the bear who is such a
bad influence that he led you right into a jail cell?

—Message from Ena Mercant to Arwen Mercant (date unknown)

THEO HAD NEVER worn such clothing in her entire life. She felt
exposed—and yet powerful at the same time. In stylistic terms, the
dress was simple: a sleeveless and strapless black sheath that shimmered
with specks of blue and came less than halfway down her thighs. That
was it. That was the entire dress.

When Nina had first offered it to her, she'd taken one look and po-
litely said, "I believe I'll need a larger size."

Nina had laughed in a way that invited Theo to share in the joke,
rather than making her the butt of it. "I promise it'll fit." The club owner
had pointed her to a little private cubicle to the side. "You can change
in there."

Still dubious about the stretching capabilities of the fabric, Theo had
nonetheless obeyed in an effort not to offend her host. It didn't take her
long to change . . . and find that the dress not only fit, but that it did so
like a glove.

She stared at herself in the mirror for a full minute, unable to relate to the Theo who looked back at her. But it was definitely her. Her fingers touched the small scar below her left inner elbow that she'd had as long as she could remember.

Yes, it was her.

But she'd spent her life learning to become invisible. This woman wasn't invisible. Her eyes were electric lightning, a flush riding her cheeks, and the tamped fury within her a voracious beast that shimmered in the air.

"Theo?" Nina's distinctive voice. "How is the fit?"

Theo swallowed, ran her hands down the dress, and stepped out of the cubicle.

Nina whistled. "Put down the hair, darling, and you're done."

Theo hesitated. The braid she wore was already her most casual look—she stuck to tight knots at the base of her head in the general course of life. But on this strange and stolen night, she did as Nina had directed and allowed her hair to fall around her face and shoulders . . . and felt concealed bindings inside her snap and drop away at the same time.

A part of her knew she should be scared, but all she felt was free.

"Such a wild energy you have under your skin, Theochka." Nina's words were an approving purr. "That much-too-good-looking bear of yours will have to fight them off with a stick."

Heart racing at the thought of Yakov seeing her this way, Theo had to concentrate to reply. "Are my shoes acceptable with this dress?"

Nina glanced over at the simple black flats she'd discarded inside the cubicle. "Next time, go for heels if you're comfortable in them. Tonight? No one will notice your shoes after they get hit with those eyes." An approving nod. "Blue fire, bright and hazardous to the body and heart."

Picking up a black tote bag emblazoned with the Club Moscow logo—a bold black letter *M* lit up from behind in neon pink, so that it was a shadow emerging from a wild night—she said, "You can put your clothes in here, and I'll leave it at coat check for you to pick up at the end of the night."

"Would you like me to transfer the credits for the dress now?"

"Dress is on the house. Have fun. Tell all your Psy friends."

"I don't have any friends." Theo wouldn't lie to Nina about the return on her investment.

The other woman leaned one hip against the doorjamb. "If you're keeping company with bears, you'll soon have more friends than you know what to do with—the bears absorb people. Like giant voracious amoebas." A scowl. "Charming assholes, one and all."

Theo couldn't tell if Nina liked bears or not. But she liked Nina. "I believe I understand now how you won the respect of the bears and the wolves."

"Oh?" A single pointed word.

"They know you won't bend, even at risk of death or injury," she said. "If they push you too hard, you'll just take the laser weapon hidden in your ankle boot and stun them with a beam to the face. No regrets. No hesitation."

Nina went motionless for a heartbeat before breaking into laughter open and husky that transformed her from sultry to flat-out breathtaking. "Oh, I *like* you, Theochka," she said with a new openness to her expression. "I'm going to put my card in the bag with your clothes. Hit me up for a coffee and you can tell me how you spotted a weapon I'm certain only the most senior members of both packs have ever noticed."

Eyes yet alive with laughter, the club owner picked up a small cylindrical tube from the basket near the door. "Gloss sample," she said, peeling off the seal. "Your lips are incredible. Play them up."

Theo dutifully slicked on the clear gloss.

To Nina's slow smile. "Oh yes, your bear is going to swallow his tongue."

HAVING caught Theo's scent, Yakov entered the club and looked to the left, in the direction she'd gone with Nina. It was a narrow corridor that led to the staff offices, all of which were walled off from the public areas.

He didn't know what he'd been expecting—but it definitely wasn't a blond bombshell with eyes of blue flame that held his with brilliant intensity, flowing hair of wavy gold, lips plush and so soft he wanted to beg her to do naughty dirty things with her mouth, and legs that went on forever.

He'd been attracted to Theo from the first, but now.

O Bozhe!

Punch to the solar plexus.

And if he was any judge of the look in those stunning eyes, she was obviously in no mood to play it safe tonight.

Striding to meet her halfway, he tugged on a loose lock of wavy hair. "Hot enough to burn, *pchelka*."

He crooked his arm.

If he'd considered it, he might've expected hesitation. But this wasn't the Theo who wore a skin that made her blend in. This was the woman of his fucking dreams. She curled her fingers possessively around his biceps, her skin a little cool to the touch and her scent an enticing blend of woman and that barely tamed fury within.

His bear rumbled to the surface of his skin.

Yasha, you're in trouble, said his inner voice.

Hell, yes he was. And he was fine with it. As he was *fine* with being claimed.

He just wasn't certain she was thinking straight after the shocks of the past couple of days. "You sure you want to do this?" he murmured against her ear, shielding her with his body when a group of laughing dancers flowed out of the dance floor in a wave of perfume and fresh sweat.

The eyes of a dangerous goddess held his. "I know who I am, Yasha, and I know what I want. Tonight, it's to live life to the limit."

His cock pulsed, the primal heart of his nature emerging to have him nuzzling her lightly at the temple. Putting his scent on her. Not much, but enough to warn off any other changelings—better that than he rip off their stupid heads if they tried to hit on her. "Let's go play, then."

Knowing he'd react aggressively if some drunken clubber banged into her—because while Yakov was generally even-tempered, he was still a dominant bear with violently protective instincts—he didn't push through to the center of the dance floor. Instead, taking her hand in his, he went left along the relatively open wall, near the part of the accordion door that was partially open—at which point he turned right and looked for an open high-top table.

Though many of the glossy black tables were cluttered with empty drink glasses and bottles the staff hadn't yet had a chance to clear away, it still wasn't hard to find clean and empty spots—people came to Club Moscow to dance and were most often on the floor, and Nina's people were efficient.

The club did have a seating area for dancers, but that was up on the partial mezzanine floor right at the back part of the warehouse. That was where tired partygoers went to put up their feet, catch up with friends, and talk over bar snacks in a more relaxed environment.

Nina being Nina, the mezzanine was set up to resemble a comfortable living area with cozy couches and even huge cushions. Just in case a changeling decided to shift form for a bit. The only rule was no nakedness post-shift. If a drunk changeling shifted while in their clothes, thus destroying their clothes, they stayed in that form.

Changelings policed that themselves. Anyone found bare-assed was quickly ordered to "put on their fur" by friends or hauled outside by the same friends to find the naked idiot some clothes.

No one wanted to be banned by association.

A movement at the corner of his eye had him glancing in that direction. Grinning when he spotted the man waving to him from three tables further along, he began to weave his way to the table.

Leaning down to Theo as they reached it, he said, "You remember Pavel and Arwen." His lips brushed the shell of her ear as he spoke . . . and she shifted closer.

Oh fuck, his Theo was *definitely* in a dangerous mood tonight.

Barely restraining the urge to haul her off to his lair, he turned and bumped fists with his twin, then did the same with Arwen. The empath had given him the skin privileges of a clanmate much earlier than he had others in StoneWater not because Yakov was Pavel's twin, but because they'd become friends independently of Arwen's relationship with Pavel.

As always, Arwen was dressed about a hundred times better than the rest of them: a long-sleeved black shirt printed with raised black patterns in what looked like fine velvet, tucked into black jeans held up by a belt of solid leather with a silver buckle in the shape of an *M*. He'd neatly folded up the sleeves of the shirt to the elbow, and his shirt was open at the collar to reveal a sliver of throat and chest.

Within that space sat a necklace with a thin and strikingly jagged centerpiece.

Pavel, meanwhile, was wearing a short-sleeved shirt of rich brown with bronze stud detailing. The shirt had a fold in the sleeves that brought attention to Pavel's biceps. It also hugged his pecs. He'd paired the shirt with his favorite blue jeans.

Wait a minute.

"New shirt?" Yakov asked his brother, his voice deadpan.

Pavel gave him the finger, because they both knew the stylish shirt had to have been a gift from Arwen. Left to his own devices, Pavel was all old checked shirts and worn T-shirts. Yakov had worried about sophisticated Arwen's tolerance for that back at the start, but the other man had never attempted to change Pavel.

This gift was something special, a piece he'd clearly been unable to resist buying because it so perfectly complemented Pavel's build and coloring. The fact that Pavel was wearing it? It meant he liked it. Because while Pavel was crazy for Arwen, he was very much his own bear.

Which was why Yakov could tease him on the point.

Noticing that Arwen had gone motionless, his face stricken, Yakov realized the E thought his words a criticism. "I like it. Might even steal it. You're still not the pretty twin, though."

"Such delusions," his brother drawled while Arwen leaned in to whisper something in Pavel's ear.

He didn't catch what it was, but he did catch Pavel's affectionate nip of Arwen's jaw before his brother murmured something back. Blushing, the Psy male relaxed. Pavel had no doubt made it clear to Arwen that no one had a chance of getting Pavel in clothes he didn't want to be in. Arwen had simply gotten his gift very, very right.

But even as Yakov had spoken with his brother, he'd kept the bulk of his attention on Theo, making sure that she got the spot next to Arwen—because behind the two was the open part of the door. To have her be the one closest to the outside, to possible danger, went against his primal instincts, but the bear was willing to tolerate it for her comfort.

"Okay?" he asked as he took position on her other side.

She nodded, her eyes scanning the room as she took in the mass of bodies gyrating to the music, the lights playing over the paleness of her skin in a dance of vivid color. "I don't believe I've ever been this proximate to so many other sentient beings in my life."

Shoulder a polite inch away from hers, Arwen put down his virgin mojito. "Hang around with bears and this is where you end up." A dire warning in his tone. "Next thing you know, you're mated and raising six cubs of your own."

Pavel nudged Arwen's hip with his own. "Six, *luchik moy*? I was aiming for an even dozen."

This time, Arwen's blush reached the tips of his ears.

Chapter 38

The changelings have a concept called skin privileges. It means that the right to touch is precious and a gift. It is never to be taken. It is to be given. We as empaths must hew to the same ethos when it comes to emotions.

We must never steal that which is not freely given.

Simply because we can read the emotions of others doesn't mean we should. There is a difference between passive absorption and active excavation.

—Excerpted from the Empathic Code of Ethics

ARWEN WANTED TO bite his playful bear back, but he remained less comfortable making public gestures of affection than Pavel. He didn't have any problems whatsoever allowing Pavel to kiss and touch him in public. He loved his bear's possessive affection. Even if it did make him all hot and flustered.

He was reaching to take a sip of his drink in an effort to cool himself down when Theo said, "How does it work in changeling society? Is it like with Psy procreation contracts? You contract with a surrogate to carry the cub?"

Arwen realized he'd have to teach Theo that such personal questions were considered rude in most human and changeling company. The other races weren't like the Psy, with their cold and pragmatic deals when it came to the next generation. But it was clear that Theo had asked the question in good faith—and she'd done so in the right company. Neither Pasha nor his brother were the type to take offense.

"Not quite," he said in response to her question, then took a drink to give himself time to get used to the emotional *sense* of her.

Arwen didn't read strangers; it went against every rule of empathic ethics. But that didn't stop certain things from just filtering in—in the same way that a changeling couldn't help picking up scents, he couldn't help picking up the outer layer of a person's emotions.

Theo's were . . . complex.

When, back at the cantina, Pavel had told him that she was a Marshall—Pax Marshall's *twin*—he'd been stupefied. She didn't feel like a Marshall to his senses. While he'd never met Pax or Theo, he had run across a number of their relatives, and to say he'd hated every single interaction would be a vast understatement.

"Cold" wasn't the right word. Many in Psy society read as cold because of Silence, but it was a cold without menace. Just a state of being, akin to the cold of a glacier or a river.

Marshall cold was . . . vicious, the ice threaded with poison.

Theo, in contrast, was a dark inferno. So hot that he was tempted to breach the ethical rules of his designation and warn Yakov. Because that intensity of heat? It came from a deep-seated rage. He'd never felt its like. You'd think the rage would repel him as much as the cold, but Theo's rage was an intensely strange thing.

There was no ugliness to it.

Arwen still hadn't figured out what that meant. Except . . . his grandmother's rage was the closest he'd felt to what lived within Theo. Ena Mercant was Silence in motion, a woman who was ice to the external world.

Inside the family, however, they knew her love to be a blade unsheathed.

The first time Arwen had felt the rage within his grandmother was right after he'd turned five. It was the first time he'd seen his grandmother's warrior avatar: a cold-eyed Valkyrie with vengeance in her heart.

"Grandmama," he'd asked, staring up at her with scared eyes. "Why do you have a black storm inside you?"

She'd crouched down, put her hands on his arms, and said, "Because a person I believed I could trust did a bad thing to one of mine. That storm is my fuel. It drives me and sustains me." Her arms wrapping around him. "Don't be scared of it, Arwen. The storm will only ever rise against bad people."

Who, he found himself wondering, did Theo's storm rise against?

Aware of her eyes on him, he put down his mojito and returned to the question she'd asked about procreation contracts. "No bear would give up all rights to a cub they'd carried," he explained. "*Especially* not a maternal bear, the ones who most often volunteer to give this gift."

"No contracts?"

He understood her shock as only another Psy could. "Their society works differently from ours, is structured in a completely dissimilar way." He felt an odd gentleness toward this woman who was a contained storm. "A pregnant clanmate is a pregnant clanmate, with access to all the usual medical services and clan resources. They don't need to insure against financial strain with a contract."

"And, at heart, a cub is always raised by the entire clan," Pavel added. "It's part of the very foundation of what it means to be clan—that any cub can go to any adult for help or a hug."

Arwen's heart grew warm as Pavel hooked his arm loosely around Arwen's back in an action as natural as breathing. Arwen wanted desperately to grab at the promise of forever that hung in the air between them, wanted to call this man his mate and also shoot anyone else who dared look at him with covetous eyes.

Perhaps he'd inherited a few of Ena's tendencies.

"Why won't you accept the mating, Arwen?"

Silver's voice, the question one she'd asked not long ago—without judgment. His sister understood the forces tearing him apart as few could.

"Because when you mated with Valya, you were as strong as he is. You knew your place in the world. I see that with Canto and Payal, too, and now, Ivan and Soleil. I'm still . . . lost."

It was no longer because of his designation. Empaths had come out of the shadows long enough ago at this point that he didn't have to hide an integral aspect of his nature. Now, it was about his family. His protective, dangerous, fiercely loving family. Ena, Silver, Canto, Ivan, and more—all of them forces of nature.

And all of them intent on shielding Arwen from harm.

"I don't want to go from sheltering under one set of wings to another," he'd said to Silver. "I want the capacity to shelter my mate, too."

His sister had given a slow nod. "I understand. But, Arwen? I think you have no idea how much you do for us. We wouldn't be the family we are without you. Don't make the mistake of underestimating your own gifts because they're different from ours." A stroke of her hand against his cheek. "You are our heart."

Arwen was still thinking over his sister's words, not sure if he believed them . . . or if he wanted to believe them because he wanted so desperately to claim Pavel as his mate.

Now, his Pasha bear's voice was a deep rumble beside Arwen as he said, "Our first port of call would be to adopt. Changeling or human—or even Psy now that your people have opened those doors—any cub that needs a home." An affectionate glance at Arwen. "This one would adopt every orphan in the world if he could."

"You talk tough but I see you sneaking the tiny gangsters cookies anytime they look sad," Arwen teased, Pavel's heart as huge as the sky.

"Lies, all lies," his bear said with a dark look that made Arwen want to kiss him.

Yakov picked up the thread of the conversation. "Where a child *is* specifically carried for a clanmate who can't bear a child themself, it becomes a new familial structure, with the clanmate who carried the child considered a bonus parent."

Arwen caught Theo's glance at Yakov, felt the vibration in the ether of a shimmering thread that was trust. He might have thought it had come into being too fast, but he'd trusted Pavel even when he'd refused to tangle with a bear. He'd known in his gut that this man would never cause him harm.

Some bonds were immediate.

"The child grows up mobbed with love," Pavel added. "And disciplined by the entire combined family as well. Combined because the maternals who give this gift are always mated with cubs of their own."

"That love, that embrace into family, is a given whether a cub is born into the clan or adopted into it," Arwen explained to Theo, because it wouldn't occur to the bears that such might even be a question. "Our race's need to achieve 'pure' genetic lines as a goal toward high-Gradient children is—"

"An abomination." Theo's statement was hard.

And the rage in her, it scalded.

Chapter 39

Welcome to the world, Neiza Nguyen Adelaja.

—Message and photo posted to Nguyen Family chat
group by Déwei Nguyen on behalf of Hien Nguyen and
the late Kanoa Adelaja (18 January 1977)

YAKOV RAN HIS hand down Theo's back, felt the quivering tension in her as she processed what she'd just learned. And he knew that her childhood had been nothing akin to that of a cub growing up in a healthy and stable clan.

When he nuzzled at her hair, she pressed back against him.

So he wrapped his arm around her and cuddled her close. He half expected a quick and firm repudiation . . . but she stayed tucked against him. And his heart kicked, tenderness flooding every cell of his body—along with the knowledge that Theo had granted him a certain level of skin privileges.

He had every intention of taking full advantage to pet her.

"You want a drink?" His twin's voice. "I'm making an order. Beer for me, a lemonade for my Arlusha." He held up his phone, which he'd linked to the Club Moscow system. With the tables all numbered, it was easier for the staff to deliver than to deal with the crush at the bar.

Yakov stroked Theo's hip with two fingers. "They have nutrient drinks as well, if you'd like that."

"Thank you, yes." A slight huskiness to her tone.

Wanting to sit her in his lap and cuddle her, then stroke her all over, he forced himself to behave. "Beer for me, too. And throw in a bunch of the heavier snacks. We only grabbed a bite from a cart for dinner."

"Yeah, we're a bit hungry, too."

Pavel had just sent through the order when a big hand came down on Yakov's back and a voice boomed, "There you are, you *mudak*! I should beat you to a pulp for that stunt you pulled."

THEO froze, her brain—which had been settling into the slumbering heat engendered by Yakov's petting—immediately switching to attack mode.

Because there were a lot of things a telekinetic who could move small objects a small distance could do to disable an attacker. For example, there was an empty glass on the table next to their own. She could easily push it to the ground, smash it into shards, then stab a shard into someone's eye.

It would wipe her out, but that person would still be bleeding from a vicious eye wound.

Perhaps these weren't things another Tk of her Gradient would think about, but those Tks hadn't been raised by Marshall Hyde. Her grandfather had twisted her in infinite ways; it was second nature for her to think with lethal intent.

The big bulky man with shaggy blond hair and an equally blond beard who'd grabbed Yakov's shoulder bared his teeth as Yakov turned and said, "You deserved it, you bag of mangy beige fur."

Theo fixed her psychic power on the glass as the man growled . . . then threw back his head and started laughing, slapping Yakov on the shoulder the whole time. "You're damn good, for a brown bear." He spoke Russian with a heavy accent she couldn't quite place.

Yakov elbowed the man in the gut—but she could see that he'd made sure there was no power behind the hit. "Get the hell out of my space, you oaf. I'm having a night out, in case you can't tell."

The big guy looked over, then leaned on the table and beamed at Theo. "Hi, I am Hakon. A polar bear out of Svalbard, Norway—with stunning *white* fur. Visiting for the season." Big white teeth against darkly tanned skin.

"I'm Theo," she said, releasing her mental hold on the glass. "Is this type of interaction normal among bears?"

Yakov tugged her closer to his body, his hand splayed over her hip and part of his body now slightly behind hers.

The contact blew life into the slumbering embers, had her tracing the line of his throat with her eyes as he said, "Only the uncivilized ones. Never trust a *beige* bear out of Svalbard is all I have to say." But his eyes were dancing.

And she realized he and the bearded male were friends. Close enough friends that they could read each other through the words spoken aloud. She'd never had friendships like that.

Her only friend her entire life had been Pax.

She felt cold all at once, though the club was warm with the heat of the bodies within. And she understood that it was the cold of being on the outside looking in, as she'd so often done as a child. Walking past restaurants and bakeries where parents stood with their children's hands in theirs, or where families sat eating. While she walked in a solitary bubble, beside the person who was paid to give her the necessities of life, nothing more.

Then Yakov squeezed her hip and gave her a smile that invited her to laugh and join in. She didn't know how to laugh, but she didn't pull away from the touch of his body. Already it had become a thing of comfort . . . of need. The latter was a terrifying realization, but she still didn't pull away.

One night, whispered the darkness inside her head, *just one night*.

When another woman joined the group a moment later, they had to shuffle around the table again, and Theo ended tucked up against Ya-kov's front on one side, with Arwen's body pressed into hers on the other. She didn't truly notice Arwen except for being aware of his pres-ence, but Yakov was a wall of delicious fire that made her breasts ache and her skin crave even more contact.

Body and mind in a state of overwhelm, she had to focus hard to hear what he was saying when he spoke against her ear. His breath was warm, his presence muscled and compact. "You okay? We can always head outside if you need space."

Theo made her mouth shape words. "I'm fine." They weren't quite the truth—her body was having trouble processing all of the input com-ing at her, but the most visceral of those inputs was the physical contact between her and Yakov.

But rather than jerking away, she wanted to push him to the wall, crawl all over him, pet his human skin as she'd petted his bear's fur. She just *wanted* with a ferocity she'd never before experienced, until it was akin to a small madness. Because this was a purloined instant of time, carved out of a life cold and lonely.

The compulsion to glut herself to the brim, like a child given treats only once in their life, it made her despise the idea of limits.

Yet she was still a Marshall, still trained in ways deadly and dan-gerous.

So she took note of the woman who'd joined them. It would've been easy not to look beyond her styled purple hair, full lips, and the volup-tuous breasts showcased to sensual effect in a plunging top of glittering gold that looked like liquid. But Theo wasn't about the surface. What she saw were the sharp eyes that had assessed Theo in a single glance, the fluid muscle on that tall frame, and the way others in the club glanced at her.

Admiration? Yes. Fear? Also a yes.

The stunning Amazon of a woman was a significant threat.

"That's Stasya," Yakov murmured to her, one of his hands coming around her waist to lie flat on her stomach with him almost fully behind her.

Theo's senses hit overload. She felt drunk. And she had no intention of moving.

"You must be Theodora?" The words shouted above the music were a buzz saw cutting through the blur of overload.

Glancing at the woman she'd all but forgotten in her primal response to Yakov, the same woman she'd tagged a significant threat, she tried to resettle her mind, find her feet again. But they kept on sliding out from under her.

Yet she refused to drop the other woman's gaze—refused to look away first.

"Just Theo," she said, without shouting—because she knew the changeling across from her would hear her.

"Stasya." A faint smile curved the other woman's lips, their eyes yet locked.

Until Pavel groaned and literally put his hand in front of—but not on—Stasya's eyes to break the silent standoff. "You two can play dominance games on your own time," he said with a bearish rumble in his voice when Theo blinked and looked over to him. "We're in party mode."

Stasya's glance toward him was deadly. "Good thing I like you."

Unbowed, Pavel said, "I'm just saving you both from eye strain and headaches." He pushed up his glasses. "Or next thing you know, I'll have to introduce you to my optometrist."

Glancing away from Pavel, Stasya caught Yakov's eye and spoke just as the music fell into a small lull. "You have a minute? I need to talk to you outside."

Theo fought down her building anger at the idea of the two of them talking about her—because all logic said it was about her—but Yakov kept his hand where it was, while angling his body to even more effectively hold Theo against him. "I'm off the clock," he drawled. "Unless it's urgent clan business?"

Stasya's eyes gleamed. "Like that, is it?" A hint of amber to her irises before she returned her attention to Theo. But whatever it was she was about to say was interrupted by a member of the waitstaff bringing over a tray of drinks. Behind them came another staff member with the food.

As everyone on that side shifted to allow them room to place the items on the table, Yakov *nibbled* at the tip of Theo's ear while moving his hand slightly up her body so that it lay on her rib cage . . . right below the taut mounds of her breasts.

Chapter 40

Dnx09: Bozhe moi! YOU GUYS!! I'm in Club Moscow and you will NEVER GUESS who I just spotted!

LvrBoo: Who????! Don't keep us in suspense!

Novemba: SPILL GIRL!

WildestW: Five minutes and no update? We gonna hunt you down and do a murder.

Dnx09: Hold on! I was trying to sneak a pic, but no luck. So my bear clanmates, obvs, wolves, too. A smokin' human or twenty—some international soccer team is in town.

LvrBoo: Brag, brag, brag.

WildestW: I'm sharpening my murder fork.

Dnx09: So, I went out to get some air, and no biggie. Not too many people outside, was chill. Then I decide to walk toward the fence—and no B.S.—I swear I saw KALEB FRICKIN' KRYCHEK talking to Nina R. (she totally owns the club) all the way out in the shadows by the fence!

Novemba: Ugh, you had me going there for a minute. I'm outa here. This Wild Woman has pups climbing out of bed and a hottie of her own to snuggle.

LvrBoo: Yeah, did you eat some magic mushrooms while out foraging? It happens.

Dnx09: I SWEAR! He totally 'ported out before I could get my proof!

WildestW: Did you also see flying pigs? Kaleb Krychek, Cardinal Tk and Too-Scary-to-Sleep-With-but-MAN IS HE HOT, is not hanging out at clubs and poofing in front of you. Nice try tho. Got us good.

—*Wild Woman* Forum

"DON'T MIND STASYA," Yakov murmured with his lips against her ear, the hard muscle of his body flexing against her. "She's protective of her clanmates. Even the ones who can look after themselves."

Theo's toes curled. "I understand. I'm an unknown," she said, and it wasn't just words; while she'd never had a true family, she'd had Pax. She'd be *exactly* the same if he showed a sudden interest in another person. Especially if that person came from a family with a reputation like their own.

Yakov moved his thumb, brushing it back and forth below her breasts. "I dunno, Theo." A nuzzle of his jaw against her hair. "You've petted my bear. We're way past the stranger stage."

She had no right to be here.

The words hit out of nowhere, slicing through her to reveal blood and bone, a brutal reminder from the part of her that would never allow her to forget or forgive what she'd done for her grandfather. That was as it should be. She shouldn't forget what she'd done. She should remember and be haunted by her actions for the rest of her life.

And even that was nowhere near enough punishment.

Yet, hypocrite that she was, she didn't move away from Yakov, and when he nudged her nutrient drink toward her, she uncapped the bottle and took a sip. She also sampled the food, her body an inferno that burned endless energy.

Rage and need and a hatred turned inward, it was a voracious mix.

"Theo?" Arwen's calm voice when Yakov leaned over to talk to someone who'd come over to their table; the other Psy's perfect face was gentle with concern. "You're in trouble."

Her fingers clenched on the nutrients.

Forcing herself to breathe in and out as she fell back on her childhood calming technique—except that it was now a bear she drew with the dots of light in her mind—she stayed silent for a full minute before responding. "And now?"

A frown, a sigh. "You've bottled it." Then he shook his head and, for such an elegant and beautiful man, looked very stern and severe as he said, "You can't keep on doing that forever. You know what happens when you just bottle things up? You explode without warning."

Theo wanted to squirm as she hadn't done since she'd been a small child in front of her tutor. Arwen was an E. No doubt about it. She might not be an expert on Designation E, but she'd spent a lot of time around Memory Aven-Rose. Despite that, tonight was the first time she understood what people meant when they said empaths could rule the world had they the inclination to do so.

Because while Memory's attention had never been focused on her, Arwen's at that instant was—and the full attention of an empath who so openly wanted only the best for her . . . and who was disappointed in her . . .

She wanted to apologize without knowing exactly why.

It was Hakon, the polar bear, who saved her. Slamming down his already empty beer bottle, he threw up his arms. "Are we dancing or having a fucking tea party?"

Stasya turned in a motion Theo could never make, it was so lethally graceful, and shoved at his chest with one hand, pushing him toward the dance floor. Though StoneWater's second-in-command weighed less than Hakon *and* was shorter than him, it was clear that she was the one in charge.

Then she began to move in a sinuous flow of muscle, and Hakon's mouth all but fell open before he grabbed her hips and began to move with her. Their motions were sensual, fluid, and primal in a way that felt far too intimate for a public venue.

Theo couldn't look away.

"Our Arctic cousin better be careful"—a grinning Pavel shook his head—"or she's going to break his wrists. An inch lower and snap, snap. Then what'll we tell Auntie Anni?"

Heart thudding, Theo turned to Yakov. It felt wildly natural to speak with her lips brushing his ear when he bent his head toward her. "Does all dancing involve physical connection?" Theo wanted to do what they were doing—and she was certain she'd explode exactly as Arwen had warned her she would.

But Yakov shook his head, the silk of his hair brushing against her cheek. "You can have as much or as little contact as you want." He nodded to the right. "Though—those two need to get a room."

Following his gaze, Theo saw two women. One wore a glittering top and equally glittering micro-shorts, while the other wore a dress similar to Theo's in shimmering silver. The couple was pressed against each other without a breath in between, a single organism in two parts.

As she watched, one of the women slid her fingers lightly along the back of her partner's neck, angled her head . . . And the couple kissed, all tongue and open mouths, while the shorter of the pair slid her hand over the curves of her partner's rear, squeezing her curves through the silver rain of her dress.

Flushed, overheated, Theo put down her nutrient drink with too much force and said, "I'd like to try dancing." If she was going to explode, she'd rather do it experiencing life than hiding away from it.

Once she knew the full truth of her past, she might never again get the chance to dance with her bear. She'd slam her own prison door shut, cut herself off from any chance of happiness.

The clock was counting down to an endless dark midnight.

Because Theo knew she was fooling herself. Rehabilitation erased a person, made them nothing, a blank surface devoid of memory or personality.

She was very much *Theo*.

So it must've been Theo who disabled cars or elevators at critical moments, sending them careening into a wall or smashing to the ground. It must've been Theo who opened all those locked doors to places where people thought they were safe. And it must've been Theo who'd switched out one pill with another.

Medication for poison.

So easy for a 2.7 with rapier control who happened to be sitting at the table right next door to her target.

Theo. Theo. Theo.

No one else.

Guilt weighed her down even as Yakov took her hand and led her to the dance floor. She shoved off the heavy stone of it with desperate hands. *Tomorrow*, she promised the ghosts that haunted her. *Tomorrow you can have your pound of flesh. I just want one night.*

One night to not be responsible for a terrible choice made by a girl hungry for acceptance.

One night to exist without the crushing awareness of what she'd done.

One night to be free.

Yakov's hand was warm and a little rough-skinned around hers, his hold firm. Because he cared about her comfort, he didn't lead her deep into the dancers. He did, however, situate them away from the table as well as Stasya and Hakon—and inside a section of the dance floor where shadows pooled, liquid and soft.

Lost in the dark.

Safe from watchful eyes.

Then he turned and put his hands on her waist, at the very edge of her hips. Having seen how other couples danced, she put her hands on his shoulders, the hard muscle of them flexing under her touch.

It was shockingly intimate.

Dimples flashing, he began to move, putting light pressure on her hips with his hands to teach her how to flow with the music, teach her how to dance. Every so often he'd speak against her ear, his lips brushing the curves of it to praise her. "Perfect. Just like that. You're a natural dancer, *pchelka*."

Her fingers dug into his shoulders, her body rubbing against his with every move. He was aroused. She could feel the hard ridge of it against her, and she wondered if he could feel her nipples the same way. They'd pebbled against the soft fabric of the dress until the friction was torturous.

But she didn't pull away. Couldn't pull away.

It felt as if she'd die of thirst if she broke this sensuous connection that was a slide of bodies on bodies, heat on heat.

SHIFTING his hold, Yakov pressed one hand against Theo's lower back, her body so close to his that he could've easily hitched her up onto his hips, slid up her dress, and—*fuck, he didn't need to be having erotic fantasies on the dance floor.*

His rigid cock didn't need any more encouragement.

The sight of Theo's pleasure was more than enough. It didn't matter that they were surrounded by others—he knew her scent, could taste the rich musk of her arousal, and it was taking everything he had not to dip his head and lick up the light layer of perspiration along her throat, eat up her taste.

But that would mean taking his eyes off the flushed beauty of her face. As they danced, he watched the black of her pupils expand, grow, and eclipse the blue until her gaze was an endless midnight.

"I don't know what's happening." Theo's voice was grit—but she made no indication she wanted distance between them.

Yet those eyes . . . He remembered too late the meaning of such an eclipse. Swearing under his breath, he said, "This is enough. I'm not going to take advantage of you when you're overwhelmed by—"

"Stop." The single word was hard, furious.

Man and bear both went motionless.

Chapter 41

—no air in my lungs, only this endless—
A brush of your finger over my—
—agony sweet and painf—
Your thighs thrusting between—
—pulse inside me, lover mi—

—"Fragments of a Torn-up Letter" by Adina Mercant, poet
(b. 1832, d. 1901)

(Original multimedia piece sold to an anonymous private collector
for ten million dollars at auction in 2047. Currently on loan
to the British Museum.)

"I'M NOT A doll to be arranged as you wish." The anger of a warrior queen in her voice. "Neither am I a child to have my decisions made for me. I know exactly who I am. And I know exactly what I want."

Yakov's entire body went rigid with need. There was no better aphrodisiac than a woman who wouldn't take his shit, and who'd go toe-to-toe with him. That didn't mean he was about to lie down and let her walk all over him.

"You might not be a child," he said. "But you are in an alien environment, smashing headlong into alien sensations. You telling me you have the capacity to process what's happening?"

One of her hands shifted to curve slightly around the column of his throat, an action not many would dare take with a bear of Yakov's dominance, her breath shallow and fast.

O Bozhe, was it arousing.

"No," she said. "But according to *Wild Woman* magazine, skin privileges of this intimacy can drive even changelings and humans crazy."

It was his turn to go mute for a moment. She was right. He'd all but lost his mind when he first experienced intimate skin privileges. And he wasn't exactly in total control right now if he was fantasizing about fucking her on the dance floor. "How far do you want to go?" It came out a bearish rumble, the human side of him giving way to the primal need within.

"I don't know." No hesitation in her words. "But I want to find out."

Yakov knew that he should stop things right now. But he didn't. It was too late. It had been too late when she walked out of the exit gate at the airport. Shifting his hold to around her waist, he said, "Then let's go play, *moya pchelka*."

Since they hadn't left anything at the table, he didn't bother to go back to it. Taking out his phone instead, he shot Pavel a quick message so his brother wouldn't hang around waiting for him when he and Arwen wanted to take off: Leaving with Theo.

His phone buzzed with a message just as they left the frenetic energy of the main dance floor: Be careful, bro. I like her, but she's not Arwen.

Yakov knew that all too well. Theo was very much not an empath; she was a dangerous woman with an anger inside her that was so deep as to be deadly—and she was the woman he'd been dreaming of all his life.

THEO felt like a runaway bullet train, picking up speed with each step she took. Every single thing she'd ever been taught told her to pull back, stop.

She ignored it all. She'd listened for so long and all it had gotten her was blood on her hands and loneliness in her bones.

Nothing good has ever come out of following the rules.

How unexpected that it was her brother, the epitome of the perfect Psy, who'd said those words to her. But of course, that was exactly it—Pax *wasn't* perfect. Not only because of the syndrome that was devastating his strong, beautiful mind, but because of her. He'd never ever let go of her, had protected her in every way he could . . . and in so doing, he'd nurtured an emotional bond that had been verboten under Silence.

What would he say if he knew the extent of the rules she was breaking tonight?

It didn't matter. This was her decision, and as maddened and out of control as it was, she owned it nonetheless.

The cold of the night air hit her as they exited the club after picking up her clothing at the coat check.

Yakov carried the bag, his free hand wrapped around hers. The heat of him was a shocking contrast to the bite of the air.

With the chill of the night came sudden clarity and the clawing swipe of guilt.

Yet . . . she'd warned Yakov, hadn't she? Shown him her full hand but for a single broken card. No doubt he'd guessed that Theo Marshall still had her secrets. He was too smart not to have done so—and he was making this decision regardless of the murkiness that surrounded her.

"It's not far to the car." Breaking their handclasp, Yakov shifted his hand to her hip.

Theo moved close, telling herself it was only sensible since he was big and warm and she was in a ridiculously short dress. His heat was a welcome burn against her, his scent a roughness against her senses. She'd never met anyone like Yakov—and she said that having met his literal twin.

Pavel might look identical to Yakov, but he *wasn't Yakov.*

Only this man, only this bear, was the one she wanted, the one she craved.

"Here you go." Having reached their heavy-duty vehicle, he unlocked it, then opened the passenger door and threw her bag over the seats into the back—only to pick her up with two hands on her hips to put her into the passenger seat.

Amber eyes hot and turbulent lingered on her lips, lips that felt swollen and sensitive. "Yasha." A breathy word.

"No," he growled. "Not here."

But then he put one hand on the naked skin of her thigh and pressed a kiss to her throat. Shoving away even as her entire body ignited, he shut the passenger door.

Three seconds later he was in his seat and pulling away from the curb, the lights of Moscow streaming on either side of their vehicle. It wasn't a long drive to the StoneWater apartment, but time crawled, Theo's skin pulsing where he'd touched her—and freezing cold where he hadn't. Yet it felt paradoxically too fast at the same time.

Dawn would come far too soon, and with it, perhaps the truth of her evil.

Again, she turned away from the reality that hovered above her, the sword waiting to fall and skewer her to the earth. The guilt wouldn't leave her alone, but it was no proof against the need within, a need that had grown for countless years. For contact, for care, for someone other than her brother to *see* Theo, scars and all.

The scars on her back were suddenly stiff and ragged. It was luck that they were located just low enough that they'd been hidden by even this dress.

Would the twisted ridges of them scare Yakov?

He was a wild being, a creature at home with imperfection.

Perhaps . . . just perhaps, he'd look at her without disgust. At least the marks were on her back. If he was disgusted, she wouldn't see the first flush of his reaction. They could pretend he'd simply changed his mind.

Because Theo wasn't stopping this runaway train until he did.

She was barely aware of them reaching the apartment building, conscious only of Yakov's hand on hers as he led her into the elevator. He looked around, as if searching for someone, though it was clear they were alone.

The elevator doors opened.

But when she turned toward him after they were inside with the doors shut, he growled. "Not in the elevator." His chest heaved. "We're doing this right."

Theo bit down hard on her lower lip, her free hand a tight fist.

The doors seemed to open in slow motion. Striding out with her hand in his, Yakov unlocked the apartment door. She walked in first, turned the instant she heard him shut the door behind himself.

His hands on her hips, his big body shoving her against the wall. Claws pricked her hips. "I'm not in control, Theo." A rumble of sound, his eyes no longer in any way human. "I could hurt you and fuck if I'll ever do that."

Theo, her skin so hot it burned, flattened both hands against the wall lest she try to rip off his clothing. "I can protect myself." All at once, the pen that had been sitting on a small table close to the door was hovering in front of his eye, point forward.

Theo could do other things with her small power, but this one tended to make the most dramatic impact. And she wanted impact, wanted this bear to stop trying to protect her, wanted him to take her with the ferocity of the creature that lived under his skin.

Grabbing the pen out of the air, Yakov threw it aside without breaking eye contact. He shifted his hand instead, to grip the side of her neck. She felt claws. Should've been afraid.

But her body clenched, the place between her thighs gushing with dampness.

"How far?" A harsh question, the roughness of it making her nipples ache.

The runaway train barreled on. "As far as you want."

Chapter 42

Tactile contact must be forbidden except for practical purposes such as medical assistance and the maintenance of children.
Sexual contact needs to be verboten. It creates too much sensation—and we have agreed that any sensation is a gateway to emotion.

—Early discussion on the possible structure of Silence
(Mercury compound, circa 1947)

YAKOV WANTED NOTHING more than to shove up her dress, rip off her panties, then drop to his knees in front of her, thrust her knees apart, put his hands on her ass, and go to town on the slick heat of her pussy. He could taste her arousal on his tongue, knew she'd come explosively for him.

But regardless of all Theo had said, he was very conscious that the balance here was skewed. She'd been in Silence most of her life, had no idea what to do with the attraction that buffeted them both. He was the experienced one, knew they couldn't go from zero to a hundred in a matter of minutes.

Especially when Theo already had a manic look about her.

She was riding overload.

Yet he knew she might just stab him for real if he tried to act the protector. He'd have to walk a very fine line.

Lightly squeezing the side of her throat, he then rubbed his thumb over the flushed cream of her skin. Her eyes were all black again, and now she shivered.

"A kiss," he said, leaning in until their breaths mingled.

Theo closed the distance between them without warning.

Lips on lips, her breasts crushed to his chest.

Groaning, he'd shoved her even harder against the wall before he could stop himself, the ridge of his erection thrusting against her stomach. Fuck, she felt good. All soft and warm and *Bozhe* but he wanted her with a raw desperation that would have her pinned up against the wall in ten seconds flat if he didn't get a grip on it.

It took everything he had to pull back, keep it slow.

He initiated the second kiss, this one a little wetter, but with both their mouths yet closed. When her hand landed on his chest, and she fisted his T-shirt between her fingers, his chest rumbled with the bear's approval.

Yakov had thought he knew all about kissing—hadn't he stolen his first kiss when he was a juvenile of barely thirteen? But this kiss, it was a bullet straight to the heart, visceral and hard. The intensity of it hit him with such fury that he had no hope in hell of resisting it.

Perhaps in some deep corner of his brain, he'd convinced himself that it would be a letdown, that his dreams had been nothing but a confused bit of foresight that had come through the genes left by his great-grandfather. That he'd misunderstood the meaning of it, and that all he'd been foreseeing was that Theo would one day come into his life.

Well, he'd been wrong.

This kiss was better than anything in the dream. It was all breath and heat and *her* and it took hold of his changeling heart and squeezed. Until he had no air and the lack didn't matter if he could keep on kissing her.

But when she tore at his T-shirt, he cupped her cheek and took a single step back. Just enough to look into her eyes, shake his head. "We are not rushing this." Not their first time.

Not *her* first time.

A hiss of air from in between her lips, her eyes flashing to blue flame.

Oh yeah, his Theo was going to drive him to distraction. But tonight, he had to hold steady, had to be the anchor.

Before she could snap at him that she'd already told him she knew what she wanted, he tugged off the hand she'd clenched in his T-shirt, lifted it to his mouth, and pressed a kiss to her knuckles. "Let me love you slow and with great attention to detail, *pchelka moya*."

Her pupils swallowed up her irises, her chest rising and falling in a ragged drumbeat. "I don't want to lose this chance." An edge of desperation. "I don't know what tomorrow will bring."

Yakov's jaw tightened. He trusted her more than she trusted herself, but he knew that nothing he said would change her mind until they had proof. So he kept it to the here and the now. "We have all night. Hours and hours." Leaning close, he nuzzled her throat, licked her up. "Endless minutes."

This time, he tasted her shiver before he pulled back and took another kiss that was a drug to his senses. They were both breathing harder, faster when he broke the kiss to say, "Do you want me to take off the T-shirt?"

THEO didn't have to think of her answer to Yakov's question. "*Yes.* I want to touch you." She didn't know how to be anything less than blunt when want was a crushing weight on her skin, a turbulent spiral in her veins.

A gleam in the amber before Yakov pulled off his T-shirt and threw it so it landed on the back of a chair. The groan that came from her throat was unbidden, feral in its lack of control.

She had her hands on him a moment later, but despite the desperation riding her, she didn't claw and scrabble. No. She spread her fingers on the silken ridges and planes of him, and she soaked him in, this man of beauty and power and warmth. So much *warmth*. Inside and out, Yakov Stepyrev was created of warmth.

It was stark need that had her pressing her lips to his skin. She wanted to absorb him into her, keep him forever in a place where no one could steal him from her. He tasted of the wild, salt, and heat, and the scent that was his. She might not be changeling, but she knew she would never mistake his scent for any other man's.

It aroused her, comforted her, made her want to cry with the loss to come.

When he put his hands on her hips, she was expecting—was ready for—a demand. But he nuzzled her throat, then nipped, and nuzzled again. Her eyes grew hot, burned. Squeezing them shut, she swallowed hard as she ran her hands over his chest. "Dimples," she managed to say when she could speak again.

A chuckle before he bent his head so she could fulfill her first fantasy: to kiss first one wicked dent in his cheek, then the other.

He groaned, nuzzled her once more.

Suckling kisses on her throat, his big body a heavy blanket.

When he began to walk backward, tugging her along with him, she went without hesitation.

Stopping at the sofa, he sat down . . . and pulled her down into his lap.

Her dress rode up, exposing nearly all of her. She didn't care. Not when she could feel the heavy muscle of him beneath her, around her. Not when his eyes were wild and he made no effort to hide the vivid evidence of his arousal.

Her skin stretched, a hot power arcing through her veins even as she felt herself losing the last vestiges of control. As if he'd felt the frenetic pulse of her energy, Yakov stroked her thigh. His touch was tiny prickles all across her body, a violent awareness that led to a clenching between her thighs, and suddenly the air was too thin, too hard to swallow.

She clutched at him, struggling to hold on as the entire world spun.

Yakov's expression altered, softened in a way she didn't understand. "Come here, Theo mine. Right here."

Her mind chaos, she couldn't process the meaning of his words, but he was nudging her head toward his shoulder, his arms warm bands around her. She wanted to resist, panicked all over again that this was it, her one and only chance, but the weight of his hand on the back of her neck, the idea of being held against his skin as if she mattered . . . she couldn't resist that.

One hand flexing against his pectoral muscle, she tucked her face against his neck and gave in to the desire to get drunk on his scent, on his warmth, on his very being.

"There you go." The rumble of his chest was a vibration against her breasts, his breath kissing her neck as she nuzzled deeper into him. "Yes, Thela. Take what you need."

He began to stroke her back.

Her dress had shifted during their embrace and she knew the instant he felt the first ripple of raised skin on her back. The slightest pause . . . before he continued on in his caresses. Exhaling, she buried her face against him and just . . . let go.

For the first time in her life, she let go without fear.

As she did so, a heavy warmth spread over her skin, through her limbs, and into her blood. The storm quieted into a sensation she'd never before felt. Was this what it felt like to be safe?

Her eyelids began to droop.

Theo wanted to fight it. She might be new at intimate sensation, but she knew sleep didn't come into it. But when she stirred, Yakov murmured to her that it was all right, and he kept on stroking her with those strong, careful hands, and she couldn't keep her eyes open any longer.

She surrendered and fell into a sleep as soft and dark as the velvet she'd once surreptitiously touched as a child.

YAKOV stroked his hands over his sleeping dream woman. What would the other unmated males in the den say if they saw him now? Probably razz him forever about the fact that his date had fallen asleep rather than exchange skin privileges with him.

He should've been annoyed, insulted.

All he felt, however, was a wave of tenderness stark and primal.

He wanted desperately to move her hair aside and look at the scars he'd touched on her back, but despite her tacit permission, he didn't. Whatever that was, it wasn't good. He'd felt it in the tension in her body, the stiffness in the line of her spine. Given her history, he had a fucking good idea of who'd done that to her—and if she never wanted to talk about it? He'd handle it. He wasn't going to push her back into the abyss.

Leaning down, he pressed his lips to her hair. "You're safe, *serdtse moyo*." His heart had never had a chance when it came to Theo. "Sleep."

He didn't know how long he'd held her when she whimpered. He immediately murmured comforting words to her, stroking his hands down her back . . . but she jolted out of sleep, staring at him with eyes that had gone an eerily flat black. Her face was sleep creased on one side, her hair mussed.

She jerked her head this way and that with wild desperation.

"Hey," he murmured, keeping his voice a low rumble. "It's Yasha. You're in a StoneWater apartment. Safe."

But when he would've raised his hand to push strands of hair off her face, she scrambled back and away so fast that she almost tumbled onto the floor as she got her trembling legs under her. "I—" A harsh gasp of air, those dark eyes staring at him as if he'd appeared out of nowhere.

Theo screamed without warning, the sound not of fear but of rage, and suddenly, Yakov went flying straight into a wall.

Chapter 43

She'll kill someone if you don't get her under control.

—Dr. Upashna Leslie to Councilor Marshall Hyde (27 November 2073)

YAKOV HIT THE wall hard but managed to take the impact with his side and leg for the most part. The only reason she'd even got him that badly was that he wasn't expecting it. But he was a bear changeling, his body built for hard knocks—and while her telekinetic throw had been far more powerful than should've been possible for a 2.7, it hadn't been as hard as an enraged bear could throw.

So he was only slightly winded when he got to his feet—to see that all the small objects in the room were swirling at deadly speed. A violent cyclone inside the apartment. "Theo!" He could see her in the midst of the chaos, her hands fisted before she screamed and gripped the bracelet on her wrist with the hand of her other.

The turbulence made it seem like it was sparking with electrical energy.

Wrenching apart the heavy metal as if it were plas, she threw it to smash against the bulletproof glass of the window.

Despite the fact he was shouting her name, she seemed unaware of him.

Not what he'd expect from a woman who was *always* aware of her surroundings. She did a good job of not making it obvious, but it was part of Yakov's job to ensure the clan's welfare—which meant *he* watched everyone without making it appear like he was doing so, unless, of course, he wanted someone to know they'd been spotted.

So he knew that Theo watched everyone and everything.

Right now, however, she appeared to have forgotten the biggest threat in the room. Whatever this was, it wasn't an attack against Yakov. He'd just happened to get in the way of the storm. With that realization in mind, he dropped lower to the ground and crept around the side of the room so that he could come up behind her.

Bears weren't the best creepers. In fact, they'd won the *Wild Woman* Award for Worst at Stealth ten years running. What an insult! Each year that stupid Award Issue came out and each year bears sat down and growled and grumped about how biased the committee was . . . until they got to the awards for Best at Parties and Biggest Hearts.

All bear. All the time.

And they forgave the award committee.

Today, Yakov didn't have to be very good at stealth—Theo was in a world of her own. Even as he came up behind her, she screamed again and literally *smashed* her hand against a mug that was flying in the air. It splintered into jagged shards against the wall.

Her blood flecked the white of the paint.

Yakov clenched his jaw.

She kept on going this way and she was going to seriously hurt herself. But he couldn't come at her full frontal—she was just powerful enough that she could disable him should she have warning that he was about to incapacitate her.

So he did the only thing he could: once he was behind her, he moved at rapid speed—because despite what the world might believe, bears could move fast when they wanted to—and took her down before she could do anything but begin to spin a little on her heel. Locking his arms around her, he pinned her own to her sides and took them both to the floor, making sure to take the brunt of the fall.

He didn't know if a Tk needed to see their target to do damage with flying objects, but he decided to act on the side of caution and—even as she screamed and unknown objects began to hit his back—he rolled so that his back was to the closest wall.

He took a few more bruising hits before he made it, but once there, the hits stopped coming. Instead, shards from the mug zeroed toward him . . . and hovered, as if she didn't know where to put them. Soon, they dropped to lie flat on the floor.

But this was far from over.

Theo twisted in his hold as if she'd become possessed of changeling strength, her rage a thing savage and bright. He spit out a curse when she turned her head and sank her teeth into his biceps, but his bear was also weirdly proud of her for thinking outside the box. She bit down hard as things smashed into the wall above his head, but he still didn't let go. Instead, he avoided the objects as best he could while protecting her from them at the same time.

"*Govno!*" He grunted as a small and heavy cube meant to hold memo paper hit his shoulder, but made sure to twist in a way that it rolled behind him rather than onto her face. Yeah, the angular thing was uncomfortable poking into his back, but far better that than its sharp edge cut her face.

The storm raged on, Theo's fists bloodless and her scream hoarse.

He'd never tasted such a depth of anger, of fury, rage in its purest form.

Then the world went silent.

All the objects that spun dropped to the carpet without a sound.

Theo's body spasmed as a wrenching shiver rippled through her . . . and then . . . nothing.

Chapter 44

I'm getting an itch at the back of my neck. Something's up at the apartment. Let's double our usual patrols in the area.

—Message from Yakov Stepyrev to Zahaan Saarinen (4 September 2083)

THE WATCHER STARED up at the window of the apartment where Theo Marshall was yet awake. The blinds had been lowered, so the Watcher couldn't see anything, but the lights were still on—and that bear was still with her.

The Watcher had thought that the bear must be staying in an adjacent apartment, but none of the other lights had come on since they went inside. Either they were planning strategy for tomorrow—or Theo was the latest Psy to fall for a bear.

The Watcher snorted. "Bears have better taste than to go for a Marshall." No, it had to be a strategy meeting.

Regardless, the Watcher couldn't get to her so long as she was in that apartment. StoneWater security was beyond even the Watcher's abilities. "She'll be alone sooner or later," the Watcher said under their breath, speaking to the person inside their mind that was their other self, the one from before. "I just have to be patient a little longer."

Chapter 45

I can't believe Neiza is already a year old! A month past it even! I tell you, my dearest D, time passes like water through the fingers when you have a child. I swear I turned around and she'd gone from sleeping fifteen hours a day to clapping her hands and laughing and making the most adorable sounds—and never wanting to sleep!

Oh, listen to me. I sound like every besotted mother there ever was! Thank you for indulging me as you do.

But that's not why I wanted to write. I suppose I could've just come over to the den, but it's our thing, isn't it? These letters? I've kept each one you've ever written to me.

Anyway, they've set the date for the Changes to Silence Referendum: July 24th next year. I'm including all available documentation listing the pros and cons, as compiled by smart people on both sides of the issue. You know how much I respect you. Please do read it with an open mind and let me know your thoughts.

Love from your favorite little sister,
Hien

—Letter from Hien Nguyen to Déwei Nguyen (20 February 1978)

. . .

THEO'S MIND FELT bruised as it always did after one of her rage attacks. She should probably find something else to call them, but why, when the words she'd chosen as a teenager described them so well?

Today, the bruise throbbed until it blurred her vision and her stomach muscles hurt, as if she'd clenched them so hard that she'd torn something. She knew the latter for an illusion; most often, the damage was limited to contusions and cuts. Once, she'd woken up after hours of unconsciousness—probably caused by a blow from a heavy object she'd sent flying.

That had been before Pax took over the family.

She'd cleaned up the blood, then gone to a medical facility for indigent street people because they wouldn't record her injuries into any system. The doctor—a human woman with gray hair—had been kind, had asked her if she was being abused.

A question come far too late.

"Theo?"

She whimpered, wanting to hide away. She'd never wanted Yakov to see her this way, as a *creature* devoid of reason or sanity, a *thing* without a mind. Just viciousness and violence.

But it was far too late for that, too. He had his arms locked around her, his body at her back. His breath brushed the hairs on the side of her face as he said, "Theo, can you hear me?"

She wanted to just shut her eyes and sink into the throbbing in her head, pretend that this humiliation hadn't taken place, but all that would do was extend the agony of it. This was her own fault. She should've told him, but she'd wanted to pretend she was normal when she wasn't normal, hadn't been any kind of normal for a long, long time.

"Yes," she answered, and it came out a throaty rasp.

Her skin heated on another hot wave of humiliation—she must've been screaming. The rages had begun while she was still living with Colette, during a time when the inside of the apartment was under full surveillance. Another attempt at control by her grandfather, one instituted because of Theo's increasing defiance.

As a result, there'd been recordings.

The worst were the ones where she screamed and screamed.

She'd slapped her own hands over her ears the first time Colette had shown her one of those videos, and she'd rocked back and forth, believing herself a madwoman. She wasn't so sure that the shocked young woman she'd been wasn't right—because she should have this under control by now. Only she didn't.

Her gaze went to her wrist.

No metal bracelet. Only a welt where the material must've scraped her skin when she tore it off. She'd have to make it stronger next time, she thought dully. Strong enough that even the stolen power of a 9 couldn't tear it off. And she had to ramp up the intensity.

Because it *had* activated right after the rage hit—she'd frozen at the painful jolt, her senses attempting to realign into sanity. Then her brother's power had poured into her in an endless wave, burning away the cold iron of control and leaving only rage in its wake.

Theo? Pax's voice in her mind, as if he'd sensed her thoughts. *I felt the power draw. Did you have an episode?*

Yes. But I'm fine. Lying in an effort to protect him was instinct. *Are you?*

Yes. Do you need help?

No. She didn't tell him that she wasn't by herself, didn't even want to acknowledge the humiliation of it. *I need to be alone in my head right now.*

Pax withdrew without further questions. He knew about her episodes not only because he sensed it when her mind began to siphon his power, but because their grandfather had made him watch the recordings of her in the worst of the rages. It had been a brutal slap to Pax's request for information about Theo.

Pax had never told her, but she could imagine what their grandfather had said to him at the time. *Your sister is an unstable liability. Look at her! Pathetic!*

Flinching inwardly, Theo tried to take her mind elsewhere, but there was no disassociation, not here, not now. Everything was too sharp, too bright, too *real* to escape. Yakov, this bear who had touched her with such tenderness that night, yet held her tight. She didn't blame him. She had no idea what she'd done to him in the midst of the vast blackness that had sporadically swamped her brain since she was sixteen years of age.

"You were born defective," her grandfather had told her after she almost killed Colette by accident. "That is the true reason why you had to be separated from your brother. Do you understand now? You could've killed him."

Theo had wanted to argue that she would never hurt her twin, had stayed silent because it would've been a lie. She had no awareness of the world in the midst of the rage storms created by her broken brain.

"I'm going to let go," Yakov said, slowly following words with action.

She felt cold, so cold as he unwrapped his arms from around her, but she forced herself to move away. He couldn't want to be near her, and the least she could do was give him his wish. Tugging down the rucked-up bottom of her short dress, she kept her back to him as she stared down at the carpet, her hair hanging around her in a curtain.

"I apologize." Her throat felt raw, lined with crushed stone. "Did I hurt you?"

"I'm a bear," he said roughly, and then he was moving to come down on his knees in front of her.

She flinched when he lifted a hand and slid it over her cheek and slightly over the back of her head to cup the side of her face. But she didn't push him away, and she didn't tell him to not touch her. He deserved whatever pound of flesh he wanted from her.

"Show me that beautiful face, *pchelka*," he murmured in a coaxing tone. "I'm pretty sure you took a hit with a flying object."

Lost, shattered, she didn't resist when he tilted up her chin. But she couldn't look him in the eye, instead looking over his shoulder at the wall she'd marked up and dented in her rage. "I'll pay to have the damage fixed." Fast, rough words. "I have the money. I can pay to fix it."

Too bad she couldn't do that for her own brain.

Ignoring her statement as if she hadn't spoken, Yakov said, "Some bruising on your left cheekbone, but it's not as bad as it could've been."

Still unable to meet his gaze, she turned her head to check the rest of the apartment—but never got there, her gaze snagging on the bite marks on his biceps. Bile burned her throat. This was her fault. Even knowing what she was, she'd allowed him to bring her here, to this place that should've been a safe haven for him.

How selfish could she be?

"I'm sorry, Yasha," she whispered, staring at the deep indentation of her teeth. "I am so sorry." Her voice threatened to break.

"Hey," he said, and waited.

Stomach churning, hurting, she met his eyes at last. Wild amber with a yellowish cast, of the bear that lived under his skin, those beautiful eyes held no disgust or anger. Unable to endure the hope that spawned in her, she scanned his face, his body, her gaze once more hitching on the bite marks on his arm.

"I'm fine," he said. "I've had worse bites than that in practice sparring sessions with some of the younger members of the clan."

Theo had never cried as an adult. "I'm not a bear," she got out past the thickness in her throat, the burning in her eyes.

"Well, you fight like one." Curved lips, gentle fingers tucking her hair behind her ear. "Come on, *milaya moya*, let's get you into warmer clothes. Your skin is chilled."

Tears barely held in check now, Theo didn't have the strength to refuse him. She allowed him to tug her up to her feet, allowed him to hold her steady as he led her to the bedroom.

She felt like nothing, a ghost without weight.

Leaving her standing by the foot of her bed, he didn't go to her suitcase and pull out a change of clothes. Instead, he walked out and grabbed the T-shirt he'd taken off during the sensual interlude that now seemed a figment of her crazed imagination.

"You like my scent, Theo," he said with a gentle rub of his beard-shadowed cheek against hers. "Don't think I haven't noticed."

Her fingers clenched tight over the soft fabric when he put the T-shirt into her hand, his muscular body a warm wall against her. It took everything she had not to crawl into him, hide away from the whole world.

"This is drenched with my scent. Snuggle into it while I make you a hot drink."

She stood there dumbly for long moments after he'd gone.

"I don't hear movement, Thela!" Yakov's voice. "Want me to come in there and help?"

Theo trembled.

Lifting his T-shirt to her nose, she took in a deep breath . . . and almost sobbed. It smelled of comfort and warmth.

Yakov, it smelled like Yakov, just like he'd promised.

Wanting it to surround her as fast as possible, she all but ripped off the dress, then put the T-shirt on over her panties. It hung off her, coming to halfway down her thighs, and it was the most wonderful piece of clothing she'd ever had.

"Come on out, *pchelka*." More coaxing words. "I've got your drink ready."

Heart thumping and the scent of Yakov the only thing holding her together, she made herself walk out and face what she'd done. But . . . the living area was no longer a scene of carnage. Not neat by any means, but just a place where a bear or two might've turned a fraction rambunctious.

Lower lip threatening to quiver, she looked over at the man who stood at the kitchen counter, holding up a glass for her.

"I'm sorry," she began, even knowing that no apologies would ever be enough. "I shouldn—"

"Don't you dare apologize for something you can't control." He pinned her with his gaze, his irises no longer bear amber, but the rich aqua green of the human part of him. "Unless you're going to lie to me and tell me that you could control that?"

Her cheeks flushed with a burst of emotion that had nothing to do with the rage attacks; she wanted to bite back a response, but she forced herself to calm down, forced herself to breathe, forced her hands to unclench.

Leaning back against the kitchenette wall, Yakov raised an eyebrow. "I survived you in full fury. I won't melt with a few harsh words."

She blinked, stared at him, and realized he was right. She hadn't killed him. She hadn't even really injured him. Impossible. The two previous times she'd been with others during an attack, the consequences had been grave. Colette had ended up with broken bones, while her grandfather's aide had needed extensive facial surgery to put her back together.

The latter, at least, hadn't been all Theo's fault. Her grandfather had pushed and pushed because he'd wanted to see what she could do. It just so happened that his aide had been in front of her when the explosion took place. And that aide had been carrying a glass of water for her grandfather.

Theo never remembered anything of an episode, but Grandfather had been taping her that day, too, and he'd shown her the results of her "defective neural structure."

Theo would never forget how the glass had shattered in a stunning starlike pattern, the shards driven upward into flesh and bone, the blood splattering onto the desk before her grandfather stunned Theo with a weapon set at maximum.

Even as Theo's body began to spasm from the blast of the weapon, the aide had begun to scream. That was how fast it had all happened. How quickly Theo had brutally wounded another living being.

But Yakov . . . Yakov was fine. "This isn't right." She ran to him, terror in her blood. "Internal injuries. It has to be internal injuries."

Chapter 46

F-Psy have some of the highest rates of insanity among our race.
It's because so many of us can see catastrophic events without the power
to change them. And so we just bear witness to terror over and over again
until our brains can no longer take it.
If the change to the Silence Protocol can alter that, if it can give
me a good night's sleep and take away my unending fear . . . I'll
be voting yes.

—Excerpt from "Insanity Is Our Destiny" by Anonymous F-8.3
(5 January 1977)

"I DON'T HAVE internal injuries, Theo mine." Despite his words, Yakov didn't stop her from pushing up the T-shirt he'd pulled on. "Couple bruises on my back and shoulders, that's about it."

Throat dry and perspiration breaking out over her skin, she finished scanning his abdominal area. Smooth, hard muscle, and flawless skin. "Your back." The words came out on top of each other. "I need to see your back."

He turned, didn't stop her from pushing up his T-shirt there, too.

A little light bruising, one spot darker—as if he'd been hit by a sharp and pointed object, and that was it.

"Internal injuries," she repeated as he began to turn around. "We should take you to a medic. Where's my phone? I need to—"

A big hand clasped her wrist, squeezed. "Theo, I'm no novice when it comes to physical injuries. I know exactly the kind of hits I took tonight—trust me, there's no chance of internal bleeding." He thrust the hot nutrient drink in her hand. "You can examine me as much as you like *after* you drink this."

Heart thunder, she nonetheless took several big gulps. "I hurt people in the rages," she blurted out. "That was a bad one. Even my reprimand device didn't work to stop it."

"What the hell is a reprimand device?" Yakov said, and Theo couldn't help her eyes going to the reddened marks on her wrist. "*Bozhe*, Theo. Was it the bracelet? It what? Electrocutes you?"

"In a way." It would take too long to explain how she'd based it off the machine her grandfather had used in an attempt to train the rages out of her. "Only enough to snap me out of the spiral so I can get to a private place. It can't hold back the rage, but it can give me a few minutes to make sure I don't break down in public."

Putting the half-finished drink on the counter, she rubbed her hand over her naked wrist. "I pulled too much of Pax's power today. The bracelet wasn't strong enough. I'll make the next iteration unbreakable even by a 9."

Yakov banged a fist on the counter, so hard that the glass of nutrients skittered to the left. "That fucking thing is never coming anywhere near you again."

Theo was feeling fragile and guilty—but she wasn't about to allow this bear to walk all over her. "No."

Yakov growled. "That thing hurts you. You put it on again and I will take it away. Every. Fucking. Time."

"It protects me from hurting others . . . and from humiliation . . . Most of the time." Suddenly deflating, she slumped against the side of the counter. "That was the worst one yet. I'm devolving, just like Grandfather predicted."

"You stop that thinking right now." His gaze on her face, his expression going soft before he hauled her into his arms. "We need to talk. But not now. It's after midnight, and you're exhausted. In the morning, on the drive."

She swallowed, almost wanting him to push so she could get this over with—but after the rage came the crash. Her legs were already shaky, her fingers trembling. "In the morning," she agreed. "What time should I set my alarm?"

"Don't you worry about that. I'll be your alarm." He pulled back so he could look at her face. "Unless you want to sleep alone tonight? In that case, I'll take the couch."

"No, stay," she said without hesitation.

Her reward was a smile that creased his cheeks, lit up his eyes. For a split second, she fell back into that time before the rage. Then he shifted to grab the glass of nutrients so she could finish it, and she saw the bite mark again.

Reality crashed into her with the force of a ten-ton truck.

She'd hurt Yakov, the one person aside from Pax who had ever mattered to her. And still she'd hurt him. Would've probably killed him if he wasn't a bear.

Murder and evil, it was in her blood.

In her genes.

She was a Marshall, after all.

YAKOV dreamed again that night, a dream of blood and fear.

He saw Theo fall to her knees, her hands rising to clasp her throat as she fought to keep her life force from draining out of her in pulses of red that streaked her hands a rich scarlet.

She stared at him with eyes that were full of a desperate need.

Help me, Yasha. Please, Yasha.

But Yakov couldn't help her. His hands were tied, his bear strength immobilized. No matter how much he struggled, he couldn't break free, couldn't do anything but scream as Theo bled darkest red in front of him.

That red stained his gaze when he jerked awake in the middle of the night. Instantly aware of Theo's responding movement, he ran one hand down her side until she calmed and fell back into deep sleep.

While she'd initially agreed to him in her bed, she'd then balked. Not because she wanted to be alone but because she was scared she'd hurt him. It had taken all his bearish charm to talk her down from that.

She'd still only acquiesced after he found her accursed bracelet and let her fix it so she could wear it again. He'd had to literally grit his teeth to not destroy that monstrous "reprimand" device, but he'd known she needed to be held. And if he was holding her, he could get that thing off her the instant it activated.

He was a smart bear. He'd watched her make the repair and knew that the seam was imperfect. One hard push from a bear's claw and it would snap open. That thing wasn't going to be hurting her on his watch.

Now, his heart thumping, he lay on his back and stared at the ceiling. *Why wasn't the vision changing?*

He still had no answer to his question by the time sleep finally found him again, some two hours later. He fell asleep curled around Theo, her heartbeat his lullaby. But that smart bear's mind kept on ticking even in sleep, kept on turning the vision this way and that.

If he couldn't alter the vision, he had to alter the end result.

Chapter 47

"How about a date, gorgeous? I promise to show you a beary good time."
"I do believe I have an urgent appointment to clip my nails tonight.
So sorry."

—"The Courtship of Arwen Mercant: A Story of Death Stares, Irresistible
Charm, and a Romantic Night in Jail" as told by Pavel Stepyrev

AT AROUND THE time that Yakov was falling back into a restless sleep, Pavel carefully unwrapped himself from around a sleeping Arwen and sat up to grab his glasses off the shelf next to the bed. Then he picked up his extremely high-spec organizer.

Produced by one of Kaleb Krychek's companies, it wasn't yet on the market and Pavel had bitten his tongue rather than ask Silver to use her connection to her former boss to get Pavel an early copy.

There were some things a good clanmate just did not do. No matter how much it pained his tech-adoring heart.

Then Ena had given it to him as a birthday present. "Arwen suggested a technological item when I asked him for ideas," the matriarch of the Mercant clan had said. "I assumed you wouldn't yet have had a chance to purchase this."

Pavel had been dumbstruck. Not only because of the coveted device in his hands, but because Ena had thought to get him a gift at all. "Thank you," he'd finally managed to say.

A steely-eyed look. "You make Arwen happy, and you're strong enough to save him from his own soft heart."

As far as compliments from Ena went, that was on par with being invited to the Sea House for dinner. Which Pavel had also now survived.

"Pasha bear?" A sleepy mumble as Arwen turned to curl himself around Pavel hip and leg.

His heart, it went all mushy. Every fucking time.

Petting his lover's naked shoulder until Arwen's breathing turned deep and even again, he pulled up the notification that had woken him. He'd set the notification to ping at a wavelength that wouldn't wake Arwen.

The results scrolled across his screen.

Medical jargon.

Didn't matter. He didn't have to know what it all *meant*. He just needed to find it. "Pasha, you're a genius," he muttered.

"Yes, you are," mumbled Arwen before falling back into sleep pressed up against Pavel.

Stupid smile on his face, Pavel leaned down to kiss Arwen's silky black hair. "I love you, you sweet, smart, and oh-so-sexy Psy."

Then he flexed his fingers and got to work.

Chapter 48

"Pasha bear? Have you been awake all night?"

"If I say yes, will you stay in bed longer and snuggle with me, my beautiful E with the prettiest lips I've ever seen?"

"Don't try that bear charm on me. I'm immu—Pasha! Stop that! I mean it! I have a meeting with Grandmother!"

"Take it back first, *moy luchik*. Say, 'Pasha bear, you are the most charming bear to ever charm his way into this world.'"

"Or maybe I'll just get revenge. Never forget my stabby ancestor."

"Did I ever tell you I read her poems to get inside intel on the Mercants when you were turning me down for dates to oil your cuticles and rearrange your spoon drawer?"

"Don't forget the time I had to walk my fish."

"That smart ass of yours needs to be spanked. Instead, I'm going to whisper 'Fragments of a Torn-up Letter' in your ear."

"My excitement knows no bounds. Such romance you give me, such passion."

"Oh, you'll be surprised, my delicious little E who I have trapped in my lair. It features the line 'Your thighs thrusting betw—'"

"You win. Kiss me right now, sexy Mr. Charming."

—Conversation between Pavel Stepyrev and Arwen Mercant
(5 September 2083)

. . .

THEO WOKE TO the sound of a phone alert.

A stir from the big body holding her, one arm reaching over her head to the bedstand to retrieve a phone. "Pasha, what is it?" was the question asked in a gruff morning voice that made her skin tighten and her toes curl into the sheets.

Whatever Pavel said had Yakov going still. "You're sure?" he asked at last.

Another silence.

Then: "Send me the address. Good work, bro."

After hanging up, he wrapped his arm around her again and said, "I know you're awake, *pchelka*." A nuzzle against her throat. "Sadly, we can't cuddle. My brother decided to be an insomniac after he had a great idea, and he's found us a lead. I'll tell you about it in the car. Ten minutes to get ready. We'll grab breakfast from the bakery."

Somehow it was easier to do this, face him again, when they were on a deadline. But once they'd picked up the food, she couldn't make herself touch the donut holes she'd previously eaten with gusto. She stuck instead to liquid nutrients. "What did your brother discover?"

Yakov finished off a breakfast roll as he drove. "You know how you looped him into the discussion with your brother regarding the pills we found?"

"Yes." It had been an easy decision, both because StoneWater was already in deep on this—and because Pavel was Yakov's twin.

Yes, she had her biases, but she would've never trusted Pavel so much without first learning to trust Yakov.

"Your brother messaged back while we were asleep, and Pasha being Pasha, he'd set up an alert for when the data came in. Once he had it, he decided to stay up all night writing a program cross-referencing any prescriptions of those drugs against people living in Moscow."

Theo frowned. "How could he get access to such sensitive data-bases?"

Coughing into his hand, Yakov said, "I can neither confirm nor deny that my twin has . . . a way with computronic security. As in, it doesn't seem to exist for him. Pasha walks through walls."

His pride in his twin was obvious. But Theo read between the lines. "He found a match." Her mouth went dry. "But Yasha, a number of those medications *are* used therapeutically."

"Yes, but that's not the match he found." Then he told her the combination of five drugs prescribed to a single *address* by two different doctors. "Two different people's names on the prescriptions, but chances are high that it's for one person. But no doctor would issue them together."

"So a partner or a friend faked symptoms to get the other part of the necessary regimen?" Theo inhaled shakily. "This would mean a *patient* is alive." That didn't make sense, not with what Theo knew of the people who'd run the facility. "How is that possible?"

"We'll find out soon—but that'll push our investigation of the possible burial sites off by hours, maybe even a day. You still don't want me to send a team out?"

Theo considered his question, shook her head. "The dead have waited for years. The living must have priority—especially if they could be a witness to what went on at the facility."

The idea of a survivor . . . Theo wanted to grip on to that hope, hold on tight, but a cold snake of uncertainty uncurled in her gut. "If they're still on the drugs," she said slowly, "they can't be free."

Yakov's arm muscles stiffened, the veins on his forearms taut. "If it's a staff member from that torture chamber holding them prisoner, then their time is up. No more hiding."

BLOOD dark and hot with the awareness that they might be about to come face-to-face with evil, Yakov brought the vehicle to a stop in front of a three-story apartment building in the suburbs of Moscow.

It wasn't one of those sleek but soulless structures that existed in certain Psy-heavy areas of the city; this was an older building, constructed of golden brick and with flourishes over the doorways and around the windows. Vines crawled up its sides, and it boasted two neat garden beds, one on each side of the pathway that led to the front entrance.

One bed held flower bushes that had been tidied up for their winter rest, with the odd tough bloomer still going in amongst them, while the other flourished with cold-weather vegetables. Yakov's father would be delighted to arrive at a property and see such thriving plants. From what Yakov could see from the street, both beds were in pristine condition, free of weeds and dead leaves.

The small but not negligible areas of lawn between the garden beds and the sidewalk provided further evidence of a gardener's care. There were no bare patches, no knots of weeds, and the area around the path had been clipped neatly.

"It feels too . . . nice?" Theo's voice lilted up at the end, as if she was searching for the right term to describe the place.

"Too homey," Yakov said. "No sense of the clinical."

"Exactly. Look there."

Following her pointed finger, he spotted the balcony that held the bright colors of a child's plas toys. "Families live here." He frowned. "No way this is a covert research facility—not unless the patient has been kept locked inside their room the entire time."

"It says a lot about my grandfather and the people he trusted that I can see that as a viable possibility." Theo's tone was taut, her eyes locked on the building.

But when he would've taken her hand, she wrenched it away.

"*Theo.*" He knew this was about the previous night, about the rage that had screamed out of her in a wave of violence.

Swallowing hard, she wrapped her arms around herself. "Did your brother uncover anything about our target residents?"

Yakov was more patient than many a bear, but he was no panda.

Except that today, he had to be; this was no place to have the conversation he and Theo needed to have. "Their trail in Moscow—in Russia overall—only begins almost exactly three years ago."

"Not long after my grandfather died." The same grating flatness to her tone.

"And," he added, "while one has more of a personal history in Italy, another in New Zealand, both those histories—and attendant records—come to an abrupt halt twenty-eight years ago." He showed her the latest ID photos of their two targets. "It's as if they vanished for a chunk of time, only to reappear in Russia."

Theo stared straight ahead now, and he wondered what she was seeing, because it surely wasn't this regular suburban street lined with trees, a passel of kids laughing in the playground only three lots down. "So," she said, her voice yet distant, "they could very well have been at the facility."

She opened the car door without waiting for him to reply, and he followed suit. When they met on the sidewalk, she said, "How should we approach this? There's no chance they'll recognize me as a Marshall, of that I'm certain. Almost no one in the world knows who I am."

"Their loss," Yakov muttered, wishing he could rip her fucking grandfather limb from limb. "I say we play it by ear." He crossed the street with Theo by his side, and it took all his years of training to keep from hauling her over and cuddling her until she melted. "Keep it friendly, see what we pick up. Most Moscow residents are happy to chat with bears, so we can use that."

The front door to the building opened right then, and a man who was maybe in his sixties shuffled out. And though he was barely middle-aged by 2083 standards, his back was slightly bowed, his brown hair thick with strands of gray.

Lines marked the tanned hue of his face, and his facial skin was lax.

He wore tough brown corduroy pants, along with a dark blue pull-over that he'd zipped up to the neck. His hands were clad in gardening gloves, and he carried a pair of clippers in his right one.

"We found the gardener," Yakov murmured, something about the man's scent nagging at him. "And our first target."

Chapter 49

I know you're sitting in the lounge downstairs, D, watching the results newscast with everyone, but I need to put my thoughts down on paper. And of course it must be in a letter to you. I'll finish it tonight and post it to you later, have it show up as a surprise.

After all this time, I can't believe it's happened. The referendum passed with a massive majority. We are to be Silent in every emotion, not only rage. The great irony of it is that on this momentous day, I sit here swamped in emotions: shock, fear, worry—but chief among them is hope.

For a better future for my baby girl. Neiza will grow up without fearing for her sanity, this I believe with every ounce of my soul.

—Letter from Hien Nguyen to Déwei Nguyen (21 August 1979)

THE GARDENER—WHOSE name was Santo Lombardi—looked up right then . . . and he had the loveliest eyes of soft green.

Eyes as guileless as a deer's.

They crinkled at the corners and it seemed as if he was about to smile. Then he flinched and took a couple of steps back. "I don't know you," he said, and turned to look over his shoulder in the direction of the door.

When no one exited, he turned back toward them. "I don't *know* you."

Fear pumped off him, reminding Yakov of a cub that had been

startled. So he went with instinct and treated Santo Lombardi with the same gentleness he would said cub. "I'm Yakov," he said. "A bear." He deliberately didn't introduce Theo, because he had the feeling this man would respond much better if he thought them both bears. "You've probably seen my clanmates around the city."

Santo peered suspiciously through narrowed eyes. "You don't have a bearskin," he said with the solemn seriousness of a young child who was sure he was being fooled.

Yakov grinned and lifted his hand. "Watch this," he said, then extended his claws.

Santo gasped and jumped back, and Yakov thought he'd made a critical mistake. Then a huge smile cracked the other man's thin face, lighting up those beautiful soft eyes. "Again!"

Laughing, Yakov retracted his claws, only to slice them back out. At the same time, he allowed his eyes to shift to the yellowish amber that came out in the bear in lower light, but that tended to be the first manifestation in his human skin of the bear rising to the surface.

"Bear," Santo said definitively.

The front door opened again right then, revealing a dark-skinned woman in her late twenties or early thirties, her hair in two neat braids that began at her temples and ended just above her shoulders. Well-fitted jeans and a poppy-red sweater outlined a compact body, her height between Theo's and Yakov's.

She wasn't looking at them, her focus on the person coming out behind her: another woman, the thinnest and smallest of the three. Closer to Santo in age. Huddled into a jacket of sunshine yellow, she wore dark brown pants.

"Janine Fong," Theo murmured. "Which one of them uses the prescriptions?"

It was impossible to tell at first glance. Janine's skin was milk pale with bluish undertones, the kind of skin that bruised with a touch. Her face, with its naturally high cheekbones and round eyes beneath epicanthic folds, didn't hold Santo's laxness, but she was more timid than him, sticking close to the side of the younger woman.

It was her hair that most struck Yakov: it was braided in the same style as her companion's, despite the clear difference in textures. Janine's braid was already slipping apart, strands escaping here and there.

Now, the younger woman shot Yakov and Theo a look of polite inquiry. "Are you here to visit a friend in the apartment building? Only, they'll have to buzz you in themselves."

That was when Yakov noticed how she balanced on her feet and realized that she wasn't a carer—or not only a carer—she was also security. "Actually, I wanted to speak to Santo." Never taking his attention off the younger woman, he smiled at the gardener. "It is Santo, isn't it?"

"He's a bear, Cissi!" Santo said to the carer-bodyguard, whose dark eyes had narrowed when Yakov stated the gardener's name. "I saw his claws!"

Suspicion morphing into worry, Cissi turned to her female charge. "Will you stay with Santo for a little while, Nene?" Her voice was kind, her tone even. "I need to talk to our new friends."

Santo opened up his arm and Janine Fong quickly shuffled over to lean against him, hiding her face in his chest.

"Why don't you show Nene your vegetables, Santo? I'll be over here with your new friend."

"Bear!" Santo said again, his grin huge. "I saw him first."

"I know, I know." Cissi laughed. "You can talk to him again after we've chatted, okay?"

It was clear from the way Santo nodded and began to lead Janine away that Cissi had built a strong bond of trust with the two. The younger woman's scent was twined into both of theirs—*Govno!*

Cold in his veins as he realized why his instincts had sparked at Santo's scent. But it had nothing to do with Santo. It had to do with someone Santo was around. *Fuck.* "I've got ID." Managing to keep his shock out of his voice as he spoke to Cissi, he reached into his pocket.

"No need, I've seen you at Club Moscow with your clanmates." A sheepish smile. "I'm sorry I didn't recognize you straight off the bat. I just wasn't expecting to see a senior bear outside our front door. You're a twin, right? I'm sure I've seen two of you at times—but that might've been the cocktails."

Chuckling took effort with his stomach in knots. "I'm Yakov. The other one is Pavel." He glanced at Theo. "And this is Theo."

Cissi's smile faded as she took in Theo. "You're not a bear. Psy."

"So are you," Theo said coolly. "You do a good job of appearing human—that comment about cocktails was excellent—but I can sense your psychic strength. I'd wager you're at least a 7."

The two women took each other's measure, before Cissi gave a crisp nod and broke the eye contact. "Why do you need to speak to Santo?" she asked Yakov.

Folding his arms, he set his feet apart. "First, I want to know who you are and what you're doing here."

No give in Cissi's expression. "StoneWater has no rights over Psy in its territory."

Woman had spine. Good. Those charged to protect should have spine.

"Per my research," he said, "Santo was a chemical analyst in his twenties." Unsurprisingly, he'd worked in an arm of the Marshall Group. "Not at the top of his field, but not at the bottom, either. Just a man doing a job and doing it well, from all his performance reviews." He held her gaze. "What happened to him?"

But Cissi stood with a gimlet expression, her hands on her hips.

Yakov groaned inwardly. He hated pulling out the big, bad bear routine, *especially* against a person he'd begun to respect. He'd much rather use charm or logic, but he had a feeling that wasn't going to work with this protective woman.

He reluctantly put on his mean face. "You live in bear territory." His voice was granite. "Do you really believe that the authorities will bother to step in to protect three random Psy from us?"

Of course StoneWater didn't just go around attacking innocent people—they weren't animals. Well . . . they were animals, but not that kind of animals. But despite the fact she'd been in Club Moscow, it was unlikely Cissi knew much more than surface information when it came to StoneWater. The vast majority of Psy still had a massive blind spot about changelings, believing violence their default.

Which reputation you haven't exactly helped with, Yakov Stepyrev.

Babushka Graciele's disappointed voice.

But his gambit worked. After glancing back at her charges, Cissi looked once more at him, then at Theo. She frowned, tilted her head, a strange confusion to her as she stared a beat too long at Theo. But when she spoke it was to Yakov.

"Name's Cecilia Bonet, but I go by Cissi. I became Santo's and Janine's carer three years ago—got the job through one of the listing sites. I had to submit to a security check, then an interview with their guardian, and I continue to be spot-checked."

"You also have security training yourself."

Cissi nodded. "That was my field in the time of Silence. I retrained as a carer afterward, and honestly, had no experience when I was given this job. Their guardian made it clear it was my security background that bagged me the position, but that I'd be out on my rear if I didn't care for them as required."

A softening in her as she looked back at Santo and Janine, who were now crouched by the garden, picking and eating what looked to be snow peas. Man had to have magic green fingers if he'd gotten a crop this early.

"I didn't know that about his work, the field he was in. Makes sense, though—every so often, he says words I don't understand, and when I look them up, they're almost always related to chemicals."

Theo stirred. "You did Janine's hair."

"What? Oh, yeah." Cissi smiled. "Neither needs assistance with hygiene, but Janine loves my braids. It's a mission to get them to hold in her hair; the strands are so slippery. I have to resort to fix-fast gel." Affection in each and every word. "Honestly, they're family now."

"Janine," Yakov said, staring at the small and skittish woman who hadn't spoken even to Santo, "she's a telekinetic."

Cissi nodded. "Used to work for a private family as a teleporter. Was groomed for the position at a young age, and the family must've had enough political power that she wasn't pulled into the Council's corps." The carer stared at Theo again, her forehead wrinkling up. "I'm sorry for being rude, but have we met?"

"Not as far as I know." Theo's voice was a touch too even. "Do you believe we have?"

Yakov understood Theo's wariness. Was it possible Cissi had been a staff member at the facility? But that didn't jibe with her relationship with her charges. Regardless, he took out his phone and tapped in a quick request to his brother: Work/residence history for Cecilia "Cissi" Bonet. Lives at the address you sent me this morning.

He slid away his phone as Cissi shook her head. "I get the strongest sense of what the humans call déjà vu when I look at you. Did you live in Missouri as a child? I grew up there."

"No," Theo answered. "I must just remind you of someone."

"Yes, that's probably it."

"Santo's and Janine's guardian," Yakov said, "you have their details?"

Cissi stiffened up again, folding her arms across her chest. "What's this all about?" A hard line to her jaw. "These two are wounded and unable to defend themselves. I won't allow you or anyone else to hurt them."

Theo spoke before Yakov could. "We're here in an effort to make restitution," she said. "There's a chance my family is responsible for their current mental and physical state. If so, we need to be paying for their expenses and any related medical costs. Our new CEO believes in accountability."

Cissi took a single step back. "Their guardian made it clear that that's already the situation. The apartment, my salary, the food, everything. Either your new CEO has the wrong information—or you're lying to me."

"Ah." Theo nodded slowly. "Yes, that explains the financial draw."

"We still need to speak to the guardian," Yakov said. "There's a chance there are more survivors in the same condition as Janine and Santo—Theo's been tasked to make sure that every single one of them is being cared for to this high standard. StoneWater has offered its support to track down the victims."

A cold chill in Cissi's eyes. "I knew it," she bit out. "I knew it wasn't an accident that hurt them. It was a Center, wasn't it? That's why the bears are involved—I've heard through the grapevine about how the former Centers now have human and changeling oversight."

She shook her head before they could answer. "Don't tell me. I don't want that nastiness in my head. As for their guardian, I won't give her up. Not when she's protected them for this long." She faced Yakov full on. "You can hurt me but that won't give you what you want."

Yakov's bear hid its head in its paws, feeling like a bully. "Look, Cissi, we mean your charges no harm, but it's critical we get in touch with their guardian. Will you pass on a message to her?"

"Yes, of course. I want only the best for Santo and Janine—and anyone else who might've survived a Center."

Yakov glanced at Theo.

Who picked up the baton. "Tell their guardian that the management has changed. And that we've found the leak. We have no intention of plugging it up, but we need all the facts."

Cissi gave a crisp nod. "I'll repeat it word for word. It might take her a few days to get back to you—she's not in the country right now and doesn't always have the best reception."

"Understood." After giving the woman their contact details, Yakov said, "One more question—other than you and their guardian, does anyone else have access to Janine or Santo?"

"Santo is friendly with others in the complex," Cissi said. "Nene—Janine—rarely talks, and tends to stick close to him or me. They're never out of my sight for longer than a few minutes except when they're asleep in their beds, if that's what you're asking."

Yakov left it at that, asking no further questions. Instead, he spoke to Santo as promised, while Janine stared at Theo for long moments before walking over to give her a snow pea pod.

Next to Yakov, Cissi whistled quietly under her breath. "I've never seen her be so friendly with a stranger."

Taking the pod, Theo said, "Thank you. Can I eat it just like this?"

Janine ran over to the patch, came back with another pod, then showed Theo how to remove the bit of "thread" along the seam that could get stuck in teeth. Discarding that bit into the garden, she mimed crunching down on the vegetable, then watched with care as Theo followed her instructions.

Her face broke out in a big smile when Theo began to eat the snow peas. A second later, Janine threw her arms around Theo and said, "Keke, I love you," in a voice soft and sweet.

Chapter 50

Cecilia Bonet began paying taxes in Moscow three years ago. Work listed as private carer of two individuals.
Prior to that, she was paying taxes in the USA. It's listed as her country of birth, and she worked there all her life before coming to Moscow. Gap of a year in her résumé that aligns with a new educational certificate in caregiving.
All looks clean and aboveboard. Full details attached.

—Message from Pavel Stepyrev to Yakov Stepyrev (11 a.m. today)

THEO WAVED FROM the car as Cissi led Santo and Janine up the walkway toward the front door of the apartment building. Janine and Santo both waved back wildly, and kept on doing so until Cissi got them inside.

Pausing on the doorstep, the carer shot them a quick wave and a smile before she entered behind her charges.

"That was an interesting day," Yakov said as he pulled away from the curb.

Because it had been a day. Janine had become so attached to Theo in the short time they'd spent together that she'd become distressed when Theo made a move to leave with Yakov.

Wishing she could read the thoughts inside the woman's deliberately damaged mind, Theo had nonetheless known one thing: she couldn't hurt this person who'd been broken by her family. If Janine, for some reason, found happiness in her, then Theo would stay with her as long as it took.

She and Yakov had ended up working in the garden with the two, then had taken the pair and Cissi out to lunch, followed by ice cream. After which, they'd gone for a long walk along the river, with Santo and Janine stopping to pet dogs, while Yakov ran into more than one person he knew.

It was after lunch, when Cissi pulled out a small bag of pills to give to Santo one by one, that they'd been given the answer to one of their questions.

"Those are strong medications," Theo had said quietly when Yakov escorted Santo to the washroom, and Janine was distracted by the aquarium wall in the restaurant. "Especially in combination."

Cissi had nodded. "When I first started the job, I figured out two by searching the marks on them. Got freaked out." A tightness to her expression, she'd said, "I brought it up to their guardian, told her I'd refuse to be part of any form of drug abuse."

"What was the response?"

"She said that she wished she could wean Santo off them as she had Nene, but that the 'accident' and the drugs he'd been given in the aftermath had permanently reset Santo's entire system. He seems to need them to remain stable and sane."

Cissi had pressed her lips together. "To put my mind at ease, to make sure I'd follow the regimen, she placed Santo on half doses for a day so I could see the impact." A shuddering breath. "I felt so awful after, even though she took full responsibility for the decision. He . . . becomes lost in nightmare. Garbled speech, whimpers, loss of physical functions, and worst of all, he screams as if he's trapped in a hellish inner landscape."

The reaction could as well have been shock at a sudden reduction of dosage, but Theo didn't believe the guardian's act showed malice, not when Janine was free of medication. "Did she say how long she tried to wean him off?"

"Longer than with Nene, but he never comes out the other side, and she couldn't stomach it anymore." Cissi's voice had been thick. "She loves them, Theo. Trust me on that. My Silence is shit because while my main ability is telepathy, I have low-level E abilities. I only survived the Council because I buried that part of me out of self-preservation."

Laughter bitter and ragged. "But I'm through with hiding—and that bit of E in me means I'm not fooled by fake Psy emotion. It's the real deal. If she could get him free of the drugs, she would. That terrible day, she got into bed with him and hugged him and rocked him until he finally fell asleep. It took hours but she never left, never gave up."

Now, with the sky growing dusky as they drove back to the apartment, and Yakov's presence a living warmth that surrounded her, she found herself thinking of this mysterious guardian. Who could it be? A staff member who'd disagreed with what was going on at the facility?

"Who's Keke?" The rumble of Yakov's voice, the pitch of it resonating deep within her, an imprint she would never forget, no matter how long she lived.

It would hurt to be away from him.

Shoving that aside because her selfish wants couldn't have priority here, she said, "I wish I knew. I've checked all my mental files and as far as I know, no one with that name—or nickname—is part of my family, worked for my family, or was otherwise connected to us."

Yakov tapped a finger on the steering wheel. "Not a stretch to assume it's their guardian. Obviously has to be a person who knew the ins and outs of the facility's finances well enough to get access to the stream of money your grandfather earmarked for it—and clever enough to have hidden it all this time."

Theo stared out the windshield. "And a good person," she found herself saying. "She saved those people, Yasha. My family doesn't save people. We hurt and kill people. She's not of our blood."

"Bullshit, Theo." His tone was harder than she'd ever before heard it. "Stop telling yourself that. You're doing exactly the same thing right now. Trying to save people, help people."

Theo wanted to believe that, believe that she had a seed of goodness in her. She had once upon a time. She'd saved that bird with Pax, had felt good about it. But it had been a long time since she was a child. A long time for her grandfather to twist her into a creature of his own making.

Unable to confront the likelihood of her own conscious involvement in evil, she thought back to something Yakov had said right at the start of the day, but that she'd let slide through the surreal beauty of what followed. "How did you know that Janine was a telekinetic? Was it in her records?"

A shake of his head. "There were far fewer records for her than for Santos. Makes sense if she was working directly for your family." His chest fell and rose in a deep inhale, followed by the rush of an exhale. "I caught her scent at the site of the murder, Theo." His words were heavy rocks falling into a glacial pond, cracking through the ice to spread chaos. "Not at the initial site, but at the pickup location in the forest. She teleported the murderer out."

Theo's skin was suddenly aflame. "Someone is taking advantage of a person who can't say no."

"No," Yakov murmured. "It's worse than that. It has to be someone she trusts. Someone to whom she *doesn't* say no. Otherwise, she'd have told Cissi. The trust there is pure—but she trusts the murderer more."

Bones grinding as she clenched her jaw, Theo forced herself to think beyond her anger. Always there, that anger, that rage. Like a furnace she couldn't switch off. "Obviously you've cleared Cissi?"

"Yes. Nothing of her scent at the site except as a secondary thread in Janine's. And Pasha found nothing suspicious in her history." He squeezed the steering wheel. "Which leaves us with their mysterious guardian."

But Theo shook her head. "If we accept that Cissi has the correct information and their guardian is out of the country, then I'd say no. It would require an immense amount of power for Janine to teleport that far to pick her up, drop her off, then return herself. She's strong, but she's not a cardinal."

At 6.1, Janine fell into the relatively rare cadre of Tks who were teleport-capable at under 8 on the Gradient. Her range was limited, as was her endurance. Quite aside from Marshall Hyde's power, that was likely why she'd ended up in private service rather than a soldier.

Thrusting a hand through his hair, Yakov frowned. "Which means either their guardian *is* nearby, or it's another person."

"Someone in the complex?"

"No hint of the killer's scent around the building. Doesn't make sense if they're a resident—it'd be embedded by dint of simple repetition."

Theo chewed on the inside of her lip, a dawning horror creeping across her vision. "What if someone else survived the Center?" she said slowly. "A person Janine trusts. Trusts enough not to tell Cissi *or* her guardian about them."

"It might not be a patient." Yakov passed a slower vehicle, his hands easy on the vehicle controls but his expression grim. "What if the sur- vivor was a member of the staff? Easy enough to gain the trust of a patient like Janine if you have constant access to her—a little kindness and she could have come to see the staff member as a friend. A twisted individual playing the long game, keeping a teleporter in their back pocket."

Theo's rage burned in her skin, was a haze in her vision. "What do we do? How do we stop it from happening again?"

"I spoke to Cissi while you and the others were looking at the ducks in the river," Yakov said. "I told Cissi that I picked up Janine's scent at the location of a brutal crime. Made it clear I didn't think she was the perpetrator, but that she *was* leaving the apartment without Cissi's knowledge.

"Turns out Cissi has access to medication intended to calm Janine and put her to sleep in the aftermath of a severe panic attack. Cissi doesn't like using it, but she also understands that it's the only way to keep Janine safe."

Theo could tell he didn't like the only viable solution. Neither did she. But whether she knew or not, Janine was an accessory to murder. Leaving her free to teleport at will could lead to another bloody scene. "Will you inform Enforcement?"

Yakov pressed his lips together. "No. Cops will try to interrogate her, and she's not capable. I also don't think she'll ever share her secret—not if she's kept it from Cissi all this time. She'll just break."

"It's a short-term solution."

"Only tonight." Yakov squeezed the steering wheel. "Tomorrow, Cissi said she'll take them to a public place, where Janine can't teleport away in secret. But she's not willing to drug her again and I'm not about to ask her to—we'll have to find another way to deal with it."

"There's really no way to keep a teleport-capable telekinetic locked up unless you cage their mind, and no one has the right to cage an innocent being's mind." Because Theo was certain that whatever it was Janine had done, she'd had no intent to participate in the brutalization and murder of others.

"We may be able to get away with intensive psychic surveillance," Yakov said. "I'll talk to Silver—she has connections upon connections. Including any number of deadly minds that'll keep her secrets."

Theo could feel control over the whole situation with the facility slipping out of her hands, panic a fluttering beast inside her. But there was no choice now. Others *were* involved. Others who'd been hurt far worse than her. She'd give them every advantage she could. "Maybe their guardian will get in touch with us tonight."

"We can hope. If she doesn't, I'll talk to Silver about arranging psychic surveillance, and we can head out to the facility."

"Yes, that sounds like a good plan," Theo said, knowing she had to update Pax and soon. "Did you get a report back on those pages we found?"

"Yes, I forgot to tell you—I forwarded it to your account. Came in while we were with the others. It's just a standard run sheet for the facility. Time of meds, time for outdoor exercise, that type of thing."

Theo felt herself deflate. She'd known it was highly unlikely those pages had anything to do with her, but still she'd hoped. Because she needed to *know*. Couldn't move forward with that hole in her memories and in her mind.

"We'll find the answers you need, Thela." A rough promise, Yakov brushing his hand over her hair as he brought the vehicle to a standstill in front of a red light.

His phone beeped before she could reply. He'd connected it to the car's system and the name on the screen in the middle of the dashboard said: *Mama Bear.*

"Ma doesn't usually call without reason," he said, then gave the command to answer the call, following with: "Ms. Mama Bear Kuznets." He said with a grin, "I have you on speaker. Theo is in the passenger seat."

"Good" was the firm response. "You can bring her to dinner with the family. In one hour. The cantina." Then she hung up.

Yakov groaned. "I do believe my mother has heard about our escapades at Club Moscow and about the fact I've been spending nights with you in the apartment. She has mother radar."

Theo felt her cheeks burn, couldn't quite understand her reaction. "She's angry."

Grinning, Yakov shook his head. "No, that's what she always sounds like when she's giving an executive order. Disobey at your own peril." But once they got going again, he glanced over at her. "If you're not up for it, I'll say no. I might be scared of my mother, but I'm not a total chicken."

Theo swallowed hard, and it was the rawness in her throat that decided her. "I'm dangerous," she said. "I shouldn't be around any of your family. Especially if there are young children." She thought of the cubs, so sweet and trusting, that she'd met in the bakery, felt her heart stop at the idea of causing them harm. "You saw how I get, Yasha. I don't know who I am. I forget how to be rational."

Yakov's bear was in his voice when he rumbled, "You can sit next to me, and if there's a wall available, we'll put you against it. I know the signs now. It'll fucking kill me, but I promise I'll knock you out the instant your expression turns vacant."

Need a keening echo in her brain, Theo resisted the temptation to just say yes. "During the rages, I siphon power from Pax. I'm not a 2.7 then."

"You're also wearing that bracelet that I want to throw into a lake. You said it's an early warning system."

Theo looked down at the metal encircling her wrist. She'd fixed it, then secretly tested it in the bathroom. The pain had stabbed right into her bones. "Yes," she said on a little bubble of hope so fragile and fine. "At its current setting, you'll have a second, maybe two at most."

"I always have a stunner on me. A second is all I need."

Theo had been looking at—admiring—his body for days now, but she'd never once spotted the weapon. He was better than good, she realized, the knowledge a breath of freedom. "No hesitation?"

"No hesitation," he promised. "The last thing I want is for a bunch of rampaging bears to pounce on you." The brush of his knuckles against her cheek. "I want you to meet my family, Theo. And I want them to meet the woman of my dreams."

Theo's reservations crumbled under the primal caress in his voice. "Okay."

Chapter 51

"Without your brother, and given the powerful influence of the Psy Council
and their mandates, we could well have crossed the line from ruthless to
cruel. He is our conscience and our soul."

—Ena Mercant to Silver Mercant (date unknown)

ARWEN WAS MORE than used to bears by now. He adored the trouble-
making, loving, loud changelings. And, following his infamous stint in
a jail cell beside Pasha and several other bears, StoneWater had decided
that he was an honorary bear—despite his "slick" suits and "shiny" shoes.

He might've taken the ribbing on his dress sense seriously if he
hadn't (a) seen Pasha himself in a suit one memorable time, and (b) met
Zahaan. Bears, with their wide shoulders and changeling-hard bodies,
could pull off suits like nobody's business. It was a crime that of all of
them, Zahaan alone seemed to appreciate that fact.

Arwen's tailor bemoaned that fact every time he went in for a fitting.

It did make it all the more special that Pasha had done it for Arwen
the day they'd gone to the Sea House for dinner. He had, in fact, been
so well-behaved that night that it was disconcerting. Arwen loved that
his bear had made the effort as a gesture of respect to Grandmother, but
chert he'd been glad to get home and see *his* Pasha again.

The jeans-wearing rogue whose idea of fancy was a new T-shirt.

Today, given the occasion, Arwen had gone for casual—possible since he hadn't come straight from a formal work commitment: a pair of dark blue jeans paired with a black shirt that had a triangular piece of detailing that angled down from one shoulder to about three quarters of the way across his chest.

That detailing echoed a weaving technique from the island of Niue in the Pacific—a nod to the designer's homeland. He'd thrown a simple black blazer over it all, albeit a blazer that had been structured to his frame by the same master tailor who had his heart broken by bears each and every day.

Pavel had whistled when he'd first emerged from the bedroom after changing, and Arwen hadn't been able to stop his pleased blush. He'd brushed nonexistent dust off Pavel's muscled shoulders, his lover dressed in a faded gray T-shirt with the emblem of a rock band and olive green cargo pants, his favorite scuffed boots on his feet.

With his metal-framed eyeglasses paired with that tight senior StoneWater dominant body, he'd looked ridiculously hot, a piercingly intelligent and competent man who could get the job done, then haul his lover back to his lair for a night of debauchery.

Arwen was quite happy to be so debauched.

But what he loved even more was the way his Pasha bear touched him. A little brush of his finger over Arwen's hip as they passed, the way his leg pressed against Arwen's after they were seated around the large family-size table at the cantina, how he put his arm over the back of Arwen's chair. The best thing was that he knew it wasn't a special effort—this was who he was: an affectionate, touchy bear.

Turning to grin at Arwen now, his killer dimples on gorgeous display, he said, "How about that? We beat everyone here."

"That's because I was in the city already, and you drove in early to run a maintenance check on the computronic security system at Yakov and Theo's building."

"Details, details."

Arwen's smile was in his heart itself. "You find anything hinky?"

"Nope. Yasha's got good instincts, but whatever is setting them off, it's not in the computronics. Clean and locked down. As it should be— it was built by the best hacker in Moscow." Slipping a finger under the edge of one blazer sleeve, he rubbed the fabric between thumb and forefinger. "I like this."

Arwen's toes curled. "You want to stay in the city tonight? No clubbing, just a walk along the river and cuddling on the couch. House is free and I already have an overnight bag there from my last visit. Complete with a spare toothbrush for my Pasha bear."

It was his grandmother who'd purchased the house, but she never used it these days now that StoneWater had given her a suite in the den—a suite so far away from the bright joy of the communal areas that no bear was excited at the thought of living there. Valentin hadn't wanted to offer it to Ena when Silver suggested it would suit better than another set of rooms that Ena had used once or twice by then.

"I don't want to insult your grandmother, Starlichka," he'd said to Silver in Arwen's hearing, his hands on his hips and his face set in confused lines. "It's so far away from the heart of the den. So quiet and lonely."

Which made it perfect for a Psy who had lived in Silence all her life—but who had come to feel great affection for the bear clan that was now part of the Mercant family. Because while the bears thought they'd co-opted the Mercants, Ena was equally certain that the Mercants now had a bear arm.

Arwen found the entire thing delightful.

As it was, his grandmother tended to stay in her den suite when she visited the city, and she was happy for her children and grandchildren to use the Moscow house as long as they left it pristine in the aftermath for the rare times she dropped by to use the living area for an informal meeting.

Arwen often deliberately left a cup out of place, or a jacket hanging on the back of the door, just to play with her. She'd always give him the most severe look when they next spoke, but he could feel her emotions and he knew he was loved. He also knew he was getting worse at the playfulness after hanging around with bears. Especially his Pasha bear.

Who leaned over to nuzzle at him now, his jaw freshly shaven in honor of the family dinner. "I'll be your river-walk-and-cuddle date—as long as you buy me ice cream from that cart along the riverside." A rumble that traveled through Arwen's bones.

Arwen felt his cheeks crease and wondered if he'd ever not smile around Pavel. "I'll even spring for a triple scoop."

"You know how to treat a man." Sitting back, Pavel took a sip of his water, all casual muscle. As if he wasn't built like a god.

"How did your phone call with Ivan go?" Pavel asked.

Arwen scowled, his happy thoughts of sinking his teeth into all that muscle flying out of his head. "My cousin told me to stop hovering. Can you believe that? I do not *hover.*"

Throwing back his head, Pavel laughed that big beautiful laugh that was a lethal weapon. "Oh, *moy luchik,*" he murmured, waves of affection blanketing Arwen's senses in a bearish caress, "you are the number one hoverer among all the hoverers I know."

Arwen tried to look affronted. It was difficult. When Pavel laughed like that, with such good humor, it lit up Arwen's entire world. "I just know how to look after my people," he said primly. "Anyway, he's fine. Settling into the pack like 'a born cat'—as per my confidential source in the pack."

Pavel rubbed his jaw. "I can see it. Mercants definitely remind me of cats. Slinky, smart, stealthy—and loyal to the core. My Mercant, though, he also has a heart big enough to love the entire world." His voice softened on that last, those gorgeous eyes of his touched by the bear's yellow-hued amber as he leaned in toward Arwen.

"So," boomed Dedushka Viktor's voice, "when are you two giving me great-grandchildren? I'm not getting any younger. And I know you already have volunteers willing to step up for the hardest part of the whole operation. Heat each other up, produce fresh seed, and next thing you know, DNA is spliced and you have a cub born of both of you and their mother."

Groaning, Pavel turned and dropped his head to the table, proceeding to bang his forehead against it in a repetitive motion. Arwen, well used to dealing with a strong-willed grandparent, rose to his feet and held out his hand to Pavel's maternal grandfather. "We're not mature enough yet," he said with a straight face. "Maybe in a decade or three."

Instead of shaking his hand, the redheaded man responsible for the astonishing aqua green of Pavel's eyes reached out to clap big tanned hands on either side of Arwen's face. "Smartass." A grin that lit up those familiar eyes. "Perfect fit for the family." Then he pressed a kiss on Arwen's forehead before releasing him from his grip.

Arwen couldn't stop smiling as he walked around the table to greet Pavel's babushka Quyen. As tall as Pavel but with bones as fine as a bird's, Pavel's grandmother—and Viktor's mate—was as sweet as her husband was salty. She also gave the most amazing hugs with those thin but strong arms.

As he received one of her magic hugs, Arwen thought again of how he loved this—that Pavel's family was as tight as his own.

The only reason Pavel's paternal grandparents weren't going to be at this dinner was that they'd gone to China to spend a couple of months with their daughter's family. She'd mated into a clan of black bears there, and had recently given birth to a cub. Which might explain Dedushka Viktor's desire to hurry Pavel and Arwen along.

Cub fever. It was contagious.

"Viktor," Babushka Quyen said after she'd greeted Arwen. "Leave the boys alone. You know it embarrasses the young generation." A confused wave of the hand at the clearly newfangled thinking. "We're not supposed to know about the sex that produces the seed," she said in a whisper no doubt heard from one end of the room to the other.

An unrelated bear out on a date doubled over in a sudden coughing fit just then.

Feeling his skin go bright red, Arwen returned to his seat beside

Pavel, then dropped his face to the table and began to bang his forehead against the honey-colored wood of it.

Pavel patted his back. "It gets better. After a while, your forehead becomes stronger, doesn't hurt as much."

Arwen's shoulders shook at his lover's commiserating tone, and he was laughing out loud by the time he sat back up. Embarrassment of their grandcub complete for the moment, Pavel's grandparents had taken the seats across from them and were discussing the menu, but the whole table erupted into movement again when Mila and Akili walked in.

Pavel's tall and stunning mother, with those brilliant Kuznets family eyes and hair as red as passion, had grilled Arwen up one side and down the other when he first began to date Pavel.

Arwen absolutely adored her.

He'd grown up in a family of powerful and loving women, and was predisposed to worship their badassery.

To his great relief, the emotion was mutual.

When he rose to greet her, she kissed him on both cheeks, then pushed one lapel of his blazer aside so she could see the detail on his shirt. "What an intricate and creative design," said the only bear in the family who cared about fashion—as evidenced by the stylish green off-the-shoulder sweater she'd paired with formfitting black jeans and black boots with visible silver zippers.

"And *ai*, my Pavka is still wearing that old T-shirt. People will think StoneWater doesn't pay you," she scolded her son, even as her love wrapped him up in a hug even before she kissed his cheeks.

Pavel's father, Akili, took Arwen's hand and drew him into a hug that ended with a companionable slap on the back. He was a few inches shorter than his mate, but built wider, with acres of heavy muscle. His skin was rich brown, his hair tight black curls that had skipped a generation, and his palm bore the calluses of a man who worked with the soil and the earth, his face creased with laugh lines.

"Oi!" Viktor said when Mila went to Quyen first. "Favoritism!" he complained morosely. "How quickly they forget which parent pretended to be a damn grass-eating horse for them."

Mila laughed, conversation overlapped, loud and vibrant, and in that moment, Arwen could all but see the luminous threads of love that crisscrossed the family. It was in this generous and affectionate soil that Pavel had been planted, and where he'd grown.

As had the man who walked in just then, Theo's hand held in his.

The movement around the table was quieter this time, the family taking in Theo with the same careful intensity with which they'd first taken in Arwen. He could feel her trepidation, the tension in every cell in her body. But Theo Marshall was used to hiding her emotions, used to putting on a stone face, and it was that face she showed Yakov's family.

O Bozhe! Arwen wanted to leap across and whisper that that wasn't the way to win the hearts of this group, but it was too late, and she was exchanging stiff greetings with each of the elders before sliding into a chair next to Pavel, with Yakov on her other side.

Chapter 52

Knew you wouldn't get back till late so made you your favorite pasta and left it on the counter. Insulated container so it'll stay hot. Watered your plant while I was there—poor abused thing looked about to keel over. I like your cat.

I don't have a cat.

I think you have a cat now. Little bitty orange ball of fluff was sunning herself inside your apartment when I walked in. I went out to the grocer and got her a fresh piece of fish.

A cat can't just move into my apartment.

I see you've never met a cat.

You're joking right? Funny. Haha. But thanks for the food, Arwen. You're a good friend.

(2 hours later)

Arwen, there's a cat on my bed. It's ... meowing. What do I do with it?

Just love her. Easy.

—Message stream between Arwen Mercant and Genara Mercant
(15 July 2083)

HE SHOULD'VE TELEPATHED her, Arwen thought too late, feeling awful about not thinking to give her a heads-up. He'd been around bears far longer, knew exactly how they reacted to coldness.

Pavel's hand on his neck, massaging with the firm strokes that he knew Arwen loved. "Stop worrying," his lover murmured in his ear, quiet enough that it would reach Arwen alone. "Yakov's Psy can take care of herself. You just look after my Psy. He's pretty special."

Arwen's heart melted.

He didn't know how he'd been lucky enough to find such an all-encompassing love—and such a *good* man. Pasha called him loyal, but no one did loyal better than a bear. Once they found their people, bears stuck like superglue.

Arwen wanted the same kind of love for Theo. Because he could see the emotional bruises on her with stark clarity now. He wasn't reading her. She'd just lowered her guard with him . . . had begun to trust him in a way subtle and unexpected. Theo might put on a stone face, but below that, she was a softness of wounds.

She needed warmth and love and acceptance.

"I want this to go well for her and for Yasha," he whispered to Pavel. "She's not like how she's portraying herself."

Pavel raised an eyebrow. "Silver," he said in a quiet reminder. "Not exactly cuddly. Ever." A chuckle. "And, you might not have noticed, but we adore her. Let Theo do her thing."

Arwen went to reply, then shut his mouth. Pavel was right. His sister wasn't only the StoneWater alpha's mate in word, she was treated that way by the entire clan. They saw past her outwardly icy demeanor to a love for the clan as deadly and protective as a blade.

Bears, he remembered, were far, far cleverer than they liked to pretend.

"So," Viktor boomed, "I hear you're taking advantage of Yakov."

Theo's eyes widened . . . but she didn't look away from the dominant bear. "I'm quite certain that there are very few people in the world who could take advantage of your grandson," she said with diction precise and tone calm, while Yakov sat beside her with a smug look on his face.

The look of a bear who was proud of the person they'd chosen as their own. And the nonchalance of a man who knew his person could handle what was being thrown at them.

"Your grandson is a man of courage and heart," Theo continued with zero fear. "I'm grateful for his assistance. You should feel lucky to have him in your family—in no situation is it acceptable to question his independence or will."

Oh. My. God. *Theo!*

Arwen was never going to forgive himself for letting her walk into this unprepared.

Viktor's eyes turned into narrow green windows. "You remind me of someone, Theo," he said after a long pause. "My mama. She also had a way of telling me I was talking bullshit in an extremely polite tone of voice."

Yakov, who'd taken a sip of water, almost spit it out. His grinning father slammed a fist helpfully on his back. Mila, on the other hand, reached over and poured Theo a glass of the nutrients they'd ordered as part of the drinks order for the table.

And Arwen finally breathed long enough to catch the emotions being broadcast . . . and realized that Theo had just won the respect of the patriarch of this family.

Pavel squeezed Arwen's thigh under the table, shooting sensation electric and exciting right to his cock. He blushed, still not used to thinking in such raw terms. But Pavel's words, when they came, were teasing and tender rather than sensual. "See, Arlusha *moy*," he murmured, "Theo's fine. You can strike her off your 'watch over and worry' list."

Arwen made a face at him. "What if I can't help it?" Worrying about the people who mattered to him was second nature—and for some reason, Theo Marshall, of all people, had made it onto his list.

It was the bruises, he thought, the ones she hid from all the world.

Pavel dropped a kiss on his ear, and Arwen could feel the heat of it going pink. "I know you can't help it," his bear murmured. "Your heart is huge and open and quite frankly"—a scowl—"gives me anxiety. I'm forever worrying about how thin you'll spread yourself if you're not careful."

Reaching for his beer, he threw back half of it in a gulp before slamming it down on the table and meeting Arwen's gaze again, his own the primal hue of his bear. "But I'm more than up for a lifetime of anxiety if I get to spend it with you."

Chapter 53

I need your help to make this work, big brother. Being Silent this way . . . it's hard. But I have to try. We all have to try. For Neiza.

I thought moving away from Mom and Dad and our younger brothers, as well as you and Marian, would make it easier, but it's still so difficult even though Kanoa's extended family pulled strings to make sure Neiza and I were in the first intake of Mercury's Fundamentals of Silence Parent/ Child course.

The Adelajas have been truly amazing in their support. You know how important they are, how much Catherine and Arif Adelaja contributed to the development of Silence. I never expected the family to offer such support to the widow of a second cousin who wasn't part of their inner circle. But they've embraced me—and especially Neiza.

In fact, the family has invited me to move into their compound.

They've lived life in Silence (as it is now) long before the referendum made it mandatory, and as such are far further along in their adherence to the Protocol. It's an extraordinary opportunity for Neiza and since my work can be done remotely, I'm going to take them up on the invitation.

This is where I need your help, D. Please don't call me, or send me any letters touched with emotion. Articles of interest, subjects we can argue about with pure logic, health updates stripped down to the medical basics, that's all I can handle as I settle into this new way of life.

Thank you from your younger sibling,
Hien

—Letter from Hien Nguyen to Déwei Nguyen (9 June 1980)

.   .   .

THEO HAD NEVER been around a family this loud and affectionate. This *open* to life. They all seemed to know what was going on with the others, multiple overlapping conversations taking place at once. Not only that, but they kept moving around the table—though Yakov never left her side, some part of his body always in contact with her own.

More movement. Now it was Yakov's delicately lovely babushka Quyen who sat at the end of the table, at a right angle from Theo. The quietest member of the family gave her a gentle smile, her uptilted eyes a kind hazel with greenish edges and her hair cut in a stylish bob. The strands were a silky and heavy brown with gold highlights. The kind of hair that fell back into place after being mussed up.

Just like Yakov's.

How extraordinary, Theo thought, to sit at this table and see so many of the people from whom Yakov and his brother had inherited pieces of their genetic makeup. Nothing cold or remote about it, DNA only a small part of the tapestry of their shared history.

"Tell me about yourself, Theo," Babushka Quyen said, and it was no demand but rather genuine interest. "Do you have any brothers or sisters?"

Theo's heart fluttered. Being able to acknowledge her relationship with Pax would never be something she took for granted. "A brother," she said, as Yakov spoke to his grandfather, the deep timbre of their voices beautiful background music. "A twin."

His grandmother's pupils flared. "Oh, that mischief bear," she said, glancing at Yakov. "He never once mentioned that."

Theo wondered when Yakov would've had time to talk to his family about her at all, but she took the words at face value. And she decided to speak the rest of her hidden truth. "We weren't allowed to grow up as twins, were separated at seven years of age." A grief that would live forever in her, but that had been tempered by her new bond with Pax even as Scarab Syndrome raised its lethal head.

Though the pain of the reminder squeezed her chest, she tried to focus on the good. "We've found each other as adults, though, and we've become a family." Odd to say that surrounded by such a loud and boisterous one, but for her and Pax, their quiet loyalty to each other was family, too.

She knew at that instant that she wanted to introduce her brother to Yakov, to show Yakov her family as he'd shown her his. It mattered to her that the two most important men in her life connect . . . that they like each other.

Babushka Quyen made no effort to hide her anger on Theo's behalf, her face set in grim lines. When she reached out a fine-boned hand toward Theo's, Theo turned hers palm up in silent welcome.

The older woman's grip was tight, her shoulders set. "I can't believe anyone would do that to any siblings, much less twins." She nodded at Pavel and Yakov. "Our two mischief bears have always been peas in a pod. Very much their own individual people right from day one, but their bond as brothers? It's extraordinary."

"I feel it anytime they're together," Theo said. "As I feel the embers of it glowing between Pax and me." It was so easy to talk to this gentle nonjudgmental woman that she added, "I want my brother and Yasha to meet. I'm not sure how it'll go, however. Pax can be protective."

"That's a good sign in a brother. As long as he's not overbearing." Babushka Quyen patted at their clasped hands with her other one, her touch warm and full of love. "Though I think you're plenty strong enough to take on even such a brother."

The elder's gaze went to her mate, her expression soft. "My love adored his mama, you know, so it's a great compliment for him to compare you to her. I wanted you to know that."

She squeezed Theo's hand. "Spine like iron, my mother-in-law. I thought for sure that she'd hate me on sight. I'm her opposite, you see. Soft and born wanting to please. But I should've known that the woman who'd raised my Vitüsha had a generous heart.

"She told me that all she'd ever wanted for her son was that his mate love him as deeply as she knew he'd love them. And that there wasn't a single doubt in her mind on that point where I was concerned." Another gentle pat of their clasped hands as Babushka Quyen turned her lovely eyes on Theo once more. "That's all we want for our grandcubs, too. Just love our Yashka, Theo."

A thousand cracks across Theo's heart, the organ fracturing under the pressure of her primal, potent emotions for Yakov. She knew she couldn't set those emotions free. She wasn't normal. Would never *be* normal. It wasn't that she had a surface scar. The damage was in her brain. The rages could strike at any moment, destroying everyone in her path.

Including this rambunctious and loving family that was Yakov's heartbeat.

YAKOV came home from the dinner happily buzzed. He could tell that, no matter their reservations, his family liked Theo. That display of steel against his grandfather had a lot to do with it—but it wasn't the entirety.

While his dedushka might be the louder one, his babushka's voice held equal weight, and she'd made it clear that she'd found a kindred spirit in Theo. "This family needs another tranquil member," she'd said at one point. "Arlushinka, Theochka, and I plan to kick the rest of you heathens out once a month and sit in a nice quiet salon over a cup of tea or coffee."

Everyone had laughed, with his mother protesting that she could be quiet, too. His babushka had rolled her eyes. "Cub of mine, if you can sit still for five minutes without twitching, I'll eat my plate, the knife, even the fork. With hot sauce."

That had made the entire table erupt into bearish laughter.

And so it was that, no matter the darkness hanging on the horizon, and despite all they'd found to date, he walked into the apartment happy and content. He'd learned long ago to treasure the moment in which he lived.

"Don't look always to the future, cublet," Babulya Quyen had said to him once, her cherished face rich with emotion. "That's what my papa taught me. For if you look only to the future, you'll lose the present. Too many of my papa's designation lived in the future and so they never lived at all."

A profound lesson. One that Yakov fought to put in practice tonight even as worries about Theo gnawed at his brain. For this moment would never again come, and he was too delighted by it to allow it to fade into the background of a future that hadn't yet come to pass.

Loose and lazy limbed, he nuzzled at Theo in the privacy of their suite. But he wasn't a bear to demand intimate skin privileges, especially not when Theo had started the day keeping a frigid distance from him. Not because she didn't want him, but because she was afraid of what she might do in a rage.

Yakov wasn't about to bulldoze past her objections.

That didn't mean he was about to leave her to stew alone. Because Theo had a lot of bleak ideas in her head, and those ideas would grow in the dark and in the cold. He'd felt them begin to take root at the cantina, only to fall again and again under the weight of his family's affection—and that family included an empath. They'd claimed Arwen as a Stepyrev (in secret, obviously, because they weren't stupid enough to annoy Ena).

"I'm going to cuddle you tonight," he murmured to Theo before she could start to listen to the dark again. "Hard-core cuddling. You ready?"

Theo gave him a funny look, a little smile flirting with her lips. "How many beers did you have?"

"Only ten." In truth, he'd nursed a single one; he had no intention of letting his guard down while they were dealing with the facility, the murderer, and her grandfather's monstrous legacy. "I'm drunk on you, *pchelka moya*."

She wrinkled up her nose in that way she had of doing. "Hard-core cuddling?" A note of intrigue in her voice.

"Bear style." After pressing a kiss to her lips, he nudged her toward the bedroom. "Ready yourself, milady. I'll do a final security sweep, lock us down for the night." He winked. "Hard-core cuddling requires total concentration. No interruptions permitted."

That adorable smile yet flirting on her lips, she walked into the bedroom but stopped in the doorway to throw him an unreadable look. "Don't be long."

Yakov groaned. The woman was going to kill him. Cause of death: lust. Bare-naked lust. The kind of lust that wanted to bite and kiss her all over, then restart from tip to toe with his tongue. Or maybe he'd go in the opposite order.

And perhaps he could talk her into petting him all over with her soft sexy mouth. Especially around his cock.

Yakov groaned again.

"Cuddling," he reminded himself before he could get too excited, then checked the locks on every window and door and made sure the computronic security system Pavel had cleared for him was set. After which, he touched base with the physical team on duty outside for the night hours.

He hadn't been able to ignore the itch in the back of his brain, the sensation that someone was watching them. Might just be his hyperprotective instincts toward Theo, but he wasn't about to take chances with the Moscow Ripper roaming the streets. The patrols hadn't felt enough—and he was old enough to listen to his instincts when they got this . . . intrusive. It was important. The F part of his genes coming out.

"All systems green," Elbek drawled. "No suspicious characters. Except you."

"Thanks for doing this." The senior soldier had stepped in at the last minute. "Where's your partner in crime?" Who also happened to be one of the most lethal fighters in StoneWater; Moon might look like a strong wind would blow her away, but yeah, Yakov wasn't about to pick a fight with their resident flower child.

Her nickname among the soldiers was Berserker for a reason.

"Doing a perimeter walk. And you're welcome. You owe us a case from that new microbrewery out west."

"I owe you two each," Yakov said. "This is the second time you've both stepped in on short notice."

"Nah," Elbek said. "You've covered for us plenty before. See you in the morning."

"Have a good night." After hanging up satisfied that Theo would be safe, he walked toward the bedroom. *He* was the biggest security measure of all. No fucking Ripper was getting through him to Theo.

"Ready or not, here comes the bear," he said as he walked in . . . and almost swallowed his tongue.

Because Theo was standing by the bed naked.

Naked.

No clothes. Not even cute little socks on her feet.

Naked.

His brain short-circuited. "*O Bozhe*, you're beautiful." All slender lines and gentle curves.

And a faint tremor.

Body and mind snapping into gear, he strode over to her—but didn't put his hands on her except to cup her cheek. "Thela, what's this?" he asked softly. "I was hoping for seminaked cuddling at best. Maybe first base if it was my lucky night."

Despite the tremor, she held his gaze, no smile in her face now, nothing but unflinching intent. "I want to finish what we started last night. I want to steal this time with you."

"*Zolotse moyo*, this morning—"

"I know. I was . . . embarrassed and scared." She leaned her face into his palm. "But spending the day with Santo and Janine . . . seeing how quickly life can change, how tomorrow I might not be the Theo I am today—"

"*Theo.*"

She pressed a finger to his lips. "Hush." Firm tone, the tremor no longer in evidence. "It's not just that. It was being surrounded by all that love and affection tonight, seeing how your family interacts, how Arwen looks at Pavel with his heart in his eyes and how Pavel does nothing to hide what he feels for Arwen in turn. I've never lived that openly in my life."

Her eyes shone, a wild fire to her. "I've been so *afraid* for so long, Yakov. So much rage inside me, but under that was fear. Of being hurt again, of being abandoned. After the rages, I'm constantly afraid of hurting people." She traced his lips with her fingers. "And now, the closer we get to finding out what was happening at the Center, the more afraid I am of what we'll find."

She stepped closer, her breath kissing his. "I want to believe my grandfather took me to that place and did something to me on which I can blame my actions as a child, but I also know that's likely a false hope. I'm afraid that I'll find out I'm a murderer created by another murderer."

"You're not." This time, he tugged away her hand when she would've stopped him from speaking. "Arwen likes you." He shook the wrist he held—gently, but enough to get her attention. "Our resident E has a marshmallow heart, but the man is also a Mercant. He's not one of those Es who thinks that even the most evil deserve a chance. He doesn't believe in forgiveness for all crimes."

Theo stared at him, her pupils huge against the blue of her irises. "He checked on me twice tonight. Telepathically."

Yakov wasn't the least surprised. Arwen had a sneaky way of looking after his people. "You know what he told me once? That he hates making telepathic contact with 'people with dark souls'—those are his exact words. He only ever does it in exigent circumstances. A dinner with my lunatic family doesn't qualify."

Theo frowned. "Your family is not lunatic." A push at his shoulders. "They're wonderful."

Somehow, his hands were at her waist now, on all that smooth and silky skin. But he was still trying to think with the head on his neck and not the one lower down. Despite the fact that Theo was *naked*. "Fine, they're wonderful lunatics," he said, laughing when she threatened to kick him.

Cuddling her closer, all those gentle curves pressed against him, he brushed her hair behind her ear. "They like you, too, and while my babushka might be kindness personified, my mother is a shark in bear's fur. She told me she'd slap me upside the head if I messed it up with you."

He rubbed his nose against hers. "Believe in yourself, Theo mine. So many other people already do."

Midnight eclipsed her eyes in front of him, her lower lip quivering a little.

"I know it's a hard thing I'm asking of you," he whispered, running his hand up the curve of her spine, then back down—and though he was aroused through the roof, it was tenderness that overwhelmed him. "Be with me not because you're afraid, Theo, but because you believe. Because you have hope."

Chapter 54

CODE RED! Cardiac arrest detected! Location data embedded.
CODE RED! Cardiac arrest detected! Location data embedded.
CODE RED! Cardiac arrest detected! Location data embedded.

—Emergency medical alert sent by personal monitoring
device assigned to Pax Marshall (18 June 2073)

HOPE.

It wasn't a word or a term that had held any meaning for Theo since she was seven years old. Before that . . . yes, she'd hoped. She'd believed. That the bird they'd found could survive, that they could escape watchful eyes to play in the grounds, that she and Pax would always be together and that they'd find a place to live with no rules, no strictures.

Childish hopes, but hopes nonetheless.

Now, this strong, honorable bear was asking her to believe in herself, in her own goodness. "It's hard," she whispered, a hot splash sliding down her cheek. "I'm *so* scared."

Tugging her even closer, not a breath between them, he rubbed his cheek against the side of her temple. She felt enfolded in him, protected by him. "I know," he said. "But you have courage upon courage, Theo mine. You survived a fucking Councilor—and you lived to dance on his nonexistent grave. Nonexistent because he was blown to pieces. Just in case you forgot. Some dreams do come true."

Laughter bubbled through the tears, her chest aching.

"Then you got tangled up with the most handsome bear you've ever seen." Rumbling words against her ear. "A good thing, because said bear might otherwise have been forced to kidnap you and steal you away to his den."

Tears continued to fall from her eyes, a faucet that once turned, couldn't be closed.

"*Theo.*" Her feet leaving the carpet as Yakov scooped her up in his arms and walked to sit on the bed, with Theo held tight against him. Managing to grab the soft blanket at the foot of the bed, he opened it out and wrapped it around her back, so that she was cradled in his warmth and the plushness of the blanket.

"Get it out, *pchelka*. Get the poison out. It doesn't belong inside you. You've paid the price for your grandfather's evil long enough. It's time to be Theo. Just Theo."

She didn't know if it was the flagrant permission, if she'd needed that, or if it was him—her Yakov, who thought more of her than she'd ever thought of herself. The dam broke. She cried for the girl she'd once been, so happy and good at heart. She cried for the girl she'd become, so lost and hurting. She cried for the teenage years that were a blur in her mind, no shape to the memories. She cried for the young woman who'd begun to realize what she'd done, the blood that stained her hands.

And she cried for the Theo who'd never had a chance to become, her trajectory forever altered . . . but that same trajectory had brought her to this moment, where she lay in the arms of a man who thought her worth the fight, who thought her *good*. And it was in that realization that she found the fragile flame of hope.

Yakov existed. And he wasn't repulsed by her though he'd seen the shadows in her heart. "My grandfather tried to train the rages out of me." Her voice was a rasp, but she wanted to speak.

Yakov's entire body grew stiff. "You don't have to go back there, not to that bastard."

"No, I want to. It's the last drop of poison."

"Hold on." Yakov kicked off his boots, then shifted them both so that he was sitting with his back to the headboard and his legs stretched out, Theo cradled against the heated muscle of him.

When she lifted her head, he sucked in a breath, his fingers trembling as he wiped away the remnants of her tears. "I love you, Theo." Firm words. Generous words. No demand to them. "I fell in puppy love with you in a dream. I could've never imagined that the reality would be so much better."

Theo took a ragged breath, unable to say those same words. Not yet. Not until she'd done this. Tucking her head against Yakov's neck and chest, she took a deep breath and walked back into the nightmare . . . only, the past didn't unravel in a painful scroll.

It was . . . faded. Like a photograph left out in the sun.

Leached of poison.

It wasn't hard to simply say it. "Initially my grandfather believed the rages to be nothing but temper tantrums, a result of my flawed Silence. So when I was seventeen, he began to punish me by tying me to a chair rigged up to deliver a shock at any hint of anger." The pain had been spiderwebs of fire, but Theo had lived a hard life by then, could bear it.

"Later, when he realized I *couldn't* control the episodes, he seemed to gain a perverse pleasure in 'punishing' me. We both knew it was something else altogether: he'd found a way to hurt me that wouldn't affect Pax. He'd always hated that I held the deciding card when it came to how far he could go with me—without my link to Pax, I would've been ash in a crematorium fire at seven years of age."

Theo would never forget her grandfather's cold expression as he sat across from her in the soundproofed concrete basement of the apartment building where she'd lived with Colette. Two chairs. One bolted to the floor and wired for power, the other sleek, black and the right size for his frame.

It was only ever the two of them in that barren place.

"Pathetic coward," Yakov snarled.

"Yes, he was." Her grandfather had been a monster to her for far too long—at last she saw him for the weak little man he'd been inside. "As for protecting Pax from the abuse," she added, "ironically enough, I did it by drawing power *from* Pax."

"I didn't realize Psy twins could do that. Share power."

"Not all twins can. In our case, our bond isn't wholly under our control. The door between our minds is instinctive and it shoves open when one of us is in need." As it had when Scarab Syndrome first took hold of Pax's brain. Theo had fed him all she could, even as she put on a front of being angered by the headaches and nosebleeds engendered by the draw.

In truth, she wouldn't have cared if he took all of it, every last drop. It had been about keeping him at a distance, her brother golden and bright who she'd believed still had a chance.

"Why didn't you drop the shield, allow the pain to reach your brother?" Yakov asked, his arms tight around her. "Not to cause harm, but as a tool to scare off Marshall."

"He protected me for so long, Yasha." Her heart ached for the young man who'd died inside each time he sensed Theo's suffering. "I just wanted to keep him safe for once. I was also a stubborn teenage girl who *hated* my grandfather. I relished taunting him about the pleasure he got from abusing a vulnerable young woman."

I guess—a breath through lingering agony—*your Silence isn't so perfect after all, old man. Are you experiencing sexual arousal? I read about such*— Another jolt, her scream echoing off the walls.

Theo shrugged on the memory of that scream. "It was stupid to taunt him, but it was the only pleasure I had in life. I'm still not sorry I did it."

"We all do stupid things as juveniles," Yakov reassured her. "It just so happens you were with a psychopath at the time."

A laugh bubbled out of her, and it was real, not forced or halfhearted. "The short of it is that I taunted him a little too much one day and he set the output to maximum. Liquid fire under my skin. You can see the results on my back." A spiderweb of scars where the current had traveled through the specially designed micro-electrodes hooked into her skin.

"I have the odd rogue scar." She touched a thin one on her inner thigh. "But the impact was mostly concentrated on my back—and it was the last time. Because I couldn't protect Pax from that. He went into cardiac arrest at the same time I did." Her last panicked thought had been her brother's name.

She'd felt him reach out desperately to her at the same time.

THEO!

Then they were both gone.

"Bozhe moi." Yakov pressed a kiss to the top of her hair, his hand shaking where it cupped the back of her head. "To know I could've lost you before I ever met you . . ." He squeezed the air out of her and she was happy to be so squeezed.

"I knew you were tough," he added in a voice rough and ragged. "This just proves it."

She soaked up the praise, a flower deprived of the sun suddenly pulled into the light. "I'm certain my grandfather would've left me to die if the medics working on Pax had managed to get his heart beating before mine. But they couldn't, even though he received near-immediate attention."

"Your brother is a stubborn fucker. He played chicken with death and won."

"Yes." She'd never be able to prove it, but she knew that Pax, a highly intelligent and well-trained Gradient 9, had done something in that final split second before flatline to link their destinies. "My brother's heart didn't start beating again until—irony of ironies—my grandfather did CPR on me and got my organ going."

"I hope the abusive coward sweated half his life away."

"I'm sure he did. It's always amused me that he was forced to bring his most hated grandchild back to life." Theo had always thought that meant she was as perverse as him, but Yakov had made her see the entire event in a different light: she'd been a *child* acting like a child, and he'd been a Councilor with all the power in the world.

Theo had taken what good she could from the situation.

"Pax has never admitted it, but I know he did it on purpose." Theo wanted Yakov to know this part of her brother, the part no one else in the world ever saw, the part that Marshall Hyde had crushed and buried and hurt. "Linked his life to mine. So our grandfather couldn't murder me without murdering him."

Yakov took a deep breath. "Never thought I'd say this, but I like your brother—at least when it comes to his relationship with you. Pax understands family." A hard nod. "But I reserve the right to look at him with suspicion in all other dealings."

"Fair enough." Theo knew Pax would expect nothing else; her brother had gone to great lengths to create an image of ice-cold power and heartless ambition.

"That's all of it," Theo murmured, her entire body liquid against Yakov. As if with the poison had gone every drop of tension in her. "Can we do hard-core cuddling now?"

Chapter 55

Subject V-1 should be decommissioned at this point. Given the amount of neural damage, there's no chance of any further useful breakthroughs. I do, of course, understand there are other considerations when it comes to this specific subject, so the call is yours.

—Dr. Upashna Leslie to Councilor Marshall Hyde (11 April 2079)

THE WATCHER SPOTTED the bear on surveillance the instant they turned the corner. No hesitation, no sharp movements, the Watcher kept on walking, just another resident of Moscow heading home after a late shift.

Head down, pace steady, somewhere to be.

The Watcher could feel eyes on their back, but no one followed and the Watcher was soon out of the zone of danger. Clearly, the Watcher had underestimated the bear with Theodora Marshall. He'd not only sensed the danger, he'd put extra security in place. And he hadn't told that security to conceal themselves: their open presence was a warning.

"Time for a change of plan," the Watcher muttered to their other self.

For tonight, however, the Watcher decided to go home, to the place where it had all begun. Where the Watcher had broken in two. The same place where the Watcher felt oddly safe. Perhaps because they'd cleared the place of all threats.

Corpse by rotting corpse.

Chapter 56

"What's this?"

"My can-do-everything handyman kit. I'm here to rearrange your spoons, forks, and knives, and build a treadmill for your fish so it can walk itself. Then I'm going to oil your cuticles, and oh yeah, climb into your nonexistent attic to get rid of the infestation of vampire bats. So, what do you think?"

"That you're a very persistent bear."

"Oh, and I brought you flowers. A bouquet of edelweiss. According to the Internet, they can represent a lot of things, chief among them the deepest love, and devotion."

"You're getting ahead of yourself."

"No, gorgeous, I'm talking about your devotion to those who are your own, your ability to love full throttle, no matter what the obstacle. I see that every time you're with Silver—she wouldn't be Valya's Starlight if you hadn't laid the foundation with your devotion and affection. Fierce heart, stubborn courage, and the most sophisticated death stare I've ever seen; my bear never had a chance against you."

—"The Courtship of Arwen Mercant: A Story of Death Stares, Irresistible Charm, and a Romantic Night in Jail" as told by Pavel Stepyrev

. . .

ARWEN ENJOYED WALKING alongside his bear as the lights of Moscow turned the river into a midnight rainbow, the air crisp but not too cold—not with Pavel's body heat next to his and Pavel's arm around his waist.

Arwen was taller by a few inches; it would've made more logical sense for him to hook his arm over Pavel's shoulders. But *this* was what felt natural. Because Arwen's lover was a bear with a protective streak a mile wide and Arwen was an empath who liked being in his bear's warm embrace.

He smiled as he fixed a cuff link on his shirt.

"What's so funny?" Pavel's fingers played over Arwen's hip as he took another lick of his ice cream cone. He'd offered Arwen as many licks as he wanted, at the reasonable price of a kiss for a lick.

"Oh, my cuff links reminded me of that day you turned up to take care of my vampire bat infestation." The links were in the shape of edelweiss blooms, a gift from Pavel. Because his brash bear lover knew how to take care of his person.

Pavel's dimples flashed. "I laughed for a good ten minutes after I got that message."

"I had washing my shoelaces and color-coordinating the weeds in the garden in reserve." Because at some point, coming up with progressively more preposterous excuses to decline Pavel's invitations to go out had turned into a flirtation that made his stomach flutter and his toes curl.

He'd become glued to his phone, waiting for his bear's next message.

"Those are good." Pavel chuckled. "Too bad you never got to use them."

Arwen hadn't had that chance because after the words Pavel had given him—*fierce heart, stubborn courage; ability to love full throttle*—he'd been a mess with no defenses left.

He was an E. He knew his Pasha bear had meant every single word and that he saw Arwen in a way that was far beyond skin and bone and lust. Not just that, but he valued who Arwen was as a person and as an E, Pavel's admiration and respect for him a caress of plush fur over his empathic senses.

Arwen's world had shifted on its axis, as an emotion potent and passionate took the place of their playful flirtation. Used to the sly machinations of the PsyNet, he'd been afraid it was a mirage, a pretty game. He hadn't understood his bear then. Blunt, honest, wild, Pavel Stepyrev had never treated Arwen's heart with anything but tender care.

All soft and happy inside as they turned around to start making their way back to their borrowed residence, he took out his phone.

"Nightly check-in on your list?" Pavel finished off the last bit of his cone in a crisp crunch.

"I *asked* Canto if he wanted me to drop by and cook him a meal or two since I know he's alone this week with Payal on that emergency trip to Singapore. He never eats well when they're apart. Just checking on his reply."

Leaning in, Pavel peered unashamedly at Arwen's phone screen . . . and chuckled. "'Dear Arwen,'" he read out, "'I still have seventeen frozen meals from your last meal prep session. And the bears keep dropping off random cakes. I found a fucking pavlova on the deck this morning. What do I need with a pavlova? No goddamn peace around here.'"

Smile on his lips, Pavel pressed a kiss to Arwen's cheek. "You're good at taking care of your people. Even ungrateful grumps like your cousin. Want me to beat him up for you?"

Mollified, Arwen said, "No, he's safe from your wrath today." Because that wasn't the end of Canto's message.

Below the grumpfest were the words: Thank you for the reminder to eat, little cousin. I do actually forget when Payal isn't here. Because when Payal *was* there, Canto was focused on taking care of her—as she was in reverse. They were adorable. Two outward hard-asses who'd found their perfect match.

Canto had also added: I'm going to try a piece of that ludicrous pavlova. It's got sliced kiwi on top of it! Where the hell did the bears get sliced kiwi, that's what I want to know.

Grinning as he read that part of the message out loud to an amused Pavel, Arwen quickly tapped back a reply, then scrolled on. Lazily content by his side, his presence that of a satisfied bear, Pavel listened as Arwen gave him updates on the others on what Pavel had named "The List."

"My little cousin—the one you met two weeks ago? She doesn't know what to study at university. I'm going to help her apply for a couple of work-study programs, help her figure out her path."

Pavel squeezed his waist, his expression tender when their eyes met. "I love how you love your people, *moy svetlyi luchik*."

Arwen was used to Pavel's affectionate words, but his heart went to mush every time his bear called him his ray of light. Leaning down, Arwen peppered his face with kisses.

Deep grooves in Pavel's cheeks, his love for Arwen a bear's hug.

Arwen loved so much about Pavel, but his generosity with Arwen's heart was a big part of it. Arwen didn't know how to be any other way, how not to "collect" people as Grandmother put it, and to look after them.

While Pavel was possessive, had actually growled at those who'd thought to hit on Arwen, he'd never once been possessive about Arwen's empathic heart. And it wasn't a case of him passively accepting that part of Arwen—no, his Pasha bear actively helped Arwen look after his people.

Whether that was by dropping off care packages when Arwen couldn't, or by checking in on certain individuals when Arwen was out of town. He'd even once put on his "big boy pants"—his own words—and bearded Ena in her den after Arwen's grandmother had gone under for a touch too long for Arwen's liking, while Arwen was on an educational retreat with fellow empaths.

"Your grandmother is flat-out terrifying," Pavel had said afterward, wiping imaginary sweat off his brow. "When she offered me tea, I was pretty sure she was going to poison me. She invited me to play a game of chess instead—and beat my ass to all hell. Brutal, man, brutal."

Arwen, meanwhile, had received a message from his grandmother in the aftermath: *You're both invited to the Sea House in a week's time, after your return from the retreat. Tell your bear that the dress code is formal—and by formal, I do not mean a new T-shirt.*

Arwen had pumped his fist in the air like a damn wind-up toy. Invitations to the Sea House were the highest possible honor in their family. His bighearted bear had done good.

"Come on, sweet stuff," Pasha said now, his cheeks still creased from the impact of the kiss storm. "You can pet me more at home."

Arwen had every intention of doing exactly that, but as a shirtless and shoeless Pavel wandered out of the guest room and into the kitchen to grab a glass of water, he found himself standing there with his designer shirt in his hands, and the words of others running through his head.

You helped me feel real, Arwen. At a time when I felt the ghost.

Thank you, little brother.

We wouldn't be the family we are without you. Don't make the mistake of underestimating your own gifts because they're different from ours.

Our family is what it is because of your heart, grandchild of mine. That's why we protect it so fiercely. Because it has been our salvation.

I love how you love your people, moy svetlyi luchik.

"Hey." Pavel stood in the doorway, a glass of water in hand. "Why so serious?" Walking over, he placed the glass on the bedstand on Arwen's side of the bed, then reached up to rub at his frown lines.

"I just figured it out," Arwen said, dropping the shirt to the bed.

Chapter 57

Look, my love
The fallen autumn leaves are laughing
And the sky, it smiles such a bright, bright blue
The cool winds kiss our cheeks as we dance
And oh, my darling, what a dance it is
In your arms I become a song
And this wild music our love story

—"Love Story" by Adina Mercant, poet (b. 1832, d. 1901)

Editorial note: "Love Story" is widely considered Adina Mercant's
sweetest and most joyful piece of poetry, with none of the usual
undertones that color her work. Some experts believe this was
written in her youth, at the very start of her career, while others
argue all indications are that it was penned in the final decade of
her life, as a monument to her infamous, passionate,
and enduring love affair with her husband.

"WHAT DID YOU figure out, my darling empath? That I am, in fact, the most charming bear you know?"

Plucking Pavel's glasses off his nose, Arwen put them on the bedside table with care. "That you're the smartest bear I know."

Pavel's cheeks dimpled. Those wicked dimples had seduced Arwen into many a bad decision, but today's decision, it was the best one he'd ever made.

"Absolute truth, right there." His lover's grin was sunshine over Arwen's senses. "But somehow I don't believe it was thoughts of my genius that put that look on your face. What's up?" Tugging him closer, Pavel nipped at his throat, their half-naked bodies rubbing against each other.

Arousal instant and rigid, Arwen wrapped his arms around his bear's more heavily muscled form and tried to find his words again. "You're scrambling my brain," he complained.

Laughter, deep and husky. But Pavel pulled back enough to look into Arwen's face. "I'll give you two minutes before I have my way with you."

Arwen pressed his forehead to Pavel's. His erection throbbed, but that wasn't the organ topmost on his mind. "I figured out that you're right. I do have my own power in the world, in my family, in Stone-Water."

Empath. Collector of wounded souls. Chief hoverer over his loved ones.

That was who he *was*.

He had no reason to search for his place in the world.

He had one that was set in stone—because he'd claimed it a long, long time ago and only made it stronger with time.

He couldn't remember giving Ivan his favorite toys as a child in an effort to make his cousin happy. He couldn't remember crawling into Ena's lap as a toddler when she was having a tough day and just patting her cheeks. He definitely couldn't remember laughing so hard as a baby that he'd "filled the room with sunshine."

Those stories had been relayed to him by others who cherished the memories. He did remember so many other things he'd done as he grew older. From ensuring that Silver didn't fall too deep into the ice of control, to kidnapping his grandmother for a walk on the cliffs, to turning up to lunch with Uncle Rufus—complete with a fully prepared lunch—when that gruffly reclusive member of his family began to go "dark" to his senses.

And now, he worked with strangers who needed an empath's gentleness, an empath's ability to heal the mind and the heart.

Small things. Necessary things. *Important* things.

"I also," he continued, "understand that I have my own power in our relationship, too." Pavel might be protective, but no one did protective like an empath—they were just cat-sneaky about it. And if Pavel was dropping off care packages for him, Arwen was lighting candles and giving Pavel a soothing massage after a tough day.

No ledger. No tit for tat.

Just . . . looking after each other. Being able to lean on each other.

Because that was the thing—his Pasha bear leaned on him as much as Arwen leaned on his bear. Whether it was worry about his twin or a concern in the den, Pavel didn't attempt to hide it from Arwen. Pavel treated Arwen as a partner, no matter if the news was good or grim.

Respect. Devotion. Love.

Arwen was so fucking lucky.

Pavel's eyes turned bear, his claws pricking at Arwen's back, as if they'd erupted without Pavel's conscious decision. "Arlusha? You saying what I think you're saying?"

"Yes." His smile felt as if it would crack his face. "Will you marry me, Pasha bear?"

That was when the mating bond smashed into them both with the force of a hurricane, a blinding vortex of love and need, affection and lust, joy and hope, memories and laughter that had been held back far too long.

The primal power of it was through with waiting.

He *saw* his Pasha bear in ways he'd never seen or known another being his entire existence. And he knew Pasha saw him in turn. Their hearts and souls exposed, stripped to the core in a feral glory that demanded *everything*.

They stood shaking in the aftermath, their bodies slick with sweat.

When Pavel shifted them drunkenly to the bed, Arwen went. They collapsed onto it side by side, his right hand linked to Pavel's left. Arwen stared at the ceiling for a full minute, until the sparks in front of his eyes were no longer a meteor shower. Then he turned to look at the bear whose chest was heaving beside him. "Wow."

The dimples flashed.

It still took three minutes before they could breathe properly again.

At which point, Pavel rose up on one arm to look down at Arwen. "Mine," he said smugly, and, one hand splayed on Arwen's abdomen, took Arwen's mouth in a kiss that was all possessive bear—wet and deep, tongue and sexual heat.

Arwen's breathing was ragged in the aftermath, but he found himself grinning, too. "Mine," he said, and leaned up to bite down on the curve of Pavel's neck.

It wasn't strictly a bear thing, the neck biting, but he'd figured out that *his* bear liked a hard bite or two. Now, Pavel groaned and ran his hand lower down Arwen's body, to the bulge in his jeans. "I think you got the wrong size." A teasing murmur that made goose bumps erupt over every inch of Arwen's skin. "They feel a bit tight."

Arwen might blush now and then, but he wasn't a virgin anymore. Though that memory? Of Pasha so playful and gentle with him? Of caresses soft and kisses upon kisses, of a bubble bath and scented oils? He'd carry that in his heart to his grave, a treasure of tenderness from his rough-around-the-edges bear.

Holding Pavel's wicked gaze, he played his bear's sexy game. "Guess you better take them off, then."

"Guess I better." A flick of his hand and Arwen's pants were undone, his zipper lowered.

Arwen went to lift his butt so that Pavel could pull off his jeans to throw them aside. Except instead of doing that, Pavel dipped his head to press a kiss on Arwen's pecs. "Look at all this sleek muscle." Another kiss, the caress of claws. "Mmm, I could eat you up."

"Pasha." Arwen wove his fingers into the thick silk of his lover's hair. "I love you until it hurts."

"Good," said the bear whose own love was fur over Arwen's senses, a knowing that his empathic heart snuggled into with delight. "Serves you right for making me crazy for you." This time, the kiss held teeth.

Laughing, aroused, and delighted at the same time, he watched as Pavel finally got rid of the too-tight jeans. His formfitting black underwear didn't last much longer—and neither did Pavel's clothes.

Skin on skin, lips on lips, they sank into intimate skin privileges with the giddy wonder of lovers who knew this was it.

Mates were forever.

"My beautiful *luchik sveta*." Growly words, Pavel's big hand on one of Arwen's more slender thighs as he braced himself over Arwen on his other arm. "You light up my world."

Cock engorged to breaking point, and heart stamped with Pavel's name, Arwen hauled him down with a hand on the back of his head, and bit down on his lower lip. That got him a bearish rumble, and a kiss as raw and untamed as the man in his arms.

His man. Forever.

Empaths could be smug, too.

By the time Pavel scraped Arwen's throat with his teeth before saying, "Where is it?" in a tone gritty with need, Arwen wanted only to have him inside him, the two of them connected in the body as they were in the heart and the soul.

"Side pocket," he gasped. "Overnight bag."

Moving with a speed startling if you didn't know bears, Pavel was back with the slender tube in hand two seconds later, all gleaming skin and taut muscle. "Delicious Berrylicious flavor? Seriously?" He groaned as he read the label. "I can feel my extremely manly balls shriveling up."

"You have nothing to worry about. You're hung like a bear."

A burst of laughter deep and familiar and oh-so-loved, and then the maligned lube was being put to good use. But today . . . today, the lust was secondary. Today, Arwen cried because they were mated, the bond between them a thing of claws and fur with a dusting of diamond gray, shining yet soft.

"You never told me it would be so beautiful," he whispered.

Pavel buried his face in Arwen's neck as he curled around Arwen from behind, his powerful body beginning to move inside Arwen in a rhythm that was no longer smooth. "I didn't know."

Arwen tried to speak, lost his words.

There was only skin and heat and need . . . and love. So much love.

When the orgasm hit, hard and deep, he was dazzled by both his pleasure and Pavel's own. The double jolt made the erotic waves last and last and last, and they were both limp and sweat-damp in the aftermath when Pavel said, "Yes, I'll marry you, *svetlyi luchik moy*. Under the sky in a slick suit, with all the people we love, all the people you look after, as our witnesses."

Chapter 58

Janine Fong has potential, despite her limitations. I suggest we assign a specific member of staff to work with her—the tests seem to show that she needs to bond to her handler in order to function at an effective level.

—Dr. Upashna Leslie to Councilor Marshall Hyde
(date corrupted, file reload required)

JANINE HEARD THE call, tried to answer. But her head was fuzzy and it felt nice to snuggle down into her blanket. *Sleepy*, she managed to telepath.

She knew they wouldn't be angry with her. They were never angry with her. Today, they said, *Rest. We can teleport tomorrow.*

Promise? Janine managed to get out past the heaviness in her mind. She loved teleporting to new places, but first she had to get the image of the place, so she could lock onto it.

Last time around, she'd gone to a forest! That had been so fun! Forests were *hard* to lock onto, because they didn't have a lot of unique things. Just tons of leaves and trees and crumbly things underfoot. But Janine had done it. She'd stared and stared at the photo she'd been sent, and found an interesting pattern of roots, then linked it to the spiral pattern on the trunk, and she'd done it!

I want to teleport again.

We will. I promise. Tomorrow night.

Janine smiled, her sleep that of the innocent.

Chapter 59

You'll never guess what just happened, Starlichka.

—A (grinning) Valentin Nikolaev to his mate, Silver Mercant (today, now)

HARD-CORE CUDDLING HAD begun in earnest when Yakov felt a jolt at the back of his brain. Not pain or a warning . . . but a shift. And he knew. Usually, only the alpha of a clan would know so soon, but Yakov fucking *knew*.

Joy, pure and unfettered, set his heart alight. "My brother just mated. About damn time!"

Big blue eyes hazy with pleasure looked up into his. He'd been lying beside Theo, petting her naked body slow and easy for a good ten minutes, and his cock was about to erupt. But this wasn't about rushing.

"How do you know when you've found your mate?" Husky words, her gaze so open that he wanted to wrap her up in titanium, protect that vulnerable core the world had wounded over and over again.

He stroked the rounded curve of her thigh, slid back up over her hip, her rib cage, to cup one plump little breast. A small handful. Just the right size to squeeze and caress and pet. "This bear," he murmured, "dreamed about his mate." He'd let her come to him in her own time as

Arwen had come to Pavel, but he wasn't about to hide who she was to him. "You're it for me, *serdtse moyo.*" His heart. Always. "Whether we mate today, or ten years from today."

A shaky exhale, her hand tugging at his T-shirt. This time he didn't resist pulling it off, and once that was off, she was insistent he get naked. "It's only fair."

As an argument, it was a compelling one. Even more compelling was the look in her eyes as she took him in once he stood bare to the skin at the side of the bed. He was a bear with no sense of modesty whatsoever, so he smiled and prowled over to lie above her, his body braced on his forearms, and the heavy weight of his cock snuggled against her stomach.

When she spread her thighs a fraction, the scent of her musk grew heavier, richer. Groaning, he leaned down to kiss her all slow and romantic. Because damn if he was just going to thrust into her like a rutting bear tonight. That could wait until his lover was comfortable with intimate skin privileges.

No scaring her off when he wanted to do this with her for the rest of her life.

Continuing to kiss her, he moved one hand down to between her thighs and began to make sensual music with his fingers, while murmuring sexy, encouraging words to her that made her skin flush and her body move rhythmically on the careful intrusion of his. And kisses slow and sweet.

His Theo liked kisses.

"Please," she whispered long before he was ready to stop playing, "I need . . ." A lost look to her.

"I have you, my Theo." And though he'd planned to draw this out, need clutched his heart, the desire to give her what she wanted his most primal driving force.

Using his knees to nudge apart her thighs, he made sure she was ready for him. "Tell me to stop if it's too much," he said, his muscles bunched and his eyes locked with her own as he began to nudge into her. "Such a pretty pussy you have, Theo." Sweat broke out along his brow. "*Bozhe*, you're tight."

Her nails dug into his arms, her breathing hitched . . . but his Theo was stubborn as all hell, and he was the one who was shaking as he sank home. She wrapped her legs and her arms around him, silky strands of her hair caught between them.

"I *love* this." A shocked little voice that made his bear strut.

Finding a fragment of control, he raised his head to look at her, and his heart, it ached at seeing the shocked pleasure, the vulnerable trust on her face. "Me, too. And we're just starting."

Theo traced his lips with her finger as she'd done once before that night. "Your smile feels like sunlight."

Throat growing unexpectedly thick, he leaned in to take another kiss as slow and deep as the movement of his body in hers. He took care, such care. Because this was his Theo, and he'd cut off his right arm before he'd ever hurt her.

But later that night, after her sobs of pleasure and his shout as his back arched, he dreamed of blood. Theo's blood. All over his hands. So slick. So much of it. Warm and fresh and unstoppable.

YAKOV was not in a good mood when he woke, that fucking dream gnawing at him. Nuzzling and cuddling with Theo did a little to temper his worry and fear, but he was forcing down toast past the fury in his throat when it struck him that the dream had changed last night.

This time, the blood had been all over *his* hands.

Halting with the toast halfway to his mouth, Theo still on the phone call with her brother that had come a minute earlier, he switched his brain into tactical mode. What had he done? Why had the dream altered? He'd been near Theo this time, no longer tied up. But not fast enough if she was still bleeding out.

When his phone rang, he almost didn't answer, not wanting to lose his train of thought. Then he recognized the personalized ringtone. "Good morning, sweetheart," he said with a grin.

"Too much charm for your own good, just like your deda," his grandmother Quyen sniffed, but beneath that bubbled unrestrained joy. "Did you hear the good news?"

He felt his cheeks crease. "Think we can officially steal Arwen now?"

"Hush! Ena, she'll rain down hell." Open admiration in her tone. "I'll invite her to tea again. Last time, she told me and Graciele about how she took over an evil man's empire as a young woman and—oh, such sad news—he had a fatal accident soon afterward."

That little tidbit didn't surprise Yakov in the least. "Have you seen the new mates?" He could just imagine Pavel's strut, Arwen's beaming joy.

"Pah! You think your babushka doesn't remember being young?" she scolded. "No disturbances until at least noon. That's my rule. But I made the new mates a big breakfast and drove out with your deda to leave it by the door of Ena's city house, then ran away and sent your brother a message telling him to open the door." A small giggle. "The insulated breakfast basket was gone when I *accidentally* passed that way five minutes later."

Yakov wished he could hold his tiny storm force of a grandmother. "We're lucky to have you in our corner, Babulya."

"Yes, you are. I didn't get these gray hairs just sitting around. I've lived a life, cublet."

Flexing his free hand, he found himself saying, "Babulya, what do you think it might mean if I dreamed I had blood on my hands?"

A long pause. "A dream or a dream like my papa used to dream?"

"It started like one of Denu's dreams . . . but this part. It feels different." Not as real. Even in the dream, he'd felt oddly disconnected from it. "I don't know how to explain it."

"Hmm." His grandmother was quiet for a moment. "Your denu told me once that he had two kinds of visions—the first kind are the ones everyone knows about, but the second were more subtle. Holding meaning but not being an exact representation of what would be."

Blood on my hands.

"My fault," Yakov murmured, his gut leaden. "It means that what's about to happen is going to be my fault."

"Well? What are you going to do to fix it?" his babushka demanded.

Yakov's panic flatlined. Because that was exactly what he needed to figure out. "I love you, sweetheart."

"I love you, too, my cheeky cublet. Give Theochka a hug for me."

After hanging up, Yakov glanced over to where Theo stood by the window, phone to her ear. He could hear most of the conversation, though he wasn't trying to listen in—just a side effect of his hearing. He'd have to tell her, so she could choose to wear an earpiece for privacy.

From what he'd picked up, Pax was warning her about a segment of their family that had apparently decided that she was a threat because of her "new" closeness to Pax. Yakov wanted to roll his eyes. He'd only known her a heartbeat of time and he could already tell that her bond with her twin was a thing old and weathered and set in stone. Just like his bond with Pavel.

"Your family is a bunch of psychopaths—I mean, seriously, a plot by your freaking mother?" he said after she hung up, tapping at his ear to let her know he'd overheard. "Er, did I just offend you?"

Looking up after sending a quick message, she gave him that sweet Theo smile that was still so rare. "No, I think they're psychopaths, too—my mother being the chief one now that her father is dead. Maybe not clinically diagnosable, but they drank of my grandfather's venom all their lives."

"I'll get you an earpiece," he said. "So you don't have a nosy-parker bear in your business all the time." Slicing up a couple of strawberries, he put them on her plate. "Your brother worries about you." Yeah, he was having to do a whole lot of rearranging of his thoughts when it came to Pax Marshall.

"He should be worrying about himself." Taking her seat opposite him, Theo sipped from the glass of nutrients he'd made for her alongside their simple breakfast of toast and eggs. "He's in the center of all that ugliness. I told him to get out, but Pax has a responsibility complex a mile long.

"Thousands of people rely on the Marshall Group's various arms for their paychecks," she explained, "and Pax knows it'll all collapse without him. Our family members have big ideas, but Pax is the only one with the training and knowledge to run the operation." Frustration and pride entwined. "I'd feel better if I knew he had someone else in the upper echelons in his corner, but it's impossible to figure out loyalties."

Yakov frowned, his fingers curled around the warmth of his coffee mug. "Huh."

"What?"

"You should hire an empath. Specifically, Arwen. Without breaking confidence, he just helped another person figure out friend from foe." Payal Rao had come from the same type of viperous family as Pax and Theo.

The PsyNet seemed to spawn them. Not surprising when Silence had rewarded a lack of emotion and punished empathy. How no one had ever seen that it would all end in tears was beyond him, but then again, as Valya often said, they were just simple bears.

Theo parted her lips, closed them, considered the suggestion. "I never thought about going to an E. Pax wouldn't, either. Trust again." The entire PsyNet might trust empaths, but the two of them had seen too much, experienced too much, to trust anyone blindly. "But Arwen . . ." She knew him, *did* trust him; he'd helped her for no reason but kindness. "Do you think he'd do it?"

"You can ask." Yakov put more scrambled eggs onto her plate. "It'll probably depend on how bad it is in there, and how much he can take. But our E's a Mercant, too—he's got steel in that sophisticated spine of his."

Theo's phone vibrated with a message. She glanced at it, swallowed. "There's another factor that might impact Arwen's decision." Taking a deep breath, she told Yakov the last secret. "My brother is sick." Having realized Yakov could probably hear her even if she spoke in a low voice, she'd messaged Pax right after hanging up.

A private question, because this was her brother's secret.

Her bear immediately took her hand. "You don't mean a cold, do you, *pchelka*?"

"No." Throat thick, she told him about Scarab Syndrome and how it threatened to swallow Pax whole. "He's stable due to considerable work by another E, but it's a tightrope that's getting slipperier day by day." She swiped the base of her palm over her eye to get rid of the moisture there—it was as if now that she'd cried once, the tears wouldn't stay put.

But she shook her head when Yakov would've risen to come to her. "No, I can't break down today. And I will if you cuddle me." His big heart, the way he held her, she felt so *safe* that it was impossible to maintain her composure. "But I want you to know all of it."

"I'm here for whatever you need." A deep rumble, his thumb brushing over the back of her hand.

Theo thought of her brother's face the day he'd knocked on her door, such a handsome man with anguish in his bones that his twin alone could feel. She'd tried her hardest to keep him at a distance, but it was an impossibility. "Here," she said to Yakov after she finished going over the entire story, "read this. It's his reply to my request to share this information with you."

Yakov frowned as he picked up her phone.

She knew the words on the screen by heart: Yes, of course, Theo. That you've found someone you trust enough to want to share this? It brings me a peace I didn't dare to hope for; the bears look after their own. I'm glad you'll have them at your back in the time to come.

When Yakov looked up, she said, "He's terrified of what'll happen to me after he's gone, worried the family will hunt me even though he's taken me out of the line of succession at my own request." Her chest squeezed, *squeezed*. "My brother is getting ready to die, Yasha."

Yakov's hand clenched on hers, the word he spoke under his breath harsh and blue. "No cure? Nothing at all?"

"Nothing anyone has discovered to date. Scarabs in the time before Silence imploded and died as children. Their brains are inherently unstable, their psychic powers a category five hurricane." Chaotic and furious and piercingly beautiful in its terrible power.

"He's not dead yet," Yakov said, his jaw grim. "Don't waste the now by living in the unknown future, Theo. Doing so will wreck both the present and the future. That's a piece of advice my great-grandfather gave my grandmother Quyen, and she in turn passed on to me."

The profound truth of Déwei Nguyen's words resonated through her bones. "I want you two to meet."

"Anytime," Yakov said at once, because this was his mate's *twin*. Of course he wanted to meet the man. "We can go to him if he can't come to us. It sounds like he's shoveling a ton of poisonous shit right now."

"I'll ask." Theo wiped away more moisture, took a shaky breath. "I feel so much better having told you. I don't want secrets between us." She swallowed. "No one talked in my family. Everything was hidden."

Yakov winced, then slapped himself in the face with his free hand.

Theo glared at him. "What are you keeping from me?"

Chapter 60

Hien, attached is an article about an engineering "miracle" in the Andes. I thought you'd find it of interest.

I'm reading through the text you sent in your last communiqué and have been making copious notes. The ethical implications of such use of natural resources are, of course, of paramount importance to me as a member of a changeling clan, but I can see the other side of the argument. I'll write more on the subject once I've finished the book.

D.

—Letter from Déwei Nguyen to Hien Nguyen (14 November 1980)

"NOTHING MUCH," YAKOV muttered in response to Theo's demand for information, but if glum had a face, it was his at that instant. "Maybe a prophetic dream that's been haunting me." His shoulders slumped. "I didn't want to tell you because it's nasty stuff."

"Of course. Being that I'm such a shrinking violet."

Those dimples flashed at her sarcastic comment. It made absolute sense that her bear would find her irritation a source of delight. Lifting their clasped hands, he kissed her knuckles before releasing her so they could both finish their meals.

Then he told her his dream of blood and death.

Theo asked question after question, digging down into every facet of his nightmare. "The Moscow Ripper?" she said at last.

"Seems the most likely." Yakov put down his coffee, his fingers bone white as he gripped the china of it. "What I can't figure out is why the dream hasn't changed despite all the security measures I've taken. I've initiated every possible countermeasure."

"No, Yasha," Theo murmured. "You didn't tell me. *Now* you've done everything."

Eyes flashing to amber, he froze for a second before releasing a stream of extremely creative expletives. "I disarmed you without meaning to. Yasha, you're a fucking *kretin* and a *mudak* to boot! I should let Hakon throw me in a hole in the ice in the frozen north."

Theo felt her lips curve. "You're not so bad. You're just a bear."

Lowered eyebrows, a heavy brow. "And you're learning how to tease me."

Yes, she was, wasn't she? Pleased by that, Theo said, "Let's rectify the lack now that I know the risk that's stalking me. Knowledge might not be enough. I need a weapon."

"What are you trained in?"

"Everything. Pax made me learn."

"I like him more with every word you say. Come on, there's a weapons safe under the floor in the bedroom."

And that was how Theo ended up with a sleek little stunner to tuck into her boot, a couple of *tiny* grenades that looked like pills but would cause minor injuries at close range, and a necklace of black beads that could be torn off and thrown on the ground to create an explosion of sparks.

"Meant to distract," Yakov told her. "No real damage, but it'll blind your opponent, gain you time."

"Who is your armorer?" she asked, astonished at the creativity of the ideas.

"Taji—one of the other seconds," he said. "I'll introduce you. Oh, take this, too." He handed her a narrow red case decorated in intricate gold.

"It looks like a vintage lighter." The kind of object people collected. "But since I know that can't be it . . ." She flicked the little tab on the side.

To find herself looking at a knife deadly and gleaming.

"Don't touch the blade," Yakov warned. "Thing's honed enough to cut through bone. Taji was in a bloodthirsty mood when he made that."

"Got it." Using the same flick of the switch to retract the blade, she took her hoard and rose. "I'll get dressed and secrete these on my body."

"Yeah, we should head out." Yakov looked out at the dawn-gray sky. "Weather's forecast to pack it in this afternoon, so we should get as much daylight time at the site as we can." He rose. "I'll call Cissi, too, see how Janine's doing."

His bear lobbied to stay in the bedroom, watch Theo get naked.

The human side of him had difficulty disagreeing, but he knew that would put paid to their plans for a quick departure. So he grabbed what he needed and went to change in the lounge instead.

After doing so, he called Cissi.

"Nene's good," the carer told him. "Her usual cheerful self. We're just discussing where we want to go today. I found a big indoor plant fair they both seem keen on."

He'd just hung up from that conversation when Theo walked out of the bedroom. She was wearing blue jeans and a gray sweater that hugged her form, over which she'd thrown his jacket—though it was clearly now *her* jacket. His bear made happy humming sounds inside him.

Her hair was in a French braid, the strands pulled neatly away from her face.

A hot buzzing in his brain, a rain of snow.

"Yasha?" Theo strode over. "What is it? What's wrong?"

Yakov touched trembling fingers to her sweater. "This is it." It came out harsh. "The clothes you're wearing in my dream, the way you've done your hair, this small snag in the wool of your sweater. Exactly this."

No fear in Theo, only cool-eyed logic. "The necklace, too?"

Bear prowling restlessly inside his skin, he touched the glossy black beads. "No," he said slowly, "the necklace wasn't in it."

"Then we've already changed the future." A triumphant smile. "Now, let's go live our today, and deal with the rest when it happens." Grabbing the back of his neck, she tugged him down for a kiss. "Forewarned, armed, and definitely not easy prey."

DESPITE the logic of Theo's words, Yakov was still on edge when they reached the facility. But if Theo was safe anywhere, it was out here in this isolated location the vast majority of people couldn't even access.

Once inside the lonely emptiness of the space, the wind a gentle howl through the trees and a faint drizzle of mist in the air, he parked by the main building. Leaves rustled across the parking area, the entire scene made even more desolate by the heavy skies that hung overhead. "Ready, *pchelka moya?*"

"Why do you call me that?" Theo's curious voice was fierce and without fear as she stared at the building that had altered the course of her existence.

"Because you buzz with a furious energy, my Theo. My bear's fur stands up around you." He tapped her nose when she wrinkled it. "Bear likes your energy. So do I. I love who you are, my potent little ball of fire."

A tug of her lips. *"Bears."*

Chuckling, he opened his door as she opened hers.

Shielded against the evil of this place by the bond of love that was a crackling storm between them, all wild changeling energy and Theo's contained fury, the two of them grabbed shovels, a sample collection kit, and a portable scanner that Stasya had dropped off this morning on her way to another meeting in the city.

"Boring city maintenance business," she'd muttered, "but I have to go since I'm the only bear who doesn't lose their mind and start suggesting multicolored tarmac or complimentary party busses in every neighborhood to liven things up."

"I dunno," Yakov had said, "I liked Zasha's idea of streetlights shaped like teddy bears. Make the city more welcoming. Adorable."

"And that"—a pointed finger—"is why none of you are in charge of repping StoneWater at the meetings. Anyway, I have to boost. Hope the scanner helps."

Yakov trusted the equipment, but he also knew it wasn't foolproof. Hence the shovels—for exploratory digging in order to get samples that could be run for evidence of decomposition as it related to the breakdown of human, Psy, or changeling remains. Yakov had a sick feeling that it might not come to that—any bodies were unlikely to be buried deep.

Took too much time to dig a deep hole, and given the number of patients Theo's brother had guessed had been housed at the facility . . .

His blood was ice fueled by pure anger at the ugliness of it all.

Slinging the scanner over one shoulder by the attached strap, while Theo took the sample kit, he closed the vehicle's trunk, then grabbed both shovels. And though the air was pervasive with the scent of old evil, he refused to surrender to it, refused to burrow into the past rather than live in today.

For himself. And for his Theo.

"You know, it's funny," he said. "I would've expected Stasya to mention Pasha's mating. It'll be the biggest news in the den today."

"It was early when she dropped by." A few fewer lines on Theo's face at the remembrance of joy. "She might've missed it."

"Maaaan, she'll be majorly pissed off if she's the last to know." He took a quick glance at his phone after realizing he hadn't checked it since his conversation with his grandmother. "Okay, this is just weird. No messages when the clan should be blowing up my phone. Half of them are in a betting pool about when the mating would happen."

"Perhaps your alpha only informed your family?"

"No, mating's a private matter. Valya wouldn't share it with anyone except Silver; he'd wait for the couple to do the sharing. And you know, that's another thing—my parents haven't called, either." He froze. "Oh. My. God."

"What?"

"Babulya Quyen is Denu's *child*." His grandmother had never shared what she'd inherited from her Psy parent, but she clearly had a few tricks up her sleeve. "That's why she called me! She knew I'd already know so she wouldn't be spilling a secret." Chuckling, he shook his head. "And she calls *us* mischief bears."

Theo's smile held impish delight. "She's my favorite," she whispered. "Other than you."

Yakov leaned over to kiss her cheek. "Acceptable. My babushka *is* pretty cute." Having reached the area Elbek and Moon had pinpointed, a desolate patch of grass with noticeable yellow patches and evidence of subsidence, he put down the shovels. "Ready?"

A reawakened grimness to her expression, Theo nodded. As the drizzle collected in glittering strands on the fine silk of her hair, she placed the sample kit next to the shovels, then stood silent watch over his bleak task.

"Nothing," he said after completing the scan of the first depression. No give in her expression, no end to the knots in his gut.

He felt no surprise when the scanner lit up on the second scan. A faint scent on the breeze tickled his brain as he showed Theo the glowing green outline. "Confirmation of buried organic material. No way to tell what at this resolution." He'd been wrong about the depth of the burial. "Could be rubbish, could be a body."

Theo stared at the outline. "We should call Enforcement. They can bring in the heavy-duty scanners," she said as Yakov began to turn in the direction of the scent that was irritating his senses. "This has now gone far beyond my family. These patients deserve—*Yasha!*"

Theo thrust her body toward his even as she screamed.

Chapter 61

The latest scans picked up a significant increase in Subject V-1's neural activity. Too much to be explained by a sudden natural regeneration. It's possible she's been avoiding her meds or feigning her apparent state.

I've put her in a locked single room for the time being, but it's imperative we do a full medical. If she *is* functional and off her meds, it's possible she has full access to the PsyNet.

I won't, of course, act without your authoriz—

—Dr. Upashna Leslie to Councilor Marshall Hyde (unsent)

DESPITE HER IMMEDIATE action, Theo couldn't move fast enough to catch Yakov as he collapsed without warning, the side of his face hitting the earth as the scanner fell to one side in a spasm of cracked green. Dropping to her knees, she placed a desperate hand on his back . . . and felt it. The residual heat of a blast from a weapon designed to deliver a jolt of energy that scrambled the nervous system.

Most targets twitched erratically as their bodies refused to obey their commands, but remained conscious.

Yakov hadn't twitched, was dead silent and motionless.

Breath short and shallow and chest feeling as if it had been crushed inward, Theo couldn't think rationally, had no room in her brain to consider who'd shot him in this lonely place filled only with the dead. She just needed to know if he was alive! She went to press her fingers to his neck, to where she should feel a strong, steady pulse.

"He's not dead," said a husky female voice. "Sorry about the hard fall, but I had no choice. He was about to scent me even though I stayed upwind."

Spinning around, Theo went for the stunner in her boot, but Yakov's assailant already had a weapon trained on her. "Hand it over or I take another shot. Even a bear can't survive two hits at max output."

Theo's pulse wanted to skitter, her mouth to go dry, but panic would get her nowhere. So she pulled on the skin of the fearless girl who'd survived a psychopathic Councilor—and became a being of ice-cold resolve. "Can I check his pulse first?"

Blank eyes, the woman's smile a painted-on facsimile that made the hairs on Theo's nape prickle. "Sure, why not."

Theo pressed her fingers to Yakov's neck, holding her breath until she felt it—the uninterrupted beat of his heart. He was a bear, she reminded herself. Heavily muscled despite his compact frame, and difficult to kill.

"Now," the woman said, "the weapon."

Ensuring she kept her hands in view at all times so as not to trigger the threat, Theo removed the weapon from her boot and threw it across to land at the other woman's own booted feet. She wore slimline black jeans and a black sweater with those lace-up boots, but it wasn't her stark choice of clothing that interested Theo.

Blue eyes.

Fine flyaway blond hair that fell below her shoulders.

A heart-shaped face.

Cheekbones that were just a fraction too rounded to be striking.

The woman's eerie smile deepened as she kicked Theo's weapon into the bushes. "It's uncanny, isn't it? The resemblance. I have to admit I gasped the first time I saw you in your adult form."

"We're mirror images of each other."

A crinkling of the woman's eyes that might even have been real. "You're being sweetly polite. I'm at least a decade your senior in looks. In reality, it's fourteen years."

Theo's mind made the connection in a fury of neural fire. "Keja." Marshall Hyde's daughter, the one marked as dead on the family tree.

"Oh, that was faster than I expected. Well done." She nudged the weapon up. "On your feet. Oh, and turn off, then throw away your phone, too. His as well. All that pesky tracking. I already took care of the system in your vehicle."

Theo did as ordered, using the opportunity offered by getting Yakov's phone out of his back pocket to once more feel the warmth of him. *Alive, he's alive*, she told herself as she threw both phones into the trees before getting to her feet.

She couldn't be emotional, couldn't show how much it hurt her to just leave him. Because Yakov had a higher chance of survival if she did abandon him—he was tough enough to survive the weather even if the clouds burst, and Keja couldn't shoot him again if he wasn't in her line of sight.

That was when Keja lowered the weapon to her side, black against black, and said, "Nene?"

Theo's heart kicked with bruising force as Janine walked out of the trees. Halting partway, she looked from Theo to Keja, back again. "Keke?" A child's thin plea.

Despite the fact that her aunt had lowered her weapon, Theo didn't make the mistake of launching an attack. Keja's fingers gripped the sleek black device tight—tight enough that Theo's minor Tk wouldn't be able to dislodge it from her grasp.

Keja could lift it and shoot Theo faster than Theo could get to her.

Then there was Janine.

She shouldn't be here, Theo said in a furious telepathic burst aimed at her aunt.

Keja's gaze flickered only a fraction. *No, but we all have to make sacrifices.* To the other woman, she said, "Can you take the bear to our old house? He's hurt." Gentle, coaxing voice. "Theo and I will follow."

"Yes, Keke. I like to teleport." Walking over to Yakov, she put a hand on his shoulder . . . and was gone, Yakov with her.

Theo's heart punched against her rib cage. "Who did you bury here, Keja?" she asked, knowing she had it right, that her aunt was behind the echoing emptiness of the facility.

"Staff." A one-shouldered shrug. "Don't tell me you feel sorry for them. I won't believe you. Bastards tried to turn you into a puppet same as they did me. Only I got the first version of the treatment, with all the hard edges and jagged shards."

Theo glanced over at the depressions in the ground. "*All* the staff?"

A curt nod. "Couple of different sites around the grounds. Janine helped me dig the holes. I told her it was for planting trees."

That explained why the holes had been deep: telekinetic assistance from a Gradient 6.1.

But Keja wasn't finished. "Considered keeping the lead doc alive, but bitch was too smart and stupidly loyal to our patriarch. And she tried to lock me up." Eyes devoid of emotion. "Nene got me out, then I bashed the doc's skull in."

"Why did no one notice her mind vanishing from the Net?"

"Time of disruption, with Father blown up that same day. Everyone flapping around about a dead Councilor. No one was watching for a few isolated minds that ceased to exist one cold and rainy night."

"I have to admit it," Theo said, "your timing was sublime."

A gleam in Keja's eyes. "Another plus was that Father had made sure his staff had airtight PsyNet shields, there was no official payroll record on Marshall systems, and that their families had no idea of their work address."

A deeper smile, but still nothing in those glacial blue eyes. "There was no trail to follow. They vanished without a trace. Just like I did, Theo. His own daughter. Erased from existence."

Theo acted on instinct. "My mother—your sister, Claire—is at this moment plotting my murder." Pax had decided, after consulting with Theo, to allow the conspiracy to continue on so he could pinpoint as many psychopathic bad apples as possible. "Our family sucks."

Barking out a laugh that was too hard, too broken, Keja said, "Want to know a secret?" The rising wind lifted strands of her hair into the air. "Twins run in the Marshall line."

It took Theo a second. "You're a twin, too." Even as she spoke the words, she knew they couldn't be true. Her mother was far older than Keja. There were no other siblings.

"My brother died in the womb," Keja said, as if reading her mind. "They didn't even note him down on the family tree, but I carry him here." A tap of her head. "He woke up after the procedure, made sure I was never alone."

Theo stared at the woman who was Theo with a little more time on her . . . and who was perhaps calmly, beautifully, insane. "How do you know so much about the back end of the operation?" she asked, both because Keja had all the answers—and because knowledge was power.

"Father had a habit of talking to me. Had no one else to boast to about his successes, I suppose—and even though I was a failed attempt, I was still functional enough to experiment on, and to serve as a control against the treatments they trialed on version 2.0." The blue turned to stone, as inhuman as the gaze of a rattlesnake. "Walk."

Version 2.0.

"That's me, isn't it? Version 2.0?" Theo said as she fell into step ahead of her aunt, soon emerging onto a familiar overgrown pathway scattered with yellow petals. She wasn't afraid of being shot in the back. If Keja had wanted to shoot Theo, she'd have done it right after she shot Yakov.

"Yes, you're the version that *worked*." Bitterness coated in a rage that glittered with ice. "You're the one who had the right brain chemistry, the *perfect* neuroplasticity."

Theo's stomach lurched, the breakfast Yakov had fed her with such affection threatening to rise up and erupt from her mouth. "Keja?" she said when she could speak again, her voice a rasp. "I don't know what they did to me. Will you tell me?"

A long pause behind her, so long that they'd reached the door to the small residence she'd explored with Yakov before Keja replied. "He never told you?"

Taking a calculated risk, Theo glanced over her shoulder at her aunt. "I didn't even know this place existed until I arrived at the gates and had a panic attack that triggered a flashback."

Eyebrows lowering, Keja said, "Get inside," but her tone was more thoughtful now.

Theo walked into the living area to find Yakov lying on the floor in the same position he'd been in on the forest floor. Janine sat beside him, patting at his arm. "He's a bear, Keke," she said in that sweet tone. "He's nice. Why won't he wake up?"

"He hit his head, Nenochka." Keja's tone was of another woman altogether, warm with compassion. "Why don't you teleport back before Cissi comes looking for you? You remember what I said?"

Janine lifted a finger to her lips. "Our secret." She giggled, then waved at them both and was gone.

"Where does Cissi think she is?"

"In the toilet at an indoor plant fair. Janine experiences stomach issues from time to time—long-term effect of the drugs they put her on here. Sorry about this."

Theo's body jerked, her nervous system overloading under the abrupt hit. Pain seared the nerves damaged by her grandfather's assault, blackness unfolding in front of her eyes.

She heard Keja swear before her aunt caught her dropping body and shoved her into a chair. "Shouldn't have had that much of an impact," she muttered, before leaving Theo.

Theo wanted to act, grab the knife in her jeans pocket, the grenades in the pocket of the jacket, but her body refused to accept her commands. Her eyes wouldn't even open.

Keja had bound Yakov's legs and arms by the time they did.

Made him helpless. Just like in his nightmare.

Chapter 62

"Something's wrong with Yasha. And neither he nor Theo are answering their phones. I'm tracking—*Govno!* Phones are either off or dead."
"Try the vehicle."
"Tracking disabled. *Fuck.*"

—Pavel Stepyrev and Valentin Nikolaev (now)

THEO'S AUNT GRABBED a chair from the dining table and dragged it to a position opposite Theo.

Theo, her nerves yet twitching, tried to use her Tk to push the weapon out of her aunt's hand, but though Keja's arm moved, she kept her grip. "Stop that." A light reprimand. "I'm you, remember? I know every trick you do. Father tested them on me first."

Breath shallow from the lingering effects of the stun, Theo decided to gather her energy and bide her time—and keep Keja's attention off Yakov. She didn't know why her aunt had spared his life, but she didn't want to remind Keja of the biggest threat in the room, bound or not.

"So," Keja murmured after taking a seat, "the old man didn't tell you."

Theo shook her head. "I have blurred memories from eight and a half to around sixteen. Distant, you could say. As if they're not quite mine."

"Interesting. I always wondered about the side effects of a successful procedure." Keja put one foot on the knee of her other leg, resting her weapon on her thigh, finger on the trigger.

"You said puppets. He was attempting mind control?" Such experiments had been run in shadowy corners of the PsyNet as long as Psy had existed.

"He always said that was a useless endeavor that demanded too many resources. He called his goal 'Enforced Malleability.'" Keja's smile turned cruel, her eyes filling with emotion for the first time. "Mind control dressed up in pretty clothes if you ask me. A sop to his ego. Marshall Hyde would never be so *common* as to try the same stupid thing as countless others over the centuries."

Theo tried not to glance at Yakov, look for any hint of movement, of waking. She couldn't risk giving him away if he did begin to come out of the stun.

"He and his pet scientist came up with the idea of rehabilitating chosen people in a *subtle* way. Janine and Santo are two examples of their first successes. Enough mind left for thought, but no ability to think on their own."

Keja sighed. "Father realized too late that the latter wouldn't work. His puppets were akin to infants, needing constant care. Hardly useful as any type of operative."

Theo's skin flushed hot, then cold, but she didn't interrupt, not wanting Keja to stop talking. Both to give Yakov more time to wake, and because she had to know the truth, no matter how twisted and brutal it turned out to be.

"The revised aim," Keja said with a tap of the weapon against her thigh, "was to make a marionette who *could* think for herself . . . but whose brain was plastic enough to mold to obey his commands. An intelligent slave—but crucially, one who thought she had free will, so would never rebel. Why should she? She wasn't being forced to do anything, after all."

The sick feeling in Theo's stomach spread through her veins, into her bones, until she couldn't contain the violence of it. "He did that to me. He took away Theo and put a doll in my place!"

One of the old books on the shelf beside them flew off to bang onto the opposite wall.

Keja flinched, but didn't threaten Theo with the weapon. Instead, she tilted her head to one side, and for the first time, her gaze was . . . normal. No flatness. No cold rage. Just curiosity, simple and explicable.

"What did you think was occurring?" she asked. "I've always wondered. With me, it was a black haze for years. I didn't even know why they'd kept me alive until after I murdered Dr. Leslie and dug through her files. Turns out I was considered a level one success despite my 'diminished mental state.'" Keja hooked the fingers of her free hand by her face to create air quotes. "Much more functional than Janine or Santo—but with an unfortunate need for an extreme level of instruction."

Theo didn't allow herself to get stuck on the casual mention of murder. Especially of a woman who'd gone along with the mutilation of minors. Because Keja was right; Theo didn't feel sorry for the staff. "I don't have any clear memories of the first years, but later, I thought I'd made the choice to please Grandfather in order to gain his approval." She met her aunt's eyes and bared her soul. "I'm haunted by that, Aunt Keja, haunted by the idea of being a willing accomplice to evil."

A sudden piercing tenderness on the other woman's face. "Well, young Theo, I can put your mind to rest on that point. Per Dr. Leslie's files you were a near-total success—you had both the malleability and the intelligence required of a subject. As a test after you'd healed, your grandfather told you multiple times that you wanted to use a hot poker to burn a small bit of your skin to see how it would feel."

Theo looked down at her arm, seeing through the jacket and her sweater to the small scar below her inner elbow that had always been a mystery. When she glanced up, Keja was nodding.

"You did it one day," her aunt said, "and when asked why, you said it was because you'd wanted to. No torture, no intensive mental control; Grandfather would just tell you things until you believed them. And you did. You thought every single act he manipulated you to do was your own idea."

Memories crashed through Theo's mind of all the doors she'd opened, all the accidents she'd caused, all the responsibility she'd accepted, all the guilt she'd carry to the end of her days. Because knowing that she'd never had a choice didn't wash away the blood he'd put on her hands. "I'm happy he's dead."

Keja's smile was deeper, more real. "I would've preferred to do it myself, but—" Another shrug. "Can't say it worked out all bad. I'd come out of the last of the fog a year or so before his assassination—"

"Wait, is that another glitch in the procedure?" Theo asked. "The fact that it wears off? I started to disobey him around sixteen."

"Yes. Not on subjects like Nene and Santo—there just isn't enough left for a recovery." Cold rage in those familiar eyes. "The good doctor downgraded you in her files after you began to act out—from Alpha Variant to Sub-optimal Variant B." Rage or not, Keja's tone was dry, as if she had humor in her, this woman who wasn't supposed to exist. "I'm sure you are most devastated."

"Why did you wait a year to act?"

"Security," Keja said. "Place was locked down. I had to plan—and I was in no immediate danger at the time, since Father continued to keep me around like a pet dog. I also wanted it so that when I did exit, they'd never find me again. Then someone blew Father dearest to bits."

Throwing back her head, she laughed. "You should've seen the panic among the staff, Theo! Headless gerbils scuttling and scrambling. Janine had already sprung me from the locked room by then—once I realized what was going on, I had to go hide in a broom closet to get my urge to laugh under control. After the first panic, though, the doctor decided that since they had the funding, they should continue their 'work' until they received further instructions from Father's successor."

Keja flicked a glance at Yakov, her attention back on Theo before Theo could move a muscle. "I decided on a change of plan. In the confusion, the doc forgot to inform the rest of the staff that I was supposed to be locked up, and they'd long ago stopped paying attention to me.

"I was furniture that could walk and do menial tasks. So I just drugged them all through the kitchen. They had me working in there, can you believe it? Idiots. I'd been hoarding medication for months, had a special spot in the grounds where I buried it.

"Janine, the others, they gave me their meds, too, because I always snuck them treats from the kitchen. The staff just fell asleep." A faint smile. "Of course, not everyone drank their nutrients at the same time, but it wasn't hard to eliminate the holdouts once I had a weapon. The perimeter guards always got their nutrients first, you see. Had to be in top shape to protect the facility."

Keja, too, Theo realized, had never had anyone to whom to boast about her exploits. And Theo wasn't only a captive audience, she was an enthralled one. "Then what? Wouldn't there have been a second shift? A third?"

"Just two. Twelve-hour shifts," Keja clarified. "After we dragged the first lot into a room and I used my new access to the injectables to make sure they'd never wake up, I dressed up in security gear to belay suspicion at the gate. I also got Janine and a few others who were a touch more functional to change into staff scrubs, so the new shift wouldn't immediately wonder where everyone was."

She winced. "It did end up a tad bloody, but I had all the weapons and I had Nene. Santo and Queenie locked the doors while the staff weren't looking. Rats in a maze. Stupid, scared rats so conditioned by Father on the importance of strict confidentiality—conditioning he reinforced by making it known that the punishment for any disclosure was death—that they never even squeaked for help on the PsyNet."

Theo could imagine the staff's terror as the conscious ones were picked off one by one, but she still couldn't make herself pity them. Unlike her and Keja, the staff members had made a choice to assist in the brutalization of countless others. "I can't believe Grandfather sacrificed a teleporter to his ambitions." Teleport-capable Tks weren't exactly thick on the ground—and Janine was a *6.1!*

"Wonder of wonders, bastard did actually admit that to be a mistake. Their initial protocol involved focusing on people with a specific brainwave pattern, and Janine was unlucky enough to display that.

"Father was so consumed by the project at the time that he green-lit her acquisition for the procedure. Poor Nene. She thought she was coming in for a mandatory health check. Instead, they killed the crisp and martial Janine she was when she walked through the door, and left our sweet Nene in her place."

Sorrow in those blue eyes so like Theo's. "I think, if it had been just me, Theo, I would've forgiven Father. Isn't that pathetic?"

"No." Theo's throat was thick; she understood this woman as no other could. "He was a charismatic man and he was the fulcrum of our world."

A blink and the softness was gone. A muscle ticked in Keja's jaw, her lip pulling up in the first whisper of a snarl.

Theo saw it then, the other dark trait that tied them together. "You're like me," she said, forcing herself not to look at Yakov even as anxiety ate through her bones. Why was her laughing, wild bear still so quiet? How hard had Keja hit him? Had her aunt miscalculated and done damage that would lead to a slow but sure death?

Keja laughed that broken laugh that grated on Theo's senses. "I was the original you," she said, her eyes bleeding to black in front of Theo— the eerie thing was that the black didn't spread outward from the pupils, but inward from the edges.

It gave the impression of a voracious virus swallowing her up.

"The perfect candidate had to be a lower gradient," Keja told her, "a Psy whose mind wasn't powerful enough to resist and thus cause unintended damage. Higher-Gradients like Santo and Janine resisted too much, and lobotomized themselves in the process."

"Why the children of the family?" Ugly as it was to think, her grandfather had had access to any number of people unconnected to him.

Yet he'd taken two young girls who'd trusted him.

Her own rage awoke. Gritting her teeth, she fought it back; she couldn't afford to be immobilized by her bracelet.

Keja's hair slid over her shoulders as she put both feet on the ground and leaned forward. "Do you really not know, Theo?"

"No. It makes no sense. Grandfather wanted the world to see the Marshall family as a power. Why would he risk that by permitting staff members to know the line could birth such weak members that they were considered disposable? He couldn't guarantee their silence beyond any shadow of a doubt; I don't care how powerful he was."

"Oh, sweet child," Keja murmured, the indicators of rage replaced by a gentle warmth. "We were trained for this. We were brought up for this. Isolated and taught certain skills. Did you never wonder why he nudged you to learn how to hack? Why you speak multiple languages? Why your caretaker taught you exercises designed to keep you flexible and nimble?"

"*No*," Theo said, even as Keja's words smashed the memories of her past into incomprehensible pieces. "*I* made those choices. That was all before the procedure."

"Adults can influence a child in countless ways. An abused and abandoned child? Give them a crumb of praise for a choice, and they'll never deviate from that path." Keja's gaze held hers. "He raised us to be cattle to the slaughter. We were nothing but meat for him to cut into, hunks of flesh he *owned*."

Chapter 63

This project is the most important of my life. It will be my legacy.

—Marshall Hyde's private notes (circa 2057)

"HE WOULD'VE KILLED you without a qualm if you hadn't had a twin who he valued."

Theo didn't react to Keja's barb—that truth was no surprise to her. "What did he make you do?"

"He made me a monster." No tone, her eyes obsidian.

Sensing the rage in her aunt rising again, Theo shook her head and leaned on the truth. "If you were a monster, Aunt Keja, Janine and Santo would be dead."

Keja looked at her, unblinking and unmoving.

"You mentioned Queenie, too," Theo continued. "Did you get all the patients out?"

A blink, and Keja leaned back in her seat. "Of course I did, Theo." That same chilling smile, of a marionette come to life. "I might be a monster, but I have standards."

Theo's blood ran cold. She knew without a single doubt that Keja *hadn't* done that. Only a minority of the patients would've been like Santo and Janine—functional to the extent that they could live under a carer's watch. The others would've needed to be institutionalized—and where would Keja have found an institution willing to take so many people without question?

"He was furious when you began to act out," Keja said all at once. "He never put it that way, of course. But if he could've murdered you to wipe out the error, he would have."

"He broke my brain," Theo said flatly. "The rages didn't come from nowhere."

"It happens with Santo and Nene as well." A raised eyebrow at Theo's inhale. "Oh, Cissi didn't tell you that? She is a loyal employee. But yes, all of the 'successes' suffer from the same unfortunate secondary effect."

Theo couldn't stop the question on her lips. "Did they ever work out a way to treat it?"

"Mood-altering drugs." Keja named three. "They work, but turn us into zombies. No mind, no life."

Her words snuffed out the tiny flicker of hope in Theo. It must've shown in her expression because Keja said, "It's all right, Theo. You don't have to worry about the rages anymore." A blank mask slipping over her, the shift so visible that it made Theo shudder.

"If you hadn't existed, if your twin hadn't existed," Keja said in a high, almost childlike voice, "he'd have taken me home. I was the first *true success*. So you see why I have to get rid of you. Then he'll have no choice. He'll take me home."

It was a terrible, heartbreaking, and horrifying glimpse into Keja's mutilated psyche. "You're the Moscow Ripper, aren't you?" she said, so stunned by the realization that she couldn't even be afraid. *"Why?"*

"I thought it would be obvious." The mask of . . . nothingness never shifted, never altered. "I thought they were you. Not rational, but I'm unfortunately not always rational. A red mist in my mind, and in that mist, they're all you."

Keja lifted her weapon. "But this time, I've got the right blonde. Father will come for me. I'm the only one left."

Theo tipped herself sideways off her chair, slamming down hard, with one arm of the chair digging into her. Pain sunburst through her damaged nerves as Keja's shot caught her a glancing blow on one hip, spreading numbness up and down along that side.

That pain awakened her simmering rage, a monstrous red beast with glowing eyes, so much anger to it that it hazed her brain. Before it could steal her mind, steal her ability to act with reason, Theo grabbed for the beads at her throat, ripped them off, and threw them at her aunt.

As Keja hissed at being blinded by the resulting shower of smoke and light, Theo managed to get out the tiny grenades, throw them at Keja's feet. But even as shards of the wooden floor flew up to embed themselves in Keja's skin, Theo saw the glitter of silver in Keja's hand . . . the blade meant for Theo's throat. And she realized she'd made a mistake in her shaking fury: the grenades had exploded a fraction too far from her aunt to do any substantial damage.

Screaming, her maddened aunt threw herself at Theo, both of them injured, both of them fighting for their lives. Only Theo couldn't get to the blade in the pocket of her jeans, her brain a cauldron of black rage incapable of reason.

YAKOV stopped playing dead the instant Keja jumped on Theo.

His body remained mostly paralyzed from the blow he'd taken. The only reason he *wasn't* dead was that he was a bear with the attendant muscle mass; he didn't know if Keja had miscalculated and given him too strong a shot, or if she'd intended for him to die, and he didn't care.

All he cared about was saving Theo.

The dream threatened to bleed into his consciousness, suffocate him in its grip. "Fuck that," he said, and took deep gulps of the air in an effort to get as much oxygen into his system as possible. His arms still felt like lead, his eyes the only part of him that he could truly move. But he wasn't about to give up.

His great-grandfather hadn't left him with a drop of foresight in his blood so that he could watch Theo die. His chest rumbled with a growl as Keja landed a punch to Theo's face that made something crunch. But Theo hit her as hard, her elbow taking out Keja's nose in a spray of blood at the same time that she managed to use her other arm to make Keja drop the knife.

That's my girl, he thought, man and bear in agreement.

His fingers flexed, sensation creeping back in razor-sharp pinpricks. Ignoring the agony, he began to crawl his hand back toward the holster positioned in the small of his back. It wasn't his favored position when he had to wear a weapon—he far preferred the shoulder, but he'd put it there the instant he'd understood that he and Theo were on a collision course with Fate.

It was the same reason he'd chosen the sound-wave weapon while they were arming themselves today. The dream had warned him that he'd be all but immobile. So he'd chosen a weapon that could be activated with the simple push of an old-fashioned button. One push. Just one.

Keja screamed as Theo slammed a flat hand against her ear, possibly rupturing her eardrum. But though Theo had managed to roll on top of her, Keja was a brutal fighter and somehow got her hands around Theo's throat.

Fight, Theo, fight!

They rolled out of his limited field of vision.

He heard Theo make a deep, wordless sound . . . then another crunch. Keja screamed again.

Followed by a grunt from Theo.

The two rolled back into view, Keja's face a mask of red from her broken nose, one side of Theo's face already slick red and swelling.

Yakov's bear raged inside his skin—he directed all that energy into his hand, into the infinitesimal crawling movement that had him touching the spot below his T-shirt that held the holster he'd altered in the kitchen that morning, cutting away the part of it designed to cushion the button in order to avoid accidental detonation.

He nudged up the T-shirt just as Keja twisted away and when she came up in a crouch across from Theo, she had the knife once more in hand. "I didn't want to do this to you," she said, her voice bloody and wet. "I wanted to give you a gentler death. But this'll do as well."

She slashed out with the blade, and it became obvious that she had the advantage. Theo had managed to grab her own knife—but her hand was too bloody and it slipped out of her grasp.

Keja swiped at her again as Theo tried to retrieve it—and got Theo on the hand, scarlet dripping to the floor. Theo slipped while scrambling backward, and fell hard, hitting her head . . . just as Yakov's fingers brushed the on button.

The sound bomb wasn't a precision device and would knock them all out, but Yakov would fall last and recover the fastest. The weapon was designed to advantage changelings. Yakov pushed the button as an eerily silent Keja jumped on a dazed Theo, her blade aimed at Theo's throat.

It *should have* worked. It should have dropped her then and there.

But Keja was a Tk in a blinding rage induced by an operation that had altered her neural structure. A Tk with just enough power to "throw" her weapon right before the sound wave reached her.

The blade sliced across Theo's throat before it spun away.

Time seemed to move in slow motion, blood pulsing over Theo's hands as her eyes met his.

No.

No one was going to hurt his Theo ever again!

He refused to let go.

Yakov *reached* and saw her lift one bloodred hand toward him as the sound wave crashed into all their brains with thunderous force. *Theo!* It was his last thought before the world went scarlet.

Then.

Nothing.

Chapter 64

Urgent request for contact from Alpha Nikolaev.

—Note passed to Silver Mercant during her live worldwide
address to members of EmNet (now)

MIDWAY THROUGH A dead run to get into a clan vehicle and drive out
to the old Psy facility, while others went to check the apartment and
Valentin tried another avenue, Pavel fell to his knees, his hands clamped
over his ears as his head vibrated with a massive boom.

On the other side of the world, Pax woke out of a troubled sleep with
an echoing emptiness in his head. *Theo!*

In the heart of Moscow, a slender Psy male with eyes an extraordinary hue between silver and blue collapsed against the wall of a building, his entire being flooded with a fear so deep it hurt.

As the phone chimed and chimed on the other end with no result,
Valentin felt the bond he shared with one of his seconds blaze hot red.

Yasha was dying.

Chapter 65

D, I'm sorry for taking so long to reply.

    The truth is, I miscalculated my ability to handle continued communication from you. I cried from missing you while reading the article you sent, and Neiza saw me. She's still so young, her mind so malleable. She was sad for me, when it's my duty to teach her not to feel emotion at all.

    I don't think that Silence can ever teach me not to love you. That bond is too deep in my heart. But I have to learn not to live that love. I have to learn to let you go.

    This will be the last time I ever send you a communication. Please help me protect my baby from her own powerful mind by never again contacting me. This, big brother, is the last thing your little sister will ever ask of you.

Good-bye, D.
Hien

                  —Letter from Hien Nguyen to Déwei Nguyen (2 April 1982)

PAX JUMPED INTO action.

He couldn't reach Theo with his mind. So he'd go to her. Never again would he stand by helpless while someone tried to separate them.

Teleport. Now! A telepathic order barked at the very expensive teleport-capable Tk he'd hired on a personal contract. At 7.9 on the Gradient, Octavio had no doubt been part of a Council unit at some point, but he was now an independent. His head might be shaved but he was no clean-cut soldier these days. Tattoos snaked up his arms and along the back of one leg, and he'd grown a beard thick and dark.

The most important thing about Octavio was that he had zero interest in politics or playing shadow games. "Had too much of that in my past" had been his clipped answer during their interview.

He also didn't want to be friends, or to bond in any other way.

To him, Pax was just a job. Exactly as Pax wanted it.

At his Gradient level and specific Tk ability, the muscular Sudanese man couldn't crisscross the globe at will, but he was plenty powerful enough for the transports Pax usually needed. San Francisco to Moscow wouldn't strain his psychic muscles.

By the time Pax ran out of his bedroom dressed only in the thin black sweatpants in which he'd fallen asleep, the teleporter was standing ready in the apartment hallway: the designated teleport meeting spot when Pax didn't give him any other direction. "My sister. Lock on her bracelet." That dull piece of jewelry that she never took off and that was marked with a unique design she'd done herself.

It had been the very first and remained the most important reference image Pax had given Octavio.

The Tk shifted until their shoulders touched, and then the world went sideways.

When it settled, Pax found himself in a small room, Theo lying at his feet. Blood coated her throat, soaked her chest. Dropping to his knees, he clamped his hand over the wound in a futile attempt to stop the flow.

His internal scream locked in the ice that was the only way he survived in the world, he went to order Octavio to take her directly to any medical facility to which he had a teleport lock, when he saw the bear who lay mere feet away. His claws were out, had cut bloody furrows into the opposing hands as he struggled against the ropes that bound him.

There was another woman, too, her face smashed up and bloody.

All three were unconscious, but while the women were obviously critically wounded, he couldn't see enough of the bear to work out his injuries.

Theo's bear.

Pax had to help him.

His entire hesitation took a second at most, but there was a flash on the edge of his vision before he could give Octavio any order at all. Octavio went for his gun, but Pax knew it for a useless piece of plas the instant he laid eyes on the man who'd just 'ported in.

Kaleb Krychek.

At his side was a tall and curvy woman in an incongruously cheerful skirt of bright yellow, paired with a white shirt and yellow high heels. Her glossy black hair curled into a flip at her shoulders, her eyes a primal amber.

"Kaleb, my sister is dying," Pax said, because he had no pride here, and this was the most powerful man in the PsyNet. If anyone knew how to save Theo, it would be Kaleb. "I'm trying to feed her power, but it's not working." As if Theo's mind had already begun to shut down.

That was when the woman in yellow rushed over and literally shoved Pax aside. "Healer," she muttered in explanation when he resisted. "She's bonded into the clan. Let me *work*!"

Hands sticky with blood, Pax went to Theo's bear and began to undo the ties around his wrists.

All the while, he talked to Theo. *Wake up, Theo. Please wake up. I have no one else if you're gone. No one.* Not a single living being who he could trust and who trusted him. Just her. Only her. *Theo, don't go. I won't make it if you go.* It would be one blow too many.

The bear groaned awake just as Pax undid the final knot in the ropes.

"Theo?" A rough word, before the bear was right next to Theo and the healer, his hand gripping her bloody one as he said, "Come on, *pchelka*, don't you give up now! You fucking hold on with all your rage, all your fury." His voice was thunder deeper than that which crashed above the house.

Rain shattered against the windows a second later.

The bear was so focused on Theo that he didn't see the other woman stir, the one who looked so much like Theo. But Pax did. Having already decided that she was the one most likely to have hurt Theo, he knocked her back out with a vicious telepathic blow.

She was lucky he didn't kill her.

The only reason he didn't was Theo. Instinct told him the woman was important, and that instinct had to be coming from Theo. Inside his mind, other voices whispered, summoned, but though Theo wouldn't speak to him, she remained the most powerful presence.

Holding them all back. Keeping him from falling into the abyss.

Theo, please.

His mental plea echoed the bear's spoken demand as he shifted to cradle Theo's head in his lap while the healer worked on her with hands that shouldn't have been able to fix a Psy. But—"She's in my head," Pax said to the bear, because the bear was Theo's and so that made him important to Pax. "She's not gone."

"I know." The bear's amber gaze met Pax's, a moment of furious understanding passing between them. "I can feel her right here." A fisted thump to his heart.

That was when Pax knew what had happened.

Theo had mated.

Which meant she had the entire StoneWater clan behind her, a primal rush of wild changeling energy pouring into her from the practiced hands of the healer.

His sister would never again be alone.

Pax didn't care that the new bonds in her life would take her further from him. Didn't even care that the bears would likely shun him. He just cared that she was safe. The bears would keep her safe long after he was gone.

A sudden gasp, Theo's eyes snapping open.

Chapter 66

"We are the foundation."

—Payal Rao, representative of Designation A on the Ruling Coalition
in the *PsyNet Beacon* (29 June 2083)

KALEB FINISHED TRANSPORTING all parties but two to the Stone-Water den infirmary. "I left Pax Marshall and his teleport assist at the site." Pax didn't need to have internal images of the StoneWater den, the home of the clan's most vulnerable.

Valentin rubbed his face. "*Chert*, what a complication. Trust Yasha to fall for a woman with Pax Marshall for a twin." Harsh words, but worry pumped off the alpha. "I'll deal with him. *Spasibo* for coming so quickly."

"I try to be a good neighbor." StoneWater was also not in the habit of asking for his help—which was why he'd cut short a critical meeting to respond to Valentin's SOS. "I apologize for not answering my phone. I had it on silent during a meeting." In the end, it was Silver who'd contacted him via the PsyNet.

Valentin waved off his apology. "You came. That's all that matters. We owe you one."

"Yes, you do," Kaleb responded, because being a good neighbor didn't mean being foolishly noble. A favor from StoneWater was valuable coin. "Good luck with the wounded."

Teleporting back to his home on the remote periphery of Moscow, he glanced outside and saw that the rain had stopped for the time being, so he stepped out onto the rain-washed deck before returning to his meeting on the PsyNet. "Apologies," he said to Payal, whose mind was laser bright next to his. "Emergency teleport request from an ally."

"I understand," said his fellow member of the Ruling Coalition, and a woman who also happened to be a cardinal telekinetic. "Everything all right?"

"I left them in an infirmary." Marshall's sister had lost so much blood that Kaleb had his doubts about her chances of survival. But he'd done all he could, and now he had to return to a problem where millions of lives hung in the balance.

He looked once more at the island on the other side of the chasm in front of him and Payal. That island was no longer an opaque blank. Rather, it sparked with energy, the connections within flickering in and out of visibility in sharp flashes—but that was because the man at the center of the island was still learning how to manage the energy that poured through his brain, then back out into the system.

"So?" he said to Payal.

"The Substrate flow is clear. Anchor energy from the main network is feeding into the island and vice versa."

"Stable?"

"Stable."

Kaleb continued to watch what was, at present, Ivan Mercant's personal fiefdom. Sahara had laughed when he'd put it that way. "He's mated to a healer, my gorgeous Mr. Krychek. He couldn't turn into a dictator if he tried."

She was right, of course, but that didn't obliterate the fact that, as of now, one man held two thousand and twenty-three lives in stable orbit around him. Which wasn't necessarily a bad thing—it was the reason why he and Payal were standing here, deep in the shadows of the Net.

"When we first brought up breaking the PsyNet into smaller units," he said, "you were adamant it wouldn't work because of the dearth of anchors." Anchors maintained and upheld the foundation of the PsyNet, the Substrate. Invisible to all but designation A, it was nonetheless *the* most critical structure in the Net. Should it collapse, so would the PsyNet—leading to the effective extinction of the Psy race.

Payal, ruthless CEO of the Rao Conglomerate, was the anchor representative on the Ruling Coalition.

"If any designation has the leverage to set themselves up as dictators, it's A," Sahara had added during that same conversation, while in the process of knotting his tie while she stood barefoot on their bedroom carpet dressed only in one of his shirts. "Lucky for us that they just want to be left alone."

While it was tempting to think about how he'd pulled off the tie soon afterward and asked for his shirt back only to throw it on the bed and haul her laughing, naked body against his, it would have to wait. Right now, his focus had to be on the continued disintegration of the psychic fabric on which he stood—because Sahara had asked him to walk in the light, to save the PsyNet rather than burning it down to the ground.

"What's your current view of the situation?" he asked Payal.

"Complex. We've assigned a team of As to study the input and output of anchor energy from the island. At this point, the island is drawing more energy per capita than the rest of the PsyNet."

Kaleb stared out at the gorge beyond his home on the physical plane, the drop sheer. Terrifying for most. But not a teleport-capable telekinetic. He'd added a safety railing nonetheless. Because this was Sahara's home, a place of utmost safety. "The Scarabs?"

"Yes. In terms of percentages, the island houses significantly more Scarabs than the rest of the PsyNet. That volume of chaotic Scarab energy would equal an inherently unstable network without conscious remediation by my As."

"Even with Ivan Mercant's containment fields?"

"He can contain them on the Net level, but the Scarabs are jacked directly into the Substrate, just like you are. No way to stop their energy from feeding into the rivers of the Substrate. My As must clean it up before it takes deeper hold and frays another part of the network. It's an exhausting process."

Kaleb considered the gleaming perfection of a drop of water that hung from the railing . . . before falling to the deck to vanish into the thin film of water already present on the boards.

Gravity was a law of nature.

As was a Psy's internal link to the psychic space that sustained the members of their race. To cut it would be to pass a sentence of death.

And the Scarabs are still us, Kaleb, said the echo of Sahara's voice, the words ones she'd spoken to him as they lay in bed one night, her head on his bare shoulder and his hand fisted in the softness of her hair. *We can't just eject our broken. That would make us no better than the Council we replaced. Monsters on a quest for genetic perfection.*

Kaleb had few scruples, his psyche damaged and brutalized too young. But Sahara was his world—and she had conscience enough for both of them. So he didn't postulate a solution that would mean the hunting and erasure of all adult Scarabs in the network. It would take time, but it could be done. A silent and sweeping genocide. But it wasn't going to be done, not under Kaleb's watch.

Not under Sahara's sky.

"Ivan Mercant is also unusual," Payal added. "His psychic ability functions in a way none of us have ever before seen."

"Most of us haven't seen it now, either," Kaleb muttered, bracing his hands on the wet railing on the physical plane.

"Ah, the man who knows everything doesn't know this. It must be most aggravating."

Had anyone told him a year ago that he'd one day be a source of amusement for the Rao Conglomerate's grim-faced and robotic CEO, Kaleb would've ordered that individual to have a drug test. "Do the anchors see it then? Ivan's power?"

"Not in the sense you mean. We are, however, aware of it in a visceral way impossible to explain to anyone but another anchor. He is exactly how his mate puts it: the heart of a system."

Kaleb didn't bother to ask for more personal information about Ivan that she might know as a result of her marriage into the Mercant family. One, Payal wouldn't tell him. And two, he could speak to Ivan himself. Kaleb would never be one of Ena's flock, but she'd accepted him into the inner circle of the family.

"What happens if the heart dies?" he asked, even as part of him grew dark at the thought of the devastation that would cause in Ena's family. The Mercants weren't like so many other families twisted by Silence. The Mercants would cut the throat of anyone who dared harm their own.

Their grief would be infinite.

"We don't know," Payal answered, "and Ivan is in the prime of his life. Let's not borrow trouble when we already have so much."

Kaleb saw the wisdom in that. "I haven't found a way to cross to the island, and now that Ivan is anchored there, he can only cross back for short periods. His network reach is effectively limited to the island."

"Yet, despite its overload of Scarabs, Ivan's island is more stable than any other section of the PsyNet."

"Yes."

"Power versus stable ground," murmured the woman who'd been raised by a man who valued power and had wielded it with an iron hand. "We need to do further research on the effect on Psy brains of a limited psychic ecosystem versus a wider one."

"A sensible precaution, but we're running out of time." The Net was unraveling around them, an increasing number of sections too threadbare to navigate. "I do know of a very tight network—less than ten individuals—that survived for a solid period." A familial network of defectors that happened to include one of Kaleb's few friends in the world. "Even if all we gain is a year, it'll be more time than we have now."

"Sadly, I have to agree." Payal's tone was solemn. "The Substrate is healthier than it's been for a long time, but we're stretched so thin, Kaleb." A more personal tone to her voice now, a hint of the exhaustion felt by every A in the system.

"The problem is Ivan Mercant—or the lack of more like him." Kaleb had sent out countless psychic bots into the PsyNet, searching for any hint of another person with the same subset of abilities. "I've hit zero. So has Aden. The empaths, too. Anchors?"

"Nothing. Yet to know that two members of a line were confirmed to have it, with a third a viable possibility, it's difficult to say it's not genetic. And it's rare for Psy abilities to be limited to a single line."

That was when Kaleb remembered when Payal had entered the Ruling Coalition. "I'm not sure it *is* genetic. After we seized his aunt's records, I looked for data to either confirm or negate a rumor I heard during the start of my term on the Council.

"I uncovered evidence that, at one stage, Scott and her former husband both chose to have experimental bioneural implants." The arrogant stupidity of it stunned him. "The aim of the implant was to control others via a forced neural link."

"Intriguing. But that doesn't explain her sister or Ivan."

"The sister was a Jax addict, and Ivan was exposed in vitro." All information Ivan had shared with the Ruling Coalition in an effort to assist their search for others with his ability. "Jax opens pathways of the mind. What if it isn't the power itself that's genetic, but rather the *predisposition* to such a specific type of expansion?"

Payal was quiet for a long time before saying, "Even if you're right, you can't use it. Jax is a psychological poison pill now."

Kaleb walked back and forth across his deck. Logic stated that such a thought was ridiculous. A medication was a medication. Used in a way not meant to cause harm, it could be a gift of life. And yet . . . how would they know it wouldn't cause harm? How could they control the exposure?

Since Kaleb would—with zero remorse and no guilt—end the life of anyone who suggested child subjects, it would have to be adult volunteers with the right brain structure. And then what? Ivan had survived because he'd been exposed in vitro, then again at a very young age. His mother, the adult user, had died.

No autopsy had ever been done, so they had no idea of the state of her brain at the time of her overdose.

"We might have to go back to the original plan," he said to Payal. "Have a powerful Gradient hold an island." A difficult—and perhaps unfeasible—task for a mind not built for it like Ivan's, but there was a chance it would work as a stopgap measure.

"I'll agree to the experiment on the understanding that if such an attempt breaks the connection to the Substrate, we call it off at once. Nothing has changed when it comes to the critical shortage of designation A—my people are spread thin, held up by each other, load sharing an integral aspect of the new system we've put in place. They'll burn out and die within days if cut off from the main streams of the Substrate."

"Agreed." Kaleb had no desire to agitate the fragile balance the As had created, one that permitted them to rest rather than working until they dropped. Healthier As meant a healthier Net; it was as simple as that.

An exhale into the psychic space. "I don't want this." Payal's voice was taut. "Every single one of our objections continues to apply. But the decision matrix has altered with the continued rise of the Scarabs and the attendant rise in chaotic energy in the Net—we have to attempt a controlled separation before an uncontainable collapse makes the decision for us."

Unspoken was that they'd have to get the agreement of all those on the Ruling Coalition, as well as the residents of the area where the experiment was to take place. But those were minor hurdles in the grand scheme of things. It was the anchors who held the veto power and they weren't going to use it.

It was time to purposefully splinter the PsyNet.

Chapter 67

"Mama, Papa made you a little cake!"

"I see that, Dimochka. You're such a good cub to carry it so carefully to me. Let's put it down here. That's it, my sweet boy. You can help me eat it after I give your papa a kiss."

"You look tired, *malyshka*."

"I already feel better now that I've had hugs from my two favorite people."

—A conversation in the office of Dr. Evanova "Nova" Nikolaev
(45 minutes ago)

YAKOV STILL HAD a pounding head six hours later, as he sat slumped in an armchair in the den's infirmary next to Theo's bed. She'd tried to get out of that bed an hour ago, and faced Nova's wrath—and her own spinning head. The end result was that she lay impatiently in it, her hand rising to brush the thick and swollen line of her new scar every so often.

Yakov knew she didn't care about the scar itself; she cared about what the state of it said of her injury. *He* cared about the scar—because every time he looked at the jagged slash in her throat, it reminded him of the horror of almost losing her.

Now she said, "I'll get it removed as soon as Nova says it's healed enough for the procedure." One side of her face a patchwork of black bruises under a healing mesh, but the blue of her gaze tender. "Until then, I'll take up wearing turtlenecks."

Lifting her hand to his lips, he pressed a kiss on it. He was still having trouble speaking, his mind awash with the final images he'd seen before the world had gone dark. Blood, so much fucking blood.

"I'm alive because we changed the future," she reminded him, her voice husky from the strain of her wound, and when he scowled, said, "We *did*. I always died in your dreams. But I'm not dead today."

"Too close," he gritted out. "She should've never got to your throat."

"Yashin'ka." A coaxing tone with a thread of steel as his Theo used his name in a way intimate and affectionate. "We can only control our decisions, no one else's. Don't be a stubborn bear and refuse to accept that we altered the trajectory of my certain death to almost-death. Big difference."

He scowled at her. "Are you sure you're not a bear under the skin? You sound smartass enough."

A grin that was his sun. "Ouch." She patted with utmost gentleness at the side of her face overlaid with the glow of the healing mesh and attendant gel.

"I need to hold my energy in reserve for any other emergencies," a tired Nova had said while Theo was unconscious, her usually perfectly set hair bedraggled and pulled back in a haphazard fashion. "Mesh takes longer but will heal her cheekbone fine."

Having witnessed the fury with which Nova had worked on Theo, Yakov had just hugged her until she'd squeaked. He'd always loved StoneWater's healer, but now he fucking worshipped her.

"Stop touching that," he ordered. "Or I'll tattle to Nova."

Theo narrowed her eyes—but dropped her hand. Because even his *pchelka* knew not to push their healer. Nova had once put Valentin himself on bed rest, then dared him to fight her when he protested.

Needless to say, Valya had stayed put—while sulking.

And his obedience hadn't been because Nova was one of the alpha's big sisters. It was because she was their healer, with the attendant power behind it.

"Am I interrupting a lover's quarrel?" A mock whisper from the doorway.

It wasn't the first time Pavel had dropped by. The rest of their family, as well as Arwen, had come for a quick visit to reassure themselves he and Theo were both fine, then ceded visiting rights to Pasha, since Nova had made it clear she did not want guests "riling up" her patients.

A bear healer had to have a firm hand—and a big stick.

Nova's stick was the sweetness of her temper. Calm was never so fucking terrifying as on the StoneWater healer.

"You want to tell me how we ended up here, bro?" Yakov asked him. "I've got no memory of anything after I detonated the aural bomb."

His twin, who'd squeezed the life out of Yakov on his first visit, his heart thumping like a drum and his breathing unsteady, then kissed Theo gently on the mouth with her smiling consent, was in a more composed frame of mind this time.

Grabbing the chair he'd left at the end of the bed, he spun it around and straddled it. "Right, so I went down like a sack of bricks—"

"Wait." Theo's voice. "You felt it?" A wonder in her tone that made Yakov want to cuddle her. "I didn't know changeling twins could do that."

"Yeah," Pavel said with a grin. "Not like Psy telepathy, but Yasha and I've always known when the other one is in trouble. I first got a glimmer of it a bit earlier, tried to track you down via your phones and the car, and couldn't. I'd said fuck it and was just going to go with my gut and drive to the facility when"—he spread his hands outward from his head—"my head went boom."

"Back when we were cubs," Yakov added, "they once had to put my arm in a sling after Pasha broke his, because I was in so much pain. Our mother still has a photo of the two of us bandaged up side by side, Pasha's other arm around my shoulders."

"Arwen loves that photo so much he asked for a copy." Pavel's smile went tender and soft for a moment. "Right, where was I? So, I crashed, then Valya felt you go down through the alpha-second bond." A nod at Yakov. "He'd already been trying to get through to Krychek, but the man wasn't picking up, so Valya got ahold of Silver and she touched base with Krychek through the Net and asked for his help."

Yakov stared at his brother. "Bullshit." StoneWater had an excellent relationship with Silver's old boss, but they were also wary of any debt to the cardinal Tk.

"It's fine. Krychek only demanded your liver and one kidney in return for his help," his brother said with a wave of his hand.

A sound from the bed had Yakov looking up. Theo's little laugh made him forgive his twin for drawing out the suspense—even when she winced again when the motion jostled her healing cheekbone.

"Did you know Krychek can lock onto faces, not just places?" Pavel raised both eyebrows. "Our local deadly telekinetic tycoon—who, by the way, I still hold is causing the minor quakes when he's bored—could've been standing in our den anytime he wanted all that time we were negotiating with him right at the start."

"Huh." Yakov rubbed his thumb over the back of Theo's hand. "Makes me like him better that he didn't. No one should enter another's home without an invitation."

Pavel gave a nod of agreement. "Short story is he locked onto Nova's face since he apparently has files on all the senior members of the clan and knows all our faces—because of course he does."

Yakov felt zero surprise; no one got to Krychek's level of power without thinking of every contingency. What mattered here was that the Tk had used the information to assist, not harm.

"Once he picked up Nova," Pavel continued, "he locked onto your face, Yasha. Said to Valya later that it might not have worked if I hadn't been wearing my glasses at the time." He nudged up the metal frames.

"Identical twins can screw up a facial teleport lock." A smug look. "*See.*
I told you specs were a better idea than surgery."

Swamped by a wave of affection for his twin, Yakov grinned. "And
it has nothing to do with your fear of lasers near your eyes?"

"*Mudak.*" A cheerful insult. "Theo appreciates my sacrifice in wearing glasses, don't you, Theo? Plus my mate says they're sexy, so you can
go scratch your furry butt with some poison ivy."

"I think you're wonderful, Pasha," Theo said with a careful grin.
"But I do also love my Yashin'ka's butt, so no poison ivy curses, if you
please."

Pavel's laugh held wild affection, while Yakov's bear prowled pleased
inside his mind. That his Theo and his brother liked each other? It made
both parts of him happy.

A smile in her voice, Theo said, "Did Krychek then bring us back here?"

"Pretty much. He left your brother to fend for himself." Pavel's voice
softened. "Said he had a teleport-capable Tk with him? So hopefully
he made it home all right. We did send people to the facility to
hold it safe until you woke up, and they knew to keep an eye out for
him, but the site was empty."

Theo nodded. "I've telepathed with him. He's at our Moscow apartment." She shifted her gaze to Yakov, the blue potent with emotion. "He
needs to see me."

Remembering Pavel's desperate embrace, Yakov nodded. "I'll talk to
Nova, see if she'll give you a pass for a short visit with your brother. We
can set up a meet near the edge of den territory. You understood why he
can't come to the den?"

"Yes. This is the home of your most vulnerable and he's an unknown
threat—he'll have no argument with the decision, either." Her brother
was just happy she was being so fiercely protected by the bears.

The reason why made her heart hurt, and she saw the knowledge of
her pain in Yakov's gaze, felt it in the kiss he pressed to her knuckles
again. "Live in the now," he murmured, reminding her of his great-
grandfather's advice.

Theo clung to it, to the now where her brother was alive and himself, and where she would see him again soon. Shifting her attention back to Pavel, who'd kept his silence during that quiet interaction, she said, "My aunt?"

"Unconscious. You have any idea why the bomb hit her so much worse?"

"It didn't. Pax slapped her with a telepathic blow when she began to come around."

Pavel whistled. "Yikes. She's going to be in a world of hurt when she wakes." No sympathy in his tone for the woman who'd tried to murder her—because while the bears were full of heart, they were also ruthlessly protective.

Pax would fit right in.

Theo released a shuddering breath at the thought of a time where her brother sat with a group of laughing bears, all of them in sync. "Where is she?" It didn't make sense that they'd keep Keja in the den, not when she was a major threat.

"Soon as Nova stabilized her, we drove her to a guarded medical facility outside den territory. Medical transport, designed for this kind of thing, so it didn't hurt her."

Theo's mind blazed hot red, an overlooked piece of information roaring to the surface. "She has access to a teleporter."

"Shit." Pavel pulled out his phone and made the call right then, telling the guards to ensure that they positioned themselves right next to Keja at all times. "That work?" he asked Theo while still on the call.

"Yes, as a stopgap. Janine can still go to her, but she can't teleport her out if she can't touch her." Tks like Kaleb Krychek didn't need physical contact, but Janine wasn't that powerful.

After passing that on, Pavel hung up. "What do Psy do about criminals like your aunt? People who can vanish out of locked rooms?"

"I don't know." She coughed, her throat dry. "I'm assuming there must be a way to block or shield certain abilities."

"Drink first, talk later." Yakov put a straw to her lips—it went into a glass of nutrients he'd arranged for her.

Theo sipped while scowling at him, but she wanted to cuddle her worried bear. She'd never forget the terror in his voice as he screamed her name.

"Ugh, goo-goo eyes, that's my cue to get out of here." Pavel rose to his feet. "But I'm fucking glad you're in the den, where we can look after you both."

Theo jerked her lips from the straw, her brain only now processing the import of her current situation. "I can't be here." The air suddenly jagged bits of stone in her lungs, she sat up, pushing aside the blanket. "I can't be here." She swung her legs over the side of the bed.

Her skin was hot, her chest compressing in on itself.

Chapter 68

"What's it like being loved by a bear?"
"Everything. It's everything."

—Conversation overheard in a Moscow café

YAKOV BLOCKED HER from getting off the bed. "Pasha, can you give us a few minutes?"

"I'll go help Arwen sort out food for you guys." Then he was gone, closing the door behind himself.

Yakov cupped the uninjured side of Theo's face. "Look at me," he said when she continued to scan the small room for an escape hatch that would spit her outside, far from the families in this den.

When he wouldn't allow her to jump off the bed, she grabbed his wrist. "You have cubs here!" Mouth dry, breath short, her skin hot. "You need to get me out—I could hurt them in a rage."

Her bear didn't budge. "Almost every single adult in this place is stronger than you," he said in a voice that held the bear's grumble. "You won't be coming into contact with any cubs on your own while you're laid up in the infirmary. Even Nova's cub isn't permitted to wander around the infirmary at will."

She fought to draw in enough air. "I—" Grabbing the glass of nutrients, she sucked hard on the straw.

The blast of energy cleared her thoughts. "Okay, okay," she said after a few deep breaths. "I won't try to escape the infirmary." He was right; she was under constant watch here, couldn't act out without being halted.

"But I can't live here." Her eyes burned, because she knew this was his home, his heart. "I'm so sorry, but I can't." She'd exist in a state of constant panic and fear—yet the idea of being torn from him?

Sharp stabs through her veins, hurt in her soul. "I could stay at the apartment," she suggested. "You wouldn't have to be with me every day, could still stay in the den whenever you wanted." Theo would never attempt to separate him from his clan and his family.

Even if she needed him with a desperation that hurt.

A growling nip of her finger. "If you think I'm not cuddling you every night forever, we're going to have a problem." Amber in those eyes now. "Because you and me, Theo? We're locked in stone now."

So much smug happiness in his expression that it cut right through her panic.

"But I know we mated in exigent circumstances," he said, searching her face. "If you need time—"

"No. I don't." Theo spread a hand over his chest, her next words blurted out. "I'm keeping you even if you gave yourself to me by accident."

A wicked grin. "I think of it more as stealing you." He nuzzled her oh-so-gently. "We'll build a place not far from the den, but far enough away that the cubs can't wander out to it without supervision.

"We can come here to eat, socialize, hang out—but until we figure out the rages, you never have to enter the den alone. You can come with me, or with Pavel, or with anyone else in the clan you trust is strong enough to overpower you." A dark glance at her bracelet. "Not that it'll be necessary if you're wearing that thing."

"You won't mind?" Theo asked, her stomach yet in knots. "Not living in the den? You love it."

"I love you more." Words so blunt it was impossible not to believe them. "Also, we'll be overrun with visitors who never want to leave, trust me." He rolled his eyes. "I'll have to kick their butts out.

"Be warned—bears don't know the meaning of personal space. But they'll respect your wish to protect the cubs, and I guarantee you'll have no surprise cub visitors, even if I have to set up a perimeter alert system to pick up any intrepid runaways. Unlikely any baby would be able to get to the area I'm considering, though."

His scent in her nose and his heart a solid beat beneath her palm, the warmth of him an embrace, Theo considered his words.

Bears.

She was in a den full of *bears.*

Strong, dangerous, bears.

With her and Yakov living outside and only coming in for communal things like meals, the risk that she'd be alone with a cub—especially if she took care *never* to be alone with a cub—was minimal. The same applied to any other more vulnerable members of StoneWater.

She trembled, fear a claw hooked into her gut. "I'm not myself when the rage takes over. I have no intentional control at all." It was an awful thing to know about herself, but she had to accept and ameliorate the risk even if she could do nothing to stop the episodes.

"Keja told me all of it while you were unconscious," she shared with Yakov. "About how my grandfather and his team damaged my brain on purpose to make me more malleable . . . but the side effect is rage. I have it, she has it, so do Santo and Janine and any others Keja got out."

She could see him struggling with her words, but what he said in return stopped her cold. "Can you rig your bracelet to dose you with a drug instead of delivering a shock?" Gritted-out words. "Can't believe I'm fucking suggesting this, but if that's what you need to feel safe, that's what you need."

Theo's brain couldn't process his words. "What?"

"*Pchelka*, you defaulted to a painful deterrent because your psychopathic grandfather used the same to torture you. There's no need for you to punish yourself with pain if the intent is to knock you out before you become dangerous." Wild amber, a rough determination. "Is there a drug that can knock you out without messing with your Psy abilities?"

"I—" She frowned, nodded. "Yes. There is. General pain meds aren't useful to us because they scramble our abilities while leaving us awake, but one class of heavy-duty narcotics does work for the opposite reason—because it shuts down both body and mind. No aftereffects."

"Then put that in a bracelet. A dose that'll knock you out seconds after it senses an oncoming episode. You'll fall where you stand. No warning. Total shutdown."

She could see that the idea of her being so helpless devastated him . . . But he loved her enough to give her this thing that to him was terrible. Chest aching, she pressed her forehead to his. "Yes, that will give me peace, let me live close to your clan." It was the only way she could ever be certain that she wouldn't hurt anyone during an episode.

"You can still use the original bracelet when you're away from the den," he said, his shoulder muscles bunched tight. "As a warning system to get to a safe place before the rage storm hits."

"No," she said. "There's no guarantee that I'll make it. And Yasha, I'd rather collapse in a public area full of strangers than have even a single more drop of blood on my hands."

But because his anguish devastated her, she took the idea further. "When I modify the bracelet," she said, "I'll insert a chip that links it to your phone. So you'll know the instant it activates. You can alert my brother to get to me with his teleporter, or send a clanmate to check on me if I'm alone in den territory."

"Link it to three other people," Yakov said at once. "Pavel and Pax. Arwen, too. I want you to have backup upon backup."

She agreed without hesitation. He'd given her what she needed to feel safe. She could give him what he needed to ease his fear of her lying helpless and alone. "It'll work," she said, because it was her turn to reassure him.

But Yakov didn't soften. His expression intent, he said, "*Serdtse moyo*, while I'll agree to this for now, I want you to keep an open mind—after you've healed and settled, I want to run an experiment where you don't wear the bracelet."

He pressed a finger to her lip when she would've spoken. "Full safety measures. Controlled monitoring."

Struggling to do as he'd asked, keep that open mind, Theo said, "Why?"

"Because we're mated now. It's possible an episode might not overwhelm you, that the load will be spread over two." His eyes narrowed. "Or . . . best-case scenario, the rage *never* actuates again, because my mind will continuously compensate for any fluctuations in yours. Minor corrections so the pressure just never builds up to an episode."

"The load on you if—"

"I'm bonded to Valya and every other second in the den, as well as to Nova. That's how a clan works. As a combined unit." Rough passion in every word. "If it works as I'm hoping, if my mind acts like a release valve on yours, then the load will spread, won't even be noticed."

Theo could barely comprehend the enormity of that possibility.

And it hit her, really hit her for the first time. "We're mated," she whispered, curling around his bearish presence inside her. "We're *mated*." To have the right to call him her own? The wonder of it stole her breath. "I don't remember it happening."

His scowl was heavy. "Me neither and I'm gonna sulk about it. Pasha tells me it's a fucking transcendental experience. I just felt you reach for me and I reached for you in return and I guess my bear took care of the rest."

Laughing wetly, she kissed the dimples she so loved. "I bet our bond is more transcendental than theirs," she said, knowing how to play with her bear now. "Plus we made it in a very dramatic fashion. That counts."

"Damn straight." He squeezed the back of her neck. "Now, get back in bed, before Nova finds you attempting an escape."

"I love you." So very easy to say that now she'd accepted that she'd never chosen evil. She didn't have to punish herself by living a life devoid of love and hope. The guilt for what she'd done while in her grandfather's control . . . that would be with her for life, but she wasn't sure that was a bad thing. It meant she was a being of heart, of empathy.

A grin from her bear. "I know." Dimples flashing again, he pretended to nip at her lower lip while avoiding the lightly bruised area. "I—"

Irises turning a primal yellow-hued amber at the same instant that he sucked in a breath of air. She'd have worried except that his lips were curved and when he returned from wherever he'd gone he said, "You know what I just saw, Theo?" Joy that bled into her cells.

"I saw you playing with a naked wild child in the long grass of a summer meadow. He was giggling and laughing and he turned into a ball of brown fur mid-roll through the grass. He's ours, Theo. Our boy. I don't know when, but I know one day you'll play with our son in a summer meadow drenched in sunshine."

The sheer wonder of his vision had her sobbing and then she was tugging him onto the bed so she could crawl into his lap, just hold him as he held her, hope a living song between them.

1988

My dear Hien,

I've done as you've asked all these years. I've never reached out to you no matter how much it hurts. The only thing that gives me comfort is that I know Mom and Dad and the boys are a presence in your life. I've never blamed our parents for cutting off contact with me to better embrace Silence so they can assist our brothers with the transition and support you in your journey with Neiza. I hope you know that, that you understand your big brother wants only the best for you and your child.

But to stop talking to you altogether? I couldn't do that. So I kept this journal, and I wrote all these letters that'll never be sent. My Mimi, she says that one day, our descendants will meet again, and that these letters will act as an archive of memories that'll bring them together. She has so much hope in her, my mate, and her courage and heart buoy mine.

Today, I write because I have news to share with you.

I have a daughter, Hien. She's so tiny and so astonishing and I cried when I first held her. We've named her Quyen Eugenia Nguyen. Such a grand name for a wee thing, but she'll grow into her name, our precious Quyen.

She looks a little like you. I wish you could see her, wish you could hold her, too. I know you would have been an adoring aunt, and that you'd have teased me for taking my time to have a cub. Mimi and I thought it would never happen, and we were content to love the children of the clan. Now we're half in shock and stunned in delight.

My mate has never begrudged me my love for you all. She is generous of heart, is my bear, has unbreakable bonds of her own with her siblings. To her, it's nothing extraordinary that a brother should care for his siblings. But her bonds make her smile, give her joy, while mine causes me only sorrow. And I won't have my child growing up in the shadow of my pain.

So today, my favorite little sister, I must let go of the last pieces of you.

I can't hold on to Otto, Grady, Mom, and Dad, either, no matter the pain of letting go. For the small and cheeky brothers who have become young men far from my eyes and about whom I know only fragments, I wish a life devoid of hurt and trauma, but filled with all the good things that exist. For our parents so loving and giving, I wish the serenity of knowing they made the only choice they could.

You, my brilliant, funny little sister, will live always in my heart and in my memories, but it's time for me to release the past and live in the joyful, vibrant present with my mate and my child. No more looking backward to what once was, and no more secret hopes for a future unseen.

As I complete this, my final letter to you, I wish you and Neiza every good thing life has to offer, and that Silence gives you the peace you desire.

Your big brother,
D.

Chapter 69

Enforcement has released new information regarding the concealed
Moscow Center, stating that the discoveries made there were as a direct
result of the Marshall family's cooperation.
"We want to make it clear that rather than hiding the crimes of former
councilor Marshall Hyde, the head of the family unit drew our attention to
them," Commissioner Yaroslav Skryabin said in his statement. "Their
integrity in this matter is beyond reproach."
The alpha of the StoneWater bears, Valentin Nikolaev, confirmed that a
senior member of his clan acted as an observer during the initial
examination of the shuttered Center, and that the bears continue to be
involved as the investigation progresses. "No one's hiding anything here,"
he stated. "Pax Marshall asked for the truth and made no attempt to
conceal it even when that truth turned out to be ugly. That says a whole
lot about the man."

—*PsyNet Beacon* (15 October 2083)

IT HAD BEEN one month since the confrontation at the site of the facility.

In that time, Enforcement had done a major forensic dig there, found a large number of bodies—but less than if Keja had killed the vast majority of the patients.

It had taken a further two weeks from that discovery to crack open Keja's finances, trace payments to multiple people who she'd set up with carers.

Fifteen.

Counting Santo and Janine, Keja had saved fifteen lives.

Theo hadn't been able to see her aunt straightaway. At first because she was healing from her injuries, and later . . . because it hurt to think of Keja. There was a big part of Theo that didn't blame her aunt for her crimes—she'd done what she had because of the damage to her brain.

If anyone could understand that, it was Theo.

But another part of her *did* blame her aunt. How could she not when Keja had been so rational for so much of their discussion? Surely Theo's aunt must've not just realized but *understood* the murderous nature of her crimes when she emerged from the fog?

It had taken her this long to work through her complex emotions— with the help of her mate and the empath who was now family—and accept that no matter how rational her aunt might've sounded at times, she hadn't been. The madness in her, the brokenness in her, it existed whether she was out murdering people or helping them.

That was who she was; she hadn't chosen that life, however. And the latter was the reason she was still alive. It was also the reason why she hadn't disappeared into the black hole of a prison, and was instead being held at a secure PsyMed facility meant to contain Psy.

Her mind had been locked down with a judicially mandated shield that meant she couldn't telepath anyone, and she only had supervised access to a "fenced-off" section of the PsyNet, the fences shields created by guard minds of significant telepathic power.

Her physical guards were all changeling, or Psy with titanium shields. No powerful patient was going to escape by mentally over-whelming them. The medics who worked intimately with the patients couldn't all be changeling—these were very Psy madnesses, very Psy problems. But the medics were always accompanied by a changeling. No exceptions.

Today, as Theo took a seat on the other side of a shatterproof glass partition, she saw two guards take position on the far wall as another guard led Keja into the room.

Theo appeared alone on this side, but her mate stood just outside the door.

Yakov had asked her if she wanted privacy and she'd nodded yes. "For her dignity," she'd said. "I'll give her that even if I can never undo what was done to her by the man who was meant to protect her."

Her bear had cupped her cheek, kissed her. "That's my Theo with her soft heart that the tiny gangsters take shameless advantage of."

"They do not," she'd said in affront.

"Ahem, do we or do we not have two dozen cupcakes in the car for the gang of cake bandits?"

When Theo had wrinkled her nose at him, he'd kissed it, then said, "Go see your aunt, *pchelka*." A solemn tenderness to his expression, this man who knew all her complicated emotions when it came to Keja. "If you need me, I'll be right here."

Theo wasn't expecting an attack. That wasn't where the danger lay with Keja.

Her aunt wore pale purple scrubs. That was a special-order item according to the information that Pax had been sent as a result of his standing as the head of the Marshall family. Since Keja had never officially been cut from the family line, just listed as dead, responsibility for her fell to the family.

Theo knew Pax would've accepted that responsibility regardless.

Now he held power of attorney over her person, as she'd been judged unable to care for herself—and, as such, he had full access to her medical records. So Theo knew that Keja's counselor had ordered the purple scrubs after Keja kept on going into psychotic meltdowns at being asked to put on the green scrubs that were the usual patient uniform at this facility.

She was fine with seeing others in them, but she would not wear a set.

Echoes of trauma. Memories of a brutal violation.

Now her aunt took a seat on the other side. Unlike in the old movie that Theo had recently watched with Yakov, they didn't have to pick up devices to talk to each other through the glass. It wasn't soundproof. Was designed to let them speak freely but without physical risk to Theo. "Aunt Keja," Theo said. "You look well."

No madness in her gaze today, Keja smiled that sad smile Theo had seen before her aunt shot her. "As we both know, looks can be deceiving." Her next words held a sharp edge. "They tell me your brother holds power of attorney over me. Seems I'm unfit to care for myself or to make my own decisions."

"You don't need to be concerned," Theo said. "Pax understands that you're eminently capable the vast majority of the time, and he has no desire to contradict your decisions or micromanage your existence. However, there are times when you are . . . unreachable."

Also in the medical records had been a notation about a recent incident where Theo's aunt had attacked a fellow inmate: a slender blue-eyed blonde. Had the guards not pulled Keja off, she'd have broken the other woman's neck.

"I'm in solitary confinement now for the safety of others," Keja said, one eye twitching slightly. Raising a hand, she pressed her finger under that eye. "Side effect of the medication they're testing on me. I asked to be part of the guinea pig group and I assume your brother must have authorized it, because they let me into the trial."

Hope for her aunt had Theo leaning forward. "What's it designed to do?"

"Regulate certain processes in the brain. I can't give you all the technical specs but they'll be in my medical records. Irritation at the twitch aside, I feel calm most of the time." Humor lit up the blue, a hint of the woman she could've been had Marshall Hyde not savaged her. "Or I think so, anyway. I might be the crazy person who doesn't know they're crazy."

Throat tight, Theo pressed a hand to the glass. "I don't know how to feel about you." It came out raw, drenched in pain. "You saved *fifteen* lives, and then you took the lives of innocents whose only crime was to look like me."

Like version 2.0.

"I love you and I understand you," Theo continued. "I also hate you for what you did . . . And I hate myself because I was the second subject. I'm only mentally better than you because you went first, took the first hit."

Keja pressed her hand against Theo's. "Don't, little niece." Severe words belied by the strange tenderness in her expression. "We are neither one of us the worst monsters. That title goes to the ones who made us."

Her eyes grew hard, black bleeding in from the edges in a creeping tide. "The counselors and shrinks want me to accept fault, but I see doing that as capitulating to what he did to me, as shifting blame from where it rightfully lies. *He* killed those women—because he created me."

Theo didn't know what to say to that. The counselors were right in that Keja couldn't move forward until she accepted culpability for her crimes. But Keja was also right—she wouldn't be this damaged being if her father hadn't mangled her brain.

"Not that it matters." Dropping her palm from the other side of the glass, Keja sat back. "I'm in this facility for the rest of my life."

She looked around. "I thought I'd hate it, but it's not so bad. The staff are kind. I heard it's because Es are the ones who do the hiring interviews. We can choose activities or a subject to study. They say I can have a garden plot in spring, can plant whatever I want. I think I'll plant flowers. Bright, pretty, happy."

Theo's soul hurt. "I'll look forward to my bouquet."

Keja smiled. "And since it's only slender blue-eyed blondes who trigger me to homicidal violence, they're working on a plan to let me out of isolation by juggling the schedule so I'm never out at the same time as any of them."

"I'm glad you won't be locked in your room." Her aunt had already suffered far more than any person should suffer.

"It's a very humane facility—especially given that so many of its residents are murderers." A shrug. "That's enough about me. How goes life with the bear?" A sparkle in eyes that had morphed from obsidian to blue once more.

"Loud, affectionate, overwhelming in the best way." Theo squeezed her hands into fists in her lap. "I wish you could have that. I wish you could know what it is to be loved exactly as you are. To have a person who sees all of you—and loves all of you."

Keja's smile was that terrible sad one. "Live for both of us, Theo. It was too late for me the first time they operated on my brain. But it's not too late for you. Forget about me and go on with your life. Live that life as a glorious insult to the man who tried to take it from us."

Theo held her aunt's gaze, her spine straight. "I will live my life," she said. "But I'm never going to leave you behind. I'll visit twice every month, and if I'm out of the area, I'll call. You're an important part of my life and my family. The only person who is like me in the entire world."

Keja blinked rapidly. Then she gave a jerky nod.

Theo had never had any intention of abandoning her aunt, not even when she was at her most confused about her emotions where Keja was concerned. That was why the other woman had been placed in a facility a mere two-hour drive from Moscow. It was the closest specialist hospital of its kind in the region.

"Before the fall of Silence," Theo told Yakov as they left the facility a half hour later, "Keja would've vanished, never to be seen again. Her life ended without discussion or consideration."

Yakov wove his fingers through hers, her bear holding her safe while she walked in nightmare.

"All because my grandfather wanted a slave." Theo lifted her face up to the cool autumn sun. "Well, fuck him." Hard words, but she felt them in every fiber of her being. "Keja isn't going to be executed, isn't going to be ignored, all memory of her buried."

Breaking their twined grip on that defiant declaration, she gripped Yakov's T-shirt with both hands and hauled him down for a kiss wild and passionate, skin privileges with her mate. "And I exist. I *thrive*."

Yakov grinned and stole another wet kiss, the bear's pleased rumble a vibration against her breasts. "That's my Theo," he said, before stepping back to open the car door for her. "Come on. We can't be late for lunch with your brother. Pretty sure the man thinks we're all insane, but he's polite and always turns up on time."

Pax's relationship with the bears was a work in progress, with both parties side-eyeing each other . . . but there was goodwill on both sides, too. Her brother would do anything to make her new life easier, while Yakov's entire clan had hearts generous and wild. Though poor Pax probably needed forty-eight hours to recover from every bear-related interaction.

Last time around, Babushka Quyen had patted his cheeks and said, "Would you like to meet a nice bear girl? My cousin Maggie, her granddaughter just made senior soldier. You two would make pretty cubs."

Theo. Help.

Laughing inwardly at the memory of his telepathic request, she jumped into the vehicle with her bear. Their life would always be complicated. Her twin fought a deadly battle day after day. Her own rages seethed on the periphery of her life. The PsyNet continued to fragment and weaken, even as Pax told her he'd heard whispers of a Ruling Coalition plan to create a second island.

The entire world was in flux.

But one thing Theo knew—she stood on solid ground with her mate by her side. He would always be by her side. Her love. Her Yakov. "Yashin'ka?"

He merged into the main flow of traffic. "Hmm?"

"I love you more than donut holes."

His cheeks creased, the dimple she could see mischievous and wicked. And then they were both laughing, delighted with each other, Theo and her bear.

Transitions

Mother? Where are you? Mother?

—Repeating whisper in the PsyNet

PAX HAD NEVER expected to end up at a lunch table with multiple bears while his twin laughed at his side and tried to tempt him into trying new dishes, but life, he'd come to learn, had a way of throwing surprises at you.

This surprise, at least, was a good one.

He could breathe now that he knew Theo was safe. Not even the most venomous member of their family was stupid enough to go after her at this point, their mother included. The Marshalls might be arrogant, many yet believing themselves better than changelings, but they also knew that the bears were allied with Kaleb Krychek.

No one in the PsyNet wanted to pick a fight with Krychek.

Tonight, hours after the lunch, he found himself standing on the roof of the apartment building where he stayed when he came to visit Theo. The air was crisp, the lights of the city glittering all around him— and best of all, he didn't have to worry about a knife in the back.

Not here. Not in his sister's home.

He rubbed at his forehead, exhausted from the viciousness of what was going on in the family. The power plays, the machinations, the political backstabbing. He was starting to believe that Theo was right, that their grandfather had poisoned them at the root, and there was no chance of salvation.

At least the current spotlight on their family had made the cockroaches scuttle back to their holes, giving him more breathing room than he'd had for months. He still wasn't certain what to do with Claire. She was a venomous snake, but even Pax couldn't simply order the assassination of his own mother.

Had to be Theo's conscience nudging him away from their grandfather's brand of psychopathic governance.

He could walk away, he thought with the cold part of his mind that had been nurtured by Marshall Hyde, let the others murder each other scrambling for control. Whoever "won" the CEO position would make a mess of it.

Pax could then buy it out from under them, with no obligation to "family" or the line. The entire empire would be his to shape, his to rebuild . . . unless the rot went even deeper than that.

Arwen Mercant had been blunt with him after Theo convinced Pax to accept empathic help. His twin had already spoken to Mercant at that point, with the E agreeing to a meeting with Pax to see if they could work together.

After that introductory contact—during which Pax had found himself taken in by too-perceptive empathic eyes—Mercant had accepted a short-term contract to offer Pax advice on which members of the family and the organization he might be able to trust.

The results hadn't been good.

"I've never met a family this disturbed, this . . . twisted." A grimness to the fine line of Mercant's jaw as they'd stood side by side on the balcony outside Pax's San Francisco office, an office that had become his default HQ after his move to the city. "There's no sense of loyalty except between you and Theo. The senior employees are cut from the same cloth, each loyal only to themselves."

His grandfather, Pax had thought, had filled the ranks in his own image.

"I'm no business consultant," Mercant had continued, "but I'd advise you to cut and run, set up your own clean operation, and offer employment to lower-level employees when the Marshall Group inevitably begins to hemorrhage. To those people, it's just a job; they have no skin in the game.

"Do *not* accept the applications of anyone in your corporate or even mid-level managerial staff." He'd made a slicing gesture with one hand. "I hate to write anyone off, but the senior ranks have been too long embedded in the organization, have absorbed too much of its ethos."

Even as Pax considered what that said about him, the person who'd been raised by the cold-eyed cobra at the center of the Marshall Group, Mercant had looked at him and said, "Theo." A quiet answer, a compelling indication of how well empaths read people. "Your devotion to Theo, your refusal to allow that bond to break? It defines you."

"More than being my grandfather's protégé?"

Piercing eyes of silver with blue undertones on his. Arwen's power was wholly different from that of Memory Aven-Rose, but the empaths had one thing in common: a spine forged of steel. Those who believed designation E weak had no idea of the strength it took to walk into the abyss time and time again.

"Yes," Arwen had said. "Your bond with Theo was there before him, and it's outlived him. I don't often tell people to dance on someone's grave, but in this case, it's more than justified." He'd slipped his hands into the pockets of his suit pants, the fabric a dark gray pinstripe that Mercant had paired with a shirt and tie in a hue caught between blue and silver, much like his eyes. "The Syndrome . . ."

Pax had waited, curious to hear what another E had to say about the condition that he could feel devouring pieces of him day after day. Theo had asked him to tell Mercant about it, so that Mercant wouldn't be unsettled by any instability he picked up in Pax's psyche, and for reasons of good faith: "He won't share the knowledge, Pax. Arwen takes empathic ethics dead seriously."

Because he trusted Theo more than any other being in this world, Pax had shared the information—even though Arwen Mercant was a member of a family who were the most dangerous information brokers in the PsyNet.

That day, on the balcony in San Francisco, Mercant had said, "I didn't believe you when you initially told me the date of onset. Your psychic signature is too unwavering."

"But?" Pax had been too long in the game not to hear the unspoken coda.

"But, now that I've been around you for longer . . . yes, I sense it." Instead of revulsion, however, his voice had held intrigue. "Not enough, though. You simply shouldn't be this mentally competent anymore."

A frank glance. "Your psychic presence is acute, clear for the vast majority of the time. That your E is a genius, that much is unquestionable, but . . . Theo. It *has* to be your bond with Theo."

Pax's shoulders had stiffened. "I don't want to pull her into this. I've done everything in my power to block the connection so that the volatility of my mind doesn't seep into hers."

"It doesn't work that way with love," Arwen had said softly. "She'll fight for you whether you like it or not." He'd stared out at the waters of the bay in the distance, the blue glittering steel. "I wonder . . ." A frown. "I'd like to speak to your E, if you're comfortable with that?"

"I'll pass on the request to her." Pax had no hope of a miracle cure, but saw no harm in allowing Arwen to consult with Memory. If nothing else, their collaboration could result in findings that might better the life of another Scarab down the line.

Ping. Ping. Ping. Ping. Ping.

Pax scowled. The idiots who'd been annoying him had gone quiet for a period, only to restart again earlier today. Busy with the lunch, followed by the work required for an upcoming acquisition, he'd ignored the irritation, but enough was enough.

He stepped out into the PsyNet, his mind in hunting mode.

No evidence of any trespassers close to him. As expected. And no impediment to the hunt. He'd kept mental track of the signatures attached to the pings, and now released psychic search bots designed to zero in on those signatures. Because the people behind this weren't exactly the cleverest in the bunch and had done nothing to obfuscate their unique psychic DNA—as was second nature to Pax.

The only reason they'd gotten away with it this long was that he'd been too busy to deal with them. Theo was right—it had to be teenagers. Well, they were about to get a fright. And he'd get some peace.

He found the first mind twenty-five minutes later, sent his own ping.

He expected to be ignored, the child scared off by actual contact. But he got an immediate response: *Hello? Can you help me? She's gone. I don't know what to do. Please help me.*

The telepathic words were curiously . . . warped.

As if fed through a blender that had mangled the shape of them.

Frowning on the physical plane, he questioned his earlier belief of this being a juvenile game. It was possible he'd simply become the inadvertent target of a mentally fragile individual who required assistance.

What do you need? he asked.

I don't know what to do, the mind repeated, a sobbing panic to it now. *She was the Mother. She told us what to do. Now she's gone and my head hurts so much and I c-c-can't focus and I just broke a table into pieces because I was angry and I'm a teacher and only a Gradient 3 but I smashed the table with my mind and I—*

An ice-cold sensation in the pit of Pax's stomach. *Have you been assessed for Scarab Syndrome?*

She said I was one of her chosen ones, that I didn't have to let the doctors drug me into compliance. That she would take care of me. But she's gone now. I'm so scared.

The ice spread in a frigid tide. *Where are you?* Pax slid out his phone. *Your physical address.*

The other mind gave it to him without hesitation, and he saw that it was only two hours out of San Francisco. Pax could ask Octavio to teleport him home, then drive out. Or, if the mind in contact with his sent him a visual for the Tk to lock onto, they could 'port directly to the location.

Octavio had brought him to Moscow and was currently in one of the other apartments in the building, so it would be well within his range.

Unless . . . should Memory Aven-Rose agree to help, she and one of the wolves could drive to the address. Given that she was part of Snow-Dancer, she also had access to an extremely high-Gradient teleport-capable Tk, so could speed things up if she deemed it necessary.

Pax went to call the empath, hesitated. He had the feeling this person wouldn't react well to a stranger walking through the door. He'd have to do the initial contact. They trusted him.

Which was a question all its own.

How did you find me?

The Mother found you. She was angry you weren't hers. I heard. I told the others. I said we should ask you. If you could say no to her, you must be strong. Will you be our Father now?

The Syndrome stirred, aroused by the promise of power, control . . . and an empire that was his and his alone. His Scarabs would never betray him. He could sense it in the raw need of the mind that spoke to his. His Scarabs would do anything he asked.

Slipping his phone back into his pocket, Pax said, *I'm coming to see you. Wait where you are.*

Yes, Father.

ACKNOWLEDGMENTS

A huge thanks to Karen Lamming and Vladimir Samozvanov for their generous help with my Russian language questions. You're both stars!

As always, any errors are mine (and I am beary, beary sorry* for them).

---

* I couldn't resist. I blame the bears. Bad influences, the whole (wonderful) furry clan of them.